GW01191644

Without A Soul
By Oisin O'Domhnaill

Contents

Chapter 1

Cannonbridge is a town in a coma, registering very few signs of life. People go about their daily business, alive but well short of living. There is, however, the occasional twitch, threatening to jolt the town awake – last Spring there were rumours of a serial killer on the prowl but it just turned out to be a series of extremely similar accidental deaths. Even the trepidation brought about by the constant threat of war in the continent does little to liven up the town. It's the kind of place where nothing happens all the time. Unfortunately for Cannonbridge things won't remain this way forever. Change, wild-eyed and grinning maniacally, has elected to have its way with the continent of Ballisca and Cannonbridge is where the wheels are set in motion. Its unwitting instrument for implication has already been chosen; his name is Vantix.

Vantix shivered involuntarily, surprised that even the large, densely packed crowd was no match for the chill. In spite of his warmest clothes he was still bitterly cold. Desperately his hands sought the warmth of his pockets only to find somebody else had beaten them to it. This town was always freezing. Added to the previously mentioned dreariness, it made Cannonbridge exactly the kind of place he didn't want to call home. Yet call it that he did, because rents were low and he'd yet to think of something witty and biting.

Large gatherings such as this were unusual in the town. Save for hangings, concert tickets and infrequent lynch mobs the townsfolk avoided the agony of congregating and small talk. Today an event taking place touched them all, or more tellingly it touched their wallets.

"*We've got Weapons*", the local weapon emporium was having a sale that promised unbelievable reductions. The proprietor, Mr Bardson, was, Vantix had assumed, either an advertising genius or had the imagination of a three legged goat. After a brief encounter, Vantix had decided the latter might be too kind. Either way the shop did a brisk trade. Demand was high, prices were low and they shifted enough merchandise to secure a rather lucrative trade. The people of Cannonbridge were quite happy to pay the prices asked for the products provided. Save, of course, for those who had no intention of paying in the first place.

Thieves in the town had long since unified into something resembling an organised body. These were divided into two categories: those who stole it in the first place and fences who resold the merchandise. Several of the former were sprinkled throughout the crowd and, for once, Vantix was actually pleased to see them.

Scanning the faces around him, his eyes eventually settled on the particular visage he sought. "Farack", he called, waving to his friend. Farack pushed his way over, ignoring the murmurs of discontent. "Good morning Vantix," he said cheerfully.

Vantix shivered again, "What's good about it?"

"Firstly, there's a sale on," Farack gestured toward the store, "and secondly, it's extremely cold for all the people here who I don't like."

"It's also freezing for the people you do like."

"I think you're willing to take one for the team."

Farack was a rhadon, the only one in Cannonbridge. Although other rhadons were known for their flaming hair and ability to manipulate fire, Farack lacked these oh-so distinguishing characteristics. As luck would have it he'd been dropped in a pond as a baby, making him uniquely devoid amongst his people. An adult rhadon would have shaken it off as a momentary unpleasantness but Farack's flame hadn't caught at the time and now it never would. As a result he resembled a slightly orange-tinged human with incredibly flammable black hair. Every opportunity to flaunt his rhadonhood was seized. Being the only person in Cannonbridge impervious to the cold was a big deal for him, even if it was a little pathetic.

"All our favourite neighbourhood thieves have surfaced", Vantix informed him. Neither of them were on the best of terms with the thieves. Both had briefly been members but had taken issue with the operating methods. The thieves were big on discretion and hadn't been pleased when Vantix burned his name into the garden of a house he was supposed to be burglarising. *Why so clandestine?* Vantix wondered, *why not leave a symbol of some kind?* That was something he just couldn't comprehend: *Why bother going to all the trouble if nobody would ever know about it?*

Their departure resulted in a grudge which manifested through the thieves penchant for ambushing the two of them on the way home from the tavern. Vantix liked to tell himself this had nothing to do with his abhorrence for them as people. If anything, it furthered served to epitomise how small town they were.

These musings were interrupted by the sound of locks being undone. Bardson appeared from within, stepping out in front of the crowd and shutting the door behind him. Feeling this was a speech worthy event, he stood proudly and announced: "Ladies and Gentleman, it's my privilege to provide for you a selection of the finest weapons and armour money can buy from Freatsrak. Not only shall you be astounded by the superlative quality of weapons, the meagre sum we ask in return shall most definitely be to your liking. In our establishment we always put you first. Should any of you have any concerns about the modest sum requested my boys will be happy to address them and discuss other means of payment."

At least that was the planned gist. What he actually said was mostly unintelligible, any words escaping Bardson's lips either half-dissolved by a mouthful of saliva or mumbled so low nobody could ascertain their meaning. He was a very self-conscious man. Deciphering anything he said was an arduous task that left all-comers confused and, more often than not, drenched in spittle. The only part Vantix understood was when Bardson opened both doors before he stepped back inside. The crowd surged forward, eager to get their grubby hands on the cheapest merchandise. Vantix and Farack were swept along with them.

"Have you got any money?" Vantix shouted, trying to be heard over the general dissonance of the raucous shoppers.

"None," was the barely audible reply.

It was true that the store was filled with high quality weapons; it was also true that they were priced very low. Another truth was that neither Vantix nor Farack had a dime between them. They didn't need it anyway.

Everything was in motion for a neat little scheme that'd get them money, weapons, and maybe even Bardson's gratitude if so inclined.

Seeing the whole village in here wasn't much of a surprise, as Cannonbridge was a town very prone to burglary. Crime had always been a problem in Fardash and the restrictions imposed by the threat of war were only making it worse. Taxes were high and the King used them to feed and equip the army. Most families couldn't cope and had to send their older children away. Pretty much all of these older children ended up as highway men, bandits or thieves. With so many turning to crime, the ability to defend themselves came very high on anybody's list of survival necessities. Locks were fine but seeing as they could be picked by any thief worth his salt and pepper, they weren't in high demand. Whereas anyone who broke into a house with an assortment of weapons was either escaping with a valuable haul or leaving parts of themselves behind.

Vantix's train of thought came to a sudden halt when Farack nudged him. Bardson's sons were solely focused on watching the two of them, allowing the thieves free rein. There were several flickers as they left the store, trying to conceal any tell-tale jingling and then dissipated into the waiting crowd with crossbows, swords, daggers, axes and maces stashed around their person. Farack and Vantix stayed to draw attention, ensuring the thieves got away with as much as they could. Quantity would make the difference later; they needed as big a hole as possible in Bardson's pocket so he'd accept their help to stitch it back up.

Vantix smiled, leaned back against a wall and watched the thieves go about their business.

There was, however, one person Vantix, the crowd and thieves didn't notice at all. Nobody saw him stroll through the crowd; nobody wondered about the lackadaisical air that made him completely incongruous amongst the fervent shoppers; and nobody saw him watching Vantix with a curiously ponderous expression. He wanted to be impressed.

* * * * *

Several hours later Vantix and Farack waited patiently for the sounds of merriment and boisterous celebration to die down. Buildings outwardly so derelict were rarely so vivacious but the inhabitants were simply delighted with their day's haul. With a little luck they'd soon drink themselves to sleep.

One person who wasn't so good natured about their success was Bardson, for obvious reasons. He was so angry that almost every word was pronounced with perfect diction. Nobody was as surprised as Vantix to hear the word "bastard" uttered so clearly and frequently. After his guards attested to both Vantix and Farack's innocence in the matter of the stolen weapons, it hadn't taken them too much time to cajole him into accepting their brand new weapon retrieval service. They'd get their pick of the weapons, a free night in the inn (bargained down from two) and 30 crowns each as long as the entire missing inventory was accounted for. Bardson was particularly avid that they secure the return of a valuable sword with a jewelled hilt. Their methods were up to their discretion.

Even if the two of them hadn't known where the thieves residence was it wouldn't have been hard to find.

Everything about the building screamed hideout. Had Vantix been in command of the town guard it would've been raided by now. Then again, that was mostly just because he hated the thieves. If a coven met there secretly he'd have no trouble keeping his nose out of their business.

After about an hour that seemed to take several laps of eternity, Farack crept to the window. The only sound to reach his ears was that of several people snoring in almost perfect harmony. A quick glance revealed that all the thieves were asleep, several of them cradling bottles. He smiled but Vantix found the cliché less amusing. The two of them climbed in, the old window giving rather easily.

It only took seconds to find the weapons, ensconced comfortably in sacks at the bottom of the stairs. Farack picked two up and slung them over his shoulder, hoisting them through the window with a grunt of exertion, before he checked the contents. His friend eyed the remaining three sacks and shook his head in dismay. *Tsk*, he thought, *we really under sold our services; must be a few hundred crowns worth of weapons here.*

Picking up the remaining three bags, he stepped quietly around the sleeping forms, resisting the urge to kick them all the while. He was close to the window when one of the thieves rolled over and his heart missed several steps and plunged down the stairs. Luckily the thief was still asleep.

Crossing to the window, Vantix heaved the bags through. Farack gave them a cursory search and then shook his head. "The sword he was on about. It's not here. " Turning back, Vantix studied the sleeping forms. After a minute he located the sword, in its sheath on the belt of an unconscious thief. Vantix drew his knife and

14

sliced through the belt. It gave a little too easy, his follow through nicking the sleeper. The thief gasped and Vantix recoiled, ready to spring out the window if the man's eyes opened. Fortunately they remained closed.

For a moment Vantix just sat there blankly. Then, with almost a mind of its own, his blade headed for the forehead of the sleeping thief. Farack intervened just in time, grabbing the blade while it descended. It sliced his palm and a few drops of blood rolled down the blade and landed on the floor just shy of the thief.

"Are you stupid or something?" Farack hissed, "Are you trying to wake him?"

"I just-".

"Thought it would be a good idea, to wake up one of the thieves by stabbing him repeatedly?"

"When you put it like that, it makes me sound sick and twisted," Vantix said in a hurt tone, "And I wasn't going to do anything. I cut him by an accident."

"The first time was an accident. The second-"

Vantix cut him off by motioning to the window, "Can we go?"

Farack nodded sullenly and climbed out. Vantix sighed and carved his name into the wall as he took his leave. They wouldn't be able to miss it. *After all, what was the point if nobody knew who was responsible?*

* * * * *

Farack and Vantix walked down the road from the thieves' hideout, neither of them noticing the dark figure walking toward them. They were engaged in their own discussion.

"..I mean, what is wrong with you? Do you think it's okay to go around disfiguring people?"

"I didn't do anything. It wasn't even me, the blade moved of its own accord."

"Amazing how often a psychopathic workman blames his tools. I seriously can't comprehend why you would have even the slightest urge to mutil-oh, sorry."

The man had seemed to step out of the night and directly into their path, too quick to avoid a collision. There was a bump but nobody fell and Vantix and Farack retained their grasp on Bardson's weapons. The man smiled from under his hood, "Heartfelt apologies, gentlemen. Enjoy your evening."

"Em, you as well."

All parties involved carried on their own way in silence.

The dark figure stopped outside the hideout before turning to watch the pair walk away. Their little ploy had entertained him, taking advantage of the situation with the thieves and Bardson to make a profit they'd no right to. They had potential. The rhadon seemed fine but he guessed the other would prove stubborn. That's why he'd taken the time to pick his pocket whilst apologising.

The hooded man regarded the knife he'd taken from the boy. The name "Vantix" was scratched into the hilt. "Perfect," he said to himself cheerfully as he walked to the thieves' hideout, "leverage."

Chapter 2

The grand chamber of Fardash castle was empty save for two figures, one perched languidly on the throne and the other standing to attention a little ways off. As usual one waited upon an answer from the other.

Welbh tapped his foot impatiently and watched as King Jandelk agonised over the choice he faced. The King was always slow and methodical. Somehow he managed to devote the same amount of deep thought to every single problem, no matter its significance. This really wore the patience of anybody who asked him a simple question.

The King finished struggling with himself and answered Welbh's question. "No," he declared, "I shall be dining momentarily and a snack would most certainly disturb my appetite."

Welbh sighed and cleared his throat before asking, "As to the other matter, my lord?"

King Jandelk looked at him lazily. "What other matter?"

"The more important matter. The reports we got from the south, sire. About the dendrid."

"You'll have to remind me," the King said wearily, "My mind was occupied."

Trying to keep his annoyance from his voice, he almost succeeded. "The village that was attacked? The massacre? It's been   indicated that the dendrid came from Derranferd. We need to know what action to take."

It was at moments like this that the King really shone. Stroking his beard and removing his crown, he relaxed in his throne and closed his eyes. Anyone unfamiliar with King Jandelk, would've assumed he'd fallen asleep. Rather the complete opposite, this was when his mind was most active.

After some time, the King reached for his crown and placed it upon his head. "This is an that act clearly calls out for retribution," he reasoned, "if it's true. I see no reason to believe that this was a military attack. We can't afford to go to war over this. The rest of Ballisca stands on the brink. We don't want to be seen notching the first arrow." At this point he turned to Welbh. "If a rogue band of dendrid are killing their way across the provinces, perhaps King Audron of Derranferd will help us bring these killers to justice. Maybe we can even lay the foundations for an allegiance. Despite our differences, he and I were once friends. There's a basis to build upon there."

His advisor bowed and made to leave. "Call the Royal Negotiator," the King called after him, "tell him to send a few letters, arrange a trip to Derranferd and whatever else it is that he does."

* * * * *

Welbh didn't like the King. In his opinion, the man lacked the right initiative to run a Kingdom; lacked the drive to make this a better place for his subjects. He'd stick to his allegiances and the Kingdom would remain in the same place it had always been. The King was okay with being poor and weak, as long as things didn't get any worse. Maintenance was his goal; keeping things tipping along. Welbh didn't understand this outlook.

Life had taught him that surviving wasn't satisfying enough. Ambitious, ruthless and merciless, there was nothing he'd let stand in the way of his quest for money, power and, time permitting, adoration.

Reaching his chamber, he entered and closed the door. Each chamber in the castle was quite sumptuous but he ignored all these comforts and settled down at his desk. Thousands of ideas filled his mind as to how he might turn the King's decision to his advantage. Each and every one of them was explored, leaving not one single outcome unfulfilled in his head.

After several minutes of solid thinking, he settled on an idea. It would make him a lot of money, didn't have that many dangerous avenues for failure and, like most of his ideas, would smudge the conscience of any honourable man. The King would hate it, he smirked to himself.

He got up and wrote a letter asking leave for family reasons. It was time to become the Royal Negotiator.

* * * * *

"To a very profitable evening," toasted Vantix, raising his glass. Farack raised his in reply. They were seated in The Smoking Flagon, Cannonbridge's most popular local tavern. They each had a flagon of the ale which had earned the tavern its name and after a couple of gulps, followed by a lot of wincing, they sat back with a satisfied sigh.

On returning to "*We've got Weapons*" to collect payment, they'd found the shop closed. A sign on the door indicated that they should deposit the weapons and collect their money later. Having predicted this eventuality, Vantix and Farack took their pick of the weapons. Twice the value of what they'd asked in payment, to teach that cheapskate a lesson.

Vantix sat back and smiled. They'd traded some weapons in at the bar to pay for the night's drinks. Even so, the day's bounty was not to be sniffed at. He'd managed to keep two pistol crossbows, a broadsword and two short swords. Farack had a new broadsword, shield and two knifes.

Just when all is going perfectly, life usually throws a lemon shaped burning brick through your window. In this case, it was an extremely suspicious looking man in a black cape, the same man they'd bumped into earlier that evening. The bar's patrons were giving him a wide berth, none too eager to make his acquaintance. A man in a dark cape always looks suspicious, and it's even worse if he's sitting on his own in a tavern without a drink.

Farack nudged Vantix with his elbow as the man approached them. Vantix began mumbling under his breath. His barely audible pleas of "Don't sit next to us. For love of the gods, please don't sit," went unanswered, as the man made his way toward them. He was looking over his shoulder repeatedly and couldn't have drawn more suspicion if he'd entered a court smeared in blood, professed his guilt and attempted to murder the jury.

Pulling up a chair at their table, he effortlessly extended his air of suspicion to the two of them. Farack just stared but Vantix threw himself back in his chair and exclaimed "Why do you hate me?" at the ceiling.

The man in black gestured toward Vantix and turned to Farack. "He's a bit of a drama queen, eh?"

The rhadon smirked and sipped his drink before replying, "And your name would be..?"

The man extended a hand. "Incognito" he answered.

Vantix rolled his eyes. "Of course it is" he muttered.

Incognito leaned forward and looked around feverishly. When he was sure they wouldn't be overheard, he spoke. "Listen", he whispered.

Before he got the chance to elaborate, Vantix cut across him. "Are you an idiot?" he hissed, before adding, "Or do you get enjoyment out of this stupidity? Gods! What is wrong with you? You know what's going to happen now? We," he indicated Farack and himself, "are now suspects 1 and 2 for every single crime for the next month, because we were seen whispering in the bar with the incredibly suspicious looking idiot. So thanks for that."

Vantix had been expecting Incognito to flounder or be taken aback for a minute but all he did was smile. "I know that," he said simply, "And I still have a proposition for you."

"Judging by your attire and your manner, I'd have to guess it's not exactly legal, is it?" concluded Farack.

Incognito shook his head. "Well it's not illegal," he smiled reassuringly, "but I would prefer the matter stayed between us."

Vantix and Farack exchanged glances. It must be illegal.

Incognito mistook this glance for apprehension. "The pay is 200 crowns. Each."

"Tw.. two hun.." Vantix spluttered and ruined a sip of his drink. It was definitely illegal.

Farack leaned in. "I'm not saying we'll do it or anything," he explained, "but what's the job?"

"Well," Incognito replied, "not only is it a chance to earn some gold it's a chance to do the right thing as well."

"Yeah, yeah fantastic," said Vantix, "Could you tell us what it actually is, please?"

"A group of dendrid attacked a small village yesterday," Incognito explained, "They slaughtered every man woman and child. I want you to kill them and retrieve something for me." He looked at them earnestly.

"You were right," Farack sighed, "He's an idiot. That's suicide"

Incognito shook his head and leaned in even closer. "Listen", he whispered, "I saw what you did tonight and I was impressed by your ingenuity." He gestured toward their new weapons, "I think you've got real potential." They both stared at him, expressions grim and resolute. "Oh come now", he said wearily, "Don't be boring. I've hired another thirteen and there's only ten dendrid." He gave them both long searching looks. Farack nodded.

Although that boring barb had touched a nerve , Vantix still refused. "Those odds still aren't that great," he shrugged, "I think I'd rather stay here and not die." Neither of them seemed to have a reply to this.

Just then there was a commotion at the doorway. A couple of the town guard walked in, pointed at the three of them and headed over to the table. Briefly Vantix considered running but knew it would only confirm his guilt in their eyes. No, better to accommodate them and let it blow over.

"Could you come with us?" called one of the guards as they neared. Vantix cursed under his breath. Judging by the guards tone and the fact that he'd neglected to say please, he knew they'd already decided he was guilty. *I should have run,* he thought. Out loud he asked, "Is there a problem?"

He winced as he saw the other guards covering all of the doors and windows, their crossbows at the ready. *Of all the nights to get caught talking to this idiot,* he thought to himself whilst glaring at Incognito, *there goes my chance of pleading innocent.*

"We're investigating a murder and you're our number one suspect," the guard wasn't explaining anything, it was an accusation.

Incognito leaned in close and whispered, "If I had to guess I'd say this town is about to get real inhospitable. Let me know if you change your mind." He retreated with an infuriating wink.

Enlightenment launched Vantix's eyebrows to the upper reaches of his forehead. Dawning on him was the realization that Incognito wasn't stupid. The extremely conspicuous cape, the appearance of the town guard, the suspicious offer; all were elements to be manipulated at his discretion in the game he was playing. The goal was unclear, but Vantix knew he was losing and decided he was damned if he was going to play.

"We found your name carved into wall of the deceased's home", this was a statement of fact from one of the guards. This time Vantix breathed a sigh of relief.

"Listen," he smiled, "I carve my name everywhere. That's not enough to convict me so there's obviously no point in us wasting each other's time." He picked up his drink and finished it off.

"Normally you'd be right," the guard replied, "but seeing as your knife was buried up to the hilt in the victim's chest we decided we'd better take it into account."

Chapter 3

Throughout Ballisca's history there are numerous tales of fantastic voyages and the ships that embark upon them, none more famous than the cautionary tale of King Midas and The Doomed Expedition. Midas was the wealthiest King to have ever lived and did so in constant fear that the rest of Ballisca would come to steal the vast riches he'd accumulated. He saw thieves lurking around every corner and decided that Ballisca had been corrupted by their desire for his wealth. In secret the building of a ship was commissioned, made of solid gold and loaded with all Midas' wealth. It was supposed to be dragged from the dock where it was built into the uncharted waters so he could search for a new, purer continent where Midas, his gold and those few he trusted could live free from the envy of Ballisca. Through his neglect to take into account the density of gold the boat sank immediately, taking all to their doom. At least they got to take the gold with them.

The news that Vantix had murdered one of the thieves took around the same time to sink in. He recovered just as a large hand reached out, knocking him from his seat.

Scrambling to his feet, Vantix took stock of the situation. Every exit was blocked by the burly shape of a man in the uniform of the town guard, several of their number advancing toward him as he backed slowly towards the bar. The patrons drank on, taking the initiative to order another round and set up an impromptu betting pool remarkably quickly. Most bets had Vantix captured within three minutes.

Farack tried to get to his feet but was restrained by Incognito. "There's no sense in you both landing in a cell," the hooded man whispered, "do as I say and we'll clear up the confusion in the morning."

Guffawing mirthlessly, Farack shook his head. "You don't realise what you've done, do you? He won't go quietly, not with all eyes on him like this."

Unarmed and with nowhere to go, Vantix was tempted to place a bet for his imminent capture himself. The nearest guard moved forward, saying "We just want to talk" in far to menacing a fashion for his liking. Sidestepping the man's lunge, a well-placed kick sent him tumbling into a table and the two patrons seated there. Cheers went up from those who'd had money on innocent bystanders getting caught in the crossfire.

One of the guards was surprised to make the acquaintance of Farack's fist before the rhadon threw Vantix his bag of weapons. "Good luck," he called over his shoulder and headed for the door Incognito was holding for him.

"After the accomplices" one of the guards snarled, mostly because he felt the moment demanded it.

Even with several of them headed after Farack, Vantix was still wildly outnumbered. All the remaining patrons had cleared to the back of the room in case a crossbow bolt should go astray. There was a distinct lack of reaction as Vantix leapt for the cover of the bar, underestimated the distance, landed on top of it, drove all the wind from his body and rolled off into cover, bag of weapons in tow. One patron muttered "made a mess of that" to his drink. It didn't reply.

Finally the guards who had them opened fire with their crossbows, peppering the bar that offered Vantix cover and the bottles on the shelves above, broken glass raining down. It seemed likely this was a distraction to afford them the opportunity to get in close and make their arrest.

Reaching into his bag, Vantix dragged out the first item that came to hand. The miniature crossbow he'd been so pleased with earlier now seemed to scream of impracticality. Although they certainly looked quite fetching and wielding both meant you could hit two targets simultaneously, unless you hit them in a very dangerous area they weren't going to suffer much damage.

He could hear the guards advancing. They liked taking people alive, meant they had someone to knock around for a few hours. Before he could think up a plan of action, an arm invaded his space behind the bar. Half out of surprise and half out of reflex, he instantly pulled the crossbow's trigger. The bolt shot forth and went clean through the arm at the elbow. It withdrew with a yelp and a cheer from those at the back.

Thinking quickly, Vantix drew the other crossbow and grabbed the nearest unbroken bottle. He tossed the bottle skyward and took aim. The guards shielded their faces as he pulled the trigger, expecting a rain of glass. Unfortunately his aim wasn't so true. There was a collective sigh of sympathetic disappointment as the bolt sailed past the bottle. Following it rather quickly was a cheer as the bottle collided with the face of a member of the guard regardless and those who had money on bottle-in-the-face collected their winnings.

Hunched down behind the bar, Vantix was afforded a moment's respite. Everything had been going perfectly until Incognito had shown up. Should have known that his brief happiness was akin to spitting in fate's face. He didn't notice the groan that accompanied the three minutes elapsing and most patrons losing their money.

Grabbing another bottle he smashed it on the bar and reached for the matches in his pocket. It took a second but then ignited, causing the guards to start back and offer him the slimmest of paths to the stairs. Vantix took it. The patrons accepted his decision to take the party upstairs and the fire as their cue to stagger home.

A bolt zipped by, cutting Vantix's shoulder but doing no permanent damage. He winced and continued up the stairs. All the doors were closed save one leading to a balcony. The guards were at the bottom of the steps as he went for it.

Only when through did he realise there was no staircase leading down in sight. Climbing onto the balustrade he decided against jumping; the square was filled with townsfolk and guards, neither of whom would be overly sympathetic towards the man who burned down the town's most popular tavern. The only way was up.

Shouts went out from below as people saw him throw his bag and then himself up onto the roof. Guards ran for the nearest buildings in search of ways to join the chase but most seemed content to fire arrows at him from the streets.

He took off at great speed, bag over his shoulder. Both the guards and flames from the tavern were making their way up and he wasn't particularly keen on either. Gathering pace as the guards emerged on the roof, he leapt the gap to the next building without turning. He didn't see the tavern's roof realise that six of his pursuers were considerably heavier than one Vantix and give way. Four took the plunge and the two who avoided it continued after him unabated.

Vantix was putting a good distance between them when he heard a crash behind him. *The Smoking Flagon*'s remaining roof collapsed into the flames, but the remaining guards pursuing him had already got clear. Eyes once more focused on his escape route, he noticed other guards had reached the surrounding buildings and seemed intent on intercepting him. Including the two behind him the guards numbered eight and, unless he lengthened his stride, would head him off easily.

Feeling the energy seep from him, he watched as three guards reached the next building and readied themselves for his arrival. Fatigue reared its ugly head but he shouted it down, yelling that there were no other options; he couldn't stop and the buildings either side of him were a good distance away. Full steam ahead to the rendezvous with the three guards.

Vantix had a great head for visualising scenarios. This is what he thought would happen next:

Landing adroitly on the next building he'd avoid the clumsy attempts to detain him and jump to one of rooftops either side. They'd be caught, dumbstruck by his skills and do naught but watch as he vanished into the night. The whole town would be in awe of his exploits.

Unfortunately, he had a pretty active imagination and was always slightly optimistic. The scenarios he visualised rarely bore any resemblance to reality. With that in mind, it was easy to see that things were going to go wrong.

The gap was wider than anticipated, turning his leap into a dive mid-air to compensate. Landing on his injured shoulder and grunting in pain, he was back on his feet mid-grunt. The guards made a move towards him and he didn't even have time to think, he just jumped at the edge. Regret followed shortly afterwards.

Without the proper run up, he obviously wasn't going anywhere. The best he could hope for was that he wouldn't break too many bones when he landed. The odds didn't look promising.

Then the most amazing thing happened; one of the guards miraculously appeared in his way. Vantix barrelled into the big man's chest, momentum sending the pair of them stumbling toward the edge. Both teetered on the brink, locked in an awkward embrace with the roof's tiles protesting the strain. The tiles creaked, moaned and went tumbling from the roof, followed shortly by the guard, still clutching Vantix to his chest.

The fall was no longer than 2 seconds with Vantix's rescuer obligingly taking the majority of the impact. After a moment Vantix sat up. When he did, it was slowly and painfully, his body chiding him for the evening's reckless shenanigans.

The guard had fared far worse. Unconscious, blood beginning to pool around his helmet, which seemed to have sustained a large amount of damage at the back. His chest was also bleeding in several places, darkening the green of his uniform.

Vantix looked up. Several of the guards were peering down at him from the rooftop. Playing the hand he was dealt seemed the most sensible course of action, so he took his leave while he was still free to, fleeing into the darkness of the night.

Chapter 4

At noon the sun shone down upon the denizens of Cannonbridge. The sky was free of clouds yet a chill wind still kept them all wrapped up. Yet none of the townsfolk commented on the weather this day. The only topic of discussion was Vantix.

The town was abuzz with news of his exploits. How he'd killed over 20 men, swindled the entire thieves guild out of a fortune and burned down the inn after he was refused a drink, all in a single evening. It just goes to show, people will lie for the sake of a good story. Already every barmaid in town was claiming to be the one who'd refused him the drink, despite only two of them actually working in "The Smoking Flagon".

Vantix didn't really mind them exaggerating his exploits and painting him as a deceitful murderer or a nefarious character in general. As long as it was him they were talking about, everything was sunshine, rainbows and bubble baths. That in hand he'd have been more satisfied with the outcome of the previous night if he'd actually managed to escape the town.

Last night several guard shaped obstacles had been stationed at every exit. Without a disguise it would have been suicide. Which made it an even bigger inconvenience that his rooms were being guarded; his coalminer's daughter costume would have gone down a treat.

All night he'd clung to the shadows in back alleys and tore down any wanted posters that crossed his path. There was no likeness or picture but the description was fairly accurate: 17 years old, sandy brown hair, blue eyes, average height, lean build, armed and dangerous. That last bit was almost recompense enough for them misspelling his name "Vanticks" at the top of the poster. It went on to claim he'd murdered a thief, burned down a tavern and been responsible for the death of 5 of the town guard. A reward of 200 crowns was offered and Vantix reckoned if caught the guard were unlikely to accept "I was a victim of circumstance" as an excuse. No, fleeing town was his only option.

Currently sitting in a bush, he watched the town's back gate, a change of clothes and few hours' sleep seriously wanting. Looking as grimy and tired as he did, he'd stick out like a sore thumb at an all fingers ball if he tried to leave. That being said one of the guards from the previous night was there so it seemed probable he'd be recognised even after a wash and a change of clothes.

As they searched a cart, Vantix eyed them wearily. They were very thorough, too much so for his liking. Still the only plan his barely functioning mind could come up with at this point, riddled with chances for failure as it was, meant he was headed out that gate. He moved off to find suitable transportation.

*　*　*　*　*

The last twelve hours hadn't gone well for Minos. It was almost enough to make him rethink his career choice. He loved being in the town guard, but at present the hours where getting to him. His shift had begun the previous evening and wouldn't finish until tomorrow evening. This massive blow to worker's rights was all down to the mess they'd made trying to arrest Vantix. According to the sergeant they'd all been lucky not to get the boot.

Scratching his bandaged eye, Minos moaned softly. A bottle thrown by Vantix had hit him in the face last night and gotten a little too intimate with his left eye. On the upside, he now had cause to get a pretty menacing eye patch.

When he'd gotten back to the barracks one of the sergeants had roared at him for hours. His stammered explanations were ignored as the sergeant drenched him in a torrent of angry spittle. It hadn't been his fault the boy had escaped. The whole group had bloody underestimated him. Yet Minos was the only one to get stuck with a double shift because of it.

A cart full of hay came toward them. Minos stepped in front and raised a hand. They'd orders to check everything and he didn't want to be shouted at again.

Motioning for others to follow him, he led the way to the cart. They took position, two on either side. One quickly checked the cart's underside. With the four of them there shouldn't be any room for an escapee. "On three," Minos whispered. The others nodded and the four of them raised their spears. "One, two—", Minos counted. He never reached three. As his tongue tried to wrap itself around the declaration of that final number, his mouth was suddenly filled with hay. Vantix had surfaced, throwing hay all over the four of them.

Minos was knocked back as Vantix leapt onto the front of the cart, spear falling from his grasp as he tumbled to the ground and fetching himself a nasty knock on the way down.

The youth cracked the reins and the cart took off, taking its contents and its owner with him. The guards were dumbstruck, managing to do little but watch as the cart sped away. Several moments too late a spear was thrown but nobody would admit to it later.

Minos sat up, head pounding. "Was that him?", shouted one of the others. "Of course it was him!" he roared back. He stopped rubbing his head and looked around. He wasn't the only one on the ground, which made him feel slightly better. *This day is not going well*, he thought to himself. However, when he drew the short straw and was forced to tell the sergeant, it got a whole lot worse

* * * * *

Vantix got off the cart about a mile from town. Its owner turned around and headed back, confident in the knowledge his story about transporting the dangerous outlaw would beat any story about refusing him a drink.

Vantix waited until the cart was out of sight before turning back the way he came. There was an emergency kit stashed in an abandoned tower on the outskirts of the town in case either Farack or himself ever had pressing need. His current situation seemed to meet the criteria.

The tower was rumoured to be haunted but in his experience that was just superstition. He did encourage the belief though, that way he could treat it as his own personal hideout.

With luck, he thought as he walked to his destination, *the guards will have reported that I've left town.* In Vantix's opinion, that was one of the best things about the guards in Cannonbridge. They didn't carry grudges and track you across entire provinces; once you left town they didn't care. As soon as he was rumoured to have left, all efforts to find him would cease. Still it wouldn't do him any favours to be seen in town for a while.

He looked up as he passed the water tower. It was basically just a large empty bucket on stilts. The water had long since gone, but this was not common knowledge. As far as the town was concerned, water from this tower quenched the thirst of their cattle. It's worth nothing almost eighty percent of all cattle in Cannonbridge die of dehydration.

Of course this wasn't actually his destination and as such, he hurried on to the supposedly haunted tower. Months had been spent building himself a cosy little nest there. Rotten floorboards had been replaced, shelves put up and a mattress dragged up two flights of stairs. Everything essential for a hasty departure from town was stored there. Eventually he'd been planning on turning it into a valuable property and selling it.

The tower's door swung open at his touch. There was no need for locks; the only other person ever here was Farack and he was gone on that foolish dendrid hunt. Moving slowly up the stairs, Vantix was a little disappointed; he'd be leaving before getting to replace them. This place could have been a lovely lair for anybody just a little shy of sane.

At the top of the stairs he threw down his bag of weapons. Grabbing a backpack from a corner, he looked around the room. So many possessions, so little room for them on the road ahead. Packing was always such sweet sorrow.

Throwing the essentials into his bag, suddenly the bed seemed to occupy his vision. It whispered enticingly of warmth, comfort and rest. *A couple of hours won't hurt*, it said. Vantix couldn't deny how tired he felt; the bags under his eyes had bags that had satchels that were wearing fanny-packs. With that stunt at the gate he was home-free anyway.

He lay down on the mattress and pulled the blankets over himself. Sleep was instant.

* * * * *

Welbh turned toward the group assembled before him. Every province in Ballisca had a branch of "The Merchants Guild" and Fardash was no different. He'd made the journey to Freatsrak in order to offer them a contract they weren't going to get anywhere else. "So you see," he picked up where he'd left off, "this really is a once in a lifetime opportunity."

Several of the congregation nodded, but Welbh wasn't paying them any attention. He only paid attention to those he hadn't convinced yet. Some people required a different sort of incentive.

"Think of your families," he said, "the King isn't going to provide for them. Are you content to watch as they starve, knowing that you could have, and should have, done something? You're the only ones who'll hear them crying with hunger in the night. The only ones who can prevent that from happening." More of the group nodded but it wasn't enough. All were needed.

Welbh was about to offer more carrot when somebody stepped forward. It was Dreyfuss, a senior member of the guild. "Need I point out to you," he motioned to Welbh, "that this is an honourable establishment. What you propose is treason!" A number of people who'd

35

nodded to him, now nodded their agreement to this statement.

Welbh smiled; Dreyfuss's interjection was one he'd anticipated. "Ah," he declared, "Is it though?"

Dreyfuss looked at him incredulously. "Trading with our enemies? Of course it-"

Welbh cut across him. "Since when is it treason to ensure the people do not starve? To bring wealth and industry to our nation? It won't be treason anyway. The King will soon be negotiating peace treaties with Derranferd. I'm simply offering you a chance to get a leg up on the competition."

Dreyfuss waved his hand dismissively at Welbh's words and asked the question on everybody's mind. "What's in it for you?"

Welbh shrugged. "Money," he said simply.

There was silence around the room. "Money," Welbh repeated before adding, "Think about this gentleman. In approximately five minutes I shall leave. Now it's all up to you. Would you rather stick steadfast to the laws of the land and some ill-conceived code of conduct, instead of saving your families and crediting yourselves as those who brought wealth and prosperity to Fardash?"

He looked at his watch again. "If you don't take advantage of my offer ," he proclaimed, "Don't worry too much about it. This deal is going ahead. There are plenty of people with extremely questionable morals who'd only love to avail of my generosity." Most of them itched to agree with him, it was clear in their faces.

"These other people won't think twice about keeping the money for themselves. They'll accumulate wealth while your children wither away and you'll ask yourself why you so selfishly clung to honour." He let that sink in for a moment and then stated, "Let's make it 2 minutes."

* * * * *

Approximately five minutes later, Welbh strode toward his carriage. There was a sheaf of signed papers under his arm. Inside he danced and screamed with smug delight but his face was a mask of composure. The merchants were still watching him and he wouldn't dare have them think he was pleased by their acquiescence to his proposition.

Pulling himself up into his carriage, he resisted the urge to count all the money he was going to make then and there. Seconds after leaning back into his chair with a satisfied sigh, he was on his feet with his knife drawn. The reason for this was the unexpected passenger seated across from him.

It was a woman. She was in her early thirties like himself but her eyes made her look older. They were cold and dead and unforgiving. These coupled with the assassin tattoo on her neck, were the cause for Welbh's agitation. She didn't even flinch as he put his knife to her neck.

"I bring a message," her voice was flat and emotionless. He didn't react. "It's from your brother."

"What does he want now?"

"The message is ten days." said the woman, "My name is Lila. You will be hearing from me again." With that she pushed his blade away, stepped out the door and was lost from view. Although Welbh hadn't noticed it the carriage was already on its way out of the city.

He cursed. What did she mean by ten days? There was an innumerable number of twisted things lurking up his brother's sleeves. Sending an assassin to deliver a message was just like him and his terrible sense of humour. Probably laugh himself to sleep when she told

37

him how Welbh had leapt out of his seat with the knife. "I thought I made myself abundantly clear last time…" Welbh mumbled, "Bloody Lintous, he ruins everything."

After several moments cursing his brother and wishing they'd been adopted by different families, he settled down. They were heading to Daichwater but there was a stop to be made on the way back that instantly brought a smile to his face. Honestly, there didn't seem any way his brother could derail his plans this time.

Chapter 5

There are a lot of things in the world people like to wake up to. Breakfast in bed, a beautiful morning and for some strange reason a slobbering pet are all on this list. Feeling the cold steel of a blade against your neck, however, is not. At least not in acceptable social circles.

Vantix felt the cold steel of a blade prick his neck. His eyes snapped open. It took a minute for them to grow accustomed to the scene before him. The knife pressed to his neck looked sharp and dangerous judging from the few droplets of blood that were already making their way toward his shirt. His gaze moved to the hand gripping the blade, then it took a stroll up the length of an arm where finally, it rested upon familiar hooded features.

Ever the showman, he had trouble resisting the urge to jump up and declare "You!", in an astonished tone. As it so happened, his neck held him back. It didn't seem overly enthusiastic about a rendezvous with the knife.

From the other end of the knife, Incognito smirked at him. Pulling back his hood and pocketing the weapon, he seemed on the verge of once again declaring he had a proposition for Vantix when he was rudely interrupted.

"I already said no," Vantix grunted.

"This time the offer's different."

"How so?"

"Well," Incognito elaborated, "before all you could hope for was money. Now, I can get you pardoned."

"Why would I want that?," Vantix retorted, "I've got a reputation now."

"You call one town a reputation?," Incognito scoffed. "With that kind of infamy you could disappear and not even your friends would notice. You're nothing. Just like your father. Now what was his name I wonder?"

The younger man looked up, face ablaze with anger. "Don't you dare speak about him"

"I don't remember him," Incognito said flatly. "Nobody does. You can be different Vantix. With my help they'll sing about you."

Vantix was silent. Much as he hated to admit it, there was truth in Incognito's words.

"To be honest, all I can really get you pardoned for is the murder," the other man went on, "The guards saw you start that fire."

"Then what's the incentive?"

"I already mentioned the renown; the fame you so desperately desire."

Normally Vantix would have jumped at this chance yet there was some satisfaction to be had in refusing the offer. Incognito's machinations irked him. Being a cog in somebody else's schemes wasn't as appealing as being the star of his own production. "Find someone else."

For a moment Incognito seemed to consider this. "Nope," he said eventually, "You're the one I want, nay need, for this job. It has to be you."

"Is that why you went to so much trouble? Why you murdered someone and put the blame on me?"

"I always get what I want."

"Not this time."

Incognito sighed. "Then I guess it is my duty, as a concerned citizen of Fardash, to take you back to town to be hung by the neck until dead," he finished flatly. His blade was at Vantix's throat again.

Vantix groaned. Since no other option presented itself, it seemed he'd have to do it. "I'll still get the money, right?"

Incognito smiled. "Of course."

*   *   *   *   *

A short while later, Vantix sat in the shadow of a boulder about a mile from the town's west gate. The few cuts and bruises from the previous evening had been easily dealt with and a wash and change of clothes had certainly left him feeling fresher. Everything he wore was a shade of green and grey. Green breeches, a grey tunic with green boots all covered by a grey cloak. He actually blended in rather well. That's why only one member of the group noticed him.

The other three were talking excitably about the 200 crowns they were about to earn. They seemed to have forgotten what was required for them to earn their shares.

Vantix stood up from his cover and grabbed his bag. Inside it were all the things he'd deemed worth taking from the tower, mostly weapons and clothes. Farack nodded to him, while the other three stared. It looked like he emerged from the rock.

"Knew you'd come," said Farack as his friend fell into step with them.

Vantix stared straight ahead whilst replying, "Didn't have much of a choice." He looked round at the others, before turning back to Farack. "Those three wouldn't happen to be the thirteen others he mentioned, would they?"

"We're meeting the other ten by Lake Glasrobe. Then the fifteen of us ambush the dendrid" Farack answered, before adding, "Nice escape the other night. The entire town was very impressed."

Vantix smiled. "Thanks, much appreciated."

They came to a crossroads. Without thinking, Vantix and Farack continued straight on, still heading westward. One of the other three called out to them, "Wrong way."

Vantix turned. The voice belonged to Osca, who worked in the local livery with his father. He was the same height as Farack, measuring up to Vantix's nose but a year older and wiry. The other two were Donre and Terif. They were twins but not identical. Both were only sixteen but tall, broad and built enough to be mistaken for men at least a decade older. Terrible beards graced both their faces. The whole time Vantix spent thinking this, Osca had been trying to explain something to him. He came to attention, just as Osca finished.

"Sorry," Vantix said, "didn't quite catch any of that."

Osca pointed out the northern path. "Shouldn't we go this way?"

Farack shook his head. "If we go that way we'll need to travel alongside the gorge and cross it at one point. It's full of vicious, slimy creatures with big teeth and non-discriminatory diets. Not exactly a nice place. Definitely not the kind of path we should take."

This time Osca shook his head. "I'm sure the five of us are more than capable of dealing with anything the gorge throws into our path."

Vantix ignored him and turned back the way he was headed. "This way it is then," he declared to Osca's chagrin. "We'd best move fast. This way brings us closer to the dendrid then I'm comfortable."

* * * * *

"I've always found something extremely sinister about people who frequent churches," whispered Incognito as he knelt in the pew, "it seems to me that penitence hides a guilty conscience."

The elf beside him neglected to respond and continued mumbling under his breath.

Port Daichwater, the smallest province in Ballisca, is a thriving port city, walled on three sides. It hosts a vast and diverse population, all with their own customs and traditions. As such there's a wider variety of religions and churches than everywhere else in the whole of Ballisca. Incognito now found himself in a Listening Shrine dedicated to Phaeris, the Nospac goddess of mercy. It wasn't his ideal venue for a business meeting; he'd have preferred somewhere with alcohol but a reliable source had informed him his quarry spent quite a bit of time here. That information had been proven correct.

"It's almost as if they resent something they've done so much," Incognito tried again, "that all they can do is provide endless supplications for the god's forgiveness."

Once again the elf refused to commit to this conversation and prayed on.

"Then again," Incognito went on, "maybe it's not something they've done. Perhaps it's concern for the welfare of their loved ones. Or rather, the souls of their loved ones."

At this the elf's ears picked up slightly. Incognito smiled; he had him right where he wanted him. "This is purely just a hypothetical now, but let's say something

43

happened that tore a family apart. What if we were to suppose that the remaining member of that family swore he'd survive to ensure sins were atoned for and a very specific debt repaid."

The tanned elf ceased his praying immediately and turned to face Incognito. The Nospac were a nomadic tribe of elves from the deserts of northern Ballisca and he was indubitably one of them. Ears were both larger and pointier than other elves while the jaw was slightly stronger. He fixed Incognito a searching look from the strange indigo eyes so many of his people possessed.

"Imagine a chance meeting with a mysterious benefactor finally afforded him the opportunity he'd been searching for all these long years," Incognito let the suggestion linger in the air for a second, "would he be inclined to seize it?"

He could see the hunger in the elf's eyes but it was tinged with caution. "You seem to know me very well," he replied quietly, "who is your source?"

Incognito looked around the dingy hall. It wasn't the kind of church that provided ample cover for eavesdroppers. Realistically it was just a hall, several statues and a few pews. Nobody lurked in the shadows, they were alone.

"While I consider myself too much of a savoury character to be his friend, Gaius Swifte was quite happy to oblige me with the information," Incognito explained. The caution was necessary; Swifte was quite touchy and it was almost impossible to tell when one of his ears were present.

"No need for the details," the elf said, "there's no task I wouldn't undertake for that reward. Whatever you need or want, I don't care. I'm just delighted to make your acquaintance." He extended his hand and Incognito shook it warmly

* * * * *

Several hours later, the group was still moving swiftly enough. Night had fallen yet they were content to keep going. A few hours had passed since they'd turned northward so Lake Glasrobe was a straight walk from their current position. When they'd walked along the north road for a little over an hour, Donre asked Vantix a question. "Farack tells us you fought a dendrid before?"

Vantix nodded but didn't say anything.

Donre stared at him for a while before asking again.

Vantix sighed. They wouldn't stop asking until he told them the story. "I tried the whole adventurer business before. It didn't end well. Suffice to say, I was the only one of the group who came back. The last one fell to a stray dendrid we encountered on the road. It was one of the scariest things I've ever seen."

The others listened, spellbound as he went on. "The feeling you get when you see one is unbelievable. I can't describe it. You'll know it before our journey is over. They can be killed by the sword just like any other man but they're much more resilient and can take a good deal more punishment then you or I. The bravest men have been known to drop their weapons at the sight of them. Worst thing about the dendrid is their breath, breathe it in just once and your soul will flee your body. Then," he shuddered, " they feed on it. If you die whilst fighting them, you'll be absolutely obliterated. There'll be no heaven or hell for you. You'll be done. Completely and utterly gone."

He clamped down and the others wondered if coming on this quest had been worth it. Money versus eternal nothingness was a difficult dilemma.

Up ahead the temple came into view. The group quickened their pace. The road went straight through the temple and as such it was a popular place to camp. Vantix had promised them they'd stay there for the night. It had once been an actual temple but it, and the god it had once been a shrine to, had long since been forgotten. It had once had arches, columns and statues. Now all that remained were the walls on either side, half the front entrance, a corner of the roof and, remarkably, several stained glass windows.

The group walked in and threw their bags down. It was past midnight and the days walking had caught up with them. Their stomachs, however, demanded to be sated before allowing them to slumber.

Terif and Donre got a fire going, as Farack produced strips of bacon from his bag. Osca had scaled the wall and was seated on the remainder of the roof, keeping lookout.

Not having got much sleep the night before, Vantix nodded off almost immediately. It was only several seconds later, that a shout disturbed his slumber. As he opened his eyes, he heard Farack calling to Osca. "What is it?" the rhadon asked.

"The dendrid," Osca shouted back, "They're coming right now."

Chapter 6

Unfortunately for Incognito the door was locked. Unfortunately for the door he didn't care in the slightest. After taking it's measure and brandishing the hatchet he'd procured for just this eventuality, he set about the task with relish. The only distraction was the landlady scurrying up to protest until he dismissed her by throwing coins down the hallway.

When he'd finished, the room beyond offered exactly the view he'd been expecting. Some people were too predictable. The furniture was all serviceable and in good taste with the occasionally completely incongruous splash of extravagance. Obviously all the better pieces had been looted from her parent's home before her departure. What seemed to elude this apartment's inhabitant was that a hovel this wretched was far past the point of no return. Dress a chicken in the finest frock you can find and it's pretty guaranteed that everybody will still know it's a chicken. The same could be said for the décor in this apartment.

Leaving the door demolished behind him, Incognito quickly lit the small stove and grabbed the nearest pan.

47

The ingredients he'd brought with him would be quite a treat to someone who'd subjected to the cuisine of Freatsrak for any extended duration. Some might say the lengths he went to for good help were a bit unwarranted but Incognito disagreed. Through the deeds they accomplished each one of his merry band would prove their worth.

As usual Incognito's timing was immaculate. No sooner had he finished laying the table, with cutlery and china from his own house, than there was a sharp intake of breath from the hallway. The familiar sound of a blade being unsheathed reached his ears as he took a seat at the far end of the table, facing the door.

Bursting into the room, it was seconds before the girl's vision locked on Incognito. "What do you want?" she demanded.

Gesturing towards the chair at the far end of the table Incognito gave her his perfected reassuring smile. "I'd very much like for you to sit."

"What about my door, you oaf?"

"I have the matter in hand," Incognito indicated the chair once more, "I'd be much obliged if you'd sit."

Warily the girl sat. Taking a sniff she eyed her meal. "None of this belongs to me."

"Neither does this." Incognito stood to get the wine only to find his feet weren't that keen on movement. The girl laughed as Incognito stared in amazement at the strange manner in which floor had grown upwards and swallowed his feet. "That," he smiled, "is damn impressive."

Slowly the floor crept back down to the corner propriety had dumped it in. The girl tucked into the meal, pleasantly surprised to find Incognito was quite the cook. "Is your name important enough to lie about?"

"Definitely," Incognito replied, "Anyway it's your name, or more specifically your last name, that interests me. What would a daughter of so noble a family as your own be doing residing in a place like this?"

The girl's expression darkened and her smile guttered. Explaining slowly and deliberately, she extolled her new life here. Far from the restrictions and intrigue of court life she'd discovered there was more to life than silk garments, horse riding and being waited on day after day. Either that or something equally disingenuous. Incognito had been too busy preparing his response to afford her the courtesy of listening.

"That's very good, almost convincing. Unfortunately no matter how good a liar you are this place gives you away." Gesturing towards an ornate vase he continued, "Pieces such as that are extremely out of place in these lugubrious surroundings. Obviously purloined from your parent's humble abode. If you were really hoping of a life here it'd be rather simple to sell it and live off the proceeds. That is your parent's favourite piece, which you took to punish them because they were ashamed, nay disgusted, by what you really are."

Tyrannical silence reigned for several moments until it was overthrown by the powers of conversation. Finishing off her meal, the girl gave Incognito a sharp look. "Disgusted was a rather strong choice of word."

"You know what would really show your parents?" Incognito sipped his wine, "Being strong enough to survive on your own. Using your talents to show how little they and their world are worth. Throwi-"

"I take it then," the girl interrupted, "that you have an opportunity with my name on it in big bold letters?"

Incognito nodded. "For which you'll be very well rewarded."

A pointy hat leapt off the hat stand and seemed to saunter through the air before placing itself graciously on the girl's head. Incognito marvelled at this display and raised his glass. The girl raised hers in turn. "I'm thrilled to accept."

* * * * *

People kill. They have since the beginning and they will in the end. A specific person might abhor violence and regard all life as sacred but taken as a whole people have blood on their hands. It's the one thing that unites all creeds, races, and species. That's what makes why they kill such an interesting question.

Some kill to protect themselves or their loved ones. Some kill for causes or beliefs. They kill out of envy, they kill out of greed, they kill because somebody looked at them the wrong way and because their brother's wife is prettier. They'll fabricate a whole multitude of reasons to justify spilling the blood of another. Yet in spite of all this, they still think themselves above anybody who kills for money.

Assassins are viewed with distaste no matter the school they've trained in; their dedication and skill, and; whether they enjoy it or not. All the general public come back to is that they're paid to kill. It's this transaction, so detached from emotion, that makes assassins so cold and methodical. Taking the measure of somebody's life, tolling up their worth and reducing them to a single sum, disconcerts people. Even if they're the life and soul of the party their job will taint them in the eyes of everybody else.

The assassin outside the Royal Negotiator's mansion wasn't like that. For him killing was necessitated every once in a while, an unavoidable aspect of life much like taxes or mothers.

Two guards brandishing torches walked straight past, not registering the eyes ostensibly hovering in the shadows. At this time of night he was practically invisible. Counting the seconds, he waited until they rounded the corner then turned to inspect the mansion.

The Royal Negotiator's abode was large, stylish and offered many avenues for intruders to take advantage of. Coming in through the roof was an option but you could never tell if these noble families would have their embarrassing, demented relative stashed up there. The front door was an obvious one but would cause something of a commotion if chosen. A balcony along with the basement and ground floor windows were all dismissed as locked. While that could be rectified, it was better to leave no trace of his presence. In the end a third floor window with a drainpipe located conveniently nearby (plumbing had just taken off in Fardash) seemed the best bet.

Ascending the drainpipe noiselessly, snatches of the patrolling guards conversations reached his ears:

"...I don't know, it just really stings when I bend over or crouch down."

"Have you put some ointment on it?"

"Don't think there's enough in all of Ballisca. I'll tell you one thing though, that's the last time I'll eat Lundion food before I meet a girl's parents."

"Must have been pretty awkward."

"I'll say. They were so busy trying to get me out of the house they wouldn't even let me wipe the seat. And I had more..."

He carried on.

On reaching his destination it was a simple matter to swing over, grab the ledge and hoist himself inside. After his eyes adjusted to the dimness of the room, the assassin paused. Thirty cats were staring at him in silence. "What the?" he breathed.

Feline eyes followed him across the floor but the cats didn't budge an inch. The door was locked. Reaching for the lock pick in his back pocket he noticed that while he'd been testing the door the cats had moved. They were still immobile, yet the distance between him and them seemed to have lessened.

Slipping his lock pick into the lock, he listened for the tell-tale click.

The cats were closer.

His lock pick broke and he reached into his pocket for the spare.

The cats began to meow. Randomly at first but they soon settled on an eerie intermittent rhythm. Ever closer they edged.

Finally the door clicked and he was through it just as paws snatched at his heels. The door closed behind him. Standing in the corridor with his back against the door, the assassin considered what had just transpired. "That was really weird," he said to nobody in particular. An answering meow sent him hurrying away.

Several days had been spent measuring the layout of the castle. Instantly he knew the room he sought was a floor lower and headed to his destination. Along the way he eyed the portraits of the Royal Negotiator's predecessors. There was a clear correlation between the times they lived and how haggard and put upon they looked. Those who lived in peace and prosperity were generously proportioned and jolly while the others looked like homeless people who'd broken into a theatre troupe's costume trunk.

Where there had been a vast number of rooms on the floor above, this floor had only one and it's entrance was guarded at all times. A single guard was on duty, at least another four hour shift ahead of him. Unfortunately, the assassin didn't have the patience to wait that long. He removed a dart from his belt and tossed it with incredible accuracy. It sped through the air and planted itself in the guard's neck. The guard grunted, before collapsing but the assassin ensured he didn't hit the ground. A big man hitting the ground makes an inconvenient amount of noise to anybody trying to be inconspicuous. The assassin lowered the man gently to the floor, before moving on.

Twisting the door's handle, he stepped inside. A brief glance around the room brought a smile to his lips. There was enough wealth in the room to feed a family for life, buy them all ponies and then pay for the surgery to turn those ponies into unicorns. Tapestries adorned the wall. Numerous bookcases were filled with gold statues and other artefacts of value. Ornate swords hung over a very intricate fireplace.

His quarry snored loudly, drawing his attention to the bed. It was absolutely huge, a four poster mountain. Not only that but runes and symbols were engraved all over. It was also made of gold. Although it must have cost a fortune, the assassin couldn't help but turn away in disgust. To him it just seemed tacky. Assassins hold style in very high regard.

Eventually he spotted what he'd been looking for: a goblet rested on a table beside the bed. It was filled with wine. He took a quick sip to quench his thirst, before emptying the contents of a small capsule into the goblet.

The wine fizzed for a moment then the surface cleared. It looked invitingly innocent.

Slitting the Royal Negotiator's throat would have been much easier but this way created less of a mess. After pocketing several valuables, he turned to leave. It was then the assassin made his only real mistake of the evening. His foot caught the leg of a table, knocking it over. Fine china flew through the air and shattered on the floor below. He fell, hitting the floor just as his target's eyes flickered open.

The Royal Negotiator sat up and his gaze darted around the room. When it landed on the assassin, it settled. The big man leapt out of bed and grabbed one of the swords from the wall. He thundered toward the intruder.

The assassin stumbled to his feet and ran toward the door. As he pulled it open, the Royal Negotiator reached him and swung the sword in a wide arc. It was very unlikely to miss.

*   *   *   *   *

Farack dragged himself onto the remaining roof. Osca was beside him and the others were hidden in different places around the ruins. These offered a slight feeling of security, even if they wouldn't generally be considered good hiding places.

There hadn't exactly been much time to get themselves hidden. Vantix lay under a cloak with some rocks and dirt thrown on it, Donre was behind a stack of rotten crates and Terif was being squeezed against the wall behind some fallen rubble.

The dendrid were obviously coming through here; it was unavoidable. From where they were perched Farack and Osca saw the dendrid before the others. Instantly they wished they hadn't.

Dendrid have clawed feet and hands and a predisposition toward wicked looking swords. Their feet went unadorned and the clothes they did wear were tattered and torn. Pallid skin was complimented by strange hair with a purplish tinge, although few had more than tufts. Their eyes, which looked out from sunken sockets, were a sickly yellow and there was not a trace of pupils. All had the same black lips that opened to reveal sharp yellow fangs. There was a savage cruelty to their features. They looked like they could do unspeakable things and then speak about them anyway.

Around them silence reigned. As if even the wind was afraid to be in their presence. The hair on the back of Farack's neck stood up as he watched them. If at all possible, it stood up even further when the dendrid came to a halt.

One of them sniffed as the others watched. A forked tongue flicked out and it seemed to taste the air. They spoke in strange hissing sounds, eerie, uncomfortable on the ear and difficult for Farack to think of a comparison that'd adequately convey how bewildering it was.

The single dendrid moved slowly back to the centre of the ruins. Beside him, Farack heard a soft click and turned around. Osca was aiming a crossbow. "What the hell do you think you're doing?", Farack asked quietly.

 "They know we're here," Osca whispered back, "I say we attack while we still can."

Farack grabbed a hold of the crossbow. "You attack and we're dead," he hissed. Osca looked daggers at him before trying to shake him off.

Unaware of the struggle going on overhead, Donre was almost rigid as the dendrid moved slowly closer to where he hid. He was sweating and his hands fumbled along the ground below him, trying to find his axe. *If I can just get a hold of it...*, a voice muttered in his head. He felt his hands wrapped themselves around the axe's handle and raised it slowly.

Had he been paying it more attention perhaps he'd have left it alone. As the axe came up, it knocked against the crates in front of him. They tumbled to the ground with a resounding thump, leaving him completely exposed to the dendrid. "Oh shi-," he managed to exclaimed as the creatures ran toward him.

His exclamation drew the attention of Farack and Osca. For a moment the struggle ceased as both turned to see what was going on. As Osca stood staring, the rhadon wrested the crossbow from his grasp. Without taking the time to aim, he pulled the trigger.

Luck was firmly on his side. The bolt flew through the air before planting itself in the creature's head. It went limp as a rag doll and crashed straight into Donre, who went down with it. Farack and Osca drew their swords and leapt from the roof, straight into the fray.

"Block your noses!" Vantix called. Remembering what he'd said about the dendrid's breath, the others pulled their shirts up. They noticed that he'd managed to pull a scarf from somewhere and tied it around his head.

Then they didn't have time to notice anything else. Farack raised his shield and a dendrid sword crashed against it. The odds weren't exactly in their favour. As he parried a sword from the other side a single thought raced through his mind; *I'm going to kill Donre.*

The others weren't faring too well either. Terif and Donre were back to back, a circle of dendrid toying with them. The dendrid kept edging slowly forward. The brothers had axes that their father had given them, but all they struck was clean air.

Vantix had two. To be fair, two had him is a more accurate description. He had a short sword in each hand, but it was all he could do to block the creatures continuous attacks. He ducked under a blow before striking at the hand, sending a sword skidding away. Underneath his makeshift bandana he smiled; it was nice to make some headway.

Osca was going toe-to-toe with one of them. The creature was faster than him and came at him from every side, but he managed to block all its attempts by flicking his wrist in one direction and then the next. He couldn't actually be said to be winning but he certainly wasn't losing.

Farack was actually doing rather well. Although he was fighting two, they only came at him from one angle. He had his back to the wall, but so far he'd given worse than he'd got. He deflected another blow with his shield, before smashing it into the creature's chest.

Then the dendrid were done playing. Donre's axe hit clean air once again, but this time it didn't go unpunished. A dendrid sword went straight through his throat. Terif spun around. "Donre!" he yelled. He leapt through the air, swinging wildly. This time he actually hit something.

Terif's swing completely missed the dendrid. It did, however, make decent contact with the wall; gave the already crumbling masonry the final push it needed. The wall collapsed. Not only on top of him, it also covered the limp body of Donre. A stray brick even hit Osca's head, sending him into unconsciousness.

While this was happening, Farack had lost the upper hand. The dendrid advanced and with every step, he was pushed farther into the corner. The horrible quality of the temple's walls does not need reiterating. So it's no surprise that when he was finally pushed back into the corner, the impact his body made against the rock caused the final section of roof to come down. He managed to bring his shield up to protect his face but the tiles covered him, too heavy to simply shrug off.

It was only as he heard this crash and saw the final two dendrid walking toward him, that Vantix realised how much trouble he was in. It was pleasantly surprising. Eight of the dendrid formed a wide circle and the other one stepped in. Granted, it wasn't a very pleasant surprise but seeing as he'd just expected the nine of them to devour him, it still counts.

Holding the other two off had been hard work. Vantix wiped his forehead with his sleeve. The scarf was making him sweat but he couldn't run the risk of not wearing it.

The creature came at him. It was quick and dangerous but lacked proper form or training. The first few attacks he parried easily, taking its measure. Ducking under a reckless swipe, he planted one of his swords deep into the creature's abdomen and tumbled away.

If he was being honest, Vantix wasn't surprised when the creature didn't fall. Dendrid are far more durable than other species, palpable through its neglect to remove his sword before attacking again.

With only one sword he found it much more difficult to block the attacks. The creature was just as comfortable lashing out with its clawed hands as its sword, even hampered by its chest wound. As soon as he parried one attack, he had to dodge another. His broadsword was sheathed across his back and both his miniature crossbows were at his belt, but he didn't have time to reach them.

The dendrid's sword came down in a diagonal arc. Sidestepping outside it, Vantix pushed this advantage and planted his other sword into the creature's chest.

An outstretched claw snagged on his scarf, ripping it from his shoulders and leaving the lower half of his face exposed when he pulled away. The creature dropped to its knees, blood dripping from the corner of its open mouth. It was finished.

Vantix reached behind his head to draw his broadsword and had an instant vision of his future:

He drew his broadsword and decapitated the monster. The other dendrid cowered in fear as he came after them, leaving not a single one alive. On meeting with Incognito, he collected payment for not only himself, but also his fallen comrades. He delivered the money to their families and the whole nation sang of his deeds. Vantix the Just! Vantix the Deliverer! Vantix Dendrid-Slayer!

As has been acknowledged before, Vantix's visions are wildly inaccurate.

His right hand tightened around the hilt of his sword. Suddenly his foe leapt up , wrapping its arms around him. Wriggling, he cursed the tight, undiminishing grasp. He lashed out, one arm was clamped under the monster's grip but the other more than capable to pummel the creature's face. It squeezed him ever tighter, not registering the two swords being pushed even further into its body.

Vantix wheezed and spluttered as the grip tightened. Struggling in vain, he sought a way out of this deadly embrace. Then his fingers found something. They closed around the trigger of his miniature crossbow, sending an arrow flying from the crossbow at his belt, along the length of his thigh and into the dendrid's kneecap.

The creature gasped. Its rank, putrid breath washed over Vantix's exposed face and then everything went black.

Chapter 7

". . . . .and apparently, he managed to strike the assassin," Jandelk explained, "but his swing was half blocked by the door and only struck the assailant's shoulder."

"So the Royal Negotiator survived, your highness?" Welbh asked.

The King shook his head. "No, he didn't. His encounter with the assassin left him understandably thirsty. Unfortunately he chose to quench it by drinking from his bedside goblet. It had been poisoned."

Welbh nodded for no particular reason. The Royal Negotiator had always been dim but drinking from a pre-filled goblet moments after chasing a fleeing assassin out of his room was stupidity in its highest form. Welbh felt it practically justified his death. It hadn't been his first crime against intelligence.

"I have decided that as the only applicant, you shall assume the role of Royal Negotiator" Jandelk informed him. Welbh nodded once more, but didn't say anything. He could tell from the king's tone that no words were necessary.

Jandelk wasn't exactly pleased with current turn of events. Lord Falisbur, the previous Royal Negotiator, had been particularly good at his job, possessing exactly the right balance of ambition, tact and deference to service the needs of their nation without insulting others. Welbh on the other hand, lacked restraint. His ambition wasn't something easily thwarted. People who stood in his way weren't able to stand very long. Obviously the King could have had him executed yet his merits outweighed this relentless ambition. When the times called for desperate measures, Welbh never shirked from the required action, no matter how questionable. It was best to give him what he wanted, at least for the time being.

Welbh was struggling to keep a smile off his face. *You've got to love royalty,* he thought. They provided ample opportunity for him to achieve all he desired.

"You may go," the King motioned for him to leave. Welbh bowed and was at the door by the time Jandelk called him again.

Turning around, he was slightly annoyed to find the King deep in thought. There were things to do, people to see and arrangements to make. Other people would have been terrified if the King gave them the same amount of consideration he dedicated to Welbh. They would have run, tried to apologise without knowing their crime but the new Royal Negotiator turned to face him without a word.

After several moments quiet contemplation, the King placed the crown upon his head before asking, "Did you hire an assassin to take care of Falisbur?"

Welbh's expression of shock was perfect. "No, my lord," he said drenching every syllable in surprise and insulted feelings.

Jandelk stared at him for a moment. "Be sure to get your shoulder seen to then. I'll need you at your best,"

Jandelk picked up a book and began to read, "You may go."

Welbh walked out into the corridor and closed the door quietly behind him.

* * * * *

Back in his chamber, Welbh checked his shoulder. It was bandaged and had long since stopped bleeding. Being a suspect in Falisbur's death was a given, being suspected of dealing the blow himself was not.

Nobody knew of his time at the academy or anything else about his past for that matter. As far as they were concerned he'd appeared at the castle looking for work six months ago with a letter of recommendation that couldn't be ignored. Jandelk must have known more than he thought. Caution would have to be exercised from this point onwards.

That idiot Falisbur had certainly left a mark on his shoulder. It'd definitely scar. It was hard for Welbh to get annoyed though. Everything was coming up his way. The plan was already well underway. All that remained was to arrange a meeting for Audron and Jandelk so he'd have an opportunity to seal the deal with the Derranferd Merchant's guild.

A parchment on the table caught his eye, dated for this evening. It hadn't been there when the King had summoned him. Glancing down at it he read the message;

Eight days, little brother. Be patient.
Lintous

Welbh's head was instantly filled with questions. What did his brother mean by eight days? More importantly, how did he get this in here?

* * * * *

Vantix was in a dark place. Everything was dark, the floor, the roof and all else that surrounded him. Curtains of darkness hung from walls of the same. They seemed to flow and ripple as if caught in the wind.

His body was moving of its own accord. Reassuming control took effort; he had to reach out and stretch himself into all his appendages before his body decided to obey him with a tingling sensation.

There was a path leading onwards through this dark corridor but Vantix's attention was diverted to the strange flowing walls. Behind them there were scenes and figures moving, too difficult to distinguish in the dim light.

He strayed from the path, making his way over to the flowing walls. They looked solid enough but his hands had no problem moving beyond them. After deciding they looked fine, he took a deep breath and walked through.

It was a passageway, carved entirely from stone and lit by torches along the walls. Vantix was sprinting full pelt down the hall. He was also standing to one side watching himself run. For a second his mind wondered how there could be two of him in the one place. It promptly gave up.

Although he wasn't moving, he was still keeping up with the running him. The walls and ground were left behind without him ever budging an inch. The other him was mumbling something. Despite sprinting at full speed, he still had enough energy to pant, "Got..to..find..her..", repeatedly.

Then Vantix knew what this was. There'd only ever been cause to utter those words whilst running down a tunnel once. Two years ago, the last time he'd tried to make it as a treasure hunter. The scene before him was a memory.

Moving away from the running figure, he headed towards the inky, forgotten blackness and stepped through it, leaving the memory behind. He didn't want to be there in a couple of moments, as it didn't end well.

The hallway looked exactly as it had moments before. All around him the memories flickered and hummed. Taking a few steps down the hall, he poked his head into a different memory. This one was even older.

For a moment he wondered if this was the afterlife. It didn't look much like any heaven he'd ever heard described. Seriously lacking in the cherubs and cello department. Could have also done with better lighting and an all-you-can-eat buffet if they asked him. For a moment he wondered if he'd died when the dendrid breathed upon him and had been sent here to consider his life. *It certainly hadn't been long enough*, was his chief complaint.

Moving up the hallway, the memories became more recent. A thought occurred to him; if he went far enough would he be able to see his future? If the memories ended with the dendrid, then he was obviously dead, but what if they continued? What if this was just in his head?

Breaking into a jog, he stopped every once in a while to check his position. A month ago, three weeks ago, ten days ago… the memories flickered behind their shrouds of darkness.

He pulled his head out of yesterday and stopped. A chill crept its way up his spine. Reaching out to touch the blanketing darkness of tomorrow, he almost didn't see something step out of today.

Vantix whirled around but saw nothing. It seemed his peripherals were deceiving him in this light. Until he turned back toward tomorrow's memory and saw it again.

The creature was the same colour as everything else here and quite difficult to keep track of. It was like a black silhouette on a black page; its movements its only distinguishing feature. As it circled him slowly, Vantix wondered at the creature's presence. It could just as easily have been a guardian of the afterlife as a figment of his imagination. No sounds were admitted as it moved, its dark shape gliding across the blackness of the floor. All he was able to discern was the creature's basic outline. It was the same height as him, with long spindly arms and legs ending in claws. A tail descended from its back to the ground. The head was triangular shaped and had horns protruding from its scalp in several places.

Its advance continued. All of a sudden it lost patience and leapt at him. Frozen to the spot, he didn't budge an inch. It knocked him over and mobility returned as he scrambled away. There was a wound on his chest from where it hit him but it didn't hurt. More pressing on his mind, was the realisation that there wasn't a floor.

He knew he'd been walking on something earlier and had been standing on something moments ago, but it didn't help. Nothing slowed his descent as he fell. The darkness swirled around him as his flailing limbs searched for a way out.

Come on, a voice in his head screamed, *there has to be a floor here somewhere….*

…..and there was. He picked himself up, unharmed. By this point it was indubitably clear this was in his head. Wishing for a floor had caused there to be one and it seemed unlikely that creature would be allowed anywhere near the heavens.

Stumbling into the nearest memory, he looked around. It was today. He shook his head incredulously, he'd been outside this memory before he'd fallen, how had he ended up here?

The scene in front of him wasn't particularly promising. His body was face down amongst the ruins of the temple and his friends were nowhere to be seen.

There was something wrong with this memory. It was too still. There were no sounds, no smells and no motion. Everything was grey.

Just then, he heard a shriek. As he turned, an indistinct shape came towards him. He had control of his feet this time and tried to run away. His foot hit a loose stone and he fell, hitting his face hard against the ground.

When he opened his eyes again things were ever so slightly different.

Chapter 8

Even in the best of us darkness lingers beneath, forever praying for that moment of weakness when it can clamber over a person's scruples and have its night on the town. Everyone's is unique, with its own slew of vices and cravings. Causes are just as unique, stemming from those little insecurities that keep us awake at night. They nurse the darkness, moulding it into the kind of monster we're afraid to let out. Obviously the extent of a darkness is relevant to the individual. As is that which it compels us to do. The deeds and misdeeds of our descent have a large bearing on who we are, yet it's our manner of dealing with them that plays a larger part. Some repress them, others drown them in alcohol, many may just wallow in regret and, of course, some people manage to deal with it. Incognito had no interest in any of these kinds of people.

Occasionally the darkness boils, froths and overflows. Any redeeming qualities are washed away, leaving only an abhorrent shell of iniquitous repugnance. Not exactly evil, but without qualms and capable of unjustifiable maleficence. Revelling in the depths of depravity and lacking the concept of having a care in the world. Owning the word villain with moustache twirling delight.

Incognito finds these people loathsome to the core, but also extremely useful in a tight situation. Still he was none too pleased to find himself in the home of such an individual.

In the basement of one of Freatsrak's more desirable homes, it was almost pitch black. Someone had taken extreme care to block any of the windows. The only light was following Incognito in through the door and seemed very reluctant to go any further. Weighing the options carefully, Incognito decided that descending the stairs would probably be a mistake and rapped loudly on the wall.

"Well, well, well," called a voice from the darkness, "looks who's back in the land of the living." Incognito was sure he also heard a faint whimpering from down there. Hopefully, negotiations would be as swift as the departure he was planning.

"Were you really fooled?" Incognito replied. He didn't like talking to space in this way but he choose it over heading down into that tenebrous basement any day of the week.

"I'll admit I was," the disembodied voice said, "but surely you didn't trouble yourself with resurrection just to pay my humble abode a visit?"

"200 crowns ," Incognito announced, "To retrieve something that was stolen from me."

"I'm more expensive than that." The voice sounded insulted.

"The money is just a gesture of good will. The real incentive is the quarry. They're dendrid."

"You know me too well; we have an accord. Can I offer you a drink to seal the deal?" The whimpers increased in volume.

Incognito shook his head with disgust. "I'm afraid our tastes still differ."

There was a muffled "Suit yourself" followed immediately by several of the most distressed screams Incognito ever had the misfortune to hear. Seconds after they ceased a figure stepped out of the darkness. "Well," he smiled as he licked blood off his lips, "should we get cracking?"

* * * * *

Vantix lay in the dirt, looking straight up at the sky. The clouds above were grey and got darker down the road. He wondered if that was symbolic then decided it wasn't. Any god trying to give him a sign surely would have done something would have done something far more creative or original.

The first thing he'd noticed was the absence of the creature. Curtains of darkness leading to corridors of memory had given way to the road ahead. When he heard the sounds of birds chirping, it seemed abundantly clear he'd left that nightmarish corridor behind.

That's all it had been, he reassured himself. A nightmare brought on by the traumatic encounter with the dendrid.

Hearing voices over to his left, he gingerly raised himself to his feet. Several feet away from him Farack, Osca and Terif were discussing something quietly. Seeing as he could see all three of them, he made an educated guess that the corpse they were huddled around had once been Donre.

"We need to bury him," Terif was saying.

"I'm sorry," Farack said sincerely, "but we honestly don't have time."

"It's eyes are really beginning to get to me," Osca stated.

"It has a name!" Terif roared.

"You know," Osca remarked, "he doesn't look soulless."

"That's because they didn't take his soul," Farack chimed in, "They just cut his neck open."

Terif said something else, but Vantix's attention had wandered. He looked around. His short swords were on the ground, both sticky with blood. Only one dead dendrid lay on the ground, the one Farack had killed. Despite multiple stab wounds Vantix's duelling partner had walked away.

They still hadn't noticed him but by this point he'd had grown tired of their arguing over whether or not the body looked like it didn't have a soul. "Look," he declared wearily, "the only thing that body looks is dead. I expect it's a look that it'll be sporting for quite some time."

The three of them whirled around and Osca drew his sword. He was, however, slightly startled and the blade was sent skittering harmlessly along the ground. Fortunately, it went nowhere near Vantix.

He shot Osca a hurt look and exclaimed, "Oh, pardon me good sir. I am dreadfully sorry. I wasn't aware that the penalty for unapproved entry into this conversation was death." On receiving startled glances, he continued. "Tell you what," he said, "If I ever tire of life, I'll initiate a conversation. On the day of such an occurrence, feel free to spin around like a maniac and stab me in the chest. Gods know actually having the conversation would be far more worse."

Osca retrieved his sword. "Sorry," he smiled sheepishly, "but we thought you were dead."

"Perhaps you've heard of this new thing I've got. It's called a pulse. Maybe next time you should check it."

"I didn't think I'd need to because of the...." Osca was interrupted by a sharp elbow in the ribs.

Vantix moved to pick up his short swords. "Just for the record," he called over his shoulder, "when we met I took you for something of a fool; you've done very little to change my mind since."

Walking over to the side of the road, Vantix cleaned his swords in the grass before sheathing them. His backpack was where'd left it last night and he heaved it onto his shoulder before turning toward his companions again.

"Why don't we pick up the bags and get going," he declared, "We're several hours behind and they're faster than us. We'll have to hurry. Farack's right Terif, we can't spare the time for a burial."

The rest of the group gathered their gear and followed him. Only Terif stopped for a moment. He placed a cloak over his brother's body and paid his tearful last respects.

* * * * *

Vantix was a good distance ahead of the others. This wasn't because he was walking extremely fast, rather more to the tentative pace they were setting.

Farack paused for a moment and watched his friend get even further ahead. Immediately Osca was by his side, hissing questions at him. "What's going on?" he hissed.

Terif joined them just in time to hear Farack's response. "I saw it," the rhadon was whispering to Osca, "the creature took his soul." Terif chose this moment to make some input, "Did you see how pale he was?"

They both nodded and Osca motioned for them to start walking. "He could be pale for any number of reasons," Osca argued, "How do we know they took his soul?"

Farack gave him an incredulous look that would have insulted a more perceptive person, before replying, "I just told you I saw it".

"But how do you know it was his soul?"

"You're right," Farack replied dryly, "The glowing, person shaped thing, that left his body when the dendrid breathed upon him, was most likely just one of his kidneys."

Osca raised his hands defensively. "Alright," he replied, "No need to have a fit."

They trudged on in silence. Farack was worried. "*Vantix will find out*", was being screamed over and over again in his head. He couldn't shake the feeling that there was something severely wrong.

As they closed in on Vantix, another thought struck the rhadon. *Why is he still alive?* Farack wondered. He'd definitely seen the dendrid take the soul.

He bit his lip and hurried on. If he was going to have a zombie as his travelling companion, they'd be keeping a close tab on it at all times.

Chapter 9

After a hard day's trudge through wet and windy conditions, the group decided to settle down for the evening. The rain had finally stopped and it seemed a good idea to get some sleep while the weather permitted it.

Vantix wasn't particularly interested in sleep. Rest still held its appeal, sleep did not. The creepy place he'd wound up the last time his mind had been left to its own devices didn't warrant another visit. Not sleeping appeared an adequate way to avoid it. However, the others weren't especially pleased when he tried to take the first watch.

"No!" Osca shouted, before composing himself, "I mean, you need your rest."

"Yeah, you look tired." Terif agreed, nodding vigorously.

"I'm fine," he reassured them, "Besides you've all been up longer than me."

Farack shook his head. "I'll take first watch."

"Me too," Osca proclaimed.

The two of them walked toward the road. Terif was left staring at Vantix in apprehension.

As any performer, entertainer, court jester or clown will tell you, awkward silences are one of the worst things that can ever happen to anybody. They're basically a desolate wasteland where nothing can endure. Any conversation that stumbles into one, is about as likely to survive as a snow flake on a sunbathing holiday. The best course of action to pursue in an awkward silence, is to excuse oneself, then leave and attempt discourse elsewhere.

"I'm sure they need your help for something," Vantix sighed. Terif nodded gratefully and stumbled off after the others.

Vantix lay down and watched the stars. He would rest for a while and then confront the others. He didn't like the way they'd been acting around him; the way their eyes were constantly on him, hands resting close to their swords. Almost as if they were scared of him.

Then there was this nonsense about keeping guard. The only other time you'd find three people on guard while one slept, was when the King went for an afternoon nap. It was blatantly obvious they didn't want him awake while they slept.

It was just plain ridiculous. Since he knew when it had started, he could feel safe blaming the dendrid. He would bet hi-

Despite reassuring himself he wouldn't, Vantix had fallen asleep.

*　*　*　*　*

The sounds of thrashing were what caught Farack's attention. He left Osca and Terif to keep watch while he checked on their companion. It sounded like his friend was fighting with some kind of wild animal. It was too dark to see where Vantix lay, but he could hear him easily enough. Lighting a match, he crouched down for a closer look.

Even in the dim glow of his match, his friend was easily distinguishable. His skin was a stark white against the muddy brown undergrowth. Farack had never seen anyone so pale.

Vantix writhed and convulsed; he seemed to be having some kind of seizure. Streams of perspiration ran down his face, barely noticeable as the clothes he wore were already soaked through from the day's rain. The noises, which Farack had initially mistaken for a scuffle between his friend and an animal, all emanated from Vantix. Hissing, growling, snarling and whimpering, he sounded like a lot of different animals having mood swings. Very few recognisable human sounds were coming from him, never mind words.

A moan escaped Vantix's lips and Farack started back in surprise. Having dropped his match, they were once more plunged into darkness. His fears now forgotten, he searched his pocket for another one. He needed to confirm what he thought he 'd just seen.

Farack reached over, trying to get a hold on his friend. It was certainly a challenge to secure his friend's head with one hand, but he managed eventually. Gingerly reaching forward, he raised the lip, to reveal a mouth full of clenched teeth, *pointed* clenched teeth. Each and every one of Vantix's teeth had somehow sharpened to a point, a remarkable new addition to his dentistry. At least Farack thought so. Teeth weren't the kind of thing he paid attention to, unless they were the kind that'd tear pieces off him given the chance.

Trying to put it together in his head, Farack didn't get anywhere. Pale skin and fangs meant vampire, yet this

76

was something different. Vampires only had two fangs, not a whole mouthful. He was also fairly certain that Vantix couldn't change shape to a colony of bats.

So extremely pale skin, pointed teeth and weird night terrors didn't add up in his head. If he had some paper he might have been able to work it out or at least draw a variety of pointless graphs. He set off towards the others. There was nothing he could do for Vantix right now.

Farack didn't know how right he was. If he really knew what was happening to Vantix, and how little time they had, he'd have got the others to collect their stuff quietly. They'd want to put as much distance between them and him as was physically possible.

Unfortunately, he didn't know. Walking quietly through the darkness, he cursed himself for not being able to remember if you used fire or silver against the undead.

* * * * *

When they set off that morning, the clouds were almost as dark as Vantix's mood. The others were obviously refraining from telling him something. They couldn't possibly have acted more suspicious.

The weather really was a pity as the countryside was rather nice. Large rolling hills, clusters of trees and long grass on every side. In fact, it was the perfect place for bandits to ambush travellers. That being said, four teenagers in torn garments probably weren't compelling quarry for bandits of any repute.

They left the road and walked up one of the many hills. At the top Vantix leaned against a tree, while Farack and Terif went to replenish their water supply in a nearby stream. Osca stood with his back to the tree, staring off into the distance. "That's Lake Glasrobe" he said, pointing afar.

His companion couldn't see what he was referring to and voiced this concern almost immediately.

"Oh, I can't see it either but it is somewhere in that direction."

Turning around, Osca tried to avoid looking in Vantix's direction. He shivered involuntarily. The pointed teeth, ghostly complexion and bloodshot eyes didn't exactly put him at ease. What's more, Osca was almost certain that human ear structure wasn't supposed to change overnight. Terif had shared his belief that they should desert their ailing companion but Farack wouldn't hear of it. True friendship is an almost incurable disease.

Without giving him time to think, Vantix grabbed a hold of his coat lapels. Osca squirmed and tried to get away to no avail. He looked around, expecting the others to come to his aid. There didn't seem to be any sign of them.

"You, my fine friend," Vantix's voice was a hushed, threatening whisper, "are going to have the pleasure of telling me what happened to me."

Vantix had caught sight of his reflection in a puddle this morning. Coupled with another nightmare last night, it had done much more than simply alert his suspicions. "Well?" he asked angrily.

Osca wasn't exactly fit for this kind of interrogation. He was half expecting to be eaten. "Th..the d...dendrid," he managed eventually.

Vantix had surmised as much, meaning Osca's answer fell under the heading 'Slightly Unsatisfactory'. "What did they do to me?" he shouted.

"Vantix," Farack demanded, "What do you think you're doing?"

He hadn't even heard them approach. Glancing over, he could see their hands were reaching toward their sheaths. He let go of Osca's coat.

"My dear friend Osca and I, were discussing the finer points of competitive knitting. Riveting subject." Vantix's explanation said it all. They knew what he was doing and he didn't care. "You'll tell me more," he leaned in and whispered to Osca, "trust me on that."

Unfortunately Osca's nerves weren't in the best state at this point. He misinterpreted Vantix's intentions and tried to manoeuvre out of the way, lost his balance, slipped, and tumbled down the hill.

Farack and Terif ran after him. Vantix was left alone at the top of the hill, a decidedly sheepish expression adorning his features.

* * * * *

It had begun to drizzle shortly after they'd left the hill. An unusually warm drizzle; made evident to them by the wind blowing it into their faces. Night had long since fallen as they walked through the trees. Normally they'd have kept to the road but the drizzle forced them to make an exception.

Having walked over 10 leagues today, they decided to stop for one of their increasingly frequent breaks atop the next ridge. The view which greeted them was quite breath-taking.

The lake was immense. Managing to stretch far away into the distance in every direction; practically a small ocean. An almost obscure green haze in the distance was the only sign of a far shore.

They decided to make their way back to the road. It led to the town, where Incognito had intended that they meet the other members of their merry band. The dendrid weren't likely to convince anyone to ferry them across; so if the group could get a boat catching them on the other side probably wouldn't be out of the question.

Arriving at the tree line, they stepped out onto the road. It led into town a couple of feet away.

Terif pulled Osca back as a horse galloped by them. It would have trampled him without a thought. Horses are callous that way.

They watched as it sped away, dragging a burning cart with it. Even more surprising than that was the corpse being dragged behind the cart. The ropes binding him didn't look comfortable. The whole thing was a tad sinister, really.

"You know," Vantix sighed wearily, "I don't get the feeling we're going to be welcomed with open arms here."

Chapter 10

Things, it is said, rarely go according to plan. There is a vast list of reasons why, which basically details all the inconveniences that suddenly occur when you try to make plans. Said list includes, but is not limited to; *the breakdown of all time telling devices in your immediate vicinity, a lack of genuine interest in your current activity, sudden unexplainable bouts of stupidity,* and *death*, to name but a few.

'Because a burning wagon dragging a corpse came from that direction' looked certain to change the group's plans and earn itself a place on that list. However, its bid was unsuccessful.

After several moments of sheer contemplation by the four of them, Osca was the first to speak. "You know," he deliberated, "we don't actually need a boat. Walking is healthier anyway. It's not as if it'll take more than a couple of...." He trailed off under Vantix's intense glare.

To be fair, Vantix had been about to suggest the same thing. Nevertheless, Osca recommending it was a decent enough reason for him to denounce it. Besides, after being attacked by the dendrid there wasn't much this town could offer to terrify him.

"We'd never catch them," Vantix returned dismissively. Farack nodded his agreement; the dendrid travelled far quicker than them.

At this point, they finally stepped out onto the road. The rain had finally ceased and the clouds had drifted away to reveal a full moon shining down. Since Osca had suggested the alternative, Vantix would be damned if he didn't march straight into town.

The road they were on led straight down to the pier and was lined by houses on either side. Another road cut across it, lined with shops and inns; the town little more than a crossroads.

The instant the four of them, Osca lagging ever so slightly behind, reached the outskirts of the town, something caught their attention and refused to let go. A man, his arms wrapped around the girl he was holding hostage.

He was at the end of the road they were on, keeping the hostage between him and the opposing buildings. he had his back to them and didn't seem to notice their advance.

"Come on then," he roared, " Scared ain't ya? Scared ta come out and face the mighty Roger, King o' the bandits!"

Vantix felt it safe to assume that this was Roger. He also felt it safe to assume that there must be someone in those buildings.

Roger held a knife to his captive's neck, restricting movement. He seemed your typical bandit; wearing trademark bandit attire and emanating the kind of awful smell it takes years of avoiding baths to perfect.

"Maybe we can reason with him?" Farack whispered, but Vantix shook his head. He pointed to the bodies which littered the street around Roger(Bandit King). Due to the torn, patched texture of their clothes it was easily discernible that most of them were bandits. After seeing what had happened to them, Roger probably wouldn't be open to negotiation.

Farack grimly drew his sword and the others followed suit. Terif's clumsiness shone through for the second time in the last three days. In an attempt to remove his axe from where it was sheathed across his back, it slipped from his grasp and clanged heavily against the ground.

For a moment, Terif lived on the impossible hope that Roger(Bandit King) hadn't heard it. This hope was crushed as the bandit whirled around.

"Aha," he exclaimed, "Sneaky fellas, eh? Big mistake." With that he drew back his arm in order to plunge the knife into the girl's neck. This was Roger's third mistake of the day. His first had been volunteering to join this raid.

As the knife descended , his captive let her legs go out from under her. She hit the floor and rolled away as his blade punctured clean air.

It was then his second mistake came back to haunt him. Several arrows flew from the windows and planted themselves in his arms, back and calf.

Now free from his grip, the girl walked over and picked up a pointy hat that was resting in the dirt. She placed it upon her head before returning to Roger's kneeling figure.

The self-proclaimed bandit King was wheezing heavily. He was in agony and more than one of the arrows seemed to have punctured his lungs. The girl knelt beside him and listened to his breathing. It was obvious he didn't have a chance.

The girl placed a hand on either side of Roger's face. His bleary, unseeing eyes didn't even notice her. She mumbled a few undistinguishable words. Osca would later swear that he saw sparks fly from her hands before Roger's lifeless body slumped forward and embraced the road.

As she stood up and walked away, Farack turned to the others. "What the hell did we just see?"

Osca and Terif couldn't come up with an explanation. They opened and closed their mouths several times without making a sound. Vantix simply stared at the departing girl with an expression of profound confusion. "I think I know her," he mumbled eventually, setting off after the pointy-hatted girl.

People had begun to appear from the buildings to occupy the street. In fact, a large host had congregated around a slightly smaller group. They probably would have been asleep were it not for the bandit attack.

There was a distinct difference between the two groups. Whereas the larger group looked like the local fisherman and trade people they were, the others were a mix of varying nationalities and race. The only thing they had in common was the amount of weapons they kept concealed beneath their cloaks. They looked just the sort you'd hire to hunt down a band of dendrid. Vantix was quick to indicate this. The others nodded their agreement.

There seemed to be a dispute between the two groups. As such disputes usually are, it was about money.

"....is just nonsense," a man who looked to be in his early forties was saying, "We've fulfilled our end of the bargain. So now you must fulfil yours."

Seeing as he was armed to the teeth, it was quite obvious he wasn't representing the townsfolk. His opposition was a man in a suit.

"Don't get me wrong," the town's spokesperson was saying, "I'm extremely grateful for everything you've done. However, I can't just give you my boat."

"You will forsake our agreement?"

"Not exactly," the boat-owner replied, "You can still have my boat. I would however, like some form of compensation." He rubbed his palm meaningfully and smiled a smile that Farack wanted to hit.

The other man seemed about to respond, until he was pushed aside by one of the members of his own group. Delegating himself as the new representative, he looked slightly ridiculous.

Whereas the others in his group were either armoured or wearing travelling leathers, his attire was mostly expensive silks. Cloaks and overcoats were also commonplace in the group, but he was wearing a cape.

"Compensation, eh? Well if you really want to, we'd be happy to accept," he cast an unpleasant gaze over the townsfolk.

"No, you misunder-" the man began, but he was cut off.

"She looks okay and maybe those two," he pointed three women out from the crowd and grinned wolfishly. The only reason for his grin, it appeared, was to showcase his teeth. To be more specific, it was to showcase his fangs. "No need to wrap them up, we'll just take them to go" the vampire sneered over the growing unease.

Silence reigned true whilst the townsfolk considered their options. It wasn't wise to argue with a vampire and their natural instincts for survival demanded they find the nearest possible exit route from this conversation.

The cloak and silk attire kind of made sense to Vantix now. Vampires have a habit for the theatrical. They loved to dress up and spend time luring young women to their doom with promises of riches and adventures. This is why most people find them excessively creepy. The rest thought they were pathetic.

After a while the vampire's intense glare began to get on the other man's nerves. "Just take the boat," he said desperately.

"Thanks," the vampire's smile never left his face, "Where is it?"

"It's docked at the pier," the man called. Trying to back away casually didn't work so he turned and ran. The vampire watched his departure with no small amount of amusement.

The villagers began to disperse. Some were intent on going to sleep; significantly more were just going home to place something substantial between them and the vampire. A few even boarded up their windows.

The only ones left after several moments were the two groups Incognito was currently employing. The larger group seemed quite content to ignore Vantix and his friends.

Vantix could see the girl again and was now certain he knew her. He was surprised to see her though. After all, they'd last parted company in such dire circumstances. He decided it was time to break the ice.

He reached forward and tapped her on the soldier. She turned around and her features lit up at the sight of him. Struggling for words, all he managed to get out was "I'm sorry." It didn't matter though, she forgave him. This job would be their first of many together and would eventually lead to better things.

Vantix's visions are wildly inaccurate.

Walking over to the other group, there wasn't a doubt in his mind that forgiveness would soon be his. It had been over a year, she'd obviously cooled down by now.

He pushed his way through the other members of her group. Tapping her on the shoulder, he adjusted his shirt while she turned around.

The first indicator that his vision wouldn't exactly pan out, was the fact that her features didn't light up. If anything they clouded over. The struggle for words was even worse than it had been in his vision. Eventually he blurted out, "Sorry?" He hadn't expected it to come out as a question, but he'd caved under her unflinching stare.

The second indicator that his vision wouldn't pan out was her fist approaching his face.

Chapter 11

Between the hours of midnight and dawn Welbh had a window of opportunity; it was the only time King Jandelk wasn't watching his every movement. So he took advantage of it to work on his personal documentation of the deal and enter all the figures into a small red notebook while constantly smirking to himself and musing at life's ease.

Though he hated to admit it, without the King there would be no deal. Nobody got through the Derranferd border, not unless they happened to be travelling in the royal carriage. The only other way into Derranferd was through Ghostwood. Those possessing their sanity would never attempt that route.

The alliance which the King intended to propose would alleviate the border patrols, making Welbh's intended trade routes available. There would still be a good bit of sneaking around but the task would then shift from beyond impossible to feasible-with-the-right-initiative. .

He couldn't help but feel pleased with himself. The merchants had agreed to pay him a fifty percent commission. Tallying the orders, he whistled contently. Even though these were the just first of many they'd make him rich soon as they were filled.

The door opened and he stopped writing for a moment. He sighed to himself; privacy was just one of the few things you couldn't have when employed in a castle. A keen interest in regicide was also forbidden.

"I don't suppose you've heard of knocking?," Welbh asked without looking up. He knew it'd be a servant, none of the royal family would even contemplate stirring at this hour.

On receiving no response, he deemed it best to look up. He was unpleasantly surprised at who he saw. Lila, his brother's favourite messenger, stood before him.

Black seemed to be her outfit's central motif. In fact, she was dressed to kill. Welbh had the same outfit hidden under his bed. It was only given to those who graduate from the prestigious Shadow Academy.

He waited for her to explain her motive for trespassing so late at night, although he was fairly certain it was another message from his brother. He changed his mind when she drew a curved knife from her belt.

She advanced slowly, ready to leap at any moment. Welbh eyes scanned the room, his mind a hive of activity. Thoughts like, *Gods, where did I put my sword?*, *What's she doing?* and *My brother would never try to kill me!*, were all vying for his immediate attention. His sword lay out of reach at the foot of his bed. Knocking over his seat he dived for it, noticing her quicken her pace out of the corner of his eye. It didn't matter; she was too late. He grasped the hilt and yanked.

The sword got halfway out before it stuck. Pulling at it desperately, this time he was too late. He could already feel her blade against his throat. As it was no use, he dropped the sheathe in frustration.

"Your brother sent me to deliver a message." Lila explained.

Welbh's gaze flickered from her to what he could see of the knife. "Some message," he spat.

The knife was removed from his neck and he heaved a sigh of relief. Lila placed the blade in his hand before turning to leave.

He paid her no heed, instead turning his attention to the etching on the blade:

Got you again little brother. I'll be dropping by in six days.
                                        Yours,
                                        Lintous

It took several readings of the message before it could be properly digested. His brother intended to visit the castle. HIS BROTHER INTENDED TO VISIT THE CASTLE!

Reaching the desk, Welbh fell back into his chair and cupped his face in his hands. His brother couldn't come here; it would ruin everything.

Sitting in silence, he racked his brain for possible outcomes. There were a few positive ones, but they all involved him being born an only child. One thing was for sure, he couldn't let his brother come here.

He fell asleep several minutes later, thoroughly exhausted.

*   *   *   *   *

Up until that point, Vantix had never been knocked into the mud by a punch to the chin. Unfortunately, this kind of affliction has a lot in common with cold sores. It leaves an unpleasant wet feeling around your mouth, makes you less appealing and is likely to happen repeatedly if it happens once. Oddly enough, it's at precisely these moments that thirty-seven percent of useless epiphanies occur.

However, Vantix ignored his sudden realisations that *the sentence: "The quick brown fox jumps over the lazy dog" uses every letter of the alphabet* and that, *women blink nearly twice as much as men.* Instead, he focused on the all too apparent fact that she packed quite a punch. Since she was the cause of his current mud-covered state, it didn't take much effort.

He raised himself up on one elbow and rubbed his chin. It didn't feel right. Switching his attention over to her, it was obvious she was not best pleased.

Terif and Farack were busy grabbing Vantix's arms. As they helped him to his feet, Farack turned to the girl. "What was that for?" he shouted.

Before she had a chance to reply, somebody else decided to join in. Osca surveyed the scene before him, unable to hide his mirth. "First impressions, eh?" he laughed cheerfully. Vantix kicked him in the shins. He pretended not to notice.

If he tried, Farack could imagine steam rising from the top of the girl's head. "You left me on the altar!" she fumed and began hitting him again; a series of blows to the chest. She didn't stop, slow down or break out in tears. Eventually one of the members of her group dragged her away. His friends would have done so sooner, had they not been pondering her outburst.

"So-," Farack elongated after a little while, "any particular reason, you didn't mention this engagement before?"

"Why did you run?" Osca piped up.

"It wasn't like that," Vantix retorted.

"Still doesn't explain why you ran," Terif pointed out, "even if you are too young."

"I wasn't going to get married," Vantix spluttered angrily.

"You could've told her that," Farack muttered disapprovingly, "Then this whole nasty scene could have been avoided."

"Explains why she hit him though," Osca remarked.

At this point Vantix gave up. He followed the other group, already making their way down to the quay. Until a statement from Terif gave him cause to stop. "This is as far as I go," the young farmer informed them.

"What? Why?" Osca wasn't particularly sure which question he wanted to ask.

"I only came because we needed 100 crowns before the end of the week, or we lose the farm," Terif explained, "Donre and I were given 100 each at the start and promised the rest when we'd finished. We have more than enough now. Without him it's going to be hard; I don't think they'll be able to manage without me as well. So I'm going to take what I've got and head home. Good luck, boys."

Osca was about to say something when somebody else stepped forward. It was the man who'd been speaking on behalf of Incognito's other group when they arrived. He took Terif's hand and shook it for a moment, then turned and walked back down the pier.

For a moment they all stared at the bag of coins the man had deposited in Terif's keeping. While he turned toward home, the others followed his generous benefactor.

Walking down the pier, they finally saw the lake stretch out before them. Despite the lateness of the hour, the fishermen were still at work. Several boats were out on the lake. Perhaps out on the lake is the wrong phrase; all of the boats lingering by the shores, almost as if they wanted to be able to make it back to dry land at a moment's notice.

Then Vantix noticed that the rest of the group had stopped. Some of them were busy cutting the rope which tethered a boat to the end of the pier while the rest were finding a comfortable corner to fall asleep. He was surprised by the boat's appearance. To be honest, that they floated was the limit of his nautical knowledge and he'd been expecting some sort of galleon. The boat had a large triangular sail that stretched across the majority of its length and a cabin set in the middle and covering approximately half its deck. Behind it was ample room for the rudder and persons to steer it. More than likely it was simply used to transport coal around the lake but for all he knew could have been a keen voyager of the open seas.

When all were aboard they cast off, a wind picking up that moved the boat away from the pier and sent it drifting across the lake.

Vantix volunteered to operate the boat while the others slept. Fear of what might happen if he went to sleep kept him awake. Death really didn't appeal to him right now; he had things to do.

Chapter 12

The sun was already past its zenith as the boat moved through the water. The wind that'd propelled it had diminished, resulting in a leisurely pace. Vantix, Farack and Osca sat on the cabin's roof. Everyone else seemed to have retreated to their own corners of the barge. The rhadon glanced to the front of the boat. The sail was limp and lifeless, but it wasn't that which caught his attention. The girl was there, along with three others. One of them seemed to be distraught, the others were offering their condolences. Looking back towards the rudder, he spotted another three. As they seemed busy steering the boat he decided introducing himself could wait.

Turning to Vantix, he decided to repeat his question. "Are you going to tell us when you were engaged?"

"I wasn't," came the familiar reply.

"Come on," Osca prompted, "She said you left her at the altar."

Vantix shook his head; he was tired of telling them they had it wrong. "There's more than one kind of altar," was all he offered.

His answer didn't help at all. "What's that supposed to mean?" Osca was genuinely bewildered.

As they clearly weren't getting anywhere, Farack decided to slightly change the subject. "What's her name?"

"Slyra" Vantix sighed.

Slyra couldn't have heard him, yet she turned at the sound of her name. She eyed them curiously for a moment, then she made her way to where they sat. Yesterday she'd been wearing the same travelling leathers as most of the others, today her outfit was almost as ridiculous as the vampire's. She still had the travelling breeches on, but was wearing a strange purple shirt. It looked just like a short robe. It wasn't, however, the part of her attire which caught the eye. Anyone who saw her in the street would only notice her good looks for a moment, then their gaze would be directed upward.

Slyra wore a tall pointy hat over her cascading blonde curls.

The thought of magic unsettles people. Everyone knew that there was no such thing as witches or wizards yet exercised a certain caution when it came to those who chose to don pointy attire. If somebody was crazy enough to go around wearing hats that jutted so accusingly at the sky they might be crazy enough to think they're a witch or a wizard. Since the general consensus was that all those involved with magic ate children, wearers of pointy hats were shunned.

Which just goes to illustrate the influence fairy tales have in Fardash. After the King heard the story of *Rumpelstiltskin,* he ordered the death of all men under five feet tall who happened to be living in the forest. The dwarves were not impressed.

Unaware that most of their parents would have tried to exorcise her and burn her pointy hat, Slyra sat down beside the three of them. She nodded to Vantix and offered her hand to Farack and Osca. They took it in turn to introduce themselves, whilst trying to think of witty things to say. She was still the first to speak. "So there are only three of you?"

"There were five," Farack replied.

"What happened?"

"One decided to go home and we lost another to the dendrid."

"The five of you attacked a band of dendrid?" Slyra asked incredulously. She almost couldn't believe how absolutely ridiculous it sounded.

"Not exactly," Farack muttered weakly. In retrospect, it stood out as an incredibly bad move.

"I won't even bother guessing who's folly that was," Slyra looked at Vantix accusingly. After several seconds her stare became one of curiosity instead.

Sensing her scrutiny, Vantix looked up. He'd been distractedly tracing the grain of the boat's wooden roof. His sudden fascination with it perplexed the others, partly because the grain had been painted over and was no longer visible.

The sun was giving him a headache. However, he was more worried about the fact that it was hurting his skin. "How many were with you?"

Slyra had been examining him until his sudden question. He was almost stark white, paler than even a ghost should be. *There's something seriously wrong here,* she thought to herself. "Ten but we lost one against the bandits," she said out loud.

Farack and Osca's thoughts instantly flashed to the corpse being dragged along behind the burning cart. They didn't say anything.

Vantix's thoughts remained fixed on the throbbing pain in his head. He was still having trouble concentrating.

"No doubt you'll tell them our names," he faked a yawn, "so let's have theirs."

Slyra gave him a cold look and pointed down toward the end she'd come from. "The grieving one is Ramos. Ned, his older brother, was killed by the bandits. He hasn't really come to terms with it yet. The small guy with the disproportionally large beard is Hemer."

"Is he a dwarf?" Osca interrupted. Although everybody had heard of dwarves, very few had ever seen one. They seemed to be in the habit of spending vast periods of time underground; a place he had no intention of visiting.

"Nope," Slyra smiled, "but he does try to pass himself off as one."

"What about him?" Farack indicated the man who'd given Terif money. Now that daylight was illuminating everything, Farack could see the intricate breastplate he wore. Making a mental note to ask about it later, he almost missed Slyra's answer.

"That's Rekil," she said, whilst turning toward the other end of the boat.

She indicated the three who seemed to be doing all the work as regards sailing. "The extremely tall one's Frank, the pale one is Sam and the tanned elf is Arsenius."

"Where's he from?" Vantix asked wearily; not due to lack of interest, his whole body felt slightly numb.

Slyra shrugged. "I don't know. Nospac, maybe."

Nospac was a desert region which stretched through three of the upper provinces. With its blistering heat, frequent sandstorms and large quantities of murderous thieves, it wasn't exactly a popular travel destination.

Pain in his head notwithstanding, Vantix worked out the numbers in his head. She'd left two out. "Where's the vampire?," he asked. Wiping his brow, it looked as if it had required a lot of effort.

The others exchanged glances. He probably needed to get out of the sun.

"Oh, the vampire," Slyra's reply was drenched with distaste, "his name's Grelow."

Vantix just about heard the end of that sentence. Darkness ate away at his vision and he passed out.

Chapter 13

Farack, Osca and Slyra hadn't exactly anticipated Vantix's sudden loss of consciousness, freezing as he collapsed. Unfortunately, in this state he couldn't be relied on to maintain his balance. The result of which, was his sudden departure from the roof of the boat.

For a moment, nothing happened. The three of them continued to stare at the place where Vantix had been sitting only seconds before. It went on until a shout from Hemer broke the trance.

"Man overboard!"

They leapt to their feet simultaneously. Farack struggled to pull off his boots, Slyra knocked her pointy hat from her head and Osca scanned the water desperately. Vantix could swim but the likelihood was he still hadn't regained conscious.

Then Rekil ran by, nudging Farack as he did. The rhadon tumbled back into the water, hands firmly lodged in his boots. That mattered little to the older man, who tossed his breastplate before diving after Vantix.

Slyra stood open mouthed, watching as Rekil disappeared beneath the surface of the lake. Hours seemed to pass as she stared at the lake's now still exterior. Fearing the worst, a splash at the end of the boat restored her hopes.

She reached the end just in time to see a drenched Rekil drag himself onto the boat, before lugging the still unconscious Vantix aboard after him. Sam helped him place the soaking youth on the deck. Without thinking, Rekil thumped him once in the chest. Despite coughing and spluttering, he still didn't wake up.

Farack dragged himself out of the water and collapsed on deck. Shooting Rekil a rather pointed look, he muttered unpleasantries under his breath.

"Get him inside," Rekil ordered. Sam and Fred grabbed Vantix's arms obligingly.

Slyra pushed in the doors to the boat's interior. It was incredibly cluttered, with a table, chairs, several cupboards and a bed all vying for space. The shutters were firmly closed, all light ostracised so that the first indication you'd receive of the furniture was when you tripped over it.

As Slyra reached to open the shutters, a hand grabbed a hold of her arm. She looked along the length of the arm, to the head and shoulders behind it. It was Fred. "A certain *friend* of ours wouldn't appreciate that," he emphasised the word friend, telling Slyra he meant Grelow.

She was about to mention that the vampire didn't appear to be in here, when he silenced her by placing a finger to his lips and pointing upwards.

Slyra looked up. The ceiling wasn't far overhead, yet none had to crouch inside the room. It wasn't the height of the ceiling which grabbed her attention. What caught her eye, was that it looked as if the roof had been carpeted. Being of a more frivolous, noble stock she was accustomed to all sorts of ridiculous whims but why

100

anyone would carpet a roof was beyond her understanding.

Then the carpet moved.

She started in surprise and raised a hand defensively. After a moment she composed herself and looked closer. *Bats*, she thought.

It is important to note at this point that there are many myths and legends circling about vampires that are slightly exaggerated. Immortality and shape-shifting into a colony of bats are perfectly true. They aren't, however, reduced to ash by sun – although they do break out with an extremely painful rash when they come in contact with it – nor do they shrink at the sight of garlic. The only thing it keeps safe from them is food; it unsettles their delicate stomachs.

The bats hung upside down, a multitude completely covering the ceiling that Slyra was too busy trying not to look at to actually count. She assumed they were sleeping.

Fred closed the door on the mistaken assumption that the bats would crumble to dust. He didn't know any better.

Slyra finally managed to move away from the bats and check on Vantix. Apart from the fact that he was wetter, he wasn't very different from when he entered the water.

This happened to be Rekil's first proper look at Vantix. He took in the pale face, cracked lips and fangs in one long look.

The word to describe the state in which he left that room, is horrified.

* * * * *

To Vantix, it was like he'd just closed his eyes for a moment. He hadn't even felt anything that had come to pass. Exactly the nap he'd been waiting for. He didn't dream, there was no corridor of memories and no creature chased him along its length. Perfectly uneventful and rejuvenating.

* * * * *

Farack and Osca were wondering about Vantix's current condition when Rekil came storming out of the boat's cabin. It was quite a good storm up; he had the perfect look in his eye. Had running been an option, the two would be in the next province right now. Since it wasn't, Farack was provided with yet another reason to detest boats.

Rekil stopped right in front of them. Although they weren't small, he towered over them. "When?" he barked.

Osca the-eternally-confused once again wasn't quite up to speed with the events unfolding around him. "Just a moment ago," he said blankly, " you pulled him out."

Rekil shook his head grimly. "When did it take him?" he asked irritably. At the sound of shouting all those aboard gathered around; leaving the boat to drift.

Osca was unable to stop his jaw from dropping. Farack sighed and looked down, "It happened three days ago."

Rekil's eyes widened. "Three days!" he spluttered. Raising a hand to his forehead, a worried expression planted itself on his face. "It's happening too fast...." he mumbled discerningly.

Slyra chose this moment to make some input. "What's happening?"

"What do you think?," growled Rekil, "Haven't you seen him lately? The ears, the skin and the teeth; he's becoming one of them."

102

This thought hadn't actually occurred to Farack and Osca. The image of their friend as a dendrid was terribly unsettling. As was being trapped on a tiny boat with one of those creatures. If there was ever any doubt, *no escape routes* cemented its position on Farack's list of reasons to hate boats.

Slyra was the first to drag herself away from such thoughts. "Can we stop it? How much time do we have?" she demanded.

Rekil rubbed his bristled chin. "It's not good," he informed them, "the only thing to do is get his soul back, but there's still no guarantee it'll work. We have about five days."

No of them were particularly thrilled with his answer.

Chapter 14

After two days of ceaseless pursuit, Welbh had finally given his new attendant the slip. King Jandelk had presented him with this irritant just after breakfast the previous day, supposedly in order to help him prepare for the journey to Derranferd. Within the first hour of servitude the man had not only gotten on Welbh's last nerve, but also jumped up and down upon it until it collapsed beneath the sheer weight of annoyance he'd been caused.

Earlier, the aforementioned attendant had thwarted all attempts by Welbh to pack the documents necessary for his business endeavours. There were no verbal warnings or remonstrations about their inclusion in the baggage; as a matter of fact, this aide never spoke. Instead he simply walked over and removed them each time they were placed inside the case. Becoming increasingly exasperated with each failed attempt Welbh hurled obscenities at his aggravator, irked even further still by the way this servant remained as impassive and aloof as ever, in spite of what he thought were some exceedingly biting witty remarks at the man's neck fat.

This type of person was essential to King Jandelk's solution to espionage. Traitors, according to the King, were just normal people afforded an opportunity for betrayal and an incentive. Therefore, if you took away their opportunities there could be no betrayal, no matter the incentive. If someone was followed at five paces all day they simply wouldn't be allowed any opportunities for deceit and would remain loyal servants of the realm.

It had also convinced Welbh that any bags he packed would most definitely be searched. Fortunately he had the perfect alternative hiding place in mind.

Guards in Derranferd wouldn't search the royal carriage; imagine the indignity. Using his knife for leverage, Welbh pulled up the rug and a piece of the wood flooring beneath before storing his papers and putting everything back into place. He then left, whistling a tune as he went.

When his attendant found him ten minutes later, it seemed there was a distressingly ominous spring in Welbh's step.

* * * * *

Even dangerous, soul-stealing creatures need to rest. Not as long or as frequent as humans, but even the dendrid needed to settle down for a few minutes. It was their first break in several days.

They'd followed his orders exactly, securing it and massacring the villagers. None could know of its existence, not yet.

Resting in the woodlands surrounding the lake, they might have noticed a boat had they looked out across the water. It was catching up.

One of the dendrid limped over to three of the others. Around its chest was wrapped a dirty, blood stained bandage. Both these injuries and the limp had been gained from that scrap a couple of days ago. "Brothers," it hissed to those present, "it's my turn."

The others nodded as one. Braegar, the one whose turn it happened to be, reached out. In his hand was placed a small wooden box.

He retreated some distance before turning his attention to it. A container only the dendrid could make; their way of capturing a soul in something no bigger than the average jewellery box.

The hadricrea, for that was its name, was made of wood. Normally wood can't hold a soul (this is the reason there aren't any wooden structures in heaven) but soaked through the grain of this receptacle were drops of purest dendrid blood, enabling it to hold the ethereal.

Braegar opened the box and grabbed its contents with his clawed hand. To grasp a soul, you have to be a soulless vessel. If you take away their vindictive nature and eventually-lethal breath, that's essentially what the dendrid are. The soul, which was a vaguely human-shaped wisp to the eye, seemed to flutter in his grasp. It was darkened and damaged by use from the other dendrid. Braegar didn't mind in the slightest.

With a twisted smile, he raised his arm and dragged his clawed hand slowly across the soul......

*　*　*　*　*

Vantix tossed and turned in his sleep. Inside his head, things had drastically changed.

The comforting darkness was gone. Instead it had been replaced by the dark hallway he'd come to loathe. The flowing, rippling walls still looked like curtains. Vantix was willing to bet his memories still lay behind them.

106

He stepped forward and stuck his head through the nearest curtain. Sure enough, he recognized the scene within. Seeing himself run down that corridor he realised he was at his usual entry point.

There was something wrong with the scene before him. There was no colour or sound; it didn't seem real. Then, the creature appeared.

It wasn't a black silhouette any more. In fact, it was the only example of colour in this memory. It was covered in vivid green scales.

The memory him ran straight into the creature's deadly embrace, barely registering it as the monstrosity tore into his chest with claws and teeth. Vantix recoiled and turned away from the grim spectacle. Watching yourself die is a horrible experience that the majority of people are lucky enough to do without.

Stumbling out of the memory, he looked up and down the corridor before running back towards his earlier memories. Going forward hadn't proven helpful last time. This time he'd go back.

* * * * *

Braegar's teeth tore free of his blistered lips and his mouth curled into something that resembled a smile only in the loosest sense of the word. He was enjoying this. Grabbing the soul he hugged it tight, enveloping it.

You had to savour the finer things in life.

* * * * *

Vantix stopped running. The creature's sounds were all around. From every direction he could hear it cackling,

107

sneering and hissing at him. Its footfalls were also loud and distinct; heralding its imminent approach.

He leapt toward the nearest memory; hoping to escape into his past. However, he was knocked back as the seemingly diaphanous curtains became as hard as stone. Desperately clutching at them, he cursed his luck.

Then there came a sound from beneath him. Looking down, he could make out a shape hurtling toward him through the darkness. It was gigantic.

* * * * *

The tortured sound the soul made as he dragged his clawed hand across it was like music to Braegar's ears. It gave him the shivers.

He raised the soul to his face. Almost choking on his own excitement, he breathed in. The soul was his!

Desire would drive him mad; he must consume it.........

* * * * *

Frozen to the spot, Vantix couldn't run. Unfortunately, the spot he was now frozen to seemed to be on the palm of a gigantic version of the creature.

Finding his feet, he threw himself off the creature's palm. Whilst falling through the air, Vantix decided he'd definitely made the best move. He changed his mind when he landed in the creature's palm again.

There was no escape. Nothing he could do. Vantix heaved a sigh and resigned himself to death-by-monstrous-creature.

The creature tossed him high and opened its mouth in anticipation. *Nasty way to go,* Vantix thought as he dropped past two rows of jagged teeth................

* * * * *

Braegar reeled as the slap caught him across the face. A clawed hand tore the soul from his grasp and shoved it into the hadricrea.

One of the other dendrid stood before him, anger clear on its features. "Fool," it reprimanded him, "Do you want the human to die?"

Braegar climbed shakily to his feet. "What do you care?", he hissed, "I caught him, he belongs to me!"

"It was your own folly that gave you those wounds, would you like it to earn you some more?"

Braegar remained silent. In his current injured state he was no match for any of the other dendrid and they knew it. He'd have to go along with them for now, but in the end he would get what was his. The others intended to turn his captive soul into one of them, but they wouldn't be able to if he had his way.

As the sun finally set, the dendrid set off once more.

* * * * *

.....and there was just warm, enticing darkness. The nightmarish creature gone, Vantix was free to enjoy his sleep. He smiled and rolled over.

Chapter 15

The sun had long since set as Farack, Slyra and Osca sat on the boat's stern rail. Feet raised just above the water, they talked of nothing in particular whilst waiting for Vantix to wake up and join them.

At the sound of a door opening, Farack and Slyra turned toward the cabin hopefully. Osca looked on with a vague interest, but in contrast to the others, wasn't disappointed in the slightest when Vantix didn't appear.

A man stepped out, covered in a long, dark cloak that concealed him from almost head to foot. His hood was raised so that apart from the tip of his sharp nose, not much else was visible.

He strode past them; intent on climbing onto the roof of the boat and heading towards the other gathering up front and as he hoisted himself onto the roof, his cloak opened momentarily. Farack caught a glimpse of expensive chainmail under a dark tunic. It certainly didn't look like standard fare.

"Where did he come from?" Farack whispered.

Slyra looked at him quizzically for several moments, antecedent to nodding in the direction of the cabin.

Farack rolled his eyes. "I know that," he acknowledged, "but he wasn't in there earlier." After a moment he added, "Was he?"

Slyra nodded. "If you didn't see him," she elucidated, "it was because he didn't want you to see him."

"Which one is he?"

"It's easy to forget about him," Slyra disclosed, "so I probably forgot to mention him earlier."

"Could you please hurry to the part where you tell me his name?" Osca replied testily. He was nothing if not impatient.

Slyra looked daggers at him and stamped on his foot. He grimaced and pretended it didn't hurt before admitting that it did by grabbing his foot in his hand when the pain overwhelmed him. She watched with a bemused smile then turned back to Farack and answered, "He goes by Elik."

* * * * *

Inside the cabin it was dark. As dark as it can possibly be. The moon, which shone down on the lake, didn't pierce the thick shutters covering the windows.

Apart from some light snoring emitted by Vantix, the only other sound was a strange rustling. It was the sound of exactly one hundred and twelve bats waking.

As they detached themselves from the roof, there were a few moments of confusion as they drifted toward the floor or groggily collided with anything in their immediate vicinity. Then the vampire decided to pull himself together.

The bats flew in circles, faster and closer together with each passing second. To the casual observer, it might have looked as if they were caught in a miniature cyclone.

111

The highest point of the whirlwind seemed to descend and the lowest to disappear into the floor as a head and shoulders were revealed. The other bats were a blur, spiralling downward until they vanished, leaving a complete vampire in their place. This entire process took little more than a couple of seconds.

Grelow yawned and licked his fangs, immediately drawing blood from his tongue. Two drops washed over his teeth, immediately rejuvenating and refreshing him.. He was among the majority of vampires who loved what they were.

Glancing around, he picked up and put on his breeches. These were followed by the rest of his attire. Bereft of the ability to check his reflection in the mirror, he was still pretty sure he was presentable. Vampires always are.

He was heading for the door when something caught his eye. Or rather, somebody caught his eye. A person lay sleeping on the small bed. He sniffed. The smell was strange, unique even. It wasn't quite human.

Well, he thought to himself, *a taste won't hurt*.

* * * * *

"So," Farack and Osca asked together, "when were you and Vantix engaged?"

Slyra shot them a sideways glance. "We weren't," she said abruptly.

"But you said he left you at the altar," Osca's response was quick, as if he'd anticipated her reply.

"I said he left me on the altar," she retorted angrily.

"Is there a difference?" Farack asked.

"It was a sacrificial altar!"

Osca and Farack shared a glance. "That sounds a lot more like Vantix."

An awkward silence ensued. Then Osca was struck by a thought. He would have been struck by another, had he not leaned forward. It went over his shoulder and landed harmlessly in the lake. "What did you do to Roger?" he asked suddenly.

A guilty expression planted itself on Slyra's face. "I didn't do anything."

"Yes you did," Osca insisted, "You whispered some mumbo-jumbo and he died."

"Did the arrows littering his body escape your notice?" Slyra's gaze was intense as she added firmly, "I didn't do anything."

Looking from her expression to her pointy hat, Osca decided to let the matter drop and then trod rather deliberately into the next touchy subject that presented itself.

"Why are you here?" he asked.

"Same reason everyone else is," Slyra replied, "money."

"That's not what I meant."

"What did you mean?" Slyra cocked her head to one side.

"Well," Osca rationalised, "as far as I can tell Incognito hired adept swordsmen or young muscle. Why would he hire a pretty girl like you in place of a young farmer's lad who's good with an axe?"

"Tactful," Farack murmured.

Osca hadn't meant to insult her, but he had. She turned, eyes ablaze and unforgiving. Fortunately for him, she didn't say anything. Instead her expression softened prior to becoming one of fear. Her eyes went wide and her lip trembled.

"What? Wha..." Osca trailed off. He turned in the direction Farack and Slyra were staring. He went pale and swallowed nervously as he spotted the cause of their unease.

Grelow was coming out of the cabin. If the fact that he was licking his lips wasn't worrying enough, the blood dripping from his fangs was slightly more distressing still.

From these signs, Osca found it easy enough to construe what had happened.

* * * * *

Grelow stood in the centre of a circle comprised entirely of people shouting abuse at him. Arsenius, Fred, Ramos, Hemer, Sam and Farack stood around trying to be heard over the sound of each other. They were fighting a losing battle. Elik and Rekil sat on the boat's stern rail, both staring angrily at Grelow. Neither of them was talking. Osca and Slyra had gone to check on Vantix. Osca wasn't particularly keen on the matter, but Slyra didn't really give him a choice.

"If anything happens to my friend you are dead! You hear me?" Farack shouted. He'd passed beyond rage and was just about ready to burn Grelow at the stake. Unfortunately, there weren't any stakes aboard. Yet another reason for Farack to despise boats.

Grelow lazily cast his gaze toward Farack. "Firstly, I'm a vampire. You'd have as much hope of killing me as you would being accepted into the rhadon community." As Farack looked down darkly, Grelow continued, "Secondly, If anything happens to your friend, you aren't going to do anything. Why is that, do you think?"

Several people were about to offer their opinions, until he shushed them. "The reason," Grelow elaborated, "is because the only thing more pathetic than a rhadon without a flame, is a fish that can't swim. I'm inclined to feel the fish would be more of a threat."

To most rhadons, it was second nature to ignite and it happened automatically when angry. It was like knowing how to breathe. There's something incredibly terrifying about a flame wielding maniac you've just insulted. Which is why people tended to stay on their good side. Grelow didn't have to worry about it though; the most Farack could do was seethe at him.

It looked as if one of the veins on Farack's forehead was about to explode. All that happened however, was a hiss and a slight steam rose from his scalp. He didn't notice the argument escalating. He was busy thinking about himself. Or more specifically, what he would do to Grelow had he not been dropped into a pond as a baby.

Osca came running out of the cabin. "He's going to make it," he panted, "but Slyra thinks he was almost drained."

The others were barely listening. They couldn't help but stare at Osca's blood stained garments. Slowly Farack turned to Grelow. "Will he become one of you?" he asked, his voice plainly showing his distaste.

Grelow stared at him and smiled a cold, unfriendly smile. "Usually I don't drink enough to turn but that taste," he chuckled and licked his lips, "I couldn't help myself. So yes, he'll be like me. What's more he's going to be hungry. He'll need at least a pint; all new vampires do. So who's it going to be," Grelow's smile widened, "the pathetic rhadon, the older warrior, the mysterious stranger, the desert elf or maybe the pretty girl who nursed him back to health. Only one thing is certain, he won't want me. You should probably decide amongst yourselves right now. It'll save you a good deal of unpleasantness later." By the time he finished, his smile stretched from ear to ear.

There was a shocked silence until Rekil spoke. He was so angry he seemed to have dug his nails into his palm and cut himself. "Pig," he spat at Grelow.

If it was possible, Grelow's smile grew even wider.

"If you like that, you'll love this," Grelow grinned, "Once when I was travelling in the desert provinces, I decided to spend the day in a cave,"-they all stared open-mouthed as he went on-"and awoke in the middle of the day to find some people rummaging through my belongings. There was a man, a woman and their son, who must have been about twelve. It just wouldn't do to have them stealing from me so I caught them, almost drained the mother and father and left all three bound and gagged. Seeing as it was the middle of the day I went back to sleep.

I rose around midnight. My unwelcome guests had also regained consciousness. The parents didn't disappoint me; they stared at their son with the familiar look of lust I'd come to know. The child was terrified, crying and trying to mumble prayers through the clothe I'd wrapped around his head.

So I set him free, gave him a five minute head start and then unleashed his mother and father. They tore after him through the night." Grelow looked around, content that he'd achieved the shock factor he'd been going for.

Arsenius, whose knuckles were white as bone despite his tanned skin, pounced. He knocked Grelow down and struck him in the face twice. Still chuckling the vampire pushed him off, stood up and began brushing the dust off his coat. Then the elf hit him again. This time the vampire was surprised. He stumbled back against the cabin as Arsenius punched him repeatedly.

He swung wildly but the tanned elf evaded it easily and struck the vampire in the abdomen, winding him. This was followed by an uppercut to the jaw.

Grelow went like a rag doll and fell back against the cabin's door.

It seemed that Arsenius wasn't quite done yet as he aimed several kicks at the defenceless vampire. Even though it went against his better judgment Rekil enlisted the help of Elik in restraining him.

Despite the beating he'd received, there were no bruises on Grelow's face. His nose, which Arsenius had broken in several places, returned to its original unbroken state as they watched. Then the vampire's eyes reopened.

Jumping to his feet and adjusting his shirts, he winked at Arsenius. "You've got quite the temper, haven't you?"

He smiled at the group in general. The sides of his mouth were constantly curled into something vaguely akin to mirth but closer inspection showed it wasn't friendly. It was smug.

Eventually, Grelow's gaze crash landed on Elik. Simply because Elik wasn't staring at him with the same look of disgust as the others. Frankly, the rather reticent warrior wasn't looking at him at all; he seemed more preoccupied with the lake.

Elik wasn't looking out across the lake for any other boats. Elik wasn't looking for any sign of the nearest shore. In fact he wouldn't have been able to see the shores if he wanted to. The night made them invisible.

The only thing to be seen on the lake's surface was the moon's reflection. It was this that had caught his eye. For the moon's reflection should be shimmering slightly on the surface of the lake, not jumping in and out of it. It also shouldn't be hurtling toward the boat at an incredible speed.

Chapter 16

"As much as I'd hate to intrude upon such a pleasant conversation, you're going to have to turn around," Elik interrupted.

The shouting abruptly ceased. Each and every one of them turned to stare at him. A considerable number of them wanted to remark about how much his deep, gruff voice suited his appearance. The others were going to comment on this being the first time they'd heard him speak. None of them were able to make any such remarks. The words died in their throats as they caught sight of what he was referring to.

Myths and fairy tales are supposed to remain in stories but occasionally they like to get out and dance around a bit. Most of the group had seen this kind of thing previously but only in story books involving voyages across the sea. Which is why they couldn't be seeing it now. The justification was very simple; *sea serpents don't exist, therefore I can't be seeing one now.* They especially don't exist on lakes miles inland.

They watched its movements in the water; dazzling as the moon caught its scales. Before it reached their boat, however, it veered off to the left and vanished beneath the lake's surface. Seconds later it emerged once more, and they could do naught but watch spellbound, as it hurtled through the air toward them.

For Farack, it seemed to happen in slow motion. He was mesmerized as the creature drifted toward him. Out of the corners of his eyes, he momentarily noticed the others diving out of the way, but then his gaze flicked back toward the serpent.

Its body was easily twenty feet long. Covered in silver scales, the only exception were its mud brown fins. They stretched from behind its gills, all the way down its entire length. The head at the top of the creature's body was wildly out of proportion. Twice the size it should have been in both length and width, it was quite the sight. Terrifying definitely, yet still somewhat remarkable. The eyes were thin and yellow with blood red pupils shining out. Two enormous nostrils were nestled just above the widest mouth Farack had ever seen. It was probably able to open at an 180 degree angle.

It seemed an eternity that the serpent's grimace filled his vision. Sure enough the mouth stretched open as far as Farack could see. A forked tongue rested in the throat's depths, behind a gum filled with sharp looking teeth. The smell of decay washed over him as the creature took a breath and he found himself staring at the pieces of rotten fish lodged between the copious teeth.

Farack's head was literally inside the cavernous mouth until someone grabbed the back of his shirt and tugged him off his feet. The monster almost passed overhead; its mouth snapped shut on empty air but the lower jaw smacked him in the forehead, depriving him of consciousness.

Its momentum carried it straight on, hitting the corner of the cabin and rocking the boat as it re-entered the water. Rather ungracefully in the opinion of those present.

Apart from the unconscious Farack, Vantix who was asleep and Slyra who was tending to his wounds, they all moved cautiously to the side and peered into the water. Twenty metres away from the boat, the serpent could be seen swimming away. It didn't give the impression of a desire to come back. They watched it intently; willing it to keep swimming. All except for Sam who couldn't see. The others were much taller than him. In a bad mood with his growth hormones, he walked to the other side of the deck.

He stared at a disturbance in the water. For a moment, he caught a glimpse of the moon.

Sam wasn't stupid. He dived to the floor and screamed. He didn't scream any words, instead going for a sound universally recognized as a sign of terror.

"Aghhh!" He hoped the others got the message.

They turned just as the serpent rose from the water and flew over Sam's head. Then they were all guilty of an almost fatal act of stupidity.

Nobody ducked. They didn't dive out of the way. None raised a sword to defend themselves. Every single last one of them, including the usually calm and composed Elik, froze in terror.

It went straight through them, teeth sinking into Fred's neck and lower abdomen. His eyes went wide and a stream of blood flew from his mouth as the creature took him into the water with it. Its tailfin swept through the air, knocking Rekil, Arsenius, Elik and Ramos overboard, then followed the rest of its body into the water.

Arsenius wasn't really aware of what was happening. He'd seen the creature coming at him but the experience had felt distant somehow. The freezing water hit him in the face as he went under, waking him up. Floundering for a moment, he managed to get above the water. Being from a vast desert hadn't helped his swimming prowess. He took a deep breath and went under again. This time he kept calm and looked around, counting silently. Arithmetic was a deep passion of his.

Osca, Hemer and Sam were busy dragging the others into the boat. Grelow looked on, sword at the ready.

Slyra came out of the cabin and looked around wildly. "Some kind of sea serpents," Osca mumbled, whilst dragging Rekil aboard.

"How many?" she replied.

Rekil shrugged. "Two, maybe three."

"There's twelve," Arsenius corrected.

Rekil grabbed Sam and Ramos and shoved them toward the sails and rudder respectively. "Get us to the nearest shore now!" he shouted after them. At that moment, whilst Sam and Ramos ran toward the front of the boat and most of the others were engaged in an unsuccessful attempt at waking Farack, the monsters deemed it best to make another appearance.

The group span in circles as serpents filled every field of vision. Trying to move the sail to every course at once, Sam and Ramos were left in a tangle of rigging as the sail tumbled down around them.

Rekil heaved himself onto the roof of the cabin at the same time one of the creatures lunged. Strange thing was, it dropped severely short of the boat. As if it was just trying to scare them. .

The others linked up with Rekil on the roof. They drew their weapons as he loosed an arrow from his bow. In this light, it was highly unlikely he'd hit anything.

Suddenly the air around them was filled with serpents, sailing over, around and in between the group. It happened in less than a second. Osca looked round in amazement. They hadn't even come close to any of them. It took another round with zero casualties for him to realise their intention. "They're toying with us," he muttered.

It was at that moment, that he realised they weren't going to get out of this in one piece. "What have I done to deserve this?" he murmured to himself. As if in answer, the countless plates of fish he'd eaten over his lifetime flashed before his eyes. He shrugged the images away. His subconscious should know when he was asking a rhetorical question.

Looking around, he could see most people clasping their swords with an expression of genuine fear that mirrored his own. There were three exceptions to this rule. They were: Elik who was staring at the serpents, his mouth set in a grim, determined line; Grelow, who was too preoccupied with cleaning his nails; and Rekil who was continuously loosing arrows out across the water. The latter didn't seem to be having any effect.

The serpents were amongst them again, passing by a hair's breathe from the group. As per usual, they didn't hit anybody but the margins grew slimmer each time. "It's almost bloody orchestrated" Osca murmured. They'd attack soon; he was sure of it. When they rose from the water again, Osca thought it was the end. After about a second he corrected this thought. The serpents were still passing around them. One went by on his left.

Out of the corner of his eye, he noticed a serpent passing by Rekil. The old soldier turned with the monster as it passed him, notching an arrow to his bow and following its passage. As the creature moved by his elbow, he loosed. The arrow flew the couple of inches from his bow to the serpent's eye.

122

Halting in mid-air is no mean feat. You have to defy the laws of physics and spit in the face of momentum. Nevertheless, the now deceased serpent accomplished it with apparent ease and landed on the boat, viscous skin immediately causing it to slide off the side and almost drag their vessel over with it.

As it rocked and shook, each member of the group tried to maintain their balance. They were largely successful; although some fell over, none of them were deposited into the lake.

The boat actually managed to put a slight distance between it and the immediate peril as the monsters shrank away. Nothing significant really, but still a distance. The group emitted a weary cheer.

Sam and Ramos finally untangled themselves from the rigging and made another attempt at steering. They caused the boat to shake a bit, but were otherwise ineffective.

"You can stop," Rekil called to Sam and Ramos. Their steering was making him nauseous.

As his stomach was not as strong as Rekil's, Osca was already leaning over the side. He stared at his queasy reflection several feet below him. Seconds later, he obliterated it with vomit. He retched several times, all his meals from the day choosing to resurface. He wiped his mouth with the back of his sleeve and spat several times into the water. As the rippling waters settled, he stared at his reflection again. In a flash it was obliterated a second time.

One of the serpents shot straight up into the air, its fin catching him on the cheek. He tumbled backwards, clutching his face in agony. Blood was rolling down his cheek and neck, soaking his collar.

In the meantime, the serpent plummeted into the water. It was immediately replaced by all its kin, soaring through the air around the boat as if they'd never left.

The group returned to their desperate attempts to wound the serpents. From where he lay on the cabin's roof, Osca watched as arrows missed their mark and swords sliced clean air. Had they not been trying to kill him, perhaps he would have admired the serpents grace and finesse. The way they twisted and turned in the air was amazing, avoiding every blow effortlessly.

In an instant they seemed to up the tempo, leaving the water as soon as they landed to leap again. Blurs of silver that barely registered.

"Down!" His shout was barely audible, but most of the group complied. They hit the deck and the serpents glided through the air above them.

Osca watched as a serpent attempted to swallow Elik. Its mouth was going to close around Elik's chest, until something strange happened.

Impossible is the best way to describe his jump. People can't jump six feet into the air. Nor can they take the time to float.

The creature went into the lake unchecked. Elik continued to float, cloak swept away to revealing his expensive chainmail. The black wings protruding from his back were also quite impressive.

As he dropped to the boat, Osca glanced around furtively. The others were picking themselves up and hadn't seen it. Slyra however, was staring open-mouthed in Elik's direction. *At least I'm not the only one,* Osca thought to himself.

Not one single person reacted when the creatures appeared again. Standing as still as she was, the serpent had no problem closing its jaws around Slyra.

Instead of the serpent's momentum carrying it and her straight into the lake, it froze in mid-air. It wasn't the only one. Every other of its kind hovered in the air, snapping desperately at the nearest members of the group. Time hadn't stopped, slowed or anything of the sort. The serpents were simply suspended in the air.

Slyra's eyes were completely white, almost luminous. Slowly pushing the serpent's jaw open, they caught sight of her robe. There were blossoming points of red all over her top as she stepped slowly from the serpent's jaws.

Her pointy hat fell from her head; she didn't seem to notice. Hemer caught it before it rolled into the lake. Wispy tendrils of energy flowed from her fingertips as the others watched in amazement. She mumbled some strange words and something slightly disturbing happened.

Each and every serpent's head made a rendezvous with their respective tailfins, the parts in between crushed and splattering outwards.

As eleven serpents worth of bloody chunks rained down on them, Slyra fainted. Fortunately, Elik caught her. Her copious puncture wounds didn't bode well.

Osca stared at the morsel of serpent in his lap. There were other pieces like it bobbing along the lake's surface. He decided to vomit again.

Rekil opened the cabin door and Elik carried Slyra inside. Placing her on the bed, he began rummaging in his pack for bandages and salves. He honestly didn't think he could do anything for her.

Having followed them in, Osca noticed something peculiar. Spinning around, scanning every inch of the room, he still didn't find what he was looking for. Even the adjoining storage room didn't yield an answer to his question. Only then did he voice his concern.

"Can any of you see Vantix?" he asked.

Chapter 17

Tode and Amph floated slowly through the water towards the boat, only their small, triangular heads visible above the lake's surface. They couldn't risk discovery.

Time and again Tode was forced to drag his companion back, signalling to him to slow down. He was making far too much noise. Amph had better not ruin this for him.

Normally he wouldn't even have been awake at this hour but his slumber had been disturbed. The Guardian's ancient voice had invaded his dreams with a message. *Come to me*, it had hissed.

Leaving his chamber, he'd arrived in the grand sanctum in a matter of minutes. Amph had given him a weary look as he bowed before the guardian. Clearly he'd also been sound asleep.

The Guardian's voice sounded like cracked parchment. It had almost a rustling quality to it. "There is a vessel on the lake," it rasped inside his head, "Something strange dwells within; it is the will of Nasrode that you bring it here."

The two of them made to leave but he drew them back. "Place this around its neck to drain it of dark magic," he instructed.

Now, Tode and Amph watched as the serpents toyed with the boat's crew. There was something oddly poetic about their pathetic attempts to defend themselves.

Watching them, he didn't see anything special. They were just a mixed group of humans, an elf and a rhadon. *Maybe the special one's in the cabin,* he thought.

As they pulled themselves quietly onto the rear deck, they took extreme care to suppress each and every sound. Even though the crew seemed occupied with the serpents, they weren't leaving anything to chance. Nobody disappointed the guardian; it would be tantamount to sacrilege.

The serpents were reaching the attack's crescendo, the big finale fast approaching. None had attention to spare, never mind pay it to the two things on the lower deck.

Tode unsheathed his dagger, indicating that Amph do the same. Whilst the other drew his blade, he caught wind of something.

It was a strange smell, oozing out from under the cabin's door. What they sought was in there, he was sure of it. Gripping his blade with his teeth he moved slowly toward the door and placed his hand upon the handle, just in time to feel it turn from the inside.

As the door opened outward, they leapt soundlessly behind it. A girl exited the cabin and looked up toward the roof. As she clambered up, the wind changed and the two of them caught her scent. It was sickly sweet, yet somehow sinister. Tode felt his nostrils creep away from it, instead fixating on the odour wafting out of the cabin. They stalked inside the cabin, seeking the source.

Amph was first to spot the figure on the bed. It looked vaguely human, but the scent indubitably originated there.

Reaching into the pouch at his belt, he withdrew the item the Guardian had given them earlier. It was a metallic black ring, lined with spikes on the inside. Handing it to Amph, he watched him place it around the thing's neck. There was a soft click, followed instantly by a gasp as each spike pierced the thing's throat. Its breathing became immediately laboured.

Amph grabbed the thing and thrust it over Tode's shoulder. Its eyes opened momentarily, but he shut them again with the butt of his knife.

Stalking out onto the deck, they noticed something exceptionally bizarre. Above them the serpents were suspended in the air, as if by magic.

There was a shout and the serpents seemed to explode. By which time they'd already plunged into the lake.

* * * * *

Vantix was underwater; that he could comprehend. What he didn't understand was how he was coping with the lack of air.

He reached for his neck. Something cold and metallic rested there, out of his line of sight. Sliding off the stone slab he lay on, he got to his feet.

The only thing that made his current location actually look like a cell were the bars on the door. Otherwise, it was rather spacious. There were stone columns, marble statues and furniture made out of some material Vantix had never seen. All were in a remarkable state of repair.

His movements around the room were slow and sluggish, lugging his legs after him as he tried to move but not as much as he'd expected. This water differed from any he'd ever encountered before. Somehow it seemed thinner, lighter than anything he'd ever swam through. In contrast to the dark surface of the lake, it was also crystal clear.

Turning his head toward the door, he experienced a sharp pain in his neck. A slight trickle of blood floated through the water in front of him.

It was only then he noticed the new garments he wore. They seemed to be made of different kinds of algae stitched together and flowed easily in the water instead of becoming cumbersome.

Reaching up and grasping the thing on his neck, he tried to remove it. Several painful seconds later, he gave up.

"I wouldn't do that," called a woman's voice. Her voice had sounded in his head, overcoming the communication difficulties presented by their submersed meeting. As it was the only entrance, he turned to the door.

There was a creature standing there, one he'd never seen before. She, for he was certain it was a she, had bright yellow skin and fins. A sharp triangular head was situated at the top of a long, angular, much gilled neck. Fins ran from its hands to its elbows and its feet to its knees. There was also one jutting out of its hair. Webbed hands and feet seemed a foregone conclusion, and Vantix was not disappointed. It wore a one piece outfit made from the same material as his own new garments.

She gave him an encouraging smile, revealing the same kind of fanged teeth he'd developed recently.

She raised a hand to her chest and nodded slightly. "My name is Deca," she announced, "and I am going to let you out now." Once again, her voice drifted into his head. He wasn't sure how he could hear her through the water, but it didn't matter. As always, he was fine with something as long as it worked; he didn't need an explanation how.

Noticing him edging toward the door, she stepped back and raised a hand. "Before you knock me senseless and make a valiant attempt at escape," she warned, "you must know there's nowhere for you to go." At her words, he visibly sagged.

The door opened and she beckoned him forward. Following her, he emerged in a vast chamber, much larger than his holding cell. Opening his mouth to speak he felt water rush in and run down his throat. He swallowed reflexively but the water didn't make it the whole way down. His new friend indicated her throat. "This device will prevent you drowning and enable you to broadcast any thoughts you desire."

Vantix took a moment to compose himself and followed her instructions. "If I were to ask where we are," he hazarded, surprised it was actually working, "would you feel inclined to give me an answer?"

Prior to answering his question, she reached the end of the chamber and opened another door. "This is Vaston," she revealed, "The city beneath the lake."

Stepping through the door she'd opened, Vantix marvelled at the surrounding architecture. Temples were on every side. Besides their state of repair, he found another thing to marvel at: their age. The statues he saw were to gods and goddesses that people had long since stopped believing in. Long forgotten commandments were written on every pillar. Some of Deca's people looked up from their plinths before these gods and eyed him suspiciously. He didn't blame them.

"But how is this possible? How can we see, talk, walk…Why doesn't the pressure of the water kill us? It doesn't make any damn sense."

Deca smiled knowingly. "It's an ancient magic, the like of which doesn't exist in the world today. The water is far thinner down here, enabling my kind to live in peace." She nodded toward the apparatus on Vantix's neck. "Your kind would still drown."

The only gap in the circle of churches was a large staircase heading up to another magnificent structure. It was easily the largest temple Vantix had ever seen.

Deca sprang lightly up the steps and Vantix followed. His movements still slow and sluggish; there was no way he could keep up with her.

This whole time, a certain question had been present at the edge of Vantix's mind. No longer bothering with tact, he finally voiced this thought, "What are you?"

Deca was genuinely surprised by his question. "You were not aware of us?"

Still waiting for an answer to his own question, Vantix shook his head. "No," he replied, "Not as such."

"But The Guardian said........." she murmured to herself for a moment. After a while, she turned back to Vantix. "Your people call it Lake Glasrobe."

Unsure of how to reply, Vantix simply went with, "And..?"

"Who do you think it was named for?" Deca stared at him before stating, "We are the glasrobes."

She sprang up the steps once more, leaving him firmly behind.

* * * * *

As a result of Vantix's restricted pace, Deca had been waiting for almost five minutes when he arrived. She didn't bother with farewells, departing just before he reached the top.

From here he had a pretty good view of the surrounding area. The entire city, for it stretched far past all he'd seen of it, was set in some sort of chasm. The temple beside him, was the only building in the vast city that actually ascended higher than the chasm's dark walls.

It had probably been above the water at some stage. Another thing he noticed, was that beyond the temples he'd seen was a much larger city. It was in dire need of repair, especially when compared to the grander buildings he had laboured past on his way here. Then again it was at the bottom of a lake so presumably safety standards and regulations didn't apply.

Deciding that Deca had probably led him there for a reason, he entered the temple. It was easily discernible as a place of worship. This was mainly due to the large quantity of glasrobes kneeling before a stone statue.

The statue itself was only as big as the average human. That still made it a considerable few inches bigger than any of the other glasrobes. Although the statues outside had been vaguely familiar, this one Vantix had never seen.

Considering that the gods outside were made up of humans mixed with an assorted range of other creatures, this one actually looked fairly normal. That being said he still possessed a rather diverse heritage.

It had a human shaped head and hair, but the same flared nostrils and skin as the glasrobes. It was wearing exactly the same clothes as Vantix, although he couldn't be sure they were the same colours. Fins ran all the way to its elbows, but there was a distinct lack of webbed appendages. Gills were also present, although only half the number other glasrobes had.

It was very obvious that the glasrobes were leaving, despite the fact that they did so noiselessly. Vantix assumed that he'd offended them, but didn't budge as they streamed out. Within moments he was on his own.

Alone in the hall he approached the statue. It was obvious it had been lovingly carved by a master stonemason. Every detail had been picked out, from it hairs to the texture of its fins. The name "Nasrode" was etched into the stone pillar on which the statue rested.

The strangest thing about it, stranger even than Nasrode's ancestry, was that a real sword rested in the stone sheath.

Vantix was intent on getting a closer look, until he was interrupted. A voice that sounded decidedly ancient echoed around the chamber. "Amazing, is it not?"

At least that's the effect it had in his head. He was pretty sure that water should prevent such an echo from occurring. Knowing he couldn't find its source, Vantix focused his gaze on the statue.

As anyone who has ever been followed will tell you, there's a difference between knowing someone's there and thinking someone's there. The hairs on your neck may rise at a feeling of observation, but an almost intense shiver all over your body lets you know someone's actually there.

An intense shiver racked Vantix's body as he sensed the presence. Seeing as it didn't bludgeon him over the head (a rather common occurrence in these situations), he assumed it either (a) meant him no harm or (b) was waiting for its cue.

Vantix decided he'd better acknowledge the presence. Turning casually, he shot the person a quizzical look.

It was another glasrobe. The main difference between this and the others he'd encountered was its advanced age. Although he didn't have an exact figure, antediluvian seemed a close enough estimate.

134

Wearing a robe and cowl covering all but a wrinkled, pointed chin, a lot of Vantix's guesswork was based on its posture. That was of course, before a gnarled hand reached out and confirmed his suspicions. However, that wasn't the only thing it did.

Just after the hand waved by, the ring on Vantix's neck unhinged and fell off. Immediately Vantix held his breath. After an extremely short period of time he was forced to let it out.

"Relax," croaked the ancient glasrobe, "you can breathe."

Vantix took several deep breaths and fumbled his neck. The wounds made by the ring were gone. Whatever the Glasrobe had done he could suddenly speak and breathe freely.

After a moments ponder, he turned in the direction of the elderly Glasrobe. "I take it you're the high priest, shaman or druid around here."

A withered hand reached up and pulled back the hood. Sure enough, it had the strange, symbolic tattoos that every decent shaman needs. He also had the one thing none of the other glasrobes had: a beard. Then again, he was the local shaman. Tradition probably dictated he be the only one with a beard. His skin was a slightly different colour to the rest. Theirs had a simple yellow hue, whilst he looked as if he'd been baked. Sort of an ancient parchment effect.

"I have waited millennia for this moment," the glasrobe declared, "I am the Guardian."

Vantix gulped. People didn't usually wait for him for good reasons.

"Of what? Sorry," he managed weakly.

The Guardian looked straight into his eye with a startling intensity. "I do not follow."

135

Vantix gave up. Chances are, he wouldn't find out what this creature was guardian of anyway. "Vantix," he said, whilst offering a hand.

The Guardian stared at it.

Gesturing toward the statue he decided to change the subject. "That's a nice statue," he offered.

The Guardian nodded, "Quite, quite." He seemed preoccupied momentarily, but then he gave Vantix an enquiring look. "You know the history?"

Just say yes, Vantix thought. *What if he wants to discuss it? Smiling and nodding never hurt. Unless lying is punishable by death here-*

"No" Vantix replied.

The Guardian sighed, "Then let us begin."

Stupid, Vantix cursed himself bitterly.

Chapter 18

Since it would have been rude to interrupt and explain that he didn't care about The Guardian's ancestry, Vantix tried to fill his head with other thoughts. This was thwarted by the ancient voice speaking directly into his mind.

"There was a time when we glasrobes roamed the land. We were many, the largest of all clans. We were also peaceful, so when The Clan Wars came we had no place there."

Vantix nodded in recognition. Although The Clan Wars had taken place thousands of years ago, everybody knew about them. In the few years he'd spent in school, they'd come up once or twice. Supposedly, they were the main reason behind the first empire. He tuned in just in time for more of The Guardian's ramblings.

"We were treated like animals," the ancient glasrobe spat, "The more barbaric of them hunted us. Used our skin for clothing, our bones as weapons. We became a means to an end. We were forced to retreat into the lakes, using our magic to sink our cities and make the depths of the lakes habitable for us.

I suppose we were fortunate. Many species without our unique abilities perished. We simply became reclusive.

Being so few in number, every single glasrobe was important to the High Guardian. When one of the them went missing, a search party was sent. I don't know what they found exactly, only that they returned with nothing but a strange looking child."

Vantix rolled his eyes; he hated fairy tales. Especially those that didn't involve him.

The Guardian didn't seem intent on returning to his story. His eyes had clouded over, probably lost in a memory. When he spoke, he sounded weary.

"Over the next eighteen years, almost everything changed. The clans fell, the empire rose and my people stayed in hiding.

The Emperor offered us peace to compensate for the sins of the clans. The High Guardian refused. He would not forgive for he had other plans in mind. Crazy as he was, nobody dared to challenge him.

The strange looking child had by now grown up. He was a young man now, named Nasrode. Being without parents he was at a disadvantage, so my father took him in. He was only a year older than I and we became friends."

Vantix shook his head dismissively. *You're not that old,* he thought to himself, *nobody is that old.* The Guardian continued unabated.

"On the eve of his 18th birthday, my father told Nasrode of how they'd found him. He explained that Nasrode's father had fallen in love with a human woman, that they'd run away together, and that her father had murdered them both because of the disgrace they caused him. After that, Nasrode disappeared for a while.

It was weeks later before the lake had a visitor. Normally we wouldn't engage with visitors, but the elf walked around and around the lake for days. Eventually, we got curious.

He informed us that the Emperor would not forgive us for what we'd done and we would pay dearly. Basically, it was a declaration of war."

I must be missing something, Vantix shrugged to himself, *Why does he think I care?* He was fairly certain the Guardian didn't drag everybody to the bottom of the lake for this history lesson.

"The next day Nasrode returned. He was cold and withdrawn for a time, but eventually my father gleaned a confession. Nasrode had always been unable to control his temper. On learning of his true parentage and their demise, he set out to find his human grandfather; intent on revenge.

As I said before, many things had changed in those eighteen years. By the time Nasrode found him, his grandfather was a baron, one of the emperor's most trusted advisors. As reward for his council, he was also in charge of a rather large estate. Nasrode slew every single man in the keep, leaving the women and children to fend for themselves. It was this act that angered the emperor so.

Nasrode offered to give himself up; a solution most of our people were happy with. My father, on the other hand, wouldn't hear of it. Apparently it was time to fight back.

With Nasrode as the figurehead and my father as his advisor, they waged war against the empire. They were surprisingly successful.

Glasrobes rose up all over Ballisca, finally shaking off the shackles of oppression. Nasrode was their inspiration, a leader who'd suffered even more than most of our people. They were, and still are, devoted to him.

139

Revenge fuelled his every waking moment. Whenever a sword was in his grasp, his thoughts immediately returned to his lost family."

"A tragic hero fuelled by revenge," Vantix muttered under his breath, "How original." The Guardian ignored him.

"The empire was shattered. In each province our people took power. It came down to a last battle on the plains of Derranferd.

On the eve of said battle, a human walked into our camp. Despite our guards putting several arrows in him, he managed to make it to Nasrode's tent and fell to his knees before us. He was a stranger to me but I knew from my father's expression that he recognised him.

In all my life, there are few conversations that I fully remember. That one, however, I will never forget.

"An assassin wouldn't make this many mistakes," Nasrode said, whilst indicating the injured man's wounds, "Who are you?"

"Surely it doesn't matter," my father interrupted, "He is obviously of no importance."

"My name is Darli," the injured man had croaked, "I'm your uncle."

Nasrode drew his sword. He was unwilling to forgive any of the family members on his mother's side; her death was their fault.

"There's something you must know," at that point blood was flowing from the corner of his mouth, in spite of which he still found the strength to go on. "My father did murder your father, but your mother, my sister, refused to come back with us.

Halfway up the road, I realised that a young woman with a new born can't survive alone in the tiny shack they'd called home. I couldn't leave her like that so I went back an-"

Darli was cut off by my father kicking him repeatedly in the chest. It was an attempt to silence him. To this day, I still remembered the horrible feeling that gripped me then. I knew everything was about to go wrong.

Nasrode shoved my father away. "What?" he shouted at his dying uncle, "What happened next?"

Darli spat a whole mouthful of blood onto the ground. "I was just in time to see her child dragged from my sister's lifeless arms by your friends here. I tried to stop them, but there was nothing I could do."

There was silence in the tent for a moment. Nasrode stared at the ground, seemingly oblivious to my father's reassurances that his uncle was lying. After a moment he asked quietly, "Is this true?"

My father leapt at the chance to deny these claims, but Nasrode's query wasn't directed at him.

Darli nodded and continued "I'm not proud of what happened that day. I just thought you should know, that your people are just as monstrous as my own. No matter who wins tomorrow, they will hunt the other to extinction. I hope you enjoyed being a pawn Nasrode, for that's not what my sister intended for you."

Those were his last words. Nasrode turned to me, placing his sword in my hands. He glared at my father for a few moments before declaring angrily, " There is no forgiveness for what you've done. When the numbers of glasrobes dwindle, when they are a forgotten race and teeter on the brink of extinction, only then shall I reclaim my sword. Only then shall you deserve me."

He stormed out into the night and was not seen again. To say he was sorely missed, would be an understatement. Without him to lead them, our army was a shamble, a rag-tag bunch who wouldn't even survive a brawl in a tavern. They were slaughtered."

As The Guardian finally lapsed into silence, Vantix breathed a sigh of relief. Maybe now they would return him to the surface. This place didn't really suit him.

After several moments of silence, he finally managed the courage to ask the question. "Can I go now?"

"All in good time," The Guardian replied. He looked at Vantix with a twinkle in his eye. "You know," he declared, "I almost lost faith several times, but...."

Vantix most definitely didn't like the way The Guardian had trailed off. "But what?" he asked hesitantly.

The Guardian smiled. "But now, you have returned."

Chapter 19

Welbh ambled cheerfully along the corridor. He even whistled a tune under his breath. Despite being called to the throne room, there wasn't a thing that could dampen his mood. They were leaving for Derranferd today.

Since they'd be spending two days in a carriage together, the King's sudden desire to speak to him was slightly unusual. It must be of some importance.

Stepping into the throne room, he surveyed the scene before him. The King sat upon his throne with two of his sons on either side. Of the four Fardashian princes, only Balithorn commanded any respect. The others were a bunch of drunken louts.

It wasn't any of these that caught Welbh's attention. That honour was reserved solely for the elf standing before the King.

Jandelk raised a hand for the elf to stop and nodded to Welbh. "You requested my presence, sire?" Welbh asked.

"Yes," the King indicated the elf, "This is Coran, he's the only survivor from the dendrid attack."

Welbh took another look at the elf. Despite the new clothes he wore, Coran was in very bad shape. There was a large bandage stretching around his head, covering up several wounds. Dried blood peeked out on his scalp regardless. A large cut stretched from just under his eye to his lip. It had been stitched up but didn't look any better. *He must have taken some beating,* Welbh winced to himself.

"I know this is painful for you," King Jandelk sympathised, "but would you mind starting again?"

The elf nodded, but Welbh could see he was on the verge of breaking down. He'd obviously been through a lot.

"They came about a week before the attack a-"

"Sorry, who did?" Welbh asked.

The elf paused uncertainly. "Th-the searchers. They came to dig."

"What were they searching for?" This time it was Balithorn asking the question.

Coran shrugged uncomfortably. "I don't know, but they found it. I don't know who they were either, only that their leader had a tattoo covering half his face. It looked like an eagle."

Welbh had been quenching his thirst with a glass of water, but at this description he spluttered. Coughing uncontrollably, he thumped himself several times in the chest. An eagle tattoo covering half the face was a favourite disguise of his brother's. What in the blazes was his involvement in this?

The others gave him a sharp look, but he raised a hand to reassure them. Coran picked up where he'd left off. "After a week of searching, they found what they were looking for. They'd paid everybody in the village to arrange a feast but it never happened.

I'd been out cutting wood, but when I saw the smoke in the sky I rushed back. I saw the dendrid cut swathes through the villagers; through my family. They were vicious, murdering everything that moved.

All attempts to defend my village were useless. A blow to the head knocked me out, left me dying outside the ruin that had been my home. Your men found me amidst the wreckage and brought me here. I awoke shortly afterwards."

The King nodded. "You have my thanks."

Coran was escorted out of the room. All except Balithorn and Welbh left the King. When it was just the three of them, Jandelk spoke: "I've received word from Derranferd. Audron claims they weren't behind the attack."

"How does that affect the negotiations?" Balithorn asked.

The King shook his head. "It doesn't. He seems quite taken with the idea of an alliance. We leave within the hour, so Welbh you should go pack. Balithorn, you shall be in charge during my absence. You are both dismissed."

Whilst the others went about their business King Jandelk sat and thought. He was still thinking an hour later when Welbh informed him that they were leaving.

* * * * *

The boat drifted lazily across the lake. There was almost no wind to fill its sails. Although the sun was out, most of the crew was asleep.

Osca and Farack were playing a game of cards. After several moments, Osca laid his on the table. Farack clucked angrily, he hadn't won a hand yet. "Are you cheating or something?" he asked.

"Nope," Osca shrugged, "Just lucky, I guess."

"That's a card in your collar, isn't it?" Farack said flatly.

"Not at all," Osca replied defensively, "So what do you think happened to Vantix?"

"I don't know," Farack murmured.

"My guess is that he woke up, stumbled out onto the deck and probably fell into the lake."

"You're quite the optimist." Farack said dryly.

A grunt caught their attention. Rekil yawned and got slowly to his feet. Apart from Elik who was tending to Slyra's wounds, he was the only one awake besides them. The others were still recuperating from the night's escapades

He gazed groggily over toward them. "How's the girl doing?"

Farack was about to inform him that he wasn't sure she'd make it, when Osca answered instead. "Hold on a minute, I'll go check." The rhadon stared after him inquisitively as he scurried toward the cabin.

Rekil emitted a dry chuckle, "He's awfully keen."

He nodded, thinking the same.

Failing in his attempt to be nonchalant, Farack found himself once again scrutinising Rekil's armour. It was of very intricate and ornate design, probably crafted by a master. He'd actually seen a picture of it once. On the front was the silhouette of a man, lantern raised and sword in hand. Around him were symbols representing all the evils he protected the world from and signifying that he was one of the Vigilant, the eternal guardians. In the old days it meant so much more, but now it epitomized infallible service as a Fardashian military commander. Rekil didn't look old enough to be a retired commander though; he was just into his forties.

"Were you a commander?" Farack asked eventually. His curiosity demanded satisfaction.

Rekil shook his head wearily. "This is my father's."

146

On seeing the other man's sad expression many would have steered clear. Farack on the other hand, couldn't help himself. "Did you serve in the army?"

"Yes, but I never made it anywhere." This was accompanied by a look. It wasn't threatening, more of an appeal not to probe any further. Unfortunately Farack was terrible at reading expressions.

"Why?"

"I was dishonourable discharged."

"What did you do?"

Rekil sighed, *Maybe if I tell him he'll leave me alone.*

"I joined the King's army when I was eighteen. My father had been a commander, and I desperately wanted to make him proud. This was twenty four years ago, when Fardash was at war with Port Daichwater."

Farack nodded. He'd heard about the war from his father, who'd been living in Port Daichwater at the time. Rekil went on.

"Port Daichwater is only a fifth the size of Fardash, by far the smallest of the provinces. It's just a big walled city, filled with smugglers, thieves, pirates, bandits and assassins."

Farack coughed, "My parents are from there."

Rekil smiled, "No offence intended. A city that big, just filled to the brim with criminals, is never going to be an easy thing to take from land or sea. They had a port, so we couldn't starve them out. Our ships were no match for theirs, so we couldn't attack from sea. We were there for seven years, by which time we'd lost the upper hand. They'd venture out in war parties, pick off some of us and scatter into the hills. They'd sneak back into the city later."

Farack shuddered. Rekil was staring straight through him, lost in the siege of Port Daichwater.

"We got word that they were being aided by Gravent. That they were getting weapons and supplies from them. Supposedly, they were seen sneaking over the border to collect these.

My father pulled some strings, got me command of a small, seven man unit to put an end to any aid they were receiving. We spent three days waiting in a copse by the nearest border before we finally saw our prey. My heart sank when we I saw they were all women and children."

Farack didn't like where this was going. By its end, the war with Port Daichwater had become incredibly dirty and a lot of the King's men were later executed for war crimes.

"They were simply trying to flee the conditions in the city so I ordered my men to leave them be. My command was questioned. Some of my men insisted we make an example of them. They wanted to show the people of Daichwater what happens to those who oppose us, to hit them where it really hurts. So I killed-"

"What!" Farack exclaimed, "No, you couldn't!"

"You didn't let me finish," Rekil responded, "I murdered two of my men. While the others were restraining me the women and children got away. My comrades dragged me back to stand trial and I would have hung for treason, if my father hadn't gone against everything he stood for and aided my escape. Duty no matter the cost was his mantra and he always put it first, save that one time. When it came down to it my father chose me. That's why I wear his armour. " He lapsed into silence.

Farack realised there was nothing he could say and resorted to the one phrase everybody loves to hear. "You did the right thing."

Rekil stared across the water. "Killing is never the right thing. War is always the same. Everybody loses. Wives lose husbands, mothers lose sons and children lose fathers. All for the selfish desires of kings and queens who've never fought a day in their lives." His two cents offered, Rekil changed the subject. "Now, where's that friend of yours got to?"

* * * * *

"How's Slyra doing?"

Elik looked up as Osca entered and shut the door behind him.

Slyra was lying on the bed and at the sound of her name, she raised herself up on her elbows. "I'm fine," she answered, "just tired." She collapsed back down.

Osca nodded to Elik. "You're a miracle worker. I wasn't sure she'd survive the night."

Elik shook his head. "I didn't do anything; she did it all herself."

"How is that possible?"

"She's a witch."

"No such thing."

"Last night you saw her reduce a pack of sea serpents to chowder and then heal herself from wounds that should have killed her. What other explanation is there?"

"Witches belong in old tales to scare children. They don't exactly just pop up in ordinary life."

They both looked to her for an answer. She looked absolutely exhausted. "Look I can't really explain," she said wearily, "but Osca you heard me mention Vantix leaving me on a sacrificial altar." He nodded, it was kind of hard to forget.

"All I remember is being chained to the altar, the knife descending and then waking up hours later. The entire cult was dead around me and I assumed Vantix had come back. He was nowhere to be seen. Without thinking, I snapped the chains and brought their temple down behind me as I left. I don't know exactly how I did it or how I managed what happened last night. Magic is difficult to harness and more often than not, I get the feeling it's controlling me. The more extraordinary feats usually involve me spectating while the magic acts of its own volition. Especially when I lose my temper."

With that she lay back and closed her eyes. She didn't seem up to much.

Elik stood in quiet contemplation. "That clears that up," he said after a while. *Why are there so many weird things on this trip,* Osca thought to himself. The other man made to leave, but not before the younger man could voice this thought. Elik stopped and turned around. "What do you mean?"

Had he been more sensible perhaps he'd have shut his mouth. Unfortunately it got the better of him.

"Well we've got a vampire, a burnt-out rhadon, a witch, whatever Vantix is," he paused momentarily and gestured to Elik, "and I don't know, the product of some sort of human-dragon love affair?"

"What?" Elik laughed, "I'm human." His face was almost perfect. Apart from his eyes, he looked genuinely confused.

The other man didn't buy it. "No, you're wrong. I know because I am human and we don't have wings."

In a flash, Elik had him pressed to the wall. Osca gulped and regretted speaking as a knife grazed his throat. "That's none of your business," Elik growled. Osca nodded vigorously. "Absolutely, of course, what

150

was I thinking? Glad we cleared that up." he managed desperately.

For a second, Elik stared straight into Osca's eyes. Then he put the knife back in its sheath. He stormed out and slammed the door behind him.

Coughing, Osca raised a hand to his throat. "I may have hit a sore spot there", he said quietly.

From where she lay on the bed, Slyra smiled and shook her head at him. "You really have a way with people."

Chapter 20

Vantix shook his head vigorously. "No, no, no, no, No!"

The Guardian nodded. "Even after four thousand years, I would recognise you anywhere."

"I'm not that guy," Vantix tried to reassure the glasrobe, "I don-"

The Guardian cut across him. "Do you deny the signs?"

Confusion reigned. "What?"

"The runes and the stars both announced your return today."

Vantix's mouth opened and closed several times. Numerous different responses were struggling to verbalise themselves. Finally, his selfishness managed to momentarily quiet the others. "I don't want to be your saviour or deliverer, or whatever it is you need."

The Guardian shook his head. "Destiny is about who we are, not who we want to be. Would you forsake both it and your heritage?"

He hadn't the faintest idea what the guardian was talking about. "My heritage," he scoffed, "I'm not exactly anything special. My father was a man and my mother was a woman. No myths, no fairy tales, no magical prophecies included."

The Guardian wanted to laugh at his naivety. "Can you truly look at yourself and think you are of human ancestry? You're a hybrid, just like Nasrode. The only difference is your human genes are overpowering your other side."

This time his words landed, leaving a crater in Vantix's aplomb. "What are you talking about?"

The Guardian smiled. Finally there was some respite in the youth's barrage of denials. "Your eyes, your mouth and the scales on the back of your neck are most definitely not human."

"Wh..What?" Scales on the back of his neck were certainly news to him.

The Guardian produced a mirror from the folds of his robe. Vantix wasted little time in snatching it and proceeded to check himself over.

When he'd caught sight of his reflection in a puddle several days earlier, it had been abundantly clear that there was something wrong with him. It was also clear that he was human. In contrast, he couldn't understand what he was seeing now.

Instead of the sandy-brown his hair had been for the last 17 years, it was dark and seemed to have a purple tinge. It looked suspiciously unnatural.

His teeth and gums were like that of some wild animal. Every last one seemed to have sharpened to a point. He ran his finger along them, it was no illusion. He stared into the eyes reflected back at him. They were narrower than he remembered and the wrong colour. The iris had expanded, almost covering the entire ocular. Apart from the white line around the edge, the only other colour besides his now dark indigo ocular was the black slit

153

taking the place of a pupil. His skin was a sickly yellow. Although he couldn't exactly manoeuvre the mirror around to give him a view of his neck, he ran a hand over it anyway. Tough and scaly like the skin of a lizard, a far cry from the norm.

With the changes to his appearance and the strange garments the glasrobes had given him, he looked an entirely different species. He lowered the mirror.

The Guardian had maintained silence during the inspection, but at the mirror's descent he spoke up. "So you see?"

Vantix nodded numbly. "There's no doubt about it," he said quietly, "I certainly don't look human."

"Then you must reclaim your sword," The Guardian intoned. His voice was like slabs of concrete crushing all hopes of future freedom.

Vantix turned toward the statue. Stepping up onto the pillar, he was precariously balanced. There wasn't really much room for him there. Almost in a trance he gripped the hilt of the sword with two hands and pulled. It didn't even budge.

He leaned back as far as he could, leaving only the tips of his toes on the pedestal. Putting all his weight behind the sword, he fell backward as it finally came free.

However, it didn't just slide out of the sheath; it did much more damage than that. It shattered the sheath and as he fell backwards, sliced clean through the statue at the knees.

It resulted in Vantix lying on the ground and clutching the sword to his chest as rubble fell through the water around him. "Careful," the Guardian called, "we wouldn't want any unnecessary damage coming to the sword."

As he got to his feet, the Guardian smiled and gestured to the shattered statue, "We'll be needing a new one anyway."

"Yes," Vantix said grimly, "but not of me." With that he swung the sword round, catching The Guardian in the face with hilt. The ancient glasrobe lost consciousness as Vantix sped away, looking for an exit.

* * * * *

The Guardian picked himself up and rubbed his jaw. It ached from where the boy had hit him.

Although he'd expected the denial, he hadn't foreseen the youth beating him and running away with the sword. There was now a distinct lack of both in the hall.

Hurrying outside, he spotted a large gathering staring up through the water. They were watching with an intense, unflinching stare as three figures swam toward the shore far above them. One was Vantix, the other two were Tode and Amph.

The Guardian raised his arm toward Vantix and began to chant.

* * * * *

Vantix knew how close he was. So close he could almost taste the fresh air. The lakebed would soon be underfoot and then it would just be a simple run to shore.

Two of the glasrobes had followed him but he had a huge lead. He'd be well on dry land by the time they even neared catching him. Whether or not they'd follow him onto the dry land was another matter. It was thoughts of this eventuality that caused him to keep Nasrode's sword.

155

Suddenly, it was as if a huge weight had been placed on his shoulders and he needed to breathe. He panicked, only the sight of his gaining pursuers enabling him to keep control and spurring him on.

His immediate thoughts were those of his imminent drowning. After a few seconds they flew toward the cause of his discomfort. Although he couldn't be perfectly sure, he would have bet the Guardian had lifted his earlier spell.

The lake water was in his mouth, his eyes and his nostrils. Firm ground was underneath his feet, but the rest of him remained beneath the surface.

It felt like he was moving in slow motion. Each movement required gargantuan effort and his lungs fit to burst as reaching the shore became imperative.

A hand grabbed his ankle and two arms wrapped themselves around his abdomen. Summoning up his last reserves of strength, he soldiered on; he'd come too far to give up.

As his head finally broke the lake's surface he sucked in a lungful of air, before it was driven out of him. A fist into the back of his neck sent him tumbling out of the water to collapse on the shore.

Taking several deep breathes, he noticed the hand still wrapped around his foot. Another was placed on his other ankle and he felt himself being dragged back into the lake. Moonlight shone down on two knife wielding glasrobes; neither seemed thrilled by Vantix's premature departure.

Groggily stabbing with Nasrode's sword, he made a lucky connection. He scrambled to his feet, wearily raising the sword despite his aching limbs and chest.

Whilst the glasrobes readied themselves, he realised he had a distinct advantage. He didn't need to take them

156

alive. Lunging at the two, his sword hacked deep into the one on the left. It fell instantly, dying without a whimper.

He sliced through the air where the other had been moments before, missing by quite a large margin. His foe had leapt back in anticipation of the blow. The glasrobe came at him from the side, trying to grab him around the neck. Since it had proven quite effective earlier, Vantix hit the glasrobe in the face with the sword's hilt. The creature stumbled and raised a hand to its face. Blood was rushing from its nose and upper lip. It hesitated momentarily, looking quite unsteady on its feet.

Vantix lunged at the Glasrobe once more, determined to finish it off. Unfortunately, it evaded easily and he felt a piercing pain in his leg. The seaweed garments had been sliced open and his thigh was bleeding.

Looking at the glasrobe, he was almost tempted to give himself up. It had a genuinely crazy expression on its face. The kind of furious expression that makes you want to apologise profusely. Instead Vantix gritted his teeth and gripped his blade every tighter. It dawned on him that the creature was no longer too pushed on taking him alive.

Thrusting his sword, he winced as the glasrobe's knife cut into his hand. The sword fell uselessly to the ground. Its knife came around again and Vantix caught the arm, pummelling it until the knife fell from its grasp. Instinctively he lashed out with his foot and sent the blade disappearing into the night.

He made a vain attempt to press this momentary advantage, but it wasn't to be. As he charged at the glasrobe, it grabbed him by the throat. Uselessly, he tugged at the hands around his neck. The supply of air was running desperately low.

"Hey!"

The glasrobe turned and Vantix kicked it in the ribs. It dropped him heavily, clutching its chest; evidently Vantix had broken something.

He fumbled around in the grass, searching for anything. Anything that would be of even the slightest bit of use. He found it.

No longer winded, the glasrobe leapt at him again. Unfortunately for it he was ready. The decent sized rock in his hand connected with the glasrobe's head. The blow was followed by a large cracking sound and the creature went limp. A second blow made sure it wouldn't get up again.

Exhausted by the exertion of the last ten minutes, Vantix panted heavily and lay down to catch his breath. He certainly owed a lot to whoever had called out.

He'd almost drifted asleep by the time the voice called again. "Well," it announced cheerfully, "what do we have here?"

Vantix didn't reply, instead collapsing into the sleep he so desperately needed.

*　*　*　*　*

The entire glasrobe tribe had gathered in the temple of Nasrode. Praying in front of the desecrated statue, they knew it was no use. He wasn't coming back.

Finally, the Guardian got to his feet. "The gods do not answer my prayers," he said angrily, "Was that what we waited for? Some spoiled brat who doesn't know the meaning of the word destiny." The tribe looked at him questioningly. "Well where is he?" The Guardian spat bitterly, "Where is our saviour?"

The venom with which he said it caught them off guard. This was sacrilege! None could deny the imminent return of Nasrode, it was unforgiveable.

Falling back to his knees, he sighed the deepest sigh the world had ever heard. It was actually quite impressive. Four thousand tiring years seemed to have caught up to him in an instant. In that moment, he doubted many things. He doubted the gods, he doubted Nasrode's return, he even doubted people in general. Therefore, it was a huge surprise when someone appeared in front of him.

"I have come," Nasrode declared triumphantly as he stepped out of nothing. He looked magnificent. Bathed in light, despite the fact that he was at the bottom of the lake. Every inch of him gleamed with an unrivalled brightness, giving off wave after wave of renewed hope.

The glasrobes fell to their knees. He was here, he was really here!

"I shall now reclaim my sword," Nasrode proclaimed, "where is it?" His glow seemed to dim slightly as he looked around for any traces of his legendary weapon.

This is the first recorded occurrence of people shuffling nervously from knee to knee. The kneeling glasrobe congregation realised they had a major problem.

A collection of nervous attempts at explanation began to fill the hall as the glasrobes squirmed beneath Nasrode's intense stare.

"Well........"

"Funny thing is.........."

"You'll laugh when you hear it, believe me...."

"It honestly wasn't our fault........"

"....and we thought he was you...."

"Silence!" Nasrode shouted angrily. "Where is my sword?"

He didn't ask them again.

Chapter 21

Darkness, and plenty of it, surrounded Vantix. As he stared at the blanketing gloom around him, only one thought went through his mind: *Damn.*

This one word echoed around the dark hallway; reverberating along its length. To Vantix it was almost deafeningly loud, but it didn't hurt his ears.

He wasn't in any particular hurry to move. Mostly because he didn't know which direction led away from the creature.

It was then he noticed the sounds, or rather the lack thereof. The low hum of his every experience mingling usually caused the place to buzz slightly. Leading to the kind of sound you wouldn't actually miss until it was gone.

Regrettably the silence didn't last. There were footsteps, odd footsteps that sounded more like two marbles bouncing off a tiled floor. Vantix didn't need to look; he just ran.

The sound of him pounding down the corridor didn't eclipse the creature's slow clacking steps. Not daring to stop, he threw a glance over his shoulder. The creature was gaining on him. What's more, it didn't seem to be moving.

How is that possible, he thought quietly. Hoping to prevent the echo, he was sorely disappointed. This and several other thoughts bounced off the walls around him.

Vantix dived into the closest memory, maybe he could lose it in here. It was a faint hope, the creature seemed to know his mind better than he did.

A familiar scene played out before him. Burning buildings, rooftop escapes; it was from the night he'd met Incognito.

He looked around desperately, aware the creature's arrival was imminent.

As he placed his feet firmly on the rooftops, the other him ran ahead. A second later, he had a somewhat jarring experience as several guards ran straight through him. He shivered involuntarily.

Then he spotted it: a patch of darkness. Not the way he'd come in, this was different. This was a patch of Cannonbridge he hadn't seen that night. More importantly, it was a patch of Cannonbridge that didn't exist in his memory.

Surely if it didn't exist then nothing could exist beyond it. It followed that should he walk through it then he wouldn't exist either. At least not here anyway. Little more than conjecture and assumption, inside the dark corridors of his mind existence was a fickle notion determined entirely by what he could remember. Save for the creature, of course.

Leaping straight off the building, he landed comfortably on the pavement below. In reality this would probably cause a broken leg. Frankly he wasn't sure he could hurt himself here.

As he approached the patch of non-existential darkness, all but it turned to grey. Whirling round, he gazed up at the other him in dismay. He knew what came next.

The creature appeared out of thin air, devouring the past him with relish. He shook his head dejectedly; there didn't seem to be any hope for him retaining any pleasant memories.

It only occurred to him then that he was wrong. The creature had infected his mind, tearing to shreds his memories and experiences. Its influence would spread across everything he'd ever done, felt or achieved until there was nothing left. The creature's dominion would extend over and corrupt all aspects of him until Vantix ceased to be.

He emitted an almost pitiful groan and stepped through the darkness that didn't exist.

* * * * *

The music was the first thing to catch his attention. A few bars were played on a lute, followed immediately by the sounds of a quill scratching on paper. Vantix took a moment to take in his surroundings.

It was a woodland clearing. Quite nice in fact, as the lute complimented the rustic effect. The trees were thick on either side, hiding the glade and affording the perfect little slice of seclusion to rest for an evening. There was a horse to one side, tied to a tree. From the look of it, it had been on the road for quite some time.

The night was still ongoing, the moon not even halfway across the sky. An intense fire next to him had caused his glasrobe garments to completely dry out. They cracked as he sat up and looked for his host.

163

The sounds of music ceased. "Would you like something to eat?" a voice called as a man stepped into view.

He couldn't have been over twenty, had long brown hair and what looked like an attempt at a beard. A lute was across his back, several sheets of paper were under his arm and he had a quill behind his ear. Since most of his attire was made from fur, adding the other elements made it only too clear what he was.

Having met several bards before Vantix knew what to expect. This was pretty much the norm. He'd have to be careful though, you could never tell when these artistic types were about to fly off the handle.

In response to the bard's question, he nodded. There happened to be a rather nice smell wafting from the pot on the fire. The bard handed him a bowl. Vantix stared at it for a moment then jumped straight in, barely stopping to chew.

The bard indicated himself, "Larents." Vantix kept eating, prompting the bard to return to his lute.

When Vantix had finished, he replied to Larent's introduction. "Vantix," he informed the bard, "How did I get here?"

"I found you fighting off two strange looking frogmen at the lake. You passed out, so I dragged you here."

Standing up, Vantix felt his now dry garments crack and several pieces fall off. "I don't suppose-" he began.

Larents shook his head. "Bards travel light."

Vantix didn't exactly know what to say. "So have you written anything I might know?"

"I'm relatively new at the whole bard thing, but I'm getting there. Give me a few years."

Vantix nodded absentmindedly, it was probably time he got out of here.

"I actually came out here for inspiration," Larents was saying, "and it looks like I've found it." He gave Vantix a meaningful look.

Vantix had always been uncomfortable around meaningful looks; it always meant people required something of him. "I really should be leaving," he told Larents.

"And you shall," Larents reassured him, "but not until after you've told me about this." He held Nasrode's sword in his hands.

"Not worth your time," Vantix protested, "It's unbelievable."

Larents removed parchment and ink from his satchel. "I'm a bard," he said blandly, "the unbelievable is my trade."

It occurred to Vantix that a little publicity wouldn't exactly do him any harm. Sitting down, he began with Incognito and the tale unfolded from there.

* * * * *

Bored of the others and their constant speculation about when they'd catch the dendrid, Arsenius had excused himself and gone to check on Slyra. "Feeling any better?" he asked upon entering the cabin.

From where she sat on the bed Slyra looked up with a smile. "Much better thanks."

Among the myths and legends in Ballisca there are countless tales of sorcery, witches and unbelievable feats accomplish through inner power, assistance from spirits, elemental energy and pacts with fae beings. Seeing it, however, was a different matter entirely to hearing it around a campfire. To say Arsenius was impressed would have been an understatement. "So you're just right as rain now?"

"No real damage done. Just a little bit tired."

"I can leave if you'd like to rest?"

"Not at all. I'll be glad of the company . After last night the others don't seem too keen on visiting. Save those who have either questions or secrets of their own. To which category do you belong?"

Arsenius pulled up a chair. "Neither."

"Meaning both, more than likely," Slyra replied.

"I wouldn't hold your lack of visitors against them. Everybody wants to be believe there are wondrous things to be found in the world. They just don't want to be confronted face first with them."

"Now I'm something wondrous?"

Arsenius shrugged once more. "Witch would probably be a more accurate description. Even without warts and a strict diet of young children, the hat and tattoo near your shoulder are a dead giveaway."

Slyra looked askance at him, "That's not a tattoo."

For a moment Arsenius wondered whether he'd made the mistake of assuming a birthmark was a tattoo, a fatal error that could do naught but stifle any conversation. Running through the options in his head didn't yield any worthwhile solutions. Immediately he thought of flattery but wasn't well versed in how to appropriately compliment birthmarks. Apologising was certainly out. Perhaps he could run.

Luckily Slyra put him out of his misery. "It's my mark of power. Or that's how I like to think of it. It appeared the day I got my powers and it darkens whenever I overextend myself magically. I suppose it could be mistaken for a tattoo."

166

"The world's grubby fingers leave none of us unblemished." Arsenius put in, " I have a mark on my back shaped exactly like a horse's hoof."

"You got kicked by a horse?" Slyra laughed.

"Almost entirely undeserved. All I did-" was as far as Arsenius got. The door opened and everybody piled in, Rekil at their head. "Get your things," he told them as the others grabbed their bags, "We've reached the shore."

* * * * *

After Vantix had finished, Larents continued scribbling. With only the sound of the quill to fill the silence, the younger man decided to further investigate the contents of pot. Perhaps it held clues as to what kind of meat he'd just eaten.

When he could see the bottom of the pot, he called over to Larents, "Well?"

Larents didn't look up. "Well, what?"

"Can you use any of it? You know, spread my name around?"

Larents sighed. "So-," he began, "We've got you recruited by a mysterious stranger, getting your soul torn out, joining a team of people with questionable morals and finally, crushing the dreams of an underwater species by stealing their magical sword."

"Is it any good?"

"The mysterious stranger part is no good-"

"And why is that?"

"It's simple," Larents elaborated, "Heroes in stories have better motives."

"Okay fine," Vantix harrumphed, "what about the rest?"

167

"Unless you go on a murderous rampage and burn down several villages, the no-soul part is useless."

"Oh, come on," Vantix challenged, "Surely, some of this is ballad material."

Larents raised a finger, "Actually," he gave his notes a quick glance, "the last part is rather good."

Vantix gave him a questioning look. "You mean the part where I hit an elderly creature in the face and run away."

Larents tutted him and waved a finger again. "Actually I was referring to the part where you defied the gods and your destiny."

Vantix hadn't thought of it like that. It sounded much better that way. He wasn't sure it was epic ballad material though. Voicing this opinion, he didn't elicit much of a reaction from Larents.

"Maybe, right now it doesn't," the bard shrugged, "but you just wait till I'm wooing audiences with tales of Vantix: the man who defied both the gods and destiny for love."

"What?"

"Obviously, love is a much better reason than selfishness."

"I'm not selfish, I just didn't want to do it."

"And yet, you didn't just leave. You also managed to steal their sacred, magical sword."

Vantix didn't say anything.

"Plus, you only told me your tale to become famous."

Vantix stared at him for a while. "There was no need to continue," he said dryly.

Larents picked up his lute and began to hum under his breath, quickly abandoning several melodies that didn't fit or were too derivative. It wouldn't do to be unoriginal.

Eventually, he placed the lute on his back and slung his bags over the horse's back. He pointed out through the trees. "There's a town that way." He looked Vantix up and down, "You could probably locate some proper clothes there. I'm heading that way myself, if you wouldn't mind the company?"

Vantix nodded his acceptance, Larents gathered the reins and they set off. The two of them were in front, with the horse carrying the bags behind them. Vantix was shivering discontentedly, whilst the bard whistled the song he'd just written. It was a pretty catchy tune.

As they neared the road, it was Larents who broke the silence that had ensued since they left the clearing. "You know," he said thoughtfully, "I think I'll try out your song on the people of this town."

Vantix blinked several times. "You've already written it?"

Larents tapped the side of his head smugly, "All up here."

Vantix didn't know how to say this next part. "You're not going to just..," he said hesitantly, "enter town and sing at them, are you?"

Larents laughed and clapped Vantix on the back. "No, but the local inn won't turn down entertainment for a night." Vantix breathed a sigh of relief.

"It's a good time to be a bard, my friend." Larents remarked cheerfully, "Magic is back, strange creatures are popping up all over Ballisca and there's tell of heroes doing wondrous deeds on a daily basis. Have you heard any of the stories from Port Daich-"

Ahead of them, the trees parted to reveal the road to town. Just as they stepped onto it, something rushed by. Vantix caught a glimpse of rags, pale skin and hair with a strange purple tinge. He leapt into a bush

169

Larents whistled. "I guess that was the dendrid," he mused. Vantix climbed gradually out of the bush.

Stepping into the road, he watched the dendrid disappear through the trees far ahead. As he stared after them, an elf sprinted by him. Two others ran by as he stared after the first. All three were instantly recognisable.

A hand grabbed his arm and he was being dragged along. Just about managing to grab Nasrode's sword from the horse, he was forced to find his feet or fall behind. He looked along the arm that was pulling him. Although they weren't exactly friends, he wasn't disappointed in the slightest to see Rekil.

Larents watched as the group disappeared into the trees after the dendrid. "That guy really is a glutton for punishment," he muttered under his breath. Then he turned his horse toward town.

Chapter 22

The carriage lurched to a halt, fetching Welbh a resounding knock to the head. Three identical carriage interiors slid across his vision until his focus returned and settled on King Jandelk's grim-faced stare. "Come on," there was nothing pleasant in the King's voice, "Let's stretch our legs."

As soon as Welbh left the carriage, the King turned to his guards, "Search the bags and the carriage, find whatever's hidden there."

"Sire?" This seemingly spontaneous search had visibly dented Welbh's inherent aplomb. Also quite vexing, was the location the King had chosen for this search. Should the documents be located and a severely detrimental punishment administered, the gods would be the only witnesses.

"Do you understand the bond Kings have with their castles?"

Jandelk's question caught Welbh off guard and he mutely shook his head. He was finding the thorough manner in which the carriage was being searched rather disconcerting.

"Castles are an extension of the King himself, and usually show what kind of King they are, whether it be humble, arrogant, ambitious, cowardly or anything else. A King knows what happens in his castle. He sees the midnight meetings, hears the whispered messages and most-"

At this point Welbh stopped listening. One of the guards had pulled up the rug, and was searching beneath it. Welbh willed him not to lift up the wood, hoping with his very being that the guard would just leave it and move on.

"So would you care to elucidate matters as regards your insidious plan?" the King's question seemed almost too polite.

The guard replaced the rug and Welbh exhaled a breath of relief. "I'm afraid I'll have to disappoint you your majesty," he said confidently, "Nothing nefarious, or anything of the sort for that matter, is going on."

One of the guards beckoned to the King. They hadn't found anything. Fortune seemed to be smiling on him right now, so Welbh smiled right back and entered the carriage.

* * * * *

Larents distractedly plucked his lute strings. This was his first gig and he was visibly shaking. He was just that nervous. The songs he'd practiced to perfection were drowned out by thoughts of broken lute strings, bum notes and booing crowds.

The tavern was absolutely packed, almost bursting at the seams. Either there was an incredibly large number of people at the inn, or every single one of the villagers had turned up. It was almost nauseating.

Larents took a seat in the corner, directly beside the window. If things turned south he might need to get out quickly.

Beginning with several drinking songs, he was off to a good start. The people danced and several even went as far as to be merry. The flagons being placed next to Larents began to build up.

The tavern creaked and threatened to burst as the villagers and guests danced. It was only then Larents noticed two groups who weren't dancing. They sat in the furthest corners of the bar and had eyes for none but each other.

One group was clothed entirely in white, the other black. Although music filled the rest of the tavern, Larents got the impression that there would be nothing but edgy silence over there. Neither group felt inclined to move so much as an inch, never mind dance. He eyed them until he finished the song, then paid them no further heed. After all, a bard has no time for those who don't appreciate his work.

The villagers loved the drinking songs, but Larents wouldn't get anywhere playing them. They simply weren't enough. Re-tuning his lute, he started a song he'd written whilst looking at the sunset over lake glasrobe.

It was a nice song, with a decent melody. Its contemplative tone was relaxing and somehow promoted equanimity. The type of music that needs to be appreciated almost as much as it needs to be listened to. Perfect for reclining at the end of the night with a glass of something too expensive to drink during the day. It was also exactly the wrong kind of song to play in a bar.

When he'd finished, he looked around. The whole place was silent as a graveyard. The villagers hadn't been able to dance, sing along or even tap their feet. They stared at him accusingly; he'd killed the atmosphere.

It was at this point that he drew a blank. Not just any blank, this was a blank of the most dangerous nature. Every single note and lyric of all the drinking songs he knew deserted him. He desperately struck a few random cords, willing the songs to come back. The crowd were going to turn. He could already feel their stares and ill-intent burning into him.

Reaching out desperately, he grabbed the nearest drink and threw it back. It was only slightly rejuvenating.

There's nothing for it, he panicked quietly, *I'm going to have to improvise.*

Leaping up on the table, he played a song he'd written earlier that evening. Even as he struck the first notes, he knew it was going to go down a treat. It had a fast, flowing rhythm and the increasingly drunken crowd loved it. They rose to their feet and danced.

Larents sang the first words that came to his head. They went a little something like this:

> *I shall tell you a story,*
> *A tale seldom told,*
> *The adventures of Vantix,*
> *A hero without a soul.*

The crowd cheered as he sang on:

> *For heaven won't take him,*
> *And he can't enter hell,*
> *Forever here his essence will dwell,*
> *He will linger forever,*
> *Outside the reach of heaven,*
> *Because he's unfit to enter.*

Thinking on his feet, he promptly composed another verse:

> *Vantix set out to do some good,*
> *To slaughter villainous dendrid,*
> *But when his courage deserted him,*
> *He promptly hid.*

The song went on for another 17 verses. Larents sang about everything Vantix had told him and made even more of it up. It was quite well received by the tavern's patrons.

In fact it was so well received that two hours later the town guard were still trying to restore order.

* * * * *

Larents counted out his money. The barkeep had given him 40 crowns and several of the bar's patrons had shown their appreciation. Unfortunately, the town guard had fined him for inciting a riot. He'd been left to pay for any damages they couldn't pin on someone else.

Larents groaned angrily. He'd only got 23 crowns left, which meant he'd lost 50 to the town guard. He cursed them under his breath; it was hardly his fault he was inspirational.

Something hit the table with a resounding clink. Larents waited a moment to acknowledge it. The clink signalled that there was a sizeable amount of money being tossed around. If this was a patron coming to offer financial support, he couldn't seem too eager. After a full minute of feigned insouciance, he looked up.

The woman was dressed completely in a brilliant white. Armour, boots, cloak, everything. Earlier Larents had mistaken them for some sort of religious zealots, but their attire made it abundantly clear they were mercenaries. Which posed the question; *Why do they wear white?* It was a nightmare to get blood out of. Larents knew as much from his attempts at hunting.

He was pondering this matter, when the woman smiled at him. Sure enough, her teeth were the whitest things the bard had ever seen. "If you don't mind," she said sweetly, "we have some inquiries about your song?"

"Such as?" Larents responded, he wasn't sure how much to give away.

"Is it true?"

"Every word."

"Then tell me," the woman continued, her tone now more business like, "Where can I find this soulless creature?"

* * * * *

No less than fifteen minutes later, Larents was disturbed from his counting once more. Having already counted the money twice, he now did it for sheer enjoyment. It was easily the quickest 100 crowns he'd ever made.

There was a dull thud as something struck the table. Looking up, Larents couldn't help but hope for another bag of coins. Instead a rather intimidating knife was lodged deep in the wood.

The other group Larents had noticed earlier, the one dressed entirely in black, now sought an audience. One of them spoke, possibly the most threatening voice Larents had ever heard snaking its way out from the

176

man's cowl. "You mentioned someone named Rekil in your song."

Larents nodded. It had been a severely minor detail in Vantix's story, but in the heat of the moment he made the spontaneous decision to include all aspects of the tale.

A different member of the group drew the knife from the table. "Unless you tell us where he went," the newcomer rasped, "I'm going to split you from head to toe."

His rasping threat was no use though. It was a third rate encore to the other man's voice. Nevertheless, Larents pointed out through the door.

"Where?"

"Outside town. Head out the west road and turn right into the woods at the bend in the road." It all came tumbling out, Larents defenceless against a voice that threatening. Every syllable dripped with unreserved menace.

The fact that he wouldn't get to spend his newly acquired wealth was also weighing on his conscience. He couldn't die, that money needed to be wasted on wine and women. The song he could provide himself.

The man smiled. "A pleasure," was all he said. He moved for the doorway and one by one his companions followed him out.

Larents sat quietly, mulling over the encounter in his head. After several minutes, he brushed all his money into his bag and asked the innkeeper to bring his horse round front. He wasn't going to be here if they came back.

Chapter 23

Dendrid are fast, a lot faster than most humans. They also seem to have hidden reserves of energy. These aspects made them incredibly difficult prey to keep up with, never mind catch.

Arsenius was exceptionally fast, so fast that he was closing in on the dendrid. His footsteps pounded in the dirt, an impressive pace that he wasn't sure how long he could keep up. Still, a few more seconds and it wouldn't make a difference.

Drawing his sword, he was already too late. Just as the dendrid leapt into the air, an arrow struck one in the neck. The way the lifeless creature fell from view certainly seemed out of the ordinary.

Arsenius skidded to a halt, almost losing his footing. The case of the disappearing dendrid had now been solved. It was just about visible at the bottom of a very deep ravine.

The ravine was wide as well, too far to jump. At the very least too far for elves and humans; the dendrid had managed easily enough. They were at the far side, lengthening the distance between them and the group.

Rekil joined him at the edge of the gorge, sheathing his bow. "Nice shot," Arsenius observed.

Everyone else arrived after a few seconds and proceeded to try regain their breath. Sam, Slyra and Farack arrived last. Slyra's wounds were now healed but had taken a lot out of her, while Sam and Farack were busy lugging the entire group's bags behind them.

Vantix took his from Sam. "You knew I'd be back?"

Farack shrugged. "Hoping for the best never did me any harm."

"Some of your things are rather valuable," Sam interjected.

Vantix rolled his eyes and a smile tugged at the corner of his mouth. He gathered his stuff and went to change out of the impractical seaweed garments. A nearby bush seemed like a promising spot. Normally he'd have changed right there but under the circumstances he decided against it. Better not to exhibit any more of the changes he'd undergone in recent weeks, especially since there was a lady present. It'd be most untoward.

Arsenius and the others looked around, searching for a path or bridge and coming up with nothing. The ravine lay in their path, an insurmountable hindrance at present.

When Vantix emerged several minutes later, he'd ditched the seaweed garments for a brown waistcoat and white shirt over. A grey long coat ended just above his knees. His lower half was covered by stout boots and burgundy linens. Both his short swords were across his back, and his pair of miniature crossbows hung from his belt. It actually felt surprisingly good to be dressed as himself rather than some amphibian deity.

Slyra looked up at him and laughed. "Look who's making an effort," she smiled.

Vantix nodded, but didn't smile back. He'd prefer to keep his fangs hidden. Indicating something behind her, he performed the neat trick of asking a question without showing a hint of his teeth. "What's that?"

Slyra shook her head. "I'm not falling for that."

"No, seriously what is that?"

The young witch sighed and looked behind her. There was nothing save the crowded tree line. "Oh," she said in mock surprise, "you got me. Well done."

She was rather surprised to see the puzzled expression that adorned Vantix's features. "Are you telling me," he said slowly, "that you don't see the massive stone doorway?"

"Are you okay?"

"I'll take that as a no, but it's clearly right there."

Slyra, Arsenius and Sam watched as he walked straight into a tree and staggered back a few feet. Whilst some burst out laughing, the others watched with concern. Vantix rubbed his forehead, before plunging on through the trees, bumping into pretty much every branch as he scrambled through the bracken. He didn't even notice it. All he could see, or think about, was the stone doorway up the hill.

The others broke through the brambles. The clearing before them was empty save for a hill, a stone doorway and Vantix clambering up one to reach the other. They watched him with more than a hint of worry.

The others came through the trees beside them. "If we don't hurry we won't...." Rekil stopped halfway. He stared at Vantix and then the stone doorway in turn.

Elik was more inquisitive. "How did you find that?" he asked.

Slyra shook her head. She couldn't explain.

"It's because he's becoming like the dendrid," Rekil's voice was barely above a whisper, "he can sense magical energy just like they can."

180

Arsenius stared at him. "How do you know it's magic?", he enquired.

Rekil smiled before replying, "Does it look natural to you?"

They climbed the hill and joined Vantix at the top. He was holding his forehead. The bracken had made quite the impression on it. Looking at the blood quizzically, he seemed unaware of where it had come from.

Up close, every detail of the doorway was palpable. It looked like a door that you would find in any building in the provinces, apart from the two main differences. The more obvious of the two was that it was made of stone, and the other was that it was covered in runes. Although the intricate runes and designs depicted several things, few were pictures of animals, strange creatures or even recognisable in the slightest. The majority of them were strange symbols that didn't exist in modern Ballisca. The gate must have been beyond ancient.

"What is it?" Sam asked quietly.

"I don't know," Vantix mumbled back.

"Then why are we here?"

"Because I can tell it's important," Vantix snapped.

At this point, Slyra caught their attention. She didn't say anything, but what she did left them speechless.

Stepping toward the doorway, she raised her palms. She whispered under her breath for a moment, and then it happened. Her pupils dilated and energy flowed down her arms. It snaked along her fingertips, before curling up into the air like pure white smoke tendrils. The tendrils drifted through the air, washing over the doorway in waves and filling every rune and carving.

Seconds later, the runes seemed to drift out from the stone. They solidified and hovered in the air before her. Then they started to spin, becoming almost a blur before the eyes of the group. Flashing momentarily, they rushed straight into her. She took a deep breath, absorbing every etched symbol and carving. For a moment light streamed from her eyes, the same brilliant white as the carvings had been.

This all happened in seconds.

"It's a gateway to the Shadowlands," her voice was pure clarity, with almost a chime like quality to it, "It comes out near the outskirts of Ghostwood." She raised her arms and blinding white energy flowed toward the doorway. The others shielded their eyes. Apart from Sam, who suffered mild retinal damage.

When the light faded they braved a look back. The stone frame still stood, each of its intricate carvings highlighted in pulsating white light. As for the door itself, it had simply vanished. Through the frame, all they could see were indistinct shades of green and red, with blue overhead stretching off into the distance. Slyra walked under the stone door frame and onto the indistinct plain, gesturing for them to follow.

For a moment there was uncertainty, as all members of the group except Grelow and Elik looked to Rekil for direction. After a moment, he nodded his consent but placed his hand on his sword.

For his part, Vantix couldn't resist running around to the other side of the doorway. From there it looked just like stone. Tapping it just to be sure, he was actually surprised when it grazed his finger. It was solid.

"You know," Sam remarked upon this newest development, "I didn't think witches existed."

Osca stared back, "After she crushed eleven sea serpents and healed herself from a fatal wound, you still doubted she was a witch?"

Sam nodded absentmindedly. He hadn't really been thinking about it.

"Then why did you think she was here?"

"I don't know," Sam shrugged, "I thought it must have something to do with gender equality."

With that he walked through, leaving Osca shaking his head with a slightly bemused look on his face. All this magic couldn't possibly bode well.

None were there to see what happened to Vantix. Suddenly gripped by an unyielding curiosity, he reached toward the pulsating white energy still on the door frame. He didn't want to, but it was like he didn't have control.

When his fingers touched the energy, it snaked up his arms before flowing straight into his chest. Something inside him felt a momentary thrill, but he knew it wasn't him.

It tried to make him reach out again, but he fought the urge. This time coming out triumphant, his smug confidence lasted no more than a second, as then he heard a gut wrenching snarl.

It sounded like some vicious creature was stalking him. He whirled around, desperately hoping to find the source of the snarl in the clearing. With a sinking feeling his suspicions were confirmed; there was nothing to be seen out here. The snarl had come from inside his head.

Suddenly it didn't seem like a good idea to be alone so he tossed his bag over his shoulder and stumbled through the gate after the others. As he disappeared across the indistinct landscape, the lights vanished and the doorway closed, becoming nothing but an ancient landmark once more.

Chapter 24

Once upon a time wizards, witches, warlocks, sorcerers, conjurers, enchanters, magicians, necromancers, occultists, witchdoctors and all other kinds of magi were in abundance throughout the land. They lived in perfect harmony with normal folk and their skills made them valued members of the community. They were the healers, advisors and leaders of the clans. People looked to them for wisdom and the greatest of them were even revered.

However, they constantly bickered amongst themselves. Their fighting wasn't the least bit ordinary though; a minor tiff between even the most junior of them could have disastrous consequences. Their command of magic and the elements could result in famine, storms, volcanic eruptions, earthquakes and tornadoes. It wasn't pretty.

When a fight between the two greatest of them got out of hand, the power produced led to catastrophic events. The energy generated was so great it tore holes in the material realms, allowing for all kinds of things to pour through.

Some of these were just new races that came through the tears to settle in Ballisca. Others, however, were far more sinister. Nightmarish creatures and demons poured through, determined to make the most of this new dimension.

They ravaged and devastated the lands, tearing across them like a plague. In each area the demons visited, nothing survived. They didn't discriminate, devouring every man, woman and child. Every clan suffered at their hands.

Eventually the leaders of the Nospac tribes banded together and pushed the demons back from their lands. They assembled an army to combat the monstrosities. From all over Ballisca, people flocked to them, no matter their race or species they were united by one goal; eradicating the demons whatever the cost.

The army spread to each of the tears, knowing the demons would follow them. Their goal was to push the monsters back from whence they came and seal each tear with enchanted stone gateways provided by the mages. A remarkable success; what few of the nightmarish creatures remained were dealt with easily.

This was the one time the clans were united of their own free will. Banishing the demons was their first act. The second, and final act of the unified clans, was to hunt down and kill every single last wizard, witch, warlock, sorcerer, conjurer, enchanter, magician, necromancer, occultist, witchdoctor and all other forms of magi. They weren't going to let anything like this ever happen again.

Several ages passed and all knowledge of these events passed from memory. They'd never been recorded save for the gateways and were only ever referred to as "The Nightmare Years". Civilisation forgot about them.

Until an eighteen year old witch absorbed all this knowledge from the runic carvings on an ancient stone doorway.

* * * * *

So Slyra was wary, constantly watching for strange movements. She'd deemed it best not to tell the others. Although they really needed to catch up to the dendrid, she couldn't be certain the others would want to risk a route through demon infested territory.

Looking down, she was surprised by her appearance. Her attire being torn on the lake had mattered little, witches tended to stock up on robed t-shirts. Anyway, it wasn't what she was wearing that caught her attention.

Luminous skin isn't exactly a recognized medical condition as there aren't many known cases. Nevertheless, it was this obscure occurrence which currently plagued Slyra. That is, of course, until she remembered one of the carvings from the stone doorway. "*What's inside will shine through*," had seemed out of place amongst the other etchings, but now she understood. Not that it made much difference to her though, she didn't hide what she was.

A spark of curiosity ignited within her as she wondered if the others were similarly afflicted. Each of them was staring at the ground, making one hesitant footstep after another. Even though there was quite a distance between them, she could already distinguish the few not too subtle differences.

However, these differences weren't present on everyone. In fact Rekil, Elik, Arsenius, Ramos, Hemer, Osca and Sam looked like a perfectly normal bunch of people out to hunt dendrid.

186

Then her gaze flickered to Grelow and remained glued there. While in real life Grelow looked like an attractive man in his late twenties, here he was a monster. Looking like a reanimated corpse is never a good thing, no matter what social circles you run in.

His skin was rotting away and stretched taut. Wounds festered all over and every once in a while, Slyra could swear she saw something crawling around various parts of his face. Eventually, she managed to drag herself away.

Deciding to shift her scrutiny somewhere else, she settled on Farack. His complexion had the same orange tinge as all rhadons. The only exceptionally different thing about him was that every single strand of his formerly ash coloured hair was now aflame. For the first time in his life, he looked like a real rhadon. As Slyra watched, he ran his hand through his hair and laughed excitedly when his shirt caught flame. Rolling up his sleeves, he began clumsily tossing fire into the air.

Farack looked up as Vantix patted him on the back. If you've ever leapt back because one of your friends surprised you, you'll be able to picture Farack's reaction. Though you probably wouldn't set the offender ablaze.

Slyra ran towards them, hoping to offer some assistance. She could hear Vantix cursing and Farack repeatedly apologising. By the time she got there, the flames were already out and minimal damage had been done.

"It's not my fault," Farack protested.

"You're right," Vantix shot back sarcastically, "it's obviously my fault you set me on fire."

"In my defence, have you seen yourself lately?"

Vantix was kind of taken aback by this response. "Yes, and so have you. There's no reason to be startled."

187

"Vantix," Slyra interjected, "the Shadowlands show what lies beneath the skin, so as of right now you're no prize." To be honest, she didn't blame Farack for trying to set him on fire.

Vantix looked at his hands, or rather, his claws. A quick look gave the impression that they were scaled, but a touch revealed otherwise. If anything, it was like the scales were beneath his skin. Spiked ears, which were twice as large as any elf's, added to the effect. Apart from those and his fanged teeth, his head still retained most of its human qualities. Even if it was a little pale.

Unfortunately, his head seemed to be the only part that was almost normal. Checking his chest he realised it looked like he was some kind of lizard creature inside a diaphanous human costume.

Beneath his skin, the scales moved. At least, he thought they moved. Hypnotised as he was by them, the rest of the world faded into obscurity. He knew where he'd seen them before. They were the exact same as those that covering the creature plaguing his nightmares. He could see it now, its imprint lingering in all the areas of his consciousness.

"Are you okay?"

Slyra's question plunged into the depths of his dream-like state, and dragged him to the surface. Flashing her the fakest smile known to man, he nodded. "Come on ," he changed the subject, "this abnormal landscape isn't going to traverse itself."

* * * * *

"Would you mind telling me what's wrong?"

Elik's question caught Slyra off guard. As did his presence; she hadn't even noticed he was walking alongside her.

"What..I-nothing," she blurted.

He feigned nonchalance. "Fair enough, but" he added perceptively, "I think the sparks flowing from your fingertips speak otherwise."

Slyra nodded guiltily and let the crackling energy she was cradling in her hand evaporate. It was only then she got a good look at Elik.

When she'd been viewing the group as a whole, she'd overlooked it. Not because it wasn't noticeable, just because the changes to the others were far more prominent.

There were several different qualities to his face. The first of which, were the colour of his eyes. They'd been brown but were now a strange golden colour. His overall features seemed to have changed slightly and now gave off an impression of majestic fierceness. If dragons hadn't already become extinct, she might have compared him to one.

"Look," Slyra explained quietly, "this may, or may not, be home to a multitude of demonic creatures."

Elik looked around, expression remaining unperturbed. "Seriously?"

Slyra gave a half-hearted shrug. "It was either this or we don't catch the dendrid."

"Good idea," he said approvingly, "Your fault if it goes wrong."

Reaching the top of a ridge, they stared out across their surroundings. The ground beneath their feet had the texture of grass but it was so vague, so inconspicuous, that it looked like the sands of a desert.

Looking down from the top, a valley was laid out before them. All the same, it was so unclear that valley didn't feel like the right word. The inclines and hills were almost impossible to see. Their gaze seemed to roll off, making it difficult to distinguish valleys from anything else. Everything they looked at seemed to be on the horizon. It was like somebody had painted the inside of a cauldron green.

The only thing that really showed it was a valley, instead of just another blurry plain, was also the first distinct thing they'd seen so far. A village lay at the bottom. The first sign of life they'd come across.

Slyra's eyes flashed white as pearls, matching the glow her skin had taken on since they'd entered this strange world. After a moment, they returned to their usual shade of light green and she turned to address the group.

"Our way out is down there," she announced. This statement elicited two reactions from the group. Most nodded in grim determination, whilst Vantix whooped for joy; the sooner his skin was back to normal, the better.

"I can feel the way out," she continued, "but I fear we may have to overcome certain obstacles."

Rekil raised an eyebrow. "Obstacles?"

"Demons," Elik explained.

"We have reason to believe there may be some sort of demonic presences," Slyra jumped in, "but how we know they're there is not of the least importance."

"Hang on a minute," Arsenius interjected, "we haven't even begun to walk anywhere near far enough, to be coming out next to Ghostwood."

"By our definition of time and space, yes, but this world moves at its own pace." The witch stated simply,

"Suffice to say we've travelled much further than you think."

Arsenius nodded in reply, content just to get out of there. The landscape was giving him a headache.

"Now," Slyra called, "Are we ready?"

Chapter 25

Vantix crept quietly around the side of the shack. Up close he could see this was barely a hamlet, numbering just a few small huts and one larger structure in its entirety. Although he hadn't seen any of the native people yet, he could hear one just around the corner.

He drew both his short swords, anything could be waiting on the other side of this hut. Dispatching it quickly would be important, you couldn't have any hesitation when fighting demons.

Demons don't play by the usual rules of form. They can have any number of arms, legs, teeth, heads, claws, mandibles, horns, and tentacles. They might even be laughable if they weren't so dangerous. Creatures consisting of one large eye atop three tentacles are simply disgusting except when any of those tentacles could crush you. Some Balliscan myths told of the man of heads, who consists entirely of working faces stacked into the shape of a man that speak dark truths and drive people mad. It was wise to take these with a pinch of salt yet stupid to ignore them entirely. You could never be certain things weren't about to go bump in the night.

Footsteps approached, preceding the arrival of somebody by less than seconds. Their owner walked into view, carrying several bundles of firewood. Vantix froze, this new arrival certainly didn't look like a demon.

In the few seconds after it caught sight of him, several things happened. Vantix remained frozen, with both hands wielding swords high above his head. The creature tossed its heavy load of firewood into the air, and took off with a shriek. Its departure spurred Vantix back into normal motion capability.

The reason behind Vantix's inability to finish the creature off was down to its appearance. Almost a foot smaller than him; having the build of a sick child; and practically transparent made him a little unwilling to lump it in the demon category.

There was an almost ghostly essence about it. It looked like some sort of sickly phantasm. A far cry from dangerous and demonic.

Vantix watched as it ran toward the wooden structure, followed closely by the rest of its kind. The doors slammed shut behind them.

As he advanced toward the building, he noticed the others congregating outside its doors. They shuffled awkwardly, none wanting to be the first to speak. Eventually, Osca broke the silence. "I always assumed demons would be scarier."

Farack nodded, "Bedtime stories really overhyped them."

Rekil cleared his throat, "Did anyone kill any?"

The group collectively shook their heads; they hadn't been able to attack the sickly looking beings.

Slyra nodded toward the door. "Our way out is through there."

"I suppose somebody had best go apologise," Vantix suggested, "I mean, we'll probably need to get on their good side if we want permission to use their magical gate."

The group nodded their assent and stared at him expectantly.

"Obviously, I can't do it," Vantix said, "have you seen me lately?"

This made perfect sense, as he didn't look quite right for the role of peaceful negotiator. It was easy to see why the creature had run from him earlier.

Rekil moved toward the door. Giving it a slight push yielded no results, so he tossed his shoulder against it.

Once inside, he saw why the door hadn't budged at first touch. Several of the natives had been leaning against it, and were now sprawled on the ground. Rekil glanced around. From those lying on the floor all the way to those huddled in corners, each and every one of the creatures was terrified.

Clearing his throat, he was surprised to see some of the creatures yelp. *I must be missing something,* Rekil thought. Unsheathing his bow evoked quite the reaction. They shrieked and stumbled over each other in an attempt to get out of his way. He dropped his bow and raised both his hands in the air. The beings moved a step closer; they still looked frightened, though now their expressions contained a tinge of curiosity.

Sensing that the slightest thing could set them off, Rekil spoke slowly and clearly. "We mean you no harm," he declared, "What happened out there was a mistake."

One of the creature's stepped forward, palpably angry. "You demons are not wanted here," it spat.

"Dermock," another of them hissed desperately, "Calm down."

Rekil hadn't been expecting this level of hostility, it threw him slightly off balance. "W..We-uh, uh," he faltered, "We're not demons."

Dermock turned to him again, "Your deception will not work," he replied, "We have seen those you travel with."

"Look, there seems to be some sort of misunderstanding."

"Why are you here?" exclaimed another of the creatures. Rekil looked around. These things were getting bolder. It would probably be best if he sorted out this matter quickly. Then a thought struck him. "I don't mean to offend, but what are you?" he asked politely.

The creatures looked at each other. The one who'd questioned Rekil's motives for being here stepped forward. A scar stretched across his face and looked incredibly strange on his semi-lucid skin. "Some call us shadows," it informed him.

"Okay, but my friends and I need to go through there." He gestured toward the back of the hall.

The shadows turned to look where he pointed. The scarred one laughed unpleasantly, "That's a wall."

Rekil smiled, "You're very wrong." He didn't like the way that one had laughed, it was unnerving. "Listen, if you'll give us your leave we'll be out of here in a moment."

The scarred one nodded. "Make it quick."

Usually, Rekil might have taught the little shadow a lesson about respect but he was doing his best to avoid any sort of conflict. Picking up his bow, he opened the door slightly and motioned the others inside.

They entered in single file, unsure as to how much space would be available. The shadows stared in amazement at Farack, awe at Slyra and disgust at Grelow and Vantix.

Whilst they moved toward the back wall, glowing white energy drifted from Slyra's hand. The gate, which the building was using as a wall, opened before them to reveal a clearing surrounded by trees. The shadows started back in surprise; they'd never seen anything like this before.

Grelow was just stepping through as a voice caught the group's attention. They turned around to see a lone shadow, stepping out from the crowd. "Please," she called, "help us."

The group exchanged glances, then turned back toward the gate.

The scarred shadow urged them on, "Go, you are not needed here." No less than a second later, the female shadow contradicted him once more.

"Please," she begged, "Why do you think we live in fear? Why do you think we cowered at the sight of you? And why do you think," she stifled a sob, "there are no children here?"

The whole room was silent, even the scarred one just stared at the floor.

Every member of the group was staring at Rekil intently. They were collectively trying to beam the thought *Let's get out of here* into his head. He cleared his throat, "We'll help you."

Many of the shadows cheered as Rekil walked back toward them. Slyra and Vantix were glaring at the back of his head again, but luckily for them he still couldn't hear their thoughts.

*　*　*　*　*

In the last hour or so, the layout of the hall had drastically changed. A large banquet table seemed to have magically appeared, along with several barrels of whatever beverage the shadows drank. The table was covered in vast quantities of meats, vegetables and deserts. Despite their small frames it was clear that the shadows certainly knew how to eat.

Vantix was sitting between Slyra and Osca, picking at his food and glancing at the other members of the group. Whilst Elik, Grelow, Ramos, Arsenius, Hemer and Sam tucked into their food, the others didn't seem to have much of an appetite.

Farack seemed content to entertain the shadows with his new found rhadon abilities. Juggling flames had long since lost its novelty in Ballisca, but the shadows ate it up. They'd probably never seen anything like this before.

On Vantix's left, Osca was picking at his food. He poked a piece of meat several times before throwing it into his mouth and giving it a cautious chew. His taste buds were not disappointed.

After noticing a slight glow under the table, Vantix was pleased to see energy still snaking around Slyra's fingers. His gaze flickered to the gate, but he already knew it was still open. It was nice to see somebody wasn't letting their guard down.

For the first time since preparations had begun, Rekil joined the group. Sitting down between Vantix and Osca, he wasted little time grabbing himself a plate and a tankard.

"Well?" Osca inquired.

"It's very good," Rekil replied thoughtfully, " I can't quite place the meat."

197

"I meant," Osca mumbled through a mouthful, "What do they expect in return for this sumptuous feast?"

Rekil shrugged, "It's a trivial matter."

Osca wiped his mouth with a cloth, "Any chance of getting it over with now?"

The older man shook his head. "They told me a demon stalks the village," he explained, "Unless they sacrifice the youngest member of the community, it will murder all of them. That's why there are no children here. It's coming to collect its next victim tomorrow and we are going to deal with it."

Osca chewed another mouthful. "Do you think that's wise?"

"I don't think it's unwise. After all, it's the least we can do seeing as they provided us with this amazing meal."

"Don't think so; I'm pretty sure the least we can do is nothing. Why should we waste time saving these people? Don't we have our own demons to worry about?"

"Good to see somebody taking the moral high ground," Rekil replied gruffly, "and I won't worry about that. Thanks to this shortcut we're days ahead of our quarry."

"Seriously, why should we fight other people's battles for them when one of our own number is fast becoming some nightmarish demon himself? Furthermore, have you ever had a thought that wasn't unreasonably altruistic?"

They turned to look at Vantix, who didn't seem to have heard them. Rekil glared at Osca momentarily, then took his meal elsewhere.

Slyra laughed, "You're just making friends left right and centre."

Osca shrugged and returned to his meal.

The young witch took this time to scan the room. It was abundantly clear that the shadows weren't really engaging in the festivities. Although there were several serving food and ale the majority of them were simply standing around. This wouldn't have seemed weird if they were dancing to the music, but none of them spoke or moved. Instead they all watched the group with the same intense gaze. Which, to be honest, was slightly disconcerting.

Leaning in close to Vantix, she whispered. "We should leave."

Osca drifted in from the other side and nodded his assent. "Rekil won't agree."

Slyra's expression was grim. "We don't have time to argue with him. We'll have to either knock him out and take him with us, or he gets left behind."

Osca didn't reply. He was staring at Vantix, who in turn was staring at his food.

A strange expression adorned Vantix's features. It looked hungry, eager and fierce all at the same time. It wasn't an expression you'd see on a human face often, looking more akin to a wild animal stalking its prey.

"Vantix, are you al-" Osca faltered. Vantix's teeth had pierced his lower lip, causing blood to mix with saliva and roll down his chin, equal parts strange and worrying.

Rising slowly out of his seat, Vantix's gaze shifted from his food to the nearest shadow. He licked his lips meaningfully.

"Vantix?" Slyra breathed worriedly. She could tell her calls were falling on deaf ears, he was only paying attention to the aforementioned shadow. Those at the table watched dumbstruck as he crouched, leapt and....

.....was poked in the eye by Elik. Stopping mid-flight, he collapsed back into his chair, clutching his eye indignantly. "What's wrong with you?" Vantix cursed at Elik, "Your nails are bloody sharp!" He got up and paced around the table, shooting Elik the occasional one-eyed dark look. A few of the shadows watched him in amusement.

"Aren't The Shadows a group in Port Daichwater?" asked Sam.

Elik nodded. "They're assassins and thieves, but they're only based in Port Daichwater. They operate all over Ballisca," he then added, "I guess we know where they got their name."

"Nobody does anything original anymore," Sam sighed before continuing, "still I don't see the connection between these guys and murderous thieves."

Elik merely shrugged in response; he honestly didn't have a clue.

Vantix sat back down as one of the shadows called a toast. Raising its glass, the shadow declared, "We will never be able to repay the deed these people are about to perform for us. To our saviours!"

As it was speaking, the group's tankards had been refilled. In response to his toast, they lifted these and took a sip.

A sip was all Vantix took. Placing his glass on the table, he attempted to voice his opinion on the beverage. "Thiiisssss ttaaassssstessss ssssstraaaangggggeee." His hung out the corner of his mouth, completely numb and refusing to aid him in forming words.

He stumbled backward out of his chair, knocking it over. However, he was faring far better than most. Slyra's head lolled forward, catching a nasty blow off the edge of the table. Grelow, Hemer, and Ramos all had their faces nestled safely in their food, whilst Sam and Osca were spread out on the floor. Besides Vantix, only Arsenius and Elik managed to actually get away from the table.

Arsenius threw a punch at the nearest shadow, but it sidestepped out of the way. Unfortunately, his momentum dragged him down and he was out for the count.

Searching around desperately, Vantix spotted Rekil across the room. The middle-aged warrior was being propped up by a couple of shadows, definitely beyond help.

Vantix was surprised to see the gate still open; Slyra was no longer conscious, after all. Eyeing the real world on the other side, he steadied himself on the table and stumbled toward it.

Elik wasn't faring any better. He'd managed to draw his sword, but his groggy swings didn't do any damage. If anything, they just sapped the last of his energy. The shadows evaded his slow swings easily, and some even managed to get under his guard to try bring him down. Wings emerged from under his cloak, knocking several of them back a few paces.

It was then he let out a shout, but it wasn't just any shout. Vantix was forced to cover his ears and watch in amazement, as Elik's shout sent the shadows tumbling through the air. Most were unscathed, but a few hit walls with particularly sickening crunches.

Elik's wings flapped lazily and he floated up in the confined space. Turning slightly, he then plummeted straight down onto the table, finally losing the battle for consciousness.

Until then, Elik had kept the shadows preoccupied. Now, as one their attention shifted to Vantix. All the same, they needn't have worried, as he'd already passed out several feet from the stone gate.

Chapter 26

Despite being awake, Slyra kept her eyes shut. She'd been pleasantly surprised to wake up in the first place. In the split second before she lost consciousness, she'd presumed it was the end.

Her feet were unbound but her arms stretched out to either side. Feeling wood on her knuckles and rope against her wrists, which were raw from chafing, she sensed this was quite the predicament. Gradually she opened her eyes.

The plains of the Shadowlands were laid out before her. Her hands were bound to a pole on either side of where she stood. The rest of the group was in the same situation. Farack and Grelow were on her left, Osca and Elik to her right. Arsenius and Vantix were immediately in front of her, whilst Hemer was ahead of them. Sam, Ramos and Rekil were just behind her, with the village a good bit behind them. She tried to move, but her wrists were firmly bound against the wood.

"It's no use," Farack sighed beside her, "These people know their knots."

Slyra stopped tugging at ropes and muttered, "We'll see", before energy snaked along her hands toward the ropes.

"I wouldn't do that," Osca called across.

She ignored him, instead opting to free herself. A second later, an arrow lodged itself into the wood alongside her hand. The energy tendrils disappeared abruptly.

There were now four shadows present, each armed with their own individual crossbow. They hadn't been there a moment ago. "How did-" she began.

"They're called the shadows," Sam interrupted, before adding "I think they've justified having an organisation of murderers and thieves named after them."

While they were saying all this, the shadows had vanished once more. "Why are we still alive?" Osca mused.

"I expect it would be because our hearts are still beating," Vantix called over his shoulder.

The others shook their heads while Osca responded. " Really? Even when we're bound and seconds away from torture or death, you have to ruin everything I say?"

Vantix nodded, prompting Osca be more specific with his question. "I meant, why haven't they killed us yet?"

Nobody bothered to answer.

Seeing as he was the only one still unconscious, Slyra decided it would be fair to wake Grelow. She called him several times but elicited no response. The others joined in, provoking the shadows to show up again, brandishing their weapons.

As soon as they disappeared again, the witch took action. She mumbled for a moment and her fingertips lit up. Electricity flew from them and zigzagged across the unconscious vampire, stinging him on the cheek.

Awaking with a sharp grunt of agitation, he tried to touch the afflicted area, only to find his hands bound.

203

The group's collective attention was torn away from the vampire's groggy surprise, to Slyra's distress after a sharp cry escaped her lips. An arrow had gone clean through her hand, embedding itself deep into the wooden pole behind it. Tears sprang to her eyes as the hand bled. The others watched in angst, but there was nothing they could do.

Grelow had long since stopped trying to free his arm. "Well," he announced after a moment's consideration, "It's been a pleasure but I trust you won't mind too much if I take my leave." With that his body seemed to break apart piece by piece and float away until there was nothing left between the posts. Although they'd seen him as his normal vampire self and as a colony of bats, this was the first time they'd witnessed one of his transformations.

Several of the shadows had appeared and were busy firing arrows at the departing bats. They didn't even come close to hitting him.

Arsenius spat in disgust, "Bastard."

This time the shadows remained. The scarred one from yesterday, who'd been identified as Craenk, strolled nonchalantly toward them. Stopping in front of Rekil, he declared "I'd like to thank you." He actually sounded sincere.

The old warrior simply stared back at him. After a moments intense silence, Craenk continued. "The creature I told you about, The Drakold, is every bit as terrifying and wonderful as I described," his eyes shone with admiration as he continued, "Our deception was necessary and you were such an obliging participant, but you could not have hoped to vanquish it. Instead, offering you will help us gain its favour."

Rekil glared. "Let us go," he grunted, "We can kill it."

"Why would we want that?" Craenk asked. "You are mere mortals like us, you cannot hope to contend with a god. The Drakold has lived for millennia; it is beyond your reach. Such is the natural order of things."

"We can help you!" This time Rekil was pleading.

"And so you shall," Craenk replied whilst leaving, " Your sacrifice shall grant us its blessing. Be grateful that you've been chosen. It's an honour."

Then they heard it. A guttural roar turned every head to the front, making them stare toward the ridge twenty feet in front of Hemer. Due to the Shadowlands vague and indistinct nature, the ridge was barely discernible, but became visible as the creature ascended from the other side. The shadows gawped in admiration. The group just gawped. The Drakold was horrifying.

Different people tend to have different opinions about what is scary. For example, some may find ravenous creatures who feed on souls horrifying, while others are terrified by the prospect of settling down and having a family. Despite their different personalities, origins, and hopes for the future, every single person there was horrified by the Drakold. Only difference was the shadows enjoyed it.

It was ten foot tall and four foot wide. On their own, the muscle in any of its appendages was easily bigger than the average man, indicating that it could not only tear a man in half, but also crush him with the slightest touch. Hands and feet ended in razor sharp claws, but didn't draw attention away from the intersecting stream of veins that ran all over its hairless chest and abdomen. Apart from its aforementioned hairless chest, its face was the only area of its body not covered in dark red hair. It only had one piece of clothing; a ragged garment reaching down from its waist to its knees. A skeletal face with a horn protruding from its forehead added to the whole horrifying effect. Its lips were thin and couldn't conceal a mouth housing far too many teeth. With blood red eyes buried in incredibly deep sockets and a single slit where its nose should have been, it probably wouldn't be winning the title of "fairest in the land" any time soon.

The Drakold advanced on them slowly, almost smugly. It seemed intent on teasing them, prolonging the inevitable just to terrify them.

Slyra couldn't take her eyes off it. The pain in her hand had faded as soon as the Drakold had come into view. Now it returned as she struggled with the ropes, desperately trying to free herself. She wouldn't be prey to that thing.

The others did the same but this time without interruption from the shadows who seemed to have vanished completely. Until one of them appeared right in front of her.

Slyra leapt back in surprise, as much as her bonds would allow. They held tight. On spotting that he had a knife, she struggled momentarily then watched in amazement as he reached up and sliced through her bonds. Reaching for the arrow, she broke the shaft in half and dragged her hand along it.

Blood dripped from the hole in her hand, rolling down both her palm and the back of her hand. Her eyes went white as the missing part of her hand healed, both sides of the cut seeming to reach out to each other as it grew back. She gave it an experimental shake; although fully healed, it still ached.

Farack watched as Slyra was joined by Osca and Elik. They set off toward the village, leaving him looking around frantically. The little shadow had moved forward to free the others, completely neglecting him.

"Hey!" he called angrily. They couldn't leave him behind, they wouldn't. And yet they were. His temper flared and before he knew it, his arms were alight from fingertip to elbow. The ropes crackled and within a few seconds, he'd burnt straight through. Now free, he glanced down at his flaming hands in wonder. "I could get used to this," he mumbled contently.

Meanwhile, Vantix's lips were quivering and he visibly shook. The Drakold drew ever closer and he'd already exhausted himself pulling at his restraints. Ahead of him, Hemer was engaged in a fruitless attempt to thrash his way out of this obstacle.

Then Vantix's left arm was free. A shadow was at his side with a rather sharp looking knife. Working quickly, the shadow crossed over and sliced into the rope restraining his right hand.

Vantix bit his lip and winced. The little shadow could have done to be a bit more careful; not only had he sliced through rope, he'd also cut deep into Vantix's arm. Blood now rolled down the wooden pole and dripped from his arm to the ground. Grimacing in pain, he tore off a piece of his shirt and wrapped it around the wound.

The Drakold was closing in, still moving with the same lazy assurance. Its approach seemed to drown out all other sound, making it impossible for any communication between the group.

Feeling a hand on his shoulder, Vantix whirled around. "Let's go," he said but it was no use, he couldn't even hear himself. Still resting one hand on Vantix's shoulder, Arsenius used the other to gesture to Hemer. They couldn't leave him; there was probably a special place in hell for those who left people to the Drakold.

The little shadow was amongst them once more, but this time he simply tossed them the knife and took off. They didn't blame him.

Hemer had been placed a good deal ahead of them and with both of them sprinting, it was Arsenius who reached him first. He sliced through one set of bindings and got no further, there just wasn't time.

Up until that moment, the Drakold hadn't shown any evidence of its immense speed, but now the prospect of losing its lunch spurred it into action. Letting out a roar of fury, it charged forward with its head down and horn raised dangerously. It could only be described as phenomenally fast.

Arsenius was lucky; Vantix dragged him from the creature's path with about half a second to spare. Hemer not so much; the Drakold drove straight into him. Piercing his chest with its horn, it lifted him high into the air. Letting out one final breath, Hemer went limp atop the monster's head. It tossed his body to the ground, before crouching and setting to work.

Arsenius and Vantix had never been more certain that there was nothing they could do. Hemer was beyond saving. The two of them backed away slowly before sprinting as fast as their legs could carry them. The Drakold paid them no heed, currently preoccupied.

* * * * *

They came upon the rest of the group, excluding Grelow, outside the banquet hall from last night. Arsenius voiced Vantix's immediate concerns, "What's wrong with you?" he shouted, "Haven't you seen that thing? We need to get out of here!"

The whole group stared at him momentarily, before Rekil spoke. "Cermus here," he indicated the helpful shadow, "says his entire tribe is in there waiting for the Drakold to leave. In case you haven't noticed, we have no weapons and they were armed to the teeth."

Arsenius tossed the knife Cermus had given him from hand to hand. "I'd rather take my chances with them, then that thing."

"Be my guest," Rekil replied grimly.

"My pleasure" Arsenius nodded. Walking slowly toward the building, he noticed movement. Throwing his knife immediately, he missed by the slightest margin imaginable.

Grelow, who'd just emerged from inside, stared at the knife next to his head, before strolling out and flashing them a smile. "So glad you all could make it," he said casually.

Rekil stared at him, "How did you..." he stopped when he noticed the flecks of blood all over Grelow's chin and clothing.

The vampire licked his lips and moved back inside, the others followed suit. Inside the group looked at Grelow's handiwork and instantly wished they hadn't. There'd been no mercy here.

Every single last shadow lay dead and drained, their blood washing over the wooden floor. Some of them had arms and legs missing. All wore an expression of extreme terror, akin to those the group had worn on first seeing the dendrid. There was no denying how thorough Grelow had been.

At this sight, Cermus vomited. Several of the group felt nauseas, but none did the same. They were definitely glad they weren't coming up against Grelow any time soon.

209

One by one the group turned away from the massacre and collected both their bags and their weapons. It was only then they noticed the arrows and crossbow bolts lodged in the walls; the shadows had tried to defend themselves.

Slyra walked toward the gate, which was still open from the night before. She stared at it uncertainly. "I didn't-," she began.

She was interrupted by Vantix and Farack. Together they grabbed an elbow each, lifting her off her feet and through the gate.

The others were already through, prompting Farack and Vantix to drop Slyra as soon as they entered the real world. "Close the bloody gate," they yelled simultaneously.

Slyra stood up and clicked her fingers. At the click, energy flowed from the gate to Slyra's palms, before disappearing. She nodded to the others, "Let's go."

A cough from Rekil stopped her in her tracks. Looking back at the gate, it was instantly obvious what was wrong.

The gate was still open and offering a view to the hall of massacred shadows. It was rather difficult to miss. Slyra sighed irritably. She clicked her fingers again, and then again as the gate still refused to close. Finally, she raised her arms and chanted, causing white energy to stream from her hands and engulf the door, rendering it invisible. Then, the orb of power imploded.

The implosion was blinding, meaning several of the group couldn't see for a few moments afterward. Even before they regained their vision, they could tell from Slyra's exasperated cries that the gate remained open.

"I can't close it," Slyra stuttered. This wasn't the first time she'd been given reason to doubt her abilities but it was still decidedly jarring. All that power at her fingertips and she couldn't close a door she'd opened in the first place.

Turning around, she noticed that the majority of the group had returned to their normal selves. In fact there were only two who hadn't. Her eyes went wide as her gaze settled on Vantix and Farack.

Vantix still had the sickly yellow skin and scales on some areas, along with the other features gifted to him from his encounter with the dendrid. As for Farack, his hair was on fire. It took a moment for them to catch her stare.

Farack ran his fingers through his flaming hair, before rubbing his hands together until they ignited. Laughing gleefully, he tossed fireballs into the air and at the gate. "Do you know what this means?" he called enthusiastically. He didn't seem to be asking anyone in particular.

"You get the customary explosion when you die?" Grelow replied coldly. There was a hint of menace in his tone, which went straight over Farack's head. Nothing could have put the now fully fledged rhadon down.

"Yes," Farack yelled cheerfully, "and it means my flame has finally taken." Whooping cheerfully, he tossed more fire into the air. He stopped when burning birds starting falling to the ground around him.

Of course, Vantix was oblivious to all this. He was staring down at his hands. They weren't exactly the same as they'd been in the Shadowlands; his nails had certainly lengthened, hardened and sharpened but couldn't be called claws in earnest yet. What really captured his attention was the wound he'd received. Where Cermus had accidentally cut whilst freeing him the skin was rapidly healing itself, leaving not a trace. The only evidence of its existence, was his darker-than-usual blood which stained the grass all around him.

He wasn't exactly thrilled by this latest development. Being that nightmare creature didn't appeal to him in the least. Trying to think of ways to get rid of this strange skin, aside from killing himself, he drew a complete blank.

Just then Rekil drew their attention. "Everybody," he called whilst glancing at the sun, "It'll be dark soon and Ghostwood is no place for the living, no matter the time of day."

Gathering their packs, the rest of the group followed him out of the clearing.

* * * * *

The Drakold's forked tongue flicked out and tasted the air. Its meal had just been finished, the taste lingering in its mouth. Human was a delicacy it hadn't tasted in millennia.

Now, its nostrils flared as it caught a new smell, something it had never smelt before. This unprecedented scent invaded its nostrils, forcing it to its feet. Following its nostrils to the source, it didn't have far to go.

A wooden pole stood as the source of the aroma, but wood couldn't smell like this. The fragrance swirled around the pole, like a cloud of intoxication.

The Drakold needed it. Sucking in breath after breath of the strange smelling fragrance until all other odours and even senses were drowned out. The exotic scent overtook the Drakold, making it act as a man – well, thing – possessed.

Then its forked tongue flicked out, going straight to where a few droplets of blood had stained the wood a darker colour. Vantix's blood to be exact, but the Drakold didn't know that.

The blood fulfilled the Drakold, engulfing and overpowering every other sense. Everything was perfect. The world came to a halt around the creature, as it savoured every single last taste of the perfect liquid. It had to have more.

After several moments, the monster's eyes unglazed and it licked its lips. There was more of the blood along the ground, leaving a trail for it to follow. The Drakold could smell it, the essence of the person whose blood it longed for and it knew where he'd gone. It set off across the vague landscape in the direction of the village.

Chapter 27

"......and that, gentlemen, concludes our business at present. You will be hearing from me." Welbh smiled and shoved the papers into his coat. The Derranferd branch of The Merchant's Guild smiled weakly back at him; they couldn't help but wonder if they'd made the right decision.

King Jandelk's carriage had reached Angelous, the Derranferd capital, that morning and Welbh hadn't wasted much time putting the finishing touches on his shiny little machination. As the deals in Port Daichwater and Fardash were already settled, it was in the Derranferd merchants' best interests to agree, and agree they had. Not that they had much of a choice.

One of the main reasons for the lacklustre conditions in Fardash, were the supplies available. In an attempt to appear self-sufficient, each province had declared a boycott on all products from the others. This was fine for the bigger provinces, but the likes of Fardash, Derranferd and Lundia weren't very well off. In times of such economic distress, honest men resorted to dishonest things in order to feed their families. Welbh rather liked that; it made them much easier to do business with.

He gave them a wink as he moved toward the door. They knew what it meant. It was the wink of a man who had them right where he wanted them, something they weren't the least bit happy about. However, they needed this desperately, which is why none had opposed him during the negotiations.

Outside, Welbh flicked through the contracts they'd signed. More importantly, he glanced at the order forms. Since his commission was half the order this first batch would easily make him one of the richest men in Fardash.

If you thought about it, he was saving lives. Without him there would be no trade, all businesses would collapse and families would starve. Taking on the law so he could employ the poor; it sounded pretty heroic in Welbh's book – noble even.

That being said, he still had to meet with King Audron's negotiator and talk about lessening the border guard but it wasn't really a problem. If they intended to be allies, and they were hardly going to say no, they'd have to lessen the guard anyway for communication between the two kings.

Wrapped up in these thoughts as he was, he almost missed the pickpocket. Feeling the bump, he reacted just in time. After mumbling "Sorry", the thief made a vain attempt to flee. Welbh caught hold of an arm, that moments before had been inside his jacket, and wrenched a piece of paper from the thief's hand. "Push off," he yelled aggressively.

It was only then he realised that the previously mentioned piece of paper hadn't been in his pocket in the first place. His gaze darted to the unsuccessful thief and recognition dawned.

Although her eyes still held their cold unblinking stare, Lila smiled at him. "I bring word from your brother."

Welbh unfolded the paper. It simply said:

Still sharp as ever brother, see you in 5.
Lintous

He instantly knew there was something wrong. Lintous had said six days four days ago. As if in answer to his thoughts, Lila spoke. "Your brother apologises for the delay," she explained, "but there were some unexpected complications, so things haven't moved quite as fast as he'd hoped."

"They never do," Welbh muttered, but she'd already left.

Still, the delays in his brother's plan boded well for him, gave him more time to organise himself. Maybe even prevent his brother from ruining all his hard work. It was with a light-hearted spring in his step that he set out for King Audron's palace.

Although there wasn't much of a spring in their step, the two men who'd been trailing him all morning moved off as well.

Unfortunately, they were also unaware of the person pursuing them.

*   *   *   *   *

"It's so strange," Slyra said to the newest member of their merry band, "You're practically invisible."

Cermus nodded. "I am a shadow, I can vanish entirely if I wish." In this world he looked even more out of place, faint and indistinct, the perfect souvenir from the Shadowlands.

"Why did you help us?"

The little shadow shrugged. "If not for you it would have been me up there."

"Nevertheless," the witch smiled, "you have my thanks."

Despite standing right beside them, their conversation went over Vantix's head. He was still deeply troubled by his appearance in the shadowlands. It didn't bode well for his future modelling career. In his head, he went through a catalogue of salves, none of which was a cure for his rather unique condition.

Aside from these three, the rest of the group were incredibly on edge. Some might say that having one of their fellows slowly turn into some kind of dendrid monster will do that to people, but Vantix wasn't the cause of their current unease. Each and every member of the party had their weapons drawn as they moved through the wood, eyes watching the immediate shadows for signs of danger. They were afraid of the forest itself.

Ghostwood is so named because of the phantoms and creatures that lurk there. They disguise themselves as loved ones or enemies; always seeking to lure travellers away from their groups with fake promises of reunions and last farewells. If someone gets lost in Ghostwood, chances are they won't be coming out.

This serves to explain the group's slow progress. Although the sun had recently gone down, an eerie light illuminated the swirling mists in the shadows. It was creepy, making the group think someone would appear out of the mists at any moment. More likely though, was that somebody would be called into the gloom by one of their relatives. They were simply waiting for the call.

"Farack......Farack..," a ghostly voice called to him from far on his left. Only it wasn't ghostly, it was soothing and

maternal. Far different from the voices Rekil had described to him. In fact, there probably was a person down there who could use his help. All the same, he should probably make sure. "Does anyone else hear that?" he asked.

Rekil replied almost instantly, as if he'd waiting to offer reassurance. "Whoever you think you're hearing," he hissed, "it's not them. Stand firm and remember where we are."

"Right," Farack said uncertainly. He could still hear the sweet voice calling out to him.

Then the barrage came.

"Rekil....Rekil..."
"Elik..."
"Osca...Osca.."
"Arsenius...."
"Grelow...."
"Sam...."
"Slyra........."
"Ramos......"
"Vantix...."
"Farack....Farack.."

Oddly enough, the voices paid absolutely no attention to Cermus, as if they didn't even notice him.

Each voice sounded in an individual person's head, tempting them beyond measure. "Don't listen!" Rekil yelled.

"But it's him," Ramos shouted back in hopeful indignation, "my brother Ned. He didn't die in that bandit attack!"

"He's dead Ramos!"

"No, he's right here," Ramos responded desperately, "Can't you hear him?"

218

Several members of the group had different reactions. Most clutched their heads and blocked their ears, while others span in circles trying to catch a glimpse of the voice's source. Slyra sang aloud, anything to drown out the voices begging for just a moment of her time.

"Ramos?" Sam whirled around hopelessly, "Where are y-" he stopped when he caught sight of the others.

Only Vantix, Cermus, Slyra and Rekil remained. The rest had disappeared into the undergrowth, searching for their mothers/fathers/families/brothers/sisters/girlfriends/wifes/children or whatever kind of illusion they were currently chasing.

Rekil grabbed Sam by the shoulders. "For the next while, we are impenetrable, got it? Nothing will take our attention from this path, will it?"

The other four nodded.

"No it will not," Rekil answered his own question. "Now stick tight, and no matter what happens follow this path. Maybe the five of us will make it out alive."

The others were staring at the ground, their mouths fixed in expressions of grim determination. They set off down the same path they were already following, intent on finding a way out.

* * * * *

Vampires are smooth, slick, cold-blooded killers. They have expensive tastes, costly attire and can call up impeccable table etiquette when the occasion demands it. Suave replies are prepared for every happenstance and all they really want is a castle they can lure people into.

The one thing they love, even more than finding reasonably priced desolate castles, is the hunt. The game, as it was. Not every game is the same, they might take place anywhere from gala balls to tiny hamlets. It's always a trick though, always a fiendishly cunning plan to snare the prey (usually a young woman) and then bask in their own glory. It's tendencies such as this that the public aren't happy about. Vampires aren't generally considered people, never mind nice.

With all these traits, it's usually a safe bet that vampires won't be following a single victim through the woods. It's also usually a safe bet that they won't nervously stumble over every single branch and outstretched root. Yet this is exactly what Grelow did.

"Grelow......Grelow, my love....." the voice belonged to a young woman. *"Come find me..."*

Brushing himself down after yet another fall, he looked around. Hoping for a glimpse of her, he would be highly disappointed if his search yielded no results. It had been sixty years since he'd heard the voice but he'd recognise it anywhere.

A flash of white caught his attention and he ran toward it. A high lilting laugh floated across the swirling mists. "Almost here, my love," her voice called again. It was just like her to tease him.

Turning a corner he reached the source of her laughter but saw nothing. He whirled around, searching for any sign of her. She had to be here, she had to!

Then she was. She was wearing her wedding gown and looked every part the beautiful bride. Moving through the strange mist, he swallowed nervously. What if it wasn't her?

She laughed and flashed him a dazzling smile, momentarily smothering any doubts he may have had. "Come here, my love," she said again.

Grelow reached out and she took his hand before wrapping him in a warm embrace.

Deep down he knew it wasn't real, but he wanted it to be.

* * * * *

Rekil, Slyra, Sam and Vantix walked slowly and deliberately. Cermus had disappeared, leaving just the four of them staring at the ground and picking their way through the forest. Until they heard a scream.

Slyra, Sam and Vantix rushed in its direction, swords at the ready. Rekil remained where he was, calling after them, "Don't go", but they weren't really listening.

The body was face down, lying against the roots of an old tree. Taking care to flip it over, Vantix noticed the wound on its neck. It looked as if some kind of wild dog had attacked him. Also quite strange, was the expression of bliss mixed with horror that adorned their now deceased companion's features.

Vantix gave a deep sigh. "Poor, poor.....eh, poor," he was stuck, unable to remember the fellow's name.

"Ramos," Slyra input.

Vantix nodded before finishing awkwardly, " Yeah, poor Ramos."

"Sam," Slyra said quietly, "I know you two were friends so-"

Vantix tapped her shoulder. Sam was gone.

Looking back at the path, it was clear Rekil had also left. He turned back to Slyra. "And then there were two," he stated simply.

* * * * *

Osca mopped his brow; work in his father's stables was certainly tiring. What was worse, his father was currently doing one of his weekly inspections and he never failed to find some aspect of Osca's work to complain about.

In contrast to his son's slight build, his father was a bear of a man. He was also the proud owner of possibly the finest beard in all of Fardash, excluding the reclusive dwarves.

The big man looked over the last horse with extreme care, before nodding approvingly. "Mighty fine job boy" he smiled at his son.

Osca shook his head. His father was notorious for withholding praise. *I must have done an incredibly job,* he thought contentedly, *Unless I'm missing something.....*

For a second, the scene before him flickered and it was just him and his father alone in a wood. As soon as he blinked, however, they were back in the stable once more.

"You okay, lad?" his father grunted, "Come here." Before he could react his father wrapped him in a bear hug. It didn't last long though, as Osca promptly shoved him away. Never mind his father complimenting him, this was absolutely unheard of.

The scene had evaporated, leaving just Osca and his father alone in the wood. He looked around franticly, there was something he needed to remember, but he just couldn't wrap his mind around it.

"Son, you're not looking well," his father grunted, "Come on, your mother's cooking will pick you right up."

That was another thing. His father's disapproving grunts made sense, it seemed all the man was able to do. These strange caring remarks weren't things you could

222

grunt at people, making them seem completely incongruous.

Occupied by these thoughts, Osca only now noticed what his father had actually said. "What did you just say?" he asked.

His father smiled, "Your mother's cooking boy, let's go get some before it's cold."

It was then Osca knew. As the big man moved to put an arm around his shoulders, Osca shrugged it off. "There's something you should know," he said quietly.

His father gave him an inquisitive look. "Aye, lad?"

Drawing his sword, Osca plunged it deep into the man's chest and buried it all the way up to the hilt, then kicked the man off the blade with his boot. "My mother died in childbirth," he hissed, before stomping away into the wood.

Behind him, the creature that had been his father assumed its natural shape.

*　*　*　*　*

Elik drank it all in; his senses all but overwhelmed by the sights, sounds and general extravagance of the scene before him. The immense hall was fantastically decorated and affluence oozed from every ornament, outfit and solid gold folly present. He thought the whole thing slightly indecorous.

There was something odd about the hall. Gold gleamed on every surface, but it seemed false. Lurking ominously beneath the lavish decor, shadows had taken up residence and made themselves quite at home. If anything, the ostentatious wealth simply made them more prominent.

Scanning the room, Elik suddenly found himself staring at his own reflection. Not because he simply spotted a mirror; somehow he was suddenly standing in front of an extremely large mirror and the party was taking place behind him.

Nevertheless, his reflection now captured his attention. He wore the garment of a servant and his wings were also noticeably absent. Trying to touch or move them yielded no result; his other senses inclined to agree with what his eyes saw. The face in the mirror was also much younger, as if the last ten years had apologised for all the worry they'd caused him and graciously taken their leave.

Of course, Elik was under no illusions as to the nature of this party. There certainly weren't any banquet halls in the middle of Ghostwood and even if there were, he doubted the boorish, self-obsessed nobility would spend time here. He'd left the group and followed the insidious call of Ghostwood in the hope it'd elucidate matters in his own head. Most people have a few skeletons nestled quietly at the back of their closets; Elik had misplaced a whole life somewhere in his. Any offers of help would be accepted, even if they came from nefarious sources.

Turning around, he found himself halfway across the hall and narrowly avoided a collision with another servant.

"Are you alright?"

Elik turned to answer but the enquirer had already vanished. That wasn't the only strange thing about the scene which greeted his eyes.

All around him the nobility who'd been drinking, dancing and enjoying themselves lay unconscious. A large number of them had fallen as they danced, whilst others lay asleep with their heads in their meals. There was but one exception and she looked around in alarm upon realising she was now alone.

All of a sudden Elik found himself closing in on her table, along with the rest of the servants. Apparently they weren't the obsequious bunch he'd originally taken them for. Then he wondered where the sword in his hand had come from.

At the table, the girl became increasingly distressed as she struggled to rouse her companions. Elik felt sorry for her; it was just like what had happened to them with the shadows.

One of the other servants was speaking, but he was only vaguely aware of it. The girl seemed familiar. She wasn't the one he'd been searching for but he knew he recognised her all the same. Attempting to sheathe his sword, his arms now proved recalcitrant.

The other was finished speaking now and despite himself, Elik raised his blade and advanced on the terrified girl. Sweat trickled down his forehead as he struggled to regain control of his limbs. "Stop it!" he roared as his blade moved of its own accord.

Everything froze as soon as the words escaped his lips. For a second the hall shimmered, before drifting away as if taken by the wind. All except the girl, who smiled reassuringly. "Elik, I knew yo- "The girl was cut off by Elik shoving her and taking off through the bracken.

Although momentarily caught off guard, Elik always kept his wits somewhere about his person and wasn't intent on succumbing to anything Ghostwood had to offer. However, their attempt to inveigle him had shaken him slightly. What was he doing in that banquet? Who were his companions? What secrets lay submerged in his sea of forgotten memories? Even if these weren't real it left him with some nagging doubts: was everything worth remembering?

Shaking these thoughts aside, Elik looked around him. In the shadows of Ghostwood scenes played out just beyond his reach. A woman cried over a coffin, a swordsman challenged him, a blood-spattered gravestone, a maniac played a broken lute and a king beckoned, yet none of these were important. There was only one question he wanted answered, only one memory that was of any importance. Then he saw them.

Elik was certain he knew them, and yet he didn't. The family before him, could have been his or anyone else's. He just couldn't remember.

Two children, a boy and a girl, and their mother stood before him in the woods. There was no doubt the boy looked like him, despite the fact Elik could only remember seeing him one other time. That had been whilst falling from an immense height and having flashes of a life he couldn't remember.

He knew they weren't real, but it couldn't hurt to gaze upon his forgotten family for a few moments. They motioned him towards them but he shook his head. Ghostwood didn't hold what he sought.

"I will find you," he promised under his breath. No matter what got in his way, no matter what he had to do, Elik couldn't stop the search. For he had nothing without them.

His wings flapped a couple times and launched him into the air, leaving Ghostwood behind.

* * * * *

Arsenius smiled at his parents, he hadn't seen them in nine years. They looked much better than their last encounter, that was certain. Life on the road had never been particularly kind to them but it seemed they'd reaped the benefits of settling down. His mother looked much healthier and his father had grown fat. "So how're things?" he asked while as he sat himself at the table.

The home they'd eventually settled in was plain enough, furniture restricted to the bare necessities. They'd never been known for extravagance. A few books lined one of the shelves, the same books his mother had in her possession all her life. To Arsenius it was heaven.

His mother looked up from the vegetables she was slicing. "We're getting by. The animals are all healthy and the crop is good. The roof is leaking though. Maybe you could take a look."

A dripping sound reached Arsenius' ears. He was almost certain it wasn't raining outside yet nodded nonetheless. "You're a good lad, Arsenius" his father mumbled, "always looking after your family."

His mother handed him a plate which was odd because only moments ago she'd been preparing the meal. Glancing down at the plate in front of him, he broke into a smile. It was her stew, his favourite meal in all the world.

"Only the best for my boy," his mother said as she was joined by his father, "Maybe you'd like to stay with us? The whole family together again."

Arsenius looked up from his food. "I'd like that very much."

"You're a good lad, Arsenius. Will you take care of us?"

Arsenius leapt out of his seat at sight of his parents. Their skin was suddenly devoid of the vivacious shine it had momentarily shown. Now they shone with a slick, pallid sheen. Death wasn't very becoming on them.

"You will help us, won't you Arsenius?" his father asked, mouth open to reveal the fangs underneath.

"Only we're so very hungry," his mother's fangs glistened, "and you've always been such a good boy."

It has been mentioned that Arsenius is extremely fast. So fast, that he'd drawn his sword, brought it round in a sweeping arc and sheathed it again before the creatures had time to react. Two heads tumbled away into the mist, leaving their bodies behind them.

"I'm sorry," Arsenius said grimly as the creature's bodies resumed their natural shape, "but I promise I'll make it up to you."

Cleaning his sword, he then strolled off in the direction of the path. Ghostwood provided him with a unique opportunity to resolve some unfinished business.

* * * * *

Farack could see them moving slowly away from him through the trees. The first other rhadons he'd seen since he was a child; letting them slip away would be a mistake, he was one of them now. "Hey," he howled joyously, unable to contain himself a moment longer.

The rhadons turned, causing him to gasp. This wasn't just any random group of rhadons, it was his family. He'd recognise them anywhere. Question was, would they recognise him?

This was incredible; his family showing up just as he achieved his birth-right. They could be together now, like it always should have been. Looking from his flaming hands and hair to his smiling face, he knew they knew him. "Farack?" they asked both tentatively and incredulously.

As he juggled flames, they ran toward him. One of them stood out from the crowd, she was moving much closer than the others. Farack's eyes glistened with tears of joy, as he avoided the outstretched arms of the others and headed straight for her. "Mother!" he cried happily.

For a second before he hugged her it looked like she was going to run away. Whilst hugging her, Farack got a sense he'd never had before. It was a sense of belonging and it ended rather abruptly.

Instantly it was over. His mother pulled away from him, screaming, or to use a more accurate word, squawking in terror. For you see, she wasn't his mother anymore.

To describe the creature as odd looking, would be an insult to odd looking things everywhere. This thing was downright ugly. From the waist down it was like a goat, with hoofed feet and a tail. From the waist up to the neck, it was feathered and had two long spindly arms that went all the way to its knees. It's head, which was entirely bald, didn't have a mouth or nose, instead just yellow eyes sat above a long serrated beak. Due to Farack's hug, it was also on fire.

The rhadon leapt back in surprise. The image of his family had faded, meaning it was just him and these things. They advanced on him with their talons outstretched.

He drew his sword and his arms lit up. As the one of the creatures dived at him, he moved out of the way and grabbed a hold of its leg. It went up in flames just like the first.

A taloned hand just missed his ear and tore into his shoulder. Yelping in pain, he shoved his sword into the creature and kicked the flimsy thing away.

Hearing sounds from two different sides, he span with his arms raised, fire flowing from both and engulfing the final two creatures. They went down without a sound.

Clutching his wounded shoulder and grimacing with pain, he moved over and yanked his sword from the dead monster. It was only then that he noticed he'd set all of the surrounding trees on fire.

He left in quite a hurry. Rhadons are immune to fire; he just didn't want the blame for this.

* * * * *

Rekil's arrow pierced her chest. It seemed to happen in slow motion, blood blossoming to spoil the white of her dress. "Grelow?" she whimpered before collapsing in a heap.

She was gone from his life once more, except this time it was through no fault of his own. Rekil! Rekil had taken her away. He couldn't be allowed get away with that, not ever! These thoughts whirled around Grelow's head, as he stared from her to the old soldier.

Grelow rose slowly from where he'd been sitting and lunged at Rekil. The old soldier was expecting the attack and evaded several of the vampire's groggy, sluggish attempts with ease.

"Listen to me," Rekil ordered as he caught Grelow's fist, "It wa-"

The vampire's other hand caught him in the face, causing him to step back and wipe the blood from his nose. "Now," said Rekil as he straightened up, "that was your only free shot, try it again and you'll regret it."

Grelow was in no mood to be reasoned with. His neck, which looked like a wild dog was feeding on it, healed before Rekil's very eyes. "You killed her," he shouted, leaping forward once more.

Rekil blocked the oncoming fist and kicked down hard on the vampire's leg. There was a loud crack as the bone broke, taking the vampire down with it. A moment later it had snapped back into place, but Grelow stayed where he was, staring at the hideous creature that had been her only moments ago. There was no point in this fight, and as such, he relented.

Rekil patted him on the shoulder. "It wasn't her," he said softly.

Grelow rose to his feet and fixed his shirt. Shooting Rekil a questioning look, he asked, "What wasn't who?"

A strange scent drifted toward him; a scent that is never a good thing to smell whilst in the woods. He was on the verge of asking if Rekil smelled something burning when Farack rushed by, leaving a trail of flaming undergrowth behind him.

Neither noticed the nearby sound of a sword being sheathed in frustration.

* * * * *

In the highest circle of Fardashian nobility it has long been acknowledged that doing your best isn't good enough. It's everyone else's best that you should be worried about.

Up there, where the wealth is tossed around like playthings in a nursery, only the best is tolerated. Housing, furniture, clothes, jewellery, horses, servants, carriages and even children are all judged and compared with those around them. In such an environment, generation long feuds begin at the slightest affront and differences are preserved just for the sake of prolonging outstanding argument. Yet despite their varying amounts of immense wealth and highly inflated egos, there's one thing all nobility agree upon: witches, and anything else their wallets can't explain, are not to be allowed within fifty feet of them.

That's why it was so surprising to see one of them out here in the middle of Ghostwood. "Slyra," the exquisitely dressed woman called, "Come home to us."

A large tree uprooted itself and flattened the pretender at Slyra's command.

"Trouble in the castle?" Vantix asked. Slyra looked angrier than he'd ever seen her.

Although still obviously furious, Slyra dismissed his question. "My parents couldn't bear the shame of a witch in the family, so I left."

As always Vantix felt the conversation required him to make an input. "So about leaving you on that alter-"

"Stay focused," Slyra said as she slapped him across the face.

"I bloody well am," Vantix shook his head. She just couldn't have fought the urge to hit him any longer. "As I was saying, I didn't mean to leave you with the murderous cult, it just sort of happened."

"This has to be one of the worst apologies I've ever heard," Slyra declared flatly.

"In my defence," Vantix shrugged, "I don't apologise often."

"How is that in your defence? You just sound like an idiot," she replied.

The sight of an opening through the trees up ahead silenced the both of them. They ran toward it.

Slyra ran ahead as Vantix came to a halt. Through the bracken he could see a man seated at a table, eating a bowl of soup. The man was in his late thirties and dressed in the travelling leathers and light chainmail he'd always worn when working. He seemed to sense Vantix watching him and looked up. For a moment they made eye contact, then the man beckoned him over. Although it was enticing, Vantix shook his head and followed Slyra.

Bursting from the shadows of Ghostwood into the fresh air beyond, they realised what they'd been putting their lungs through. In comparison to out here, the air in there was dank and stale, putrid even.

Elik eyed them thoughtfully and took a bite out of an apple, as they swallowed mouthful after mouthful of the air. The others were nowhere to be seen.

After catching his breath, Vantix walked over to Elik. "How did you get out so fast?"

"As soon as I'd had my fill, I decided it was best to fly out of there," Elik responded casually.

It took Vantix a moment to digest this. "Had your fill? What does...," his eyes went wide, "You ate them!"

"What? No," Elik hadn't actually been expecting a reply that stupid.

Fortunately Sam, Osca and Arsenius came tearing out of the woods almost simultaneously, ending the conversation between Vantix and Elik. The three of them were coughing, and mumbling something about fire.

"It was nice of you all to abandon us, by the way," Slyra muttered indignantly.

At that moment, Farack came running out of the trees. He looked extremely guilty. Rekil and Grelow trailed him by a few seconds.

"Ramos?" Elik asked, he wasn't expecting much of an answer. Vantix shook his head.

Cermus appeared next to his elbow, causing Elik to fall off the rock he was perched on. "Where did he come from?"

Nobody felt inclined to offer a reply.

"There's a town that way," Elik offered as he climbed to his feet, "Probably good for some food, rest and beds for the night."

The group nodded as one and set off without delay. Smoke billowed up behind them as Ghostwood burned. The blaze would eventually wear itself down, but not before it took half of Ghostwood with it.

Chapter 28

By the time they reached the town, it was an hour after midnight. As such the desertion of its streets was understandable. Perhaps a little more out of the ordinary were the eyes peering out at them from every household, vainly engaged in attempts to hide behind the curtains when really they should have been sleeping. They didn't seem pleased to see them, but then again, people generally weren't.

Rekil nodded to Arsenius. "Find somewhere for us to stay," he dropped a few coins into the elf's hand. "You three go with him."

Osca, Elik, Grelow and Arsenius set off in search of an inn. The other five followed Rekil.

After another minute's walk of drawing curious glances, Rekil slowed to a halt. He opened his bag and tossed several articles of clothing at Vantix. "Put these on," the old soldier instructed.

Slightly bemused, Vantix did as he was told. Pulling on the gloves and throwing on the sleeveless-hooded shirt, all the scale inflicted areas were no longer visible. The garments were strangely fashionable, meaning it didn't look like he was trying to cover anything up, just that style meant a lot to him. He tossed his jacket on over these; it was terribly cold.

Since Rekil was undoubtedly the leader, none questioned his motivations as they stumbled into the building in his wake. Intent on sweeping the doors open and giving the shopkeeper quite a look, convey the sense that he was not to be trifled with and all that. Unfortunately there was no sign of a shopkeeper and Rekil found himself staring at a wall that didn't flinch beneath his gaze.

Despite this momentary setback, he didn't waste time in moving to the counter and ringing the bell. When nobody appeared, he tutted irritably and hit it again.

Hair, a forehead and eyes slowly raised themselves up and peered at the group over the counter. This was then joined by the lower half of the same face and a body followed suit, until a whole man stood before them. Dusting himself down, he treated them to a weary smile. "Good evening," he said whilst stifling a yawn, "What can I get for you?"

Rekil unstrapped his quiver and set it on the counter. "I need this filled." Turning around, he caught Cermus playing with a sword. "We'll take that as well."

The shopkeeper nodded. Cermus smiled his thanks as Rekil reached for the now full quiver. He handed over payment before asking, "Could you tell the rest of the town that we mean them no harm?"

It took the other man several moments to catch on. When he did, he gave a throaty chuckle and shook his head. "We're not hiding from you," he explained, "We have troubles of our own."

Vantix and Slyra shook their heads, they knew what Rekil's response would be. He seemed to have this unnecessary desire to waste time, offering aid to every sob-story, wounded duck and vaguely downtrodden person to cross his path. It was almost as if he wanted the dendrid to get away.

"Maybe we can offer you our services?" They'd all seen Rekil's suggestion coming.

The shopkeeper inspected them a little closer, taking in their weapons, attire and accumulation of cuts and bruises. "Maybe you can," he agreed, "A group of eight dendrid were seen heading this way. They'll be here shortly after dawn."

For the next few seconds there was absolute silence, then the village became a hive of activity.

* * * * *

Working for The Dark Horse provided both men with quite a lot of opportunities. Granted, a lot of these opportunities weren't exactly considered legal and the main allure for them was not the hope of cultivating a diverse work portfolio, but rather the chance to do what they truly excelled at. In most cases this involved inflicting pain on others.

And thus the purpose for their presence in the tavern was easily deduced. They were intent on having a meeting with one of its occupants. Both bore the title "enforcer" with pride, so obviously their concept of what a meeting entails isn't exactly the norm.

They pushed their way through the publicans and merrymakers, sitting themselves down at a table. This wasn't where their meeting was to take place. Instead this was where the preliminary threatening stares would be given from.

Welbh finished yet another drink before looking up, it wouldn't do him any harm to take his time; he had all night to celebrate. Two extremely large men caught his eye, as they seemed to be staring right at him. To be certain he gestured toward himself and cocked his head to one side in askance. Both men nodded and resumed their intense glares. Either one could probably have snapped him in half, but they wouldn't have a chance if he could get them somewhere less crowded.

Even so, he was happy to see them now. If they'd intended to kill him he wouldn't see them at all. Which meant the current likelihood was they'd just break his arm, maybe his leg. This wasn't exactly an uplifting thought but Welbh wasn't exactly sober.

He called for another, fully aware that his apparent carelessness was infuriating the two thugs. Giving them a mock salute he chuckled softly into his ale, not currently at his best.

It took him a while to notice that someone had sat down at his table, and a while longer for him to recognise said person. Lila sat across from him, looking less threatening than usual. Wearing a dress and make-up, she was a far cry from the cold assassin of their other encounters. In the state he was in, Welbh decided it would be best to voice these thoughts. "You know," he remarked, "You're much pretty than usual tonight." It had sounded so much better in his head.

Despite this Lila smiled. "Let's go somewhere," she said warmly.

Her smile actually dazzled him. Almost enabling him to forget that she was an assassin. Before he could think of a suave response she was knocked off her seat.

The "enforcers" seated themselves across from him. "We work for The Dark Horse," one of them declared. The other gave a mean grunt.

Welbh shrugged casually, "That's unfortunate."

The more articulate enforcer smiled, "For you, maybe." The other managed to nod in agreement with both menace and vigour. This is actually quite difficult to achieve, especially if you want to avoid looking ridiculous.

"You see," the talkative thug elaborated, "there are many things in this world that seem unattainable to the ordinary man. Occasionally the need for such an unattainable item will be far more pressing than abiding by the law and that's where The Dark Horse comes in. Now it looks to us that somebody neglected to inform you and you're trying to take business that rightfully belongs to him. That just doesn't sit well with us, does it Harold?"

The other thug, whose was actually Bertram but felt it wasn't imposing enough, shook his head once more.

"We think it would be best for all involved if you stopped." This last sentence dripped with menace.

Welbh was slightly oblivious to all this, but mostly because he simply hadn't been listening. "I think you two gentlemen need drinks," he waved a barmaid over and two new flagons joined his own on the table.

Never quick to turn down a free drink, both of them sipped their drinks nonchalantly. After a moment they spoke again, "We feel it would be best if you hand over the contracts no-"

He didn't get to finish. This was due to Welbh, in his infinite wisdom, interrupting him. "Hold that thought."

Lila was leaving and as she passed through the door she turned for an instant and waved, beckoning him. Welbh got up and made for the door. The enforcers stared after him, this time it was in disbelief; nobody treated them this way.

Welbh burst through the door and out into the cold night beyond. Looking up and down the street didn't reveal any sign of his brother's favourite messenger.

Drunken stupor is the case behind a lot of erratic, and sometimes stupid, behaviour. It is the reason for missing road signs, house fires stemming from alcohol -induced comas while cooking, impromptu haircuts/piercings/tattoos, etc. etc. It's also behind a craze involving sheep, racing and fireworks that has gripped Fardash in recent weeks. Welbh's case of it wasn't that bad and as such, neither were the penalties.

Still, forgetting that your standing in front of a door isn't the most ingenious move. Welbh was quite surprised when it swung open, caught him in the small of the back and sent him sprawling.

The two enforcers stormed out into the street, looked up and down before spotting him at their feet on the pavement. Then, they joined him, only difference being they wouldn't be getting up again.

Welbh dragged himself up, but he was too late; blood already stained his garments. The thugs had rather inconsiderately allowed their necks to be opened and spurt blood, to the ruination of his both his favourite jacket and trousers. Nonetheless he was glad it wasn't him down there, making a mess of the street.

Lila stepped into view. Although she still wore the dress, her friendly demeanour had vanished. "Your safety is your brother's concern," she stated blandly.

Welbh looked from the deceased thugs to the knives lodged in their throats. He gave his own blood-stained garments a quick look, before finally moving onto Lila. Mustering up all the courage he could, and with enough alcohol he could muster quite a lot, he realised he was drunk enough not to care. "Still what to go somewhere?" he asked without regard for his own safety.

She glared at him icily.

An ear-piercingly high scream forced Welbh to clutch at his head. A woman had walked out of the bar and drawn entirely the wrong conclusion from the scene before her.

Welbh almost turned around to explain, then realised he must be absolutely inebriated to even contemplate doing any such thing.

As luck would have it she didn't get a proper look at him before he ran, later informing the police that the murderer had been a "blood-stained person".

* * * * *

Somewhere near the eastern edge of Ghostwood, there's a clearing among the trees. However, the clearing itself is insignificant.

In this clearing there's a small hill, but the hill itself is of no consequence. Atop this hill though, there happens to be a doorway.

The most remarkable thing about this doorway isn't that it's eight foot high and made of stone, or that it's lined and covered in glowing runes. The truly outstanding thing about this gate, is that it's one of the few ways to enter the Shadowlands. Also outstanding, was that some idiot had left it open.

Looking through the doorway, three things were immediately visible. One was what looked like a banquet hall. Another was the bones of the shadows, completely picked clean by the third, and most noticeable, thing: the Drakold.

The Drakold moved toward the gate. The dead shadows had proven quite a substantial meal, and its movements were now slow and content. However, it couldn't be said to be fulfilled.

Its mind kept returning to that blood on the wooden pole. That sweet, sweet, exotic substance plagued its every waking thought. It wanted and needed and craved and longed for more. There was no alternative.

It could still smell it, permeating the air.

Following the trail of blood had led it here, and now was going to lead it further, the Drakold eyed the gate uneasily; it didn't smell right. It was living and yet made of stone. Exactly the opposite of what it should be.

Yet the trail went beyond it. Therefore, the Drakold was obligated to pursue it, even into the strange land beyond the gate.

As the ten foot tall creature emerged in Ghostwood, the masonry of the gate came crashing down around it. There would be no going back.

New sights, sounds and smells greeted the monster, but overpowering all of these was the scent of its prey. The Drakold took a rapacious whiff, then followed the scent into Ghostwood.

This was far different from the clearing and the hill within. For this, well, this was significant.

Chapter 29

Vantix was decidedly restless; he hadn't slept at all last night. In fact he hadn't gotten any actual sleep for a while. Apparent from when he was deprived of consciousness against his will – which obviously didn't count because he didn't get the same refreshed feeling afterward – it had been a while since he'd had an honest to gods night's slumber.

Obviously part of the reason he didn't want to sleep was the nightmare but there was more to it than that; he also barely felt the need anymore. Though he was currently agitated and jittery, there were few other detrimental effects. Had he decided to miss out on this much sleep a month ago, he'd probably lack the strength to keep his mouth closed and be swimming in drool.

Sleep wasn't the only thing he hadn't felt the need for recently. His appetite and the need to blink had deserted him entirely.

The others had set about making preparations as soon as the dendrid's arrival time had been confirmed. They had something planned, something that would ensure things were back to normal soon enough.

It was only after these preparations had begun that the subject of where they actually were had come up.

Ghostwood is vast, stretching into at least four different provinces. Although they'd kind of taken it for granted that they'd still be in Fardash, they were wrong. Somehow they'd managed to cross into Derranferd.

The town had sent for help but it was unlikely they'd receive any. In an attempt to stop discrimination the dendrid had been made citizens of Derranferd, meaning the villagers had to claim there were bandits terrorizing them. Even if they got any help, it was extremely unlikely it'd arrive in time. Until the group arrived they'd been like an honest gambler in Port Daichwater; in danger, out of luck, and likely to be dead in the morning.

As such, it was easy to see why they'd been so keen on Rekil's offer of aid. In return for free equipment, accommodation for several nights and food, they let the villagers convince them to undertake the task Incognito was already paying them to complete. Rekil had attempted to offer their help for free, but the rest of the group overruled him. Altruism just wasn't their forte.

The majority of the group were hidden in houses lining the road the dendrid would come in on. The exception to this rule, Farack was hidden out on one of the rooftops. A few hours had been given to him for sleep and then he'd been thrust atop this roof. To be fair, it was because he had a special task to perform. However, he didn't see why he had to be lookout as well.

Vantix had watched ten minutes earlier when the sun rose and now he remained vigilant. This was it, there was no time for hesitation or anything of its sort. He had to stay focused and get the job done.

The garments Rekil had given him still covered up his scales. None of the villagers had seen his skin's deterioration and he'd like to keep it that way. At least until he'd reacquired his soul.

Anybody who lost all their friends because they suddenly became a genius, had to walk home naked because somebody stole their clothes, or were forced to recite poetry to them by an overbearing parent, can tell you of the need which drove Vantix on. It isn't a complex, elaborate or even obscure need. He simply needed to be normal again.

His friend's mangled attempt at cawing directed his attention to the road. The dendrid were about to enter the street.

On the roof above him, Farack eyed the dendrid nervously. Even from up there it was abundantly clear they were on edge. They'd probably expected a representative of the townsfolk to meet them at the entrance and ask them to walk around in return for supplies. Unfortunately, this town didn't have any extra supplies to give.

Reaching the midway point in the street, the creatures were surprised to see a rhadon appear on the rooftops to their left. His arms flared up and flames soared from them.

The flames headed in two different directions, neither of them at the dendrid. Instead it headed for the opposite ends of the street, igniting the two pools of oil that lay there and cutting off any escape routes. There would be no running.

Although some of the roofs had tiles, the preference here seemed to be thatch, meaning Farack had a small problem. Thatch roofing is a major inconvenience for rhadons. Whilst hiding he had managed to keep his blaze in check, however, as the dendrid wheeled on him his concentration slipped, causing a few stray sparks to drift down to the thatch.

Sliding down from where he stood, Farack made a flawless landing. Vantix emerged from the building almost immediately and stood at his friend's side. They drew their swords.

From all along the street members of Incognito's hunting party emerged, finally ready to earn their 200 crowns . Despite a clear effort from Grelow, Rekil still looked the most impressive. The vampire's silk suit and cloak came nowhere close to Rekil's buffed and polished armour. He looked every bit the commander his father had been.

For some strange reason, Slyra seemed to have stuck a flower on the rim of her pointy hat. Since Vantix was pretty sure the dendrid didn't have an irrational fear of floral arrangements, he guessed she'd opted for the flower to brighten up her outfit or something along those lines.

One by one the group drew their weapons, nodding determinately to each other. Rekil had given quite an inspirational speech last night about what these creatures had done and what they deserved to have done back to them, though it had mostly gone over Vantix's head. He'd been staring at his scales again; they seemed to be appearing all over his skin. The entire effect was somewhat nauseating.

The soul-stealers turned to face their foes. One of them caught Vantix's eye. It had a strange sort of belt, unlike anything its fellows wore. To be exact, his eye was drawn to a certain wooden box on said belt. The realisation of what it contained was almost instantaneous.

With a slight smile tugging at the corners of his lips, he raised both swords and sprinted at the creature.

* * * * *

"What in the name of the gods is going on here?" Trune whispered incredulously.

The preparations for war had meant an increase in the amount of soldiers each province was taking in. It also meant these soldiers had between little and nothing to do outside of the expected training exercises. As he'd been pestering his superiors incessantly it'd been decided that Trune would be sent to investigate a call for help from the village of Oakhead. Normally a call for help wouldn't even be acknowledged by the king's soldiers, but Trune's constant request for orders and relentless insistence that he was waiting with alacrity to show his commitment to the nation had quickly fostered a desire to get him out of the barracks so they could enjoy a moment of peace.

Staring down at his new uniform once again, which was blue and yellow just like the rest of the Derranferd army's, he felt as if he'd finally made it somewhere worth being. These feelings were brushed aside as smoke caught his attention. It drifted into the air far above the village, indicating that there was some degree of unpleasantness afoot. He frowned, though eager to prove himself he'd been almost certain this detail was a waste of time.

He left his horse and strolled into town, sword at the ready. Having not experienced actual combat yet, it was probably fair to say he was out of his depth. Amongst the new influx of recruits he was easily the most enthusiastic swordsman, though that was nothing compared to actual combat experience.

Deserted is the manner in which he found the town, not a single person to be seen. All doors and windows were shut, meaning he couldn't tell if there was anybody inside. Knocking on the windows didn't elicit a response anywhere he checked. Getting the impression he'd find

247

something grim, he set off toward the source of the smoke.

A wall of flame blocked his path. That was just typical; the only street worth investigating was beyond his reach. Through the flames he spotted several of the thatch rooftops alight.

Intent on calling out, possibly waking anybody who happened to be asleep in the fiery death-traps, his words caught in his throat at the scene before him. What looked like a group of mercenaries, seemed to be in some sort of skirmish with a band of dendrid.

His eyes settled on one of the mercenaries. Or rather, his attire. With his mouth forming an expression of surprise, he recognised it. This armour belonged to a commander of the Fardashian army.

This complicated things to no extreme. It meant this wasn't just a random group of bandits or mercenaries; this was a Fardashian war party.

The rhadon with them explained the fire, and the dendrid were clearly attempting to save the village. This was a declaration of war.

Stumbling over his own feet, Trune sprinted back toward his horse. He had to get out of here; to warn someone of the imminent threat Fardash posed. If they were already burning villages down then there obviously wasn't much time

Mounting his horse, he spurred it into a gallop back the way he'd come.

* * * * *

Between the two immense walls of flame, the fight seemed to be going well. Although they didn't have the numerical advantage Incognito had originally intended,

248

the two dendrid missing almost evened it up. They weren't exactly thinking about this though, as they were understandably preoccupied.

Kerchiefs adorned the lower faces of all those present, protecting them from the soul stealing breath of their foes. The only exception was Vantix, who didn't need it.

Forced to rely on his sword and shield, Farack's vexation increased with every blow that was thwarted. Given the chance he'd have burnt this monstrosity to a crisp, but it hadn't any intention of handing him that opportunity. The creature's constant onslaught meant it required all his skill in order to defend himself. Parrying a downward thrust, he used his shield to ram his opponent. Unfortunately, it was largely a futile endeavour. Although it would have wounded a lesser man, this wasn't even a man. Pressed back by another barrage of blows, Farack realised this was going to require something special.

Across from him, Slyra and Cermus were having the same problem. Since neither of them was an accomplished swordsman, it would have made far more sense to partner either of them with Elik or Grelow. Currently the two of them were just about able to withstand the monster's advances. Slyra's efforts at muttering incantations were constantly interrupted by the need to defend herself. Her decision to wear armoured leathers in favour of her mini robe stood to her; dents already covered them from she'd been unable to evade her opponent's attacks. She was trying to manoeuvre herself away from the creature, desperately searching for the time to cast some sort of spell.

To be frank, Cermus wasn't up to much. Rekil had told him to stay out of the fight but the little shadow had been adamant; he wanted to be like them.

Osca and Sam were faring a lot better. Combined the two of them were more than a match for this swine, almost toying with it as they prodded and poked it backward. Sam went left and Osca right, not leaving any room for a sidestep. Parrying Sam's thrust, it just had time to throw an arm up in front of Osca's. The two of them exchanged a quick glance. The gash running down the monster's arm signalled one thing; it didn't have much longer.

Vantix watched as the creature skirted to one side, a smile tugging at the corners of his mouth. The first moments of this encounter had been spent testing his opponent, watching and learning its reactions. Now it was time to inflict some pain.

Not only had he anticipated his foe's evasion, but also its intended reprisal. As the blade came toward him, he ducked under it and planted one of his short swords into his opponent's open left flank. For a moment he thought that was it, that it was over. Almost toppling, the dendrid recovered in time and yanked his sword out. Flinging his sword across the road, the wound stretched and blood poured from it. Yet the dendrid remained on its feet. Vantix tossed his other sword from hand to hand casually; he wasn't sure whether to be pleased or upset with how much he was enjoying this.

Arsenius' curved blade crashed against the dendrid's serrated sword. Unfortunately he momentarily let his guard down, giving the dendrid a chance to grab him. Its pale, twisted features neared his own and its rank breath washed over him. It was the first time he'd ever thanked the gods that he'd chosen to wear a kerchief, but it was well deserved. Not one single piece of that oblivion-inducing breath reached his nostrils. Lashing out with his feet, he slipped from the fiend's grasp. Spinning away, Arsenius readied himself once more. It wasn't over yet.

Rekil is by nature an archer. That being so, the close quarters combat here honestly didn't suit him. It was clear he wasn't exactly in his comfort zone with his axe. Not that it matter much, the creature only just outclassed him.

An ear bounced along the road several times before coming to a halt, a clear indication that somebody very nearby was about to become incredibly hard of hearing. That person was a dendrid who'd had the misfortune to come up against Elik. Wounds bled all over and soaked its ragged garments. In fact it was a miracle it was still standing.

Contrary to popular belief, vampires have hearts, souls, and will eventually face eternal damnation. The trick is getting them to die. Which is why Grelow's scuffle with the dendrid was almost unfair. With his kerchief blocking his nose and his sword preventing damage to his heart, he was almost untouchable. His clothes were slightly shredded but you can't win them all.

Osca and Sam had the creature in the palm of their hands. It was backed up against one of the houses, desperately trying to make some progress against them. However, it was far too late. As they advanced upon it, the dendrid let out a strange hissing sound.

Vantix was truly horrified. Not that the other dendrid had joined in the hissing, only that he could understand their strange dialect. This newfound ability prompted him to end this with renewed vigour.

Sam cried out as a desperate swipe from the abnormal opponent caught his shoulder. Thinking this was its chance, the fiend leapt at him. A moment later its body crashed to the ground. No more than a second afterward,

251

this was joined by its head. Osca had decapitated it mid-lunge. Leaving Sam to recuperate, he made toward another scream.

Elik closed in for the kill, taking the offensive and bringing his sword around in a wide arc. Inexplicably, this time his foe outmanoeuvred him. With an astute shuffle inside his guard, it stretched out a leg and kicked his sword from his grasp. The creature closed in, bringing its sword around diagonally.

Too close to elude the swipes, it seemed his only option was up. His cloak billowed out behind him as two wings emerged. They flapped once, throwing him high into the air and beyond the reach of his hideous adversary. As he landed, nobody spared the time to notice how practical wings were. They could really benefit from acquiring some.

The dendrid wheeled on him slowly; it seemed appropriate. Besides, he didn't even have a sword; what possible harm could he do?

Evidently quite a lot. Before his villager-massacring opposition even turned around, Elik let out a roar. A deep, deafening roar. Exactly the type of roar, that picks dendrid up and tosses them through the front of a nearby burning building whose flaming masonry then comes crashing down on top of the unfortunate dendrid. Had all this happened in some sort of gladiatorial arena it would have won a standing ovation. As it was nobody even noticed.

Arsenius ducked under his adversary's guard, sword flashing straight across its chest. The tattered rags fell away as blood poured from the wound, giving Arsenius a rather unpleasant view of a heart which just happened to be three sizes too small. The tanned Nospac elf immediately found someone else to help.

This new opponent parried Arsenius' first blow, finally giving Farack the opportunity he'd been waiting for. His arms burst into flames that he immediately channelled in the opposing fiend's general direction. Within seconds of Arsenius backing off, the creature was engulfed in flame. The heat increased, reducing the monster to cinder and leaving almost no trace of its existence. Arsenius patted Farack on the back and nodded toward the others; they could probably use their help.

Looking around, Farack spotted something that made him feel a pang of regret. Cermus lay on the ground, eyes wide and mouth forming a perfect circle. The little shadow had drawn his last breath.

Slyra was pretty high on the list of prime candidates for assistance. Without Cermus she didn't have a hope of fending off the dendrid. Certainly not without magic anyway. Diving away from a downward swipe, she lost her hat in the process. She tumbled to her feet immediately, but the dendrid was even faster still. Its foot came across, sweeping her off her feet.

This was pretty easy to distinguish from the romantic sort of "sweeping her off her feet", mainly because the romantic sort didn't involve hideous soul-stealing monsters. The romantic kind also didn't usually involve landing on a dusty road either.

Slyra lay in the dirt, paralysed with fear. Able to do naught but watch, as the dendrid raised its sword high and......

...........Osca cut its arm off. Both sword and arm clattered to the ground, leaving a rather surprised look on the monster's face.

Slyra smiled her thanks. Osca smiled back and offered his hand. A moment later his hand went to his chest and his smile turned into a grimace of absolute agony.

253

For Osca had made a rookie mistake. Cutting off one arm isn't enough, it just makes them angry. A fact made clear by the taloned fingers, currently protruding from his abdomen. He gave Slyra a rather quizzical look, as if he was surprised by what had happened.

Slyra's eyes went white with fury as Osca fell to his knees, energy flying down her arm and exploding from her fingertips. She didn't need any words, her intent was enough.

Although it couldn't be seen, the energy picked the dendrid up and suspended it in the air as the fiend reached out, searching in vain for something to grab.

Slyra clicked her fingers. The monstrosity's remaining arm snapped to the accompaniment of a wail of terror audible several provinces over. The witch was oblivious to this as she picked her hat out of the dirt. Clicking her fingers again caused both legs to break simultaneously. The creature moaned and whimpered, unaccustomed to the terror that gripped it. Her mouth forming into a sneer, the young witch clicked her fingers a third and final time. Every single bone left in the terrified soul-stealers body cracked, piercing and jutting out of its skin in horrific positions before she let it drop. A dead, mangled, mess was the most accurate way to describe the heap of blood and bones that landed in the road.

The whites faded from her eyes and Slyra stared at the bloody mess. She seemed confused by it, as if it had been beyond her control. Then she hurried over to Osca.

Vantix danced around the monster's angry swipes. It couldn't hit him; he moved with a newfound speed. Spinning away from a blow, he dragged his sword across the back of the creature's legs, bringing it to its knees.

Rekil lashed out with all the force he could muster, sending its sword out of his opposition's hand. There's a lot to be said for ending things quickly, which was exactly what Rekil intended to do, but the old soldier wasn't going to get the chance. Bringing the axe up, he had the wind knocked out of him.

His axe fell from his hand as he wrestled with the demon. It was fast, but unused to hand-to-hand combat. Still, its clawed hands could do plenty of damage once given the chance.

Punching its monstrous face, he managed to knock it off. The dendrid rose to its feet, wiping away a trickle of blood that Rekil had caused. It lunged at him and he reached for the nearest possible weapon; an arrow from his quiver.

As his adversary attempted to wrap its clawed arms around him, he rammed the arrow into its head behind the ear. It didn't have any major immediate effect besides slowing the creature down. Exerting a monumental amount of pressure, he forced the arrow deep into the head, instantly killing his assailant.

Whilst picking up his axe, he saw something quite disturbing. Vantix's opponent was on its knees, unarmed, and the thoroughly disturbed youth was stabbing it repeatedly. Rekil shook his head, they'd need to have a little chat later.

Many of the others had gathered around Osca, so Rekil decided to join them. Mainly because the alternative was talk to Grelow.

The dendrid crumpled, dead by all standards. Vantix removed his sword one final time. That had gotten ever so slightly out of hand. Looking around, he realised the fight was over. The only dendrid showing any vitals was the one desperately trying to push Grelow off its neck. It went still as the vampire pulled away, smacking his lips.

Vantix heard him mumble "exquisite" before turning back to his fallen foe. He needed his soul back.

Osca was kneeling on the ground, his shirt and hands soaked in his own blood. Breathing was becoming an extreme effort and blood was trickling out of the corner of his mouth. The others, apart from Vantix and Grelow, knelt around him.

Farack nudged Slyra. "Isn't there anything you can do?" he asked quietly.

The witch shook her head. "I've already closed the wounds, but I can't fix the internal damage." Her face set in a grim expression, "He doesn't have long."

Osca exhaled heavily. He was completely numb, everything sounded and felt distant. *I can't believe it ends like this,* was his only thought, but he couldn't seem to voice it. "Can we get you anything?" Slyra asked tenderly.

Osca's head lolled forward and the group gasped, but he wasn't ready to leave yet. Looking at the ground and speaking laboriously , "I really don't want to die. I want to go home. I want to see my father. B-but I'll settle for a kiss."

Slyra leaned forward and placed a small kiss upon his forehead. He was dead before she pulled away.

Vantix was busy rifling through the deceased dendrid's few possessions. Trying to get the box free, he was interrupted by a tap on his shoulder. Grelow pointed out an item on the fiend's belt. "Would you mind handing me that?"

Not really paying much attention, Vantix handed him the aforementioned item.

It was then he finally got a hold of the wooden box. Paying no attention to the elaborate carvings, he released the clasp and lifted the lid.

Light flew from it and engulfed him. He felt it cover him, soaking into every single aspect of his physical being. It seemed quite obvious he'd finally regained his soul.

That was it; his soul finally his once more. He was free to return to normality with no fears of getting assaulted by nightmarish creatures, or worries about whether or not he'd change into a monster. His life went on, filled to the brim with normality.

Vantix's visions are distressingly inaccurate.

*   *   *   *   *

"You're certain, Private Trune?" his superior asked him incredulously. It couldn't be happening.

"Positive, lieutenant," Trune replied respectfully, "I observed a Fardashian war party burn Oakhead to the ground. They attacked while the people were sleeping, the act of a coward."

"Then the king needs to know," lieutenant Hawthorne replied, "Take whatever personal belongings you require, you leave as soon as possible."

In the next couple of moments, the lieutenant got him the finest horse available, promoted him, gave him the few provisions he'd need for the short trip and gave him an order for the king's eyes only.

For the king was the only person who could know; he had many enemies who'd use it to their advantage. Probably to spread dissent and nurture thoughts that the king wasn't a strong enough leader. Which meant he valued loyalty above all else. Who knew how he'd react to the Fardash's betrayal?

Trune smiled to himself. He was fairly sure it meant another promotion for him. As the horse raced toward the city, one thing was certain; he was definitely going places.

Chapter 30

It was well into the afternoon by the time Incognito appeared. One minute he wasn't there, the next he was strolling down the street toward them.

In what seemed an effort to appear less conspicuous, he'd ditched the feature-concealing cloak in favour of expensive looking travelling silks. Like a more practical version of Grelow's attire. He eyed the site of the skirmish with an amused smile.

The fires had long since been extinguished and most of the damages were superficial, apart from two houses. One of these had crumbled because of Elik, the other had simply burned for too long. As such, the villagers had already set about making the repairs needed to make their homes habitable once more. Rekil and Elik had offered their help, an offer which the villagers had been quick to take advantage of.

Only moments beforehand, they'd lowered the shrouded bodies of both Osca and Cermus into separate graves. A silence had been held in honour of the departed, but few of them dallied there. Although saddened by the loss of their friend, the majority of them didn't feel inclined to depress themselves by hanging around graves.

Rekil on the other hand, didn't seem bothered by it. He'd not only kept a short vigil on the graves, but also built a small memorial to everyone they'd lost over the course of their travels before going to help the villagers rebuild.

Apart from Rekil and Elik, who were busy tending to the townsfolk's every whim, the entire group looked up in surprise at Incognito's sudden appearance. However, Grelow was the only one to rush forward and seek a quiet conference with their employer.

The vampire was wearing a thick hood to shield himself from the sun. As has been said before, it wouldn't have reduced him to ash or any of that superstitious nonsense. It'd just leave him with an excruciatingly painful rash. In fact, the only reason nonsense of this kind circulated was because the truth was so ordinary.

Of course, that being said a stake through the heart would kill them. Then again, a stake through the heart would kill anything. Unless, of course, it possessed several hearts.

The rest of the group watched curiously as Grelow removed something from the folds of his cloak. They were too far away to see it clearly and the same went for their ability to hear the conversation. A few stray words managed to make it over the hustle and bustle of the village being rebuilt and land upon their ears.

"....as soon as.."

"..three days.."

Since these phrases were of absolutely no use to them the group returned to their own business.

Farack turned to Vantix, instantly stifling the thought that his friend still looked as soulless as ever. "What do you think they're talking about?"

"Me," Vantix shrugged back.

"Everything isn't about you," Arsenius called across.

"It should be," Vantix sighed, "It might be more interesting."

Farack surmised that they wouldn't get any good theories about the Grelow -Incognito discussion from Vantix. Turning to ask Slyra, he was just in time to see her rubbing her eyes. Immediately the nature of his inquiry shifted. "Are you okay?"

Slyra tried to smile and nod but she didn't quite pull it off.

"It wasn't your fault," Farack intoned.

"Don't, she replied firmly, "You know it was. He saved me," she sniffed, "and I couldn't save him."

For a time Farack had been under the impression that Slyra had feelings for Osca. Now, he saw it for what it really was: guilt. "Trust me," the rhadon said slowly, "These sort of things happen, you can't save everyone."

Slyra honestly couldn't be sure if he'd been trying to comfort her or not, as she didn't feel any better. Still, she nodded uncertainly and gave him a slight wave of acknowledgement. It would take time.

It was several moments more before Incognito decided to grace them with his presence, Grelow in tow. Their employer smiled at them. "Firstly, I'd like to thank all of you for the parts you've played. Secondly, it's understandable that you'd all like to be paid immediately but due to," he glanced sideways at Grelow, "unforeseen additional costs, you'll have to meet me in Ghostwood castle in three days. In the meantime, the locals have informed me they'd like to throw you a banquet."

As they'd done quite a bit of damage to the homes of all those currently living in the town, this came as quite the surprise. A few members of the group could be heard say, "They what?"

Incognito waved his hands defensively. "Okay so maybe I informed them they'd like to throw you a banquet, but there'll be food, drinking, music and dancing galore. So I suspect you'll all have a good time. Remember, Ghostwood castle in three days." He then departed, just as suddenly as he'd appeared.

* * * * *

"The king shall see you now."

Jandelk gestured to Welbh, indicating that he accompany him inside. He was Royal Negotiator after all.

The chamber they now entered was rather nice. Spaciously furnished, bookcases and tapestries adorned the walls and a roaring fire warmed the room from the large fireplace. The setting sun's light streamed in through a massive window that offered a magnificent view of the city of Angelous. In front of this was a desk, but King Audron didn't sit there. He was gazing lovingly out the window; in this light Angelous looked everything its name meant, heavenly.

In contrast to Jandelk, Audron wasn't a big man. He was small and skinny, with a clean shaven face and grey-blonde hair nestled beneath an oversized crown. Not exactly the type of king who led his men into battle and was renowned for his bravery in every conquest. No, Audron ruled out of sheer ability to govern. He turned toward them as the two declined an offer of drinks.

"Ah, Jandelk," he smiled, "it has been quite a long time."

"Indeed, old friend," the king of Fardash said in reply.

262

So this is what it's like among kings, Welbh thought to himself. He didn't like it; it seemed uncomfortable and rigid, as if both men were scrutinizing not just each other but also him. Nor had he liked their exchange. Audron's smile was most definitely fake and he'd visible tensed upon hearing the word friend. It seemed as if the men were testing each other, looking for any signs of weakness.

Being the amazing improviser that he was, Welbh desperately searched for anything to comment on, anything to fill the everlasting silence between the two kings. Eventually his gaze settled on the only painting in the room. "That's an interesting painting," he said vaguely.

Audron stared at the painting, almost as if seeing it for the first time. "Yes, it is," he concluded, before adding quietly, "Most curious."

"How so?" Jandelk asked politely.

"It's nothing important," Audron replied dismissively, "Now to what do I owe the pleasure of your company?"

Jandelk didn't mince his words. "We're willing to forgive and forget what happened in Southrook," he proposed, "if you're willing to negotiate. We think it would be mutually beneficial to form an alliance."

For several moments, Audron just stared ahead, mumbling the words "mutually beneficial", "forget" and "alliance" over and over again. "Tell me," he said eventually, "Do you know what that painting is called?" His question was directed at Welbh, who shook his head. "It's called The Sin of Langora and shows in painfully clear strokes, how the people of Langora were punished when they murdered the followers of the Goddess Archtex. If you look closely you can even see the individual people being swallowed up by flame. An eye

263

for an eye as it goes." He paused here for quite some time.

Jandelk's patience was beginning to wear thin, Audron was acting strange and he'd rather sign the treaties and get out of here. "I see. Tell me; is any of this relevant to our negotiations?"

Audron let out a loud humourless laugh, completely devoid of all mirth. It ended abruptly and he said in tones of undisguised anger, "This is relevant because you made the same mistake they did."

Although unsure as to what they'd actually done to warrant this strange behaviour from the king, Welbh had been listening and got the wrong end of the stick. He began to back away slowly, variations of the same thought repeating in his head over and over: *Audron thinks he's a god! This crazy fool thinks he's a god!* You did not mess with people who had delusions of self-deity. It was suicide.

He was wrong though, Audron was in fact referring to the other part of his explanation.

Jandelk was the next person to speak. He simply said, "What?"

"Don't deny it!" Audron shouted, "I know what you did in Oakhead."

"What happened in Oakhead?"

"If you intend to persist with this tiresome facade of ignorance, then fine," a wave of his hand brought a young man into the room, "but you cannot deny the facts. Sergeant Trune here, was recently promoted. Would you care to tell them why, Sergeant Trune?"

The young sergeant, who couldn't have been more than nineteen, cleared his throat and stated, "I observed a Fardashian war-party, who I recognised by their armour, burning Oakhead to the ground and murdering citizens

264

of Derranferd. I deemed it my duty to ride here and inform the king of the imminent threat Fardash posed."

There was silence for a moment before Audron spoke again. "I told you the attack wasn't us and you go behind my back to do this. Did you think I wouldn't find out?"

"We didn't do it," Jandelk managed lamely. Things, admittedly, were not looking good for them.

"Really," Audron sneered, "how original. It must have been the other Fardash."

Suddenly the room was filled with armed soldiers, each grabbing either Welbh or Jandelk to restrain them.

"My heartfelt felicitations gentlemen," Audron said coldly, "You've successfully started a war." He turned to the guards. "Take them away," he ordered.

It was at this moment that Welbh realised his whole plan was up in flames. There would be no vast quantities of wealth, no smuggling operations with him at the head. If he was lucky he'd spend the rest of his life in the confines of a dungeon, something that didn't appeal to him in the slightest.

As they were being escorted from the room, Welbh reached inside his left sleeve and grasped the hilt of a sword fastened to his flank. With his other hand, he threw a small capsule at the floor. It smashed immediately, emitting a large cloud of smoke. His shirt tore as he wrenched the sword from its sheath and through his clothing.

Smoke clouded the view of all those present as he brought the sword round in a wide sweep.

* * * * *

The man known as Incognito strolled nonchalantly through Ghostwood. Although this was something

265

normal people tended to avoid, he didn't mind it. The swirling mists and strange trees intrigued him, meaning he actually enjoyed the occasional stroll through this idyllic forest.

For Incognito had no regrets, no people he missed and no unfinished business. Both his parents and his grandparents were all alive, so the creatures here had absolutely nothing to work with. Other supporting players may have come into his life and also made their exits, sometimes in exceedingly grisly manners, but he was at peace with it. Life was neither an endless struggle nor a delightful fandango. It simply was.

Whistling an upbeat tune, he ambled along in the direction of the rendezvous point. She'd be waiting with horses for the two of them. It was actually hard not to smile, his plan was coming together almost exactly as he'd anticipated.

Certain people would point out that Grelow had refused to relinquish his property, but certain people didn't know that's what he'd expected. Name any of them, Grelow, Vantix, Rekil, they were all so easy to read. Predicting their every reaction was a cinch, all down to the psychology of the individual. That being said, everyone was easy to read when you knew their mind.

Surprising as it may seem, Incognito was genuine about paying them in three days. They'd done well, earned their paltry rewards. An elaborate scheme to have all murdered for the sake of discretion would just be stupid. It'd probably take time, effort, an even larger group of mercenaries and be far more expensive than just paying them. And then he'd have to hire even further mercenaries to shush the first crowd and a third to shush them and so on; an endless cycle of ambushes and sky-rocketing costs. Better to just wait the three days.

By his reckoning the prize was worth waiting an eternity for. With it in his grasp things would change; Ballisca would be free of the old divisions; every species would be treated equally and respected; no more famines, drought or senseless deaths. A world of altruism, prosperity and unity. A perfect world.

Then there were bodies all around him. Bodies in white armour under white cloaks. They didn't belong in this dank, treacherous forest. If anything, they looked like the guardians for some kind of extremely religious, mountain dwelling cult.

Normally Incognito would have drawn his sword in a flash, but he was in no danger here. The Divine, as these white clad were known, had a reputation for only hunting the wicked and he'd been on his best behaviour of late. Not to mention they owed him a favour. Still, he was quite startled by their sudden appearance.

A woman's voice called out, but he couldn't tell which one of them it came from. "You wouldn't have seen a demonic creature by the name of Vantix around here, would you?" the feminine voice asked.

Not intent on having any sort of conversation with them, Incognito did naught but point over his shoulder. The voice spoke its thanks and the white figures moved on, leaving him alone once more.

As they moved off, he put up his hood. It helped him to think. Pondering the matter for five minutes led to this conclusion. Eventually, The Divine would probably catch up with his merry band and judging from Vantix's complexion on their last encounter, it wouldn't end well. The likelihood was Rekil, Farack and Slyra would campaign to save him but the others would give him to the Divine. Unfortunate as it was, it didn't put a single dent in his plans; his investment was safe for now.

Dismissing these thoughts only took a second. It may have taken longer, had something else not demanded his immediate attention. He unsheathed his sword.

Multiple clicks sounded all around him, making him spin full circle. Figures in armour and cloaks of the darkest black surrounded him, aiming their crossbows at his chest. Not only did he recognise this group, he was also on first name terms with the older members. They hadn't parted on kind terms and as such, he was exceedingly grateful for the hood which shrouded his face.

"We hear there's a demon this way," an incredibly threatening voice announced. The kind of voice that frightens children, sends shivers down the spine and manages to drag a blood soaked extra syllable from every word.

Incognito replied in a voice at a far higher pitch than his own to prevent them from recognising him. "That's true enough."

The man with the threatening voice, or Carl to his friends, was among the most bloodthirsty, fierce, villainous and irascible people Incognito had the displeasure of knowing. He needed a way out of this conversation and away from these people. They went by "The Heretics" and were not renowned for their warm and caring nature. As anybody could have construed by now, these were not nice people.

"I hear this so called demon is travelling with Rekil the merciful," Carl's nightmare inducing voice spat this last name and unofficial title as if they were dirty words. Which just goes to show how The Heretics view those that upset the status quo. One prodigious act of mercy earned people a knife in the belly as far as they were concerned.

Incognito nodded and pointed over his shoulder. To him at least, his life far outweighed theirs.

Carl's voice spoke once more, his tone ice cold. "Thank you very much, Lintous."

Incognito whirled around, cloak flying off his shoulders. They'd said his bloody name! They knew it was him!

His sword already drawn, he leapt through the air at his nearest assailant. The blade sliced through the dark armour, only seconds before fourteen crossbows were fired as one. There was not a single miss.

Incognito/Lintous stood resolute for a minute, as if he still intended to take them on even with his arrow riddled body. Then his sword fell from his hand and his body toppled backward to its final resting place amidst the gnarled roots of the Ghostwood trees.

The Heretics moved off in the direction he'd pointed. Their business with him had been settled once and for all.

Chapter 31

The village of Oakhead certainly knew it's way around festivities. Large tables had been produced and vast quantities of meats, vegetables, fish, desserts and a number of ales placed upon them. Singing and dancing all took place around a roaring fire under the moonlight.

At one such food-laden table, Incognito's hired help enjoyed themselves. The drink was flowing freely, and the majority of them had reached the stage where all food was flawless.

"So," Farack asked no one in particular, "What are you going to do with your 200 crowns ?"

"Spend it," Arsenius replied instantly.

"Really? That's amazing," Slyra returned, emptying yet another tankard of the strongest ale available. In an attempt to stand up, she knocked her chair over before stumbling away groggily.

The others watched her in dismay, she clearly wasn't coping very well. Rekil voiced these thoughts, "She's taking his death pretty hard."

Farack finished the last piece of his meal and excused himself. "She can't seem to draw any conclusion other than it was her fault," the rhadon called over his shoulder. He walked over to Slyra and offer her his hand; without help she'd probably end up asleep in a ditch.

Arsenius turned to Rekil. "So what are you going to do with your share?"

The old warrior shrugged, "The money is nothing more than a bonus for me. Incognito promised me a pardon for my crimes, that was the only incentive I needed." He spat the word "crimes" with unrivalled venom.

It was as if Elik could sense Arsenius's vocal chords beginning to form the question. "Our dear employer promised me information," he declared between sips of his drink.

"Then we have something in common," Arsenius raised his tankard and Elik hit with his own, Arsenius then continued. "He promised me information about the man who killed my family."

At this point Grelow interjected. "Well," the vampire sneered in annoyance, "isn't this just delightful. The drunken wench leaves and I get stuck with three maidens desperate to pour their hearts out and show how good they are by declaring themselves above the money."

Elik was on his feet, sword drawn in an instant. "Don't call her that," he said firmly, "I'll kill you if you go near her."

"Same goes for me," Arsenius growled, "Even the gods won't be able to protect you."

Rekil nodded, showing the ramifications would be the same if it was up to him. Then he gestured for them all to relax and sit down.

In the awkward silence that ensued Grelow announced for all to hear. "I came on this trip for the dendrid blood; it's exquisite," his smile irritated them no end, "Not that anyone's interested."

"We also don't care," Arsenius offered ahead of asking Rekil another question. "Where did Vantix and Sam go?"

Elik pointed vaguely in the direction of the clearing. "Some girls came looking for dance partners when you were relieving yourself earlier."

"Typical," the tanned elf mumbled into his drink. As an afterthought he asked, "Didn't they see his face?"

"He kept his hood up."

Arsenius laughed dryly. "Only he could get a dance while looking like that."

"It's true," Elik nodded, "apart from the whole soulless thing, he's extraordinarily lucky. Who else could escape from the captivity of some underwater amphibian race who mistook him for their deity?"

Rekil nodded, "He told you about that, eh?"

Arsenius rolled his eyes, "He told everyone about it, twice."

"While we're on the subject," Elik turned the conversation his way, "Why hasn't Vantix returned to human form?"

Rekil scratched his chin ponderously. "I've been wondering about that myself and there's a lot to consider. The amount of time it took us to get his soul back, Grelow's bite and so on. I must admit I'm torn between several conclusions. What I hope, is that it's simply taking time. Vampire bites don't affect the dendrid, but now that he's no longer turning into one it could complicate his transformation back to human. That's only another possibility though. What I fear is most likely, is that the damage to his soul is irreversible and that he'll remain the way he is now."

Arsenius shuddered and took a sip from his drink. "I don't envy him."

"There may be other options." Elik pointed out, "Who's to say it won't all just be fin-"

At this point there was a scream. Not the playful laughing screams you sometimes hear at dances; this was a scream of downright terror. The table was knocked over by the force of the four of them getting to their feet.

A girl thundered past them, screaming at the top of her lungs. "That's the girl Vantix was dancing with," Elik said uneasily. There was a certain degree of foreboding in his voice.

"Oh gods," Arsenius gulped nervously. This was not going to end well.

That lone girl running from Vantix had in fact started a stampede. It was all the four warriors could do to stand and avoid being swept away amidst the mass of fleeing people. Men, women and children ran, dragging each other back in their attempts to get away. They were all successful, leaving the group on their own with a view of the cause of the village's distress.

Sam and Vantix were fighting. However this wasn't two friends tousling over a girl, Sam was fighting for hus very survival. Fending Vantix off clearly wasn't going well, as several already bleeding wounds could attest.

This was mostly because he wasn't fighting Vantix anymore. Vantix couldn't move that fast, nor could he shape-shift into a colony of bats and avoid Sam's wild swings. Rolling out of the way of a thrust caused his hood to roll back, exposing his face.

The transformation that had begun when the dendrid took his soul was finally complete. It was only moments ago that'd he'd looked vaguely normal, but now his translucent skin seemed to have mixed with the scales that had been underneath since the Shadowlands. Another factor which added to its overall monstrous

273

effect, was the two massive fangs protruding from its gums. Brave men have faced numerous dendrid and would take one on without a second thought, but even they would run from what Vantix had become. Uniquely horrific is the most accurate way to describe it.

What had happened was simple: initially his dendrid transformation had prevented the vampire bite taking effect, now the bite was preventing him from regaining his humanity.

Arsenius was the first to speak. "What the hell is this? He got his bloody soul back!" On receiving no answer he added, "He looks like some kind of vampire dendrid."

"He is," Rekil replied solemnly.

Arsenius flapped around, looking for some kind of response. He eventually settled on, "WHAT? How is that even possible?"

Rekil shoved Grelow. " Ask this idiot," he hissed, "He bit him." The old warrior drew his axe and thundered over to Sam. It was clear he needed assistance.

Cuts lined Sam's arms and ran across his cheek and forehead. The creature formerly known as Vantix was too fast and he could tell it enjoyed toying with him. Whenever he got a clean swipe under its guard, it seemed to disintegrate and appear behind him. It knew this wouldn't take much longer; he barely had enough strength left to lift his sword.

And then he didn't have to. Rekil, Elik, Arsenius and Grelow were suddenly in there, taking the monster off his hands. Without the fight to keep him going he collapsed, thoroughly exhausted.

The others didn't fare much better. Rekil's forceful swings were put to an abrupt halt as the vampire-dendrid scratched deep into his brow, causing blood to drip into his eyes.

Elik jumped in, sword coming around in a wide arc but it was largely an ineffectual move. The creature dispersed, bats flying out in every direction. Elik span around, ready for it to come down behind him but it anticipated his blow. Instinct caused the wings on Elik to flap out, covering him entirely. A second later the creature landed on top of him, then flew away in frustration at its attack being stopped.

Arsenius could do almost nothing as a cloud of bats latched onto his clothes, his arms, everything. Dragging him up into the air, they paid his squirming attempts at freedom no heed. Shouting and tugging at them proved useless, the tanned elf closed his eyes in expectation. This was it, the end.

Then he felt warmth against his face and singeing the tips of his hair. The next moment he was falling, finally free of the bat's fatal embrace. He crashed to the ground, clothes still smouldering.

Farack paid no attention to any of them, instead focusing on the colony of bats flying overhead. His arms were lit up in proper rhadon fashion and he used these god given abilities to drive the creature back.

What had once been Vantix evidently decided they weren't worth the effort. It fled into the darkness, not content with the present company anymore.

The group was left wounded, humiliated and angry. They also realised they'd have to abscond immediately; the villagers were probably going to show up with torches and pitchforks momentarily and it doesn't pay to underestimate angry peasants. Especially when you've just ruined one of their parties.

The general consensus was that the night could not be saved.

* * * * *

It had been an eventful few hours for the newly crowned King Athrin. To say his father's meeting with the Fardashian representatives had taken a turn for the worst was an understatement; the negotiation of peace treaties simply wasn't supposed to end with a mountain of corpses.

In fact, the only survivors were Sergeant Trune and the Fardashian Royal Negotiator. The latter had miraculously escaped.

Thanks to them, Athrin now sat on the Derranferd throne. They had placed him in a tricky position though; the assassination of his father called for swift and merciless vengeance. However the Fardashian king also lay dead, meaning that retribution wouldn't even be felt by those who'd sanctioned this assassination.

It then occurred to him that without a king Fardash would be in disarray, vulnerable even. Obviously it was the perfect time to strike, yet he didn't want to risk his crown so soon.

It was then he looked up, finally becoming aware of how many people were in the room. Packed to the brim with advisors and well-wishers, all offering fake sympathy and demanding his attention. They awaited his next move.

He raised his hand and was surprised at the silence that descended immediately. Even as a prince he hadn't had this much power. Power to do whatever he wanted, but right now he just wanted to mourn his father, as Prince Balithorn of Fardash was probably doing.

Then it was clear to him. Prince Balithorn wouldn't be mourning his father. Nobody in Fardash knew what had transpired here today.

Although King Athrin sounded nice, Emperor Athrin was much more alluring. Should he start an empire there seemed no more fitting a place than the lands of those who'd killed his father. Balithorn wouldn't see this coming. It was the perfect opportunity. He cleared his throat.

"Ready the army, they march on Fardash immediately."

* * * * *

The fire Farack had started had burned down over half of Ghostwood, leaving the whole eastern portion severely lacking in the tree department. Environmental officers were outraged by this and sent Farack several nasty letters, but he never got around to reading them.

More importantly, the depleted tree line made it far easier for the Drakold to follow its prey. He'd been here, that much was certain. A village lay in the distance, maybe about a mile or so. The Drakold's prey was there; the demonic creature was sure of it.

It was intent on paying the village a visit, until the wind changed. It brought with it a rather distinctive aroma, the one aroma the Drakold craved beyond measure. It was much stronger in the air than it was on the ground, which meant the prey was coming this way.

The Drakold licked its lips delightedly, thinking of him and his delicious blood. Judging by the intensity of the fragrance, very soon the hunted would become a meal for the monster to feast upon. The Drakold began to drool.

All the while, a cloud had been rushing toward it, heralding his approach. Only it wasn't a cloud. As it screeched overhead, the Drakold realised it was a swarm. The intense aroma was coming from this cloud. It was him!

They flew past, back over the forest. The Drakold dismissed the light scent coming from the village and set off after the swarm. It was after the bigger prize.

* * * * *

Welbh hit the ground hard. His face connected with the road first and he swallowed a mouthful of dirt. He didn't get up immediately, instead content with groaning and rubbing his face. The force of impact left him with a burst lip.

His horse had carried on without him and was now several feet up the road. As for the assailant who'd knocked him off his horse, she was busy fixing her hair.

"Can't this wait," Welbh shouted indignantly, "It's been made quite clear that my safety is my brother's concern and in case you haven't noticed, I'm currently trying to make good my escape."

"Your brother is dead," Lila called, finally getting her hair under control.

"What?" he asked in his despair. His plans up in smoke and his brother dead; this definitely wasn't his best day of recent times. It didn't feel real, more like an imagined disaster was trespassing on the plains of his reality.

"He wanted you to have this," Lila handed him a book and as she did so, he noticed how red her eyes were.

278

She'd obviously been crying, which didn't seem in character for her. Welbh didn't comment upon it.

"Everything you need to know is in there," Lila continued, "Lintous was going to do amazing things, Welbh. The world needed him."

Welbh just nodded; Lintous had always set out to accomplish the extraordinary. It'd always set him apart no matter where he went. Yet this was neither the time nor the place for such thoughts. Welbh ran and hopped back on his horse. "Thanks," he shouted over his shoulder as the horse took off, leaving her far behind. He never saw her again.

Chapter 32

When one of your friends has been possessed by a demon there are always several courses of action available. Abandoning them is obviously one, unless they're engaged to your sister and you want to have to hear about it for the rest of your life. Going after them is another, but that usually gets complicated and causes the death of several other friends in the process. Alternatively, you get that group of friends together and stage an intervention, but demons aren't known for respecting such things. This coupled with the fact that most of them really weren't that close to Vantix, meant the majority of the group opted for the first option. Nevertheless, Slyra still wasn't too happy with this outcome and vocalised her thoughts on the matter repeatedly, until even those on her side were sick of hearing it.

"For the last time," Grelow said wearily, "unless you've got soul replenishing powers under that hat, could you do us a favour and shut up about it?"

Slyra strolled off in a huff, joining Farack who'd already given up trying to find a logical reason for them to go after Vantix. Friendship wasn't sufficient for any of the others save Rekil. At present, everyone else had returned their attention to the pig roasting on the spit.

They'd left Oakhead without a moment to spare, the leaders of an angry mob of villagers throwing rocks at them and waving their pitchforks threateningly. Which, coincidently, is the only way a pitchfork can be waved. Indubitably an indicator that they'd outstayed their welcome.

Travelling along the outskirts of Ghostwood was taking longer than simply going through it but considering the perils involved none complained. The direct road to the castle was around here somewhere and they'd find it eventually.

Slyra had proved rather useful as regards healing their wounds from the short tousle with Vantix. Said wounds hadn't been anywhere near life threatening but the fact that she'd effectively healed them seemed to pick her up a bit.

"Is there any hope for V-," Sam stopped himself as he caught Rekil shaking his head dejectedly.

"I thought we'd saved him when we caught up with the dendrid," the old soldier sighed, "but, that creature isn't him. There's nothing of Vantix left anymore. I think our only option now is to finish this miserable job and put the whole thing behind us."

Arsenius poked the pig and shrugged, "Seems a decent enough job to me."

Rekil didn't say anything, thinking about how of the fifteen that had been hired, only seven would return. Eight if he included Terif. Still, it would be a sad day in many households.

"Speaking of this job," Sam broadcast for all to hear, "Grelow, refused to relinquish something to our employer. Care to enlighten us?"

281

The vampire shrugged and removed a strange looking object from a pouch on his belt. It looked like a ring belonging to some kind of paper thin giant. It was long and narrow, around the same size as a bracelet. Only there wasn't a clasp, its side was solid and unblemished. A long rhombus shaped emerald ran along one side, possessing a strange dull sheen.

Grelow slid it along his hand until it nestled in his palm, showing how this jewellery was supposed to be worn.

"So," Sam surmised, "it's some sort of palm-ring-bracelet-thing?"

"It's funny," Rekil mused, "I didn't pick Incognito as the jewellery obsessed type."

The vampire slipped it off and put it in his pocket. Their attention returned to the pig. Pronouncing it cooked, Arsenius cut two slices and carried one to where Slyra sat while the others quarrelled over their portions. "You should keep your strength up," he said, offering her a slice. She took it and bit into it absentmindedly, thoughts clearly vacationing elsewhere.

"I didn't realise you were such an avid fan of Vantix," Arsenius said quietly.

Slyra looked up at this. "I'm not," she sighed, "there's more to it than that."

"It's not about Osca then, is it?" Arsenius wasn't sure if this was a sensitive area so he decided to continue on a trial and error basis. "It's a dangerous world, Slyra, and Lady Death is far more likely to dance with those of us making eyes at her across the dance floor. Honestly I don't understand the sway his death has over you. Did you have feelings for him?"

Slyra looked up more with pity than anything else. "Nothing as grand as that. In spite of all my ridiculous, mystical abilities I couldn't save Osca the way he saved me. His blood is on my hands."

Arsenius shook his head. "Sometime in the future, hopefully the distant future, we're all going to die. Having magical powers doesn't make saving everybody your responsibility."

"It does when they're your friends."

Spending all your life wandering, made it extremely difficult to be an authority on friends. Most of the people Arsenius knew nestled quietly under the heading "acquaintances" in his address book.

Slyra carried on in the face of his silence. "Friends are the only people we can truly rely on when things take a bad turn. So we should be there in return when they need us most. I couldn't do it for Osca but I will save Vantix, no matter the cost."

A little taken aback by the way she finished this sentence, Arsenius casually nudged a stick with his foot. "He's lucky to have a friend like you," he said quietly before returning to the others.

* * * * *

Welbh literally had to fight his way through legions of refugees. Wasn't it just typical of the wretched masses to get in his way? God forbid they should ever come into power, as the grudge wielding maniacs would probably execute everybody richer than them out of spite. At least that was the view Welbh took; he simply didn't trust anybody who wouldn't feel it when he touched their wallets.

He couldn't help but wonder why they were there, mucking up the plains in front of the castle with their unkempt dress sense and endless panicked supplications.

283

Pushing his way through the throng, he caught snatches of conversation:

"Burned Freatsrak to the ground...."

".....no prisoners....."

"...even women and children...."

"....two days..."

Eventually one of the guards recognised him and dragged him inside, freeing him from the mass of struggling refugees.

The throne room was a mess, all the way from new curtains to the refugees that had set up camp in here and covered almost all free space. Prince Balithorn sat upon his father's throne, taking in any news the refugees could offer. It was all the same thing; the Derranferd army had invaded and was cutting some sort of destructive swath through Fardash.

When the prince caught sight of Welbh he dismissed all others. "Where is my father?"

Welbh stood to attention, "The treacherous King Audron sought to imprison both your father and I, but we defied them and drew our swords. King Jandelk fought bravely, yet fell beneath the blade of Audron."

Balithorn stared down at his feet for several moments before asking quietly, "Did he suffer?"

"No, my lord ," Welbh offered, "and if it makes you feel any better, I slew Audron myself."

Balithorn gave him a meaningful look, "It does," he declared after several moments of silence, "now go get yourself cleaned up."

Welbh bowed and left to find a bath.

* * * * *

Vantix sprinted down the curtained hallways of his mind. Not sleeping in quite a while had lit the tiny flame of hope that maybe this place had simply ceased to exist; that he'd never have to grace it with his presence ever again. Yet here he was. Unfortunately, a certain heinous lizard creature was also in the vicinity.

This whole matter was incomprehensible to him. Having reclaimed his soul, he'd been under the impression it was only a matter of time before he turned into a dazzling example of a human being. Or at the very least he'd be himself again. The last thing he could remember was dancing with that girl. About midway through whatever jig or fandango they'd been doing he'd awoke here.

It felt like he'd been running for hours, every single escape method he tried failing miserably. Both leaping into dark space he couldn't remember and running into places beyond his memories had proven inadequate. Cliché as it sounded he'd even resorted to pinching himself repeatedly. Hell, he'd even let the creature catch him at one stage.

The first time the creature had caught him, on his first visit to this realm of unconscious shenanigans, the descent of its clawed hands had caused him to wake, only slightly the worse for wear. This time however, it had cut a piece of him away. Not off, away.

Where the demonic monstrosity struck him, there was nothing. Its claws had simply erased a part of him. Not only did it sting beyond measure, there were now three tears along his left shoulder. They weren't even bleeding. Anybody looking at him could have easily drawn a comparison with a painting that had been gone unfinished because the artist died or vanished in mysterious circumstances.

285

Needless to say, he'd run like some sort of monstrous lizard from his nightmares was after him. Even though he'd left it far behind him, he didn't let his guard down.

Glancing down at his chest he tried to avoid thoughts of what would happen if his whole body disappeared. When he was unable to avoid these thoughts, something else occurred to him. His thoughts were no longer bouncing along the length of the hallway. He must have gotten better at concealing them.

Or this isn't your head anymore.....

Whirling around he looked for the origin of this statement, but he couldn't find it. "Who's there?" he called out desperately.

A moment later he realised the only other person here to answer his question was of the homicidal lizard persuasion. Hearing its hissing shrieks, he bounded in the other direction. If he could just stay out of its way long enough his friends would find a way to cure him. He was sure of it.

* * * * *

Welbh put on a clean tunic and let out a sigh of relief, loving the fresh feeling. Hours on the road had tired him and the warmth of his rooms was doing little to alleviate this. It was the kind of evening where all that was required was a hot chocolate and blankets to reach paradise.

Nevertheless, he grabbed a case and began piling all his important belongings in there. If Derranferd came calling, Fardash probably wouldn't be able to hold them off.

As he moved to throw his dirty clothes away, he noticed something poking out of the bundle. Pulling out his brother's diary, he experienced a momentary pang of denial. His brother couldn't be dead; he'd always seemed so vivacious, never bound by concerns of mortality.

Lila had wanted him to read this, which really meant Lintous had wanted him to read it. He couldn't deny his brother's dying wish.

Welbh flicked to the first entry; a foreword from his brother addressed specifically to him. The date showed it had been started a little over a month ago. Making himself comfortable, he began to read.

* * * * *

The creature formerly known as Vantix stalked through Ghostwood. It was going nowhere in particular, awaiting orders from higher up. Dendrid don't do anything without reason.

Many people wouldn't believe it, but dendrid aren't mindless killers. In fact, they're among the most loyal soldiers in all of creation. They may seem eerie and diabolical but the only sinister thing about the matter was their tendency to steal souls at every opportunity. As for their master, well, almost no one even knew he existed.

"HAVE YOU REQUISITIONED THE ITEM?"

Despite the vast distance between where it was and where its master sat, the voice thundered in its head instantaneously. The vampire dendrid, although uniquely dangerous among dendrid, was nothing compared to its master. Bowing its head it replied, *"It's lost to us."*

"THEN YOU KNOW WHAT MUST BE DONE."

This was absolutely true, without the item it couldn't return to its master. That simply wasn't an option.

287

The creature formerly known as Vantix set off after his erstwhile teammates.

* * * * *

Frank's wife and children were already inside around the roaring fire. He was intent on joining them until, for the second time that evening, his walk to the house was interrupted. An incredibly threatening voice called out:

"Has anyone by the name of Rekil passed this way?"

Frank turned to survey the voice's owner. Sure enough, he was suitably impressed. Fourteen men in armour blacker than the darkest night stood before him. Although he couldn't see faces, he expected they'd be sporting rather intimidating grimaces.

"Strange, that," Frank grunted.

"Strange, what?" the gruff voice shot back.

"You're the second group in five minutes to ask me that."

For a moment there was deathly silence, it seemed as if the dark robed figures were holding their breath.

"They wore shining white armour and white cloaks," Frank continued.

At this point the silence changed. It became threatening and sinister.

"They went that way," Frank indicated a direction and turned and sprinted for the door.

He'd made it inside and had just slammed the door, when a knife lodged itself in the wood. His family stared at him, but they needn't have worried. It was only for effect.

* * * * *

288

Approximately an hour after he'd begun, Welbh put the book down. It was a startlingly good read.

In that instant, a plan formed in his mind. Money, then power and then adoration had been fine before, but if Lintous' diary spoke the truth he could have all at once and anything else that took his fancy. His brother may have had much grander intentions; world peace, ample food for all and the end of child labour, etcetera, yet Welbh knew them to be folly. People were a horrible, flawed bunch and the world would never be the perfect place his sibling had imagined. That's why Welbh had simpler goals. In contrast to his brother's plans, his were actually capable of being realised.

Grabbing a coat, he rushed downstairs and shouted for any nearby servants. There were plenty of arrangements to be made for his trip. His brother would be avenged.

Normally he wouldn't consider himself the vengeful type, but this was different. This was personal. And there was money involved.

Chapter 33

It didn't take them that long to find the road to Ghostwood castle, and it was an even briefer period of time before they embarked down it. Although it was a good while before they came to a halt, the sun still shone when they arrived at the village.

They still couldn't see the castle yet, this ostensibly just a random village on the road to nowhere. It looked just like any other adorable little hamlet except it was in the middle of Ghostwood and completely deserted. Evidently it had been abandoned in a hurry. Quite recently in fact.

Several carts lay in various positions of immobility; some were on their sides as if they'd been pushed over whilst others were completely overturned. Their contents, which ranged from hay to fruit and vegetables, littered the road all around the fallen carts.

Sam was first to embrace the situation, running to the nearest pile of hay and throwing himself in. He gave a relaxed sigh and looked at the others. They took his meaning; this was as good a place as any for them to rest. Even if its emptiness was slightly unnerving.

It didn't take long to get a fire going and the group didn't hesitate when it came to taking a few of the vegetables from the carts. It wasn't like anybody else was using them. The aroma of the meal they were preparing drifted up to where Sam sat atop a cart which lay on its side. This caused him to visibly sag and spin the wheel he sat beside dejectedly.

"Great," he said with very apparent apathy, "stew again."

"You don't have to have any," Arsenius shot back.

"I won't," Sam replied triumphantly, "Toss me some of those apples."

Slyra threw him an apple and he moved in order to catch it.

Several things happened as the apple made the seemingly short journey from Slyra's palm to Sam's hand: 1) A rare species of butterfly which was flying by descended to avoid the apple and landed in the stew, effectively becoming extinct; 2) somewhere in eastern Gravent a Baker had an epiphany that would revolutionise the world of pastry, and; 3) an arrow went straight into Sam's back and exited through his chest before smashing on the road. He wheezed once and fell backwards off the cart.

Only Farack reacted immediately. Leaping up in order to grab a hold of Sam's feet, he was just a second too late. Arsenius pulled him back down, two arrows sailing by. He needn't have worried though, they were both at least a foot above the rhadon's head.

The entire group was huddling behind the cart, all thoughts of food forgotten. Arrows thudded into the cart's exposed underside but they seemed to be safe on this side. "Well?" Rekil shouted at Farack.

"Well what?"

"Who is it?"

"Fifteen people with crossbows in shining white everything."

"Then why the hell are they firing at us?" Rekil growled to himself. This puzzled the majority of the others no end.

For a moment the constant din of arrows hitting wood stopped. A women's voice called out to them, "Give us Vantix and this can all be avoided."

"What in the name of the gods do you think you're doing?" Rekil had poked his head over the top of their makeshift shelter and was roaring at their assailants. The others tried to calm and drag him back to safety, but he wouldn't be stopped, "You're supposed to fire a warning shot first."

Much to the surprise of the group, who'd been expecting Rekil to get riddled with arrows, the woman called again. "It wasn't my fault," she replied weakly, "he moved into the arrow's path at the last second. There was nothing I could do."

For The Divine, their white clad opposition, had strict rules. Sam's death would be viewed as the killing of an innocent, which could mean either expulsion for the woman or an accusation of bloodlust topped off with a sentence of death for malevolent behaviour. That's exactly why The Divine existed, to punish the wicked so that the scales on which the world rested wouldn't tip toward evil. As to how Rekil came to know this, that's anyone's guess.

"Listen," the woman offered, "just give us Vantix and we'll forget you were all travelling with a demon." With Sam's blood on her hands she was already in a precarious position, more blood wouldn't really help.

"He's not with us anymore," Rekil responded while taking a seat with his comrades.

The barrage of arrows recommenced.

"I don't think they believe us," Slyra sighed.

"Okay," Rekil readied his bow, "on three."

Farack's arms flared up and energy crackled from Slyra's fingertips as she set her hat firmly upon her head.

"One"

Arsenius and Grelow rooted around in Vantix's bag for his miniature crossbows. He was hardly likely to use them any time soon.

"Two"

Elik's wings appeared as he ditched his cloak. He'd go straight over the top; The Divine wouldn't know what hit them.

"Thre-"

As he tried to say three, an arrow lodged itself into their side of the cart. It just about missed Slyra's hat.

"Blraenk," Arsenius cursed in his native tongue, "They've surrounded us."

"Not exactly," Farack swallowed nervously.

The others looked to where he stared. Approaching them were fourteen figures clad entirely in black. They also had crossbows.

Time seemed to move in slow motion as the menacing figures reached for the triggers. Elik was the only one to react, taking decisive action just before these new assailants took the shot. He stepped in front of the group with his back to the assailants and his wings spread out in all their glory. No more than a second later, thirteen arrows pierced them. He fell to the ground, wounded but very far from dead.

Rekil grabbed a hold of a wing and dragged the wounded man back to his friends. Using his free hand, he reached up and pulled the cart down over his merry band. All light was shut out as they cowered beneath the arrow studded cart.

Arrows continued to crash into both sides of the cart without respite, until eventually their number diminished and finally came to a stop. A deathly silence ensued. It went on for what seemed like an eternity, but then again, anything can seem like an eternity when your trapped under an overturned cart. In fact, it stretched on for so long that Rekil was tempted to take a peek. As he was reaching to do so, two shouts rang out:

"Heretics!"

"Divine!"

They could hear the sound of crossbows firing, but the arrows no longer hit the cart. There was also the sound of running feet, followed closely by clashing swords.

Outside the cart, the Heretics and the Divine were evenly matched. Pretty much every thrust and swing was parried or blocked. Both groups only recruited from the elite, but both recruited people of a different mind-set. They were opposites who both sought to balance the world. For just as the Divine kept the wicked in check, the Heretics ensured no outbursts of selfless good would be tolerated. They did not get on very well, or mix socially.

"I don't think they like each other," Arsenius whispered. The others ignored him, busy tending to Elik.

There were thuds above them, as a duelling pair's contest took a slightly more elevated platform.

Slyra reached forward, grabbed an arrow lodged in Elik's back and pulled. Intense pain racked his body and he screamed. It was not a human scream. The others had to cover their ears and the cart was blown high into the air. It soared higher than any cart had ever soared before, taking those on top of it along for its record-breaking flight.

The duelling pair who'd accompanied the cart up also came back down with it. The Heretic hit his head off a nearby building and went limp; the Divine landed on his knee, shattering it. Which was funny really, because a second later the cart shattered on him.

The fighting ceased as both the Heretics and the Divine wheeled on the group. From where they lay in the dirt, Slyra and the others shot apologetic looks at their assailants.

The female spokesperson for the divine was the first to speak. "I think we've forgotten the real reason we're here," she said quietly.

The Heretics nodded.

"They've killed one of our number," the woman continued, "the penalty for such an action is death. I trust you honour the same rule?"

Once again, the Heretics nodded.

No more words were necessary and as such, no more words were spoken. Both opposing groups aimed their crossbows at those seated on the ground. They wouldn't miss.

Arsenius and the others were at a loss. Apart from Grelow, who could fly away any time he wanted, there didn't seem to be a way out. On his right Slyra desperately racked her brain for a spell that could stop 27 arrows fired at point blank range, to his left Elik tried uselessly to bring his wounded wings under control. All the others tried something, whilst he just closed his eyes and waited for the inevitable click to signal oblivion.

On hearing the screeching of bats, he assumed that either a) Grelow had taken his leave or b) he was already dead and about to be introduced to the underworld's thriving bat population. Sensing that he was wrong on both accounts, Arsenius opened his eyes.

The Heretics and the Divine seemed to lose interest in them. Which wasn't hard, because compared to what was happening at the end of the street they were practically a wet painting of grass growing. What everyone was now staring at was a colony of bats swirling down to the ground in an almost tornado looking formation.

As the bats merged together and formed the truculent, monstrous features of Vantix, the group let out a collective groan. The amount of people trying to kill them was becoming distressingly large.

"He's come back to save us," Slyra whispered excitedly, for she hadn't seen his display the other night. As far as she was concerned he was back to deliver them, and in doing so redeem himself for his indiscretions for the previously mentioned night. She was so very wrong.

The creature formerly known as Vantix, was a mess. Its clothes hung about it in rags, dirt covered its skin and seemed to have been used to oil its hair. They had all his weapons, but he didn't need them anymore; sharp talons protruded from his fingertips. All in all, he certainly wouldn't be used as a mascot for any sort of benign organisation any time soon. Letting out a bloodcurdling howl, the creature rushed at them.

Neither the Heretics nor the Divine hesitated, firing their crossbows immediately. It looked almost like an explosion, bats flying out in all directions to avoid the arrows. It wove a path through them with the utmost ease, adding a much more menacing air to this vampire-dendrid. The bats amalgamated once more, no more than ten paces from them. A horrible twisted smile adorned the monster's features.

The remaining Heretics, numbering thirteen, and the remaining Divine, numbering fourteen, drew their swords. Some of them looked fairly nervous.

The creature sprinted toward the nearest swordsman. He swung his sword in anticipation, but struck naught but air. He looked down with an almost unbelieving expression to stare at the gashes the demon inflicted upon his chest.

One of the divine ran up, intent on catching Vantix unaware, but he was unsuccessful. It was suddenly behind him, sinking the elongated fangs Grelow had given it deep into the man's neck. No more than a second later, countless bats hoisted two of the Heretics high into the air. They were dropped from such a height that there wasn't the slightest chance of survival.

Slyra watched as the monster evaded another sword thrust and sunk its teeth deep into yet another swordsman. It was beyond gruesome and now abundantly clear that Vantix had left the building.

Arsenius stared in silence as what had once been their companion leapt up and rammed one of its clawed hands deep into someone's neck, whilst still managing to impale the swordsman behind it. This vampire-dendrid could teach any mercenary, trained assassin or veteran warrior something about the fine art of massacre.

It picked them off in pairs, rarely killing less than two at a time. It side-stepped and weaved between swords, untouched by any blade. It was clear that they'd lost all hope and would have fled, but the monstrous creature didn't give them the chance.

Farack wanted to jump in; to try and help them. *Nobody should have to endure this*, he thought to himself. Of course, he didn't jump in. If he had, he would just be another corpse amongst the increasing large pile this demon seemed intent upon building.

After several minutes only two of the Heretics remained, both trying to back away from conflict. The monster walked straight up to one, making absolutely no attempt at evasion when his sword came round just above waist high. For a second he thought that was it and a smile tugged at the corners of his lips. He was about to be disappointed.

The vampire-dendrid split in half, straight across the waist. Bats billowed out in both directions for the fraction of a second it took the sword to pass through him. He shifted to bats and back in the blink of an eye, just long enough to allow a tiny space to open up amongst the bats and let the sword pass through. The last two Heretics' jaws dropped and they gawked as the creature slew them.

"Can you do that?" Farack asked Grelow.

"No," the vampire replied in awe, "That kind of shift is too quick, like being both forms at once. It's impossible."

The group rose cautiously to their feet. The vampire dendrid was now soaked in blood, which seemed to multiply its whole terrifying thing tenfold. It didn't look at them though.

Grelow broke into a wide grin and strolled toward the crouching demon. Farack tried to pull him back, but the vampire shrugged him off. "Can't you see," Grelow laughed, "A mindless creature couldn't do all that with such finesse. That must be Vantix."

As has been stated before, dendrid are not mindless creatures. They are among the most cunning, vicious and bloodthirsty of all the peoples in Ballisca.

Grelow was made very aware of this as the monster leapt at him, sinking its talons deep into his stomach and tearing out a handful. "What?" Grelow exclaimed incredulously as he collapsed into the dirt.

The vampire-dendrid, formerly known as Vantix, ignored the vampire's writhing as it reached for his belt and picked up a strange gold item with a large rhombus running along one side. This was what its master wanted and it should deliver it to him immediately.

Slyra stepped forward, energy flowing from her fingertips. It rolled over the creature, which tried to flee but couldn't. Her power seemed to restrict it, confining it to the one shape. It wouldn't be flying out of here.

Advancing in her direction also proved futile, as the monster seemed to hit an invisible wall. Slyra wasn't taking any chances. Glowing streams of energy flew from her palms and wrapped themselves around the creature. The intensity of that power burned the demon's skin.

The creature formerly known as Vantix threw its head back and wailed at the sky.

* * * * *

Vantix thundered down the dark corridors of his memories, trying to put some distance between himself and the creature that stalked his dreams. He had no idea how long he'd been running, but it had been ineffectual. He hadn't been able to lose the monster anywhere.

It would result in a confrontation, he knew that. He also knew he'd need some sort of advantage. Or at very least a weapon of some kind.

Taking the steps two at a time, he was at the top before he realised they hadn't been here before. It was some sort of pyramid, stairs descending on four sides. There was a decent amount of room up here, enough for him and maybe seven other people to stand comfortably.

The creature's shrieking was all around him and he could see why. There was hundreds of it, legions surrounding him on every side. Exact replicas of the creature, every single one of them intent on killing him.

Glancing at his shoulder, he saw the part of him the demon had cut away hadn't grown back. It was just empty space, and once again his thoughts went to what would happen when he disappeared entirely.

The shrieks became synchronised as one of the creatures began its ascent of the steps. Seeming to tire of the intense build up, it sprinted the stairs and hurled itself at him, claws outstretched.

Shuffling to one side, he evaded the claws and grabbed a hold of the creature's head. Pulling furiously to one side, he heard a loud snap. The monster went limp and tumbled back down the steps.

And that was it, Vantix knew he could beat them. They weren't invincible after all. He'd be fine, so long as they kept coming one by one.

At this point each and every last one of them bounded up the steps toward him.

* * * * *

The entire group watched as the vampire-dendrid writhed and convulsed upon the ground. Parts of the creature swelled up, returned to normal size and swelled up again a moment later. It's breathing became incredibly rapid and laboured, not sounding the least bit healthy.

None of them had the faintest idea what was going on. This was simply unheard of. Exorcisms didn't usually involve the demon swelling up and then shrinking repeatedly. This was more akin to one of those diets that involved ballooning, tears and drastic weight loss.

Unsurprisingly, Farack had definitely had enough. Grabbing Slyra's arm he yelled, "Stop it! You're killing him!"

The young witch raised her hands defensively. "It's not me anymore," she protested, "He's doing this himself."

Apart from the thrashings of the creature, an eerie silence descended. They all waited in anticipation for it to get up and attack them, but no such thing happened.

Then, much to their surprise, the creature formerly known as Vantix began to glow.

* * * * *

Vantix punched, kicked and cursed. The relentless tides of oncoming monsters were overwhelming him. For every one he knocked down there were another three ready to take its place.

Anywhere their claws touched him the skin blotted and faded away. Already he was missing parts of his chest, legs and a line of nothingness ran straight across his right arm. Nonetheless he still retained control over his hands.

Gathering all the strength he could muster, a massive push sent several of the monstrosities tumbling down the side to be crushed under the feet of their brethren. There was no time to feel pleased with himself, four of the monsters pounced on him. He was dragged to the ground, their claws tearing into him. Parts of his body began to disappear as he struggled to push them off.

Then the creatures whirled around, something else commanding their attention. Vantix managed to pull himself to his feet, the rapidly evaporating parts of his body stinging like heck. Catching sight of what the creatures were looking at, he was hypnotised.

The silhouette of a man, featureless and shining with an intense brightness was walking toward them. It moved with purpose, the legions of creatures spontaneously combusting as they came near his refulgence. As they did so, his light grew.

The creatures wheeled on Vantix, intent on finishing the job before his glowing saviour arrived. Fortunately they were too late, their shrieks ringing out as the glowing figure burned them away.

Intense light forced Vantix to shield his eyes. He got the impression the figure was staring at him, even if it didn't have a face. "Thanks," he murmured uncertainly.

As if in response the light increased, undeniably coruscant . It filled Vantix's vision, the dark hallways melting away forever as his soul returned triumphantly.

* * * * *

As the light faded, it was easy to see that the vampire-dendrid was no more. Vantix lay there, as normal as he'd been before the first unpleasant encounter with the dendrid. He opened his eyes and surveyed the damage before him.

He was only slightly more impressed than horrified.

Chapter 34

Prince Balithorn sat atop his father's throne. It was uncomfortable; the actual seat itself and the enormity of responsibility that came with it. Everyone was somehow relying on him, as if his every word could feed the hungry, or demolished homeless shelters. The slightest shift in his seat could bring about calamity or social reform, so instead he sat, quietly determined not to fundamentally alter the kingdom with an accidental gesture.

One thing he couldn't comprehend, was Welbh's insane ability to disappear. It was unfathomable; his father's Royal Negotiator had gone for a bath and never returned. These things weren't supposed to happen to Balithorn. Usually people exercised more caution to stay on his good side.

Eyeing his advisors warily he beckoned them over. As with most royal advisors, they constantly sought attention. They needed everyone to hang on their every word whilst they informed him of the matters of little importance, and resented anyone who attempted to hijack their spotlight. Balithorn couldn't hear a thing when they all voiced their opinions in raucous discord. He cut them off abruptly.

"The situation in Freatsrak is....?" Balithorn prompted them to finish this statement.

"Burned to the ground, sire."

"The people are....?" This was actually the most effective way to deal with advisors.

"Are either here or dead, your highness," replied one of the attention seeking congregation.

"The Derranferdian Army is....?"

"A day and a half away at most, my lord."

"So our plan is...?"

One of the advisors stepped forward, but before he could speak he was interrupted by another of his scrutiny craving brethren. "If you'll permit me, my lord," the second advisor suggested, "I have a most cunning plan."

Prince Balithorn gestured for him to continue.

"We've had word that it is in fact the entire Derranferd army on its way here," he paused for effect, "as such, if we send our army into Derranferd, it'll be ours for the taking."

Balithorn stared at the man for some time, trying to determine if he'd been fully serious. On realising he was, Balithorn cursed his inability to justify stupidity as a executable offense. "There is only one major flaw with your plan," he explained slowly, "It involves the death of pretty much everyone here. Get out of my sight." Turning to the other advisors, the prince issued his commands. "Leave about a hundred men to occupy the castle and find somebody to build barricades throughout the keep, preferably tall ones. I want two hundred men behind the eastern ridge, lying in ambush and the rest of the army on the plains. Fit as many refugees into the cellars and dungeons as is humanly possible, and send the overflow to Nivoldn." Nivoldn was a city in the north east of Fardash, there was no way Derranferd could have reached it yet.

The advisors scuttled off to carry out these orders, leaving Balithorn alone for the first time in days. Almost automatically, his eyes closed and he was on the verge of dozing off when a small voice intruded upon his attempted slumber.

"Sire," it called uncertainly.

Balithorn opened his eyes. A small boy stood before him, possibly one of the stable hands. "Yes?" the prince asked irritably. Although usually renowned as a man of the people, sleep deprivation was getting to Balithorn.

"I heard you were looking for Welbh, your highness."

"You know of his whereabouts?" The Prince was suddenly upright in his seat; this could be interesting.

"He left for Ghostwood yesterday, your majesty."

"Thank you," Balithorn said absentmindedly, "Your family are welcome to a place in my cellar."

The stable hand strolled off, unsure whether he'd just been threatened or if he should be pleased with himself.

Balithorn however, was not pleased. His thoughts remained focused on Welbh, asking himself the same question repeatedly. *What was that damn fool up to?*

* * * * *

Vantix made no effort to hide his jubilation at being back. He kept running his fingers over his teeth, delighted not to find fangs there. The fact that he was supremely pleased with his skin and hair was beginning to get on everyone's nerves save Farack and Slyra, who seemed almost as happy at the situation's resolution as he was.

They'd left the mountain of corpses Vantix was responsible for behind them, burying Sam and setting off along the road once more. The only sounds to be heard were Vantix greedily helping himself to any food available; being that demon had left him with quite the appetite. He was also trying to get the taste of blood out of his mouth. How vampires enjoyed it was beyond him.

Apart from these sounds, Ghostwood was extremely quiet and not because Farack had burned it down either. The lack of sound was due to the Drakold's presence somewhere in the woods, but they didn't know that.

"What I don't understand," Arsenius pondered aloud, "is how he isn't a vampire anymore? I mean I get why he isn't a dendrid, but the vampire part doesn't make any sense."

Rekil shrugged. "Don't question a good thing," was the inadequate explanation he provided, "I assume his soul purging his system of the dendrid taint took the vampire infliction along with it". Despite this hypothesis he still cast suspicious glances at Vantix every now and then.

"Slyra seems happy he's back," Arsenius changed subject, "She didn't think much of him before."

"You're underestimating the power of near death experiences."

"Eh?" the old warrior's response seemed rather irrelevant and obfuscating to Arsenius.

"It's actually quite simple," Rekil explained, "He left her to die on some sort of sacrificial alter, she was right to be mad at him. Since he was possessed by a demon and she managed to save him, that's overruled his wrongdoing. When our friends are truly in need it behoves us to ignore their faults. You can't hold grudges if you want to be friends."

"Ah-," despite not fully comprehending Arsenius elongated his response to indicate understanding.

Rekil gave him a knowing wink. "Is someone jealous she's paying him so much attention?"

Arsenius didn't even need to say anything. It seemed Rekil was more perceptive than he'd thought.

Ahead of the two of them, Vantix was busy removing things from Grelow's possession. The first he'd actually heard of the vampire biting him was after he'd woken up cleansed of his demons. Stealing his belongings was a decent enough revenge that probably wouldn't incur the vampire's wrath. Vantix didn't want Grelow going crazy and biting him again. His self-preservation instincts were still intact, after all.

"What did you get this time?" Farack laughed.

Vantix pulled all number of items from his pockets. "Two compasses, a pouch of herbs, a locket and this." He held up a slim bracelet looking object with an emerald stretching across one of its surfaces.

"Ah, Grelow showed us that," Farack informed him, "It's Incognito's prize. Hardly worth all the trouble and expense. The side with the jewel slides onto your palm."

Vantix nodded and slid it onto his hand. It was a perfect fit and nestled in his palm rather nicely.

Farack's eyebrows furrowed. "That's odd."

Vantix was still admiring the shining emerald. "What?" He asked absentmindedly.

"Yesterday the emerald didn't shine, it was dull, lifeless even."

"Maybe Grelow gave it a polish."

The rhadon shook his head. "It looks like an entirely different stone."

As Vantix removed it and put the item into his pocket, their attention was grabbed by something else. A castle had come into view at the end of the road. They'd both heard about Ghostwood castle. Although a perfectly serviceable castle, it had been abandoned fifty years ago in mysterious circumstances. It stood tall, high above the trees but this was partially because it had been built on a hill, which placed only its lowest level amongst the forest.

The group quickened their pace, as only those expecting payment can. Even so, it would still be another while before they reached it.

* * * * *

As Welbh walked along the corridor, he wrestled with a sneer. These people killed his brother, they deserved to die right now!

Unfortunately business and manners restricted him, forcing him to wait. Business because they had something he needed, and manners because it just wasn't polite to go around killing people. Unless it was part of business, of course.

The archway into the room was behind a curtain. Welbh peered through, eyeing these murderers. His brother's diary had said he'd hired fifteen to begin with. Seven was not a decent return by anyone's standards.

None of them had seen him yet; they were all staring at a raised stage in front of a door. It was literally effortless for Welbh to move up behind them. Intent on getting their attention, he cleared his throat.

Vantix, Slyra, Grelow, Rekil, Elik, Farack and Arsenius wheeled around. A few of them drew their swords.

Chapter 35

"Relax," the man raised his arms for calm, "My name is Welbh. I'm Lintous's brother."

Slyra watched as Vantix, Arsenius, Elik and Grelow refused to sheath their swords. "Who's Lintous?" Arsenius growled.

"The man you know as Incognito."

As they sheathed their swords, Welbh had to work to keep the welcoming smile on his face. Their guilty reaction had basically confirmed his suspicions. It had *we killed your brother* written all over it.

"Aren't you the king's right hand man?"

Welbh stopped, surprised somebody had recognised him. "Yes, that's me," he said to the Rekil. His brother's journal had names and detailed descriptions of these people. There was, however, one of them he knew already.

He nodded to Elik, "It's been a while."

It took Elik a minute to realise Welbh was speaking to him. "You know me?" he asked incredulously.

Welbh smiled uncertainly. "Of course, we went to school together."

Elik ran forward and grabbed him by the shoulders, prompting Welbh to reach for the dagger up his sleeve.

He needn't have bothered though, the other man meant him no harm. "What about my family?" Elik catechized, "Do you know them?"

This level of intensity was too much for Welbh, who was visibly uncomfortable. "Your parents are dead, that's all I know."

"What about my wife and children?"

Rekil placed a reassuring hand on Elik's shoulder. "He doesn't know," he said softly. Elik reluctantly let go of Welbh.

Welbh hurried up onto the small stage he'd had placed here. Things weren't exactly going according to plan but up here he'd have their full attention. Since the encounter was fast diverging from the route he'd had in mind, he dropped the small talk. "Have you got the item?" he inquired.

Grelow nodded and reached for his pocket. A moment later he was patting himself in a frenzy. When it had gone on for far too long, one of the other members of the group coughed.

Welbh stared at him, searching in his brother's notes in his head for clues to the teenager's identity. "Vantix, I presume?"

The youth nodded and handed Grelow the item in question. "I think you dropped this." As Grelow handed it to Welbh, Vantix brought out the rest of the vampire's possessions he'd confiscated on the way here. "You may also have dropped these."

The vampire scowled at him, causing Slyra, Farack and Arsenius to stifle sniggers. Welbh took no notice. He was busy staring at this wonderful item, turning it over and over in his hands. "Do you know what this is called?"

The group sensed it was a rhetorical question and waited for Welbh to answer it. "It's called the Solus," he informed them.

"Fantastic," Grelow replied impatiently. He just wanted to take his money and go.

"Anyway," Welbh said dismissively, "How much did my brother promise all of you?"

"300 crowns ," Grelow's response was almost instant.

Welbh tapped his lip. "Since he hired 15 of you this was worth almost 4500 crowns to him."

Vantix whistled. It was a massive sum.

"You have fulfilled the bargain and earned your fee."

Rekil was next to speak. "Some of us were promised more than just a fee."

Welbh rolled his eyes wearily and produced a small leather bound book from his pocket. "My brother got Rekil and Vantix their pardons soon after you agreed to help him. As for the information some of you requested, Elik will find what he seeks in Port Daichwater and Arsenius received his from the get go."

The aforementioned nodded their thanks. Then Welbh caught them all off guard with a somewhat strange question. "How much do you think my brother was worth?"

None of group knew how to answer that.

"Obviously," Welbh began to answer his own question, "he had the money to pay you, meaning he was worth at least 4500 crowns . Plus, he had several large business endeavours and ships all worth around 60,000 crowns . Adding in his houses and possessions will probably bring the total up to 85,000 crowns ."

Vantix whistled again. It was his automatic reaction to hearing large amounts of money mentioned. And 85,000 crowns was a monumental amount; several families could live off that for the entirety of their lives.

"I think he was worth more than that," Welbh continued, "He was my brother. Something that I think outweighs monetary value. It's priceless." For a moment his eyes glistened, forcing him to wipe them with his sleeve. An awkward silence ensued. Farack tried to break it by clapping at Welbh's speech, but only managed to make it worse. It would take an outstanding display of charisma to banish a situation this awkward.

"Which is why," Welbh managed eventually, "Lintous was well worth the price of the mercenaries I hired. Enjoy." He turned and left through the door behind the stage. It happened suddenly, not giving the group any time to react.

"I'm having trouble following this," Arsenius declared, "Does he think we killed his brother?"

"I wonder," Slyra announced thoughtfully, " If there's any chance we could convince him there's been a misunderstanding?"

At that point, several moments after their cue, the windows around them smashed.

* * * * *

Welbh slid the Solus onto his palm. His brother's diary had explained everything. How to use it, what it could bring him, everything.

If he left now, he could make it to the castle long before the Derranferd army attacked. With the Solus to help him, he could easily stop the invasion.

He could also become king, but that was just a bonus. Leaping onto his horse, he mumbled a few words at the

Solus. It's emerald shone with an almost unsettling brightness and his horse took off at an unnatural speed.

* * * * *

Misunderstandings are commonplace in the world. From selling a year's supply of stock at knock down price because of an accent misinterpretation with a foreign merchant, to scuttling your own boat because you mistook a friendly vessel for a group of pirates, all the way to making fun of someone when they're right behind and thus ruining your chances of getting an invitation to subsequent parties they might have. Misunderstandings are everywhere, and so are their consequences.

Derranferd laying waste to the cities and towns of Fardash, has its roots in a false report sent to King Audron that Fardash had attacked Oakhead. The entire underwater population of Lake Glasrobe was killed because they gave their messiah's sword to the wrong person. Actions have reactions, but what people sometimes forget is so do misunderstandings.

Your employer's brother hiring people to kill you because he thinks you murdered your employer, is a rather rare occurrence, but Vantix put it down to the company he was keeping. Things just seemed to get as bad as they possibly could around them. He tossed it on the pile of misunderstandings that had built up on this journey.

It seemed to him that they'd not been given a fair say. Like the trial had been skipped and they were right at the execution. He wanted to indicate that this wasn't legal but realised nobody cared.

The glass from the windows hit the floor and he realised the last few seconds had taken their time to pass. Then everything sped up.

313

Armed mercenaries leapt from every window, door and available opening. One came down the chimney, showing an inspiring level of dedication to surprise attacks.

Vantix realised his akimbo crossbows would be no use here and drew both his short swords. Knowing this still wouldn't be enough, he ran for the nearest exit even though mercenaries were piling through.

Given the chance he'd have probably tried to pass himself off as an undercover mercenary, but then he'd probably have to show them some sort of ridiculous tattoo to prove his credentials. Any group that required him to have a massive picture of a dolphin fighting an eagle on his back just wasn't for him.

His comrades also ran for the exits only to find each one of them blocked, they then cursed and drew their weapons. It was abundantly clear that this was going to get messy. Four skirmishes broke out at each of the exits.

It might have been because he didn't feel like tackling all those steps, or because of the vast amounts of mercenaries coming up them, but Vantix ruled the staircase out. In an attempt to back away, he bumped into something warm which set his sleeves alight. He'd recognise Farack anywhere. "Back to back?" he called over his shoulder whilst putting out his smoking sleeves.

"As it should be," the rhadon replied firmly, mouth set in a grim determined line.

Rekil and Arsenius had made a break for the door behind the stage, both intent on giving Welbh a piece of their mind. Or stabbing him, whichever seems more appropriate. Unfortunately the door had been locked. Even more unfortunate, was that now they had their backs up against a wall. Surrounded as they were, they drew their weapons. There was a lot to be said for prolonging the inevitable.

Slyra and Elik headed for the doorway behind the curtain. Some of the mercenaries had got caught in the curtains on their way through, dragging it down on top of themselves. It was quite a sight; a bunch of the men sprawled beneath a curtain, desperately struggling to fight their way out. Elik plunged his sword into each one of them before moving on to enemies that posed an actual threat.

Grelow was the only one who hadn't made any movements to the exits. He could head for the windows and fly out of here any time he wanted, but there wasn't much point as it didn't really matter anyway. The chances of anybody hitting his heart were slim to none and any other injuries could just heal. The reality, was that he could have some fun here.

Vantix parried an attack with one sword and sliced open a chest with another. Any gaps he made in the line were instantly filled, indicating a surplus of assailants. It was just like his nightmare, only he wasn't fighting monsters. Well not in a physical sense anyway, even if they didn't have the horns and demonic haircuts who was to say they weren't monstrosities in some sort of spiritual or domestic sense. Another reason this wasn't like his fight with the creatures was no glowing savio-

"Duck," Farack called. Vantix obeyed and a huge broadsword passed over first his friend's head and then his own. Rolling over, he blocked another descending sword and planted his own into somebody's knee.

Farack rushed at the wielder of the broadsword, pummelling the man's chest with his shield. The weapon clattered to the ground but Farack's shield was torn from his grasp as the opposition managed to wrap his hands around it. Reacting instinctively, Farack grabbed his opponent's face with his flaming hands. The assailant went down, clutching his face and screaming. He wouldn't be using those eyes to see any time in the near future.

Out of the corner of his eye he saw a raised axe and leapt out of the way. He needn't have worried though. Vantix had sliced the back of the man's calf, causing him to fall.

Farack had misjudged his leap and crashed against the wall. His sword smashed one of the many hanging lamps and oil spilled over his blade. The flames from his hands drifted up and ignited it instantly. Now wielding an impressive flaming blade, he re-joined the fray.

Rekil and Arsenius didn't even have room to swing a sword. They just stabbed everything wildly. Which was in fact extremely difficult, considering Rekil wielded an axe.

Since Rekil was in front of him, Arsenius seized this opportunity to aim a few kicks at the door. Marking it off as a lost cause, he returned to his comrade's side.

Slyra shook as lightning flew from her fingertips. Elemental magic was tiring and using it repeatedly wasn't healthy. She couldn't keep electrocuting people, even it was yielding phenomenal results. Fortunately, she had Elik by her side. His attacks were all precise and critical, not one missed its mark. Every time his sword moved through the air somebody fell, either spraying blood or already dead. Sometimes both.

Grelow's clothes hung in shreds, torn apart by the enemies' swords. After all that had happened over the last week, he'd need an entirely new wardrobe. It was slightly depressing, mostly because his shirts came all the way from the northern provinces.

It was his own fault really, he hadn't even tried to stop their attacks unless they'd come near his heart. His sword was still in its sheath, he preferred using his teeth.

Catching an incoming blade, he used it to propel himself to his next victim's neck. Although victim wasn't exactly the right word. If anything, he was only massacring them in self -defence. The victim fell to the ground and Grelow spat out a chunk of throat. Despite the destruction of one of his favourite shirts, this was turning out to be an enjoyable evening.

Farack's flaming sword was really going down a treat. It swept around in an arc, cutting, burning and setting alight all in its path. Any who managed to block it could still rely on the flame throwing prowess of its wielder.

Now that those in front of him were busy trying to extinguish themselves. Farack whirled around to help Vantix. "Look out," he called whilst cradling flames in his hands.

Vantix hurled himself to one side, crashing into one of the assailants. The two of them fell, both losing their weapons. They struggled, each trying to get the upper hand and put the other down.

Rekil and Arsenius were faring much better. They'd managed to move out from the wall, giving them the space necessary to inflict some damage. As a result five of their opponents lay wounded and three seemed to have fled, leaving them with only two to deal with. They finished them off almost simultaneously.

They'd been about to head for another exit route, when they were faced with a problem. The three foes they'd thought had fled were standing just out of reach, crossbows at the ready. The crossbows went off.

Sir Ralph the Faint-Hearted of Gravent was horrified to hear of what happened next, but only because his wife was compiling a list of people braver than him. This was all an attempt to entice him into retrieving a very rare

317

diamond from a dragon's hoard, which he was too sensible to even attempt.

Arsenius froze and Rekil moved in front of him, effectively shielding the Nospac elf from all danger. Three arrows struck Rekil, who provided ample protection for his petrified friend. This solidified Rekil in the third position on the aforementioned list, just behind the artist Alex DeReggino whose bravery took pottery in exciting new directions. First place went to Mascal of Derranferd, renowned for taking on a hydra whilst armed with nothing but two pairs of shoes and a wooden spoon. He was later disqualified for suicidal levels of stupidity.

As Rekil fell, Arsenius leapt up and brought his cutlass around in a wide swing, decapitating two of the opposition and cutting off the third's arm. He didn't aim to cut off the arm; this one just happened to be significantly taller than the other two. They didn't even have a chance to draw their weapons.

Arsenius slid to Rekil's side, expecting some sort of last wishes monologue that he didn't have the time or the patience to sit through. Rekil, on the other hand, was intent on keeping this short and sweet. "Get them out of here," he yelled whilst spitting out a mouthful of blood.

Slyra was almost as horrified as she was tired when her latest attempt at lightning trickled from her fingertips and vanished in front of her. Sensing that this was their chance several of the mercenaries rushed at her and she raised her dagger defensively.

Elik came to her rescue, his wings billowing out from under his cloak and knocking all around him off their feet, Slyra included. He extended a hand and pulled her up; this wasn't over yet.

Vantix finally managed to grasp the hilt of one of his swords, using it to smash his opposition in the face. The man crumpled as Vantix picked up his other sword and dragged himself to his feet.

Farack was still cutting/burning swaths through the mercenaries in front of him. Unfortunately, he wasn't paying much attention to those behind him. "Farack!" Vantix shouted, but his friend didn't hear him.

As another of the hired arms advanced he tried to evade, to find some way to make it to his friend's side, but to no avail. All he could do was block an attack and watch as one of the opposition jammed their sword through Farack's back.

The rhadon gasped in shock and stared down at the sword protruding from his stomach. He fell to his knees, surprise evident all over his face. Warm, oily blood poured from his wounds. His flames didn't die out, instead getting hotter, brighter and more intense.

Vantix leapt at his friend's killer, plunging his swords deep into the man's neck before Arsenius appeared at his side. As Arsenius kept the enemies off his back, Vantix knelt by Farack's side.

"I'm sorry," he croaked, his voice raw with emotion. They'd always been a team, now it was gone.

Farack's eyes looked glassy as he replied, "You're forgiven."

"It's all my fault," Vantix moaned, "I should have had your back."

"Get out of here," Farack roared. His flames had begun to singe Vantix's clothes. "I'm a rhadon," Farack winced involuntarily, "Can you guess what happens next?"

"He's dying?" Arsenius asked over his shoulder, his eyes filled with worry. Pulling Vantix to his feet, he announced, "We're leaving."

The room was still filled with mercenaries, who either didn't know what a rhadon death entailed or didn't care, forcing Arsenius and Vantix to cut their way through until they caught sight of Slyra beckoning them her way.

All the while Farack's heat got more intense, flames ignited his highly flammable blood. There wasn't much time before a stray spark ran up his blood stream and reached his heart.

Elik ran down the corridor that had been hidden behind the curtain and didn't hesitate when he saw an open doorway. Masterful swordsman or not, it would be hazardous for the health of anyone to remain around here.

Slyra followed him and was in turn followed by Vantix. Arsenius didn't rush through it like them though, he waited at the door. Grelow ran toward him, intent on following them but the elf punched him in the face, slammed and bolted the door, then set off after the others. This was ranked number twelve on Sir Ralph's list of most justifiable betrayals.

The punch caught Grelow off guard, sending him reeling and tumbling back into the mercenary filled room. They were trying desperately to escape, blocking up every doorway and condemning themselves in their haste. Grelow struggled with them momentarily, then gave up. The actual exits were useless.

Turning toward the windows he finally drew his sword, severing the limbs of two advancing mercenaries. Then he caught sight of Farack.

The rhadon knelt in a pool of blinding white flame. Grelow's presence confused him, but then he realised he didn't need to think about it anymore. "See you in another life," he managed.

As the vampire changed into bats and headed for the windows, Farack got one of the items on a long list of things he thought he'd never acquire. His head slumped forward and his hands, which he'd been using to shield his wounds from the flames, hung limply at his side. The heat intensified, melting all furniture in the room and blackening the walls.

A stray spark drifted through the air and landed upon Farack's now open wounds. It ignited the blood inside of his stomach before splintering, flames going in all directions. Everything inside him was aflame, his veins, his arteries and all other major organs. Lastly, the flames hit his heart. The explosion was immense.

The colony of bats that indicated Grelow's presence only had seconds to reflect on what they would do to Arsenius if they ever got the chance. No life flashed before the vampire's eyes, and he got the feeling that this wasn't the end, that he'd have another chance to wreak havoc and furious vengeance upon a certain treacherous elf from Nospac.

One or two of the bats almost made it out before the flames engulfed them. Then the flames engulfed everything else.

Farack had quite the send-off, in true rhadon fashion.

Chapter 36

Welbh arrived at the castle in record time. He'd expected to just about beat the Derranferd army here, but he'd definitely underestimated the power of the Solus. A journey that should have taken several hours had been completed in under forty-five minutes. The significance of this was not lost on him; he could see why his brother had been willing to spend so much.

The mass rabble had been replaced by soldiers of the king's army, the majority of whom were asleep on the ground. Only a few sentries stood guard, the moonlight picking out the glint of the chainmail beneath their green tunics against the otherwise dark night.

His horse finally slowed, as if it knew galloping at supernatural speeds would arouse suspicion. After he was briefly halted and commanded to verify his identification, the gates opened and he went through. At this point he was forced to dismount, due to the lack of mobility caused by all the barricades.

They were all about ten paces apart, ranging in heights from three to six feet. Poorly constructed would be a generous way to describe them, but only because they were so ridiculous. Built out of a mixture of wood and furniture that on their own would probably be sturdy, the barricades themselves looked like it wouldn't take much to overwhelm them. An impediment, but one that enough of the enemy could probably push over.

No craftsman in the world would want to take responsibility for these, which was fine because they'd been constructed by soldiers. Large gaps at one side allowed Welbh to simply walk through. The gaps had been tactfully placed at opposite ends of every second barricade, clearly the intention was to use them to filter the enemy in. This might slow opposition forces down but certainly not for any considerable amount of time.

Entering the castle, he stepped over the three foot barricade. *God forbid we have to rely on that,* he thought to himself. He didn't dwell on it though, as it mattered little. The situation was under his control.

Going straight down the hallway would lead him to the staircase to the upper floors, turning left would lead him to the kitchens. As it was he turned right, in the direction of the throne room

It was several hours after midnight, but Welbh had no doubts about who he'd find there. In times of war there was no respite for the ruler of the realm; they could spend days in here. Pushing open the doors, he found it hard to distinguish where Prince Balithorn began and the throne ended. The prince had been sitting so long the chair had almost conformed to his general shape. He was treasuring a rare moment of peace, but worries of tomorrow were intruding on any attempts he made at sleep. Welbh cleared his throat.

Balithorn woke with a start, almost jumping out of his seat at the noise. Huge bags hung beneath his eyes, and his face looked painfully haggard. Despite his lack of sleep when he saw who came calling his full attention was focused on Welbh. "You," he snapped, "where have you been?"

"Ghostwood," Welbh replied succinctly.

Unfortunately, Balithorn was not in the mood for Welbh's games and he proved rather irascible when tired. "Did you enjoy it?" he barked.

Welbh remained silent. Like everything else, anger passes.

He was correct. Having failed to elicit a response, Balithorn sagged back into his seat. "I trust," he said slowly whilst rubbing his forehead, "that there was at least some pertinence in this impromptu trip?"

Welbh nodded, "Of course, your majesty."

"Care to elaborate?"

"Suffice to say, I simply wished to guarantee victory tomorrow."

"And?" Balithorn gestured for his father's advisor to continue.

"I succeeded."

Something his father had said returned to him. "Welbh always has ulterior motives and is selective about the truth he tells but he can be relied upon," the old king would say, "Be on your toes around him." Only the part about his reliability managed to stick.

Getting out of his chair for the first time in several days, he wrapped Welbh in a friendly hug. After all, he was the saviour of the nation. Breaking away, Balithorn tapped the end of his nose in a decidedly conspiring manner. "I look forward to seeing what you have in store."

With that Balithorn went to bed. Thanks to Welbh's reassurances, he slept soundly.

Welbh spent several moments in the throne room. He inspected everything from the throne, to the chandeliers, to the rug. This could be his; all the wealth, power and everything he desired.

He'd just have to wait for the opportune moment. Said moment would most definitely come tomorrow, there was no doubt about that.

As for now, exhaustion didn't just catch up with Welbh, a brick of solid lassitude seemed to hit him in the face and he dragged himself to bed.

*   *   *   *   *

The Drakold sniffed every individual pile of scorched remains, its plight so intense that panic was actually evident despite it horrendous face. He couldn't be here; it couldn't end like this.

All sorts had been here; it could smell them. Elves, men, rhadons, vampires and possible a witch. That last smell was only lingering, she probably hadn't died here.

More importantly, its prey had been here. Not too long ago either. Despite the stink of burnt everything, ·his aroma seemed to pave a path through all others.

There was something fundamentally different about his scent. The Drakold couldn't make much sense of it, but just knew it couldn't give up. The thought of that blood filled it with a burning desire.

His fragrance led to a closed door. The Drakold pulled apart the masonry surrounding it, creating an opening big enough for it to get through. The corridor wouldn't exactly be comfortable either, but it didn't matter. He was worth it.

*   *   *   *   *

Considering that hordes of mercenaries had travelled to Ghostwood on horses, it would have been remiss of the group not to avail of their generosity. They'd ridden for several hours, not taking a break until the mercenaries were firmly behind them. They needn't have worried; dead men don't give pursuit.

Right now the horses were enjoying a well-deserved, if soon to be short-lived, rest. They'd settled down to recuperate, but thanks to Vantix, not to relax.

"Okay," he demanded, "What the hell was that?"

"He killed the three of them," Slyra answered.

"He tried to kill us," Elik replied.

"We didn't get paid," Arsenius sighed.

Vantix shook his head. "I wasn't talking about that," he informed them, "I was referring to our friend Arsenius here, murdering our own people."

Arsenius stared at the ground. "He deserved it."

"What?" Slyra asked in confusion. This was pretty much going over her head.

"Grelow," Elik responded.

Vantix stared at Arsenius for a moment. "You can't just go around killing regular people," he exasperated, "even if they deserve it. I wasn't particularly fond of that blood sucking parasite eith-"

At this point he was interrupted by a shouted question from Arsenius. "Who are you to lecture me on morality?"

"At least I don't go around murdering people on my own team!" Vantix replied indignantly.

Arsenius punched Vantix right in the mouth, knocking him off his feet. It was the first time it had happened since Slyra had hit him upon their reunion after the Roger(bandit king) incident, but it was still happening too often for his tastes.

Massaging his mouth in order for it to regain some feeling, Vantix subsequently ignored the realisations that, *"Caligynephobia is the fear of beautiful women,"* and *"Rabbits can't sweat."* Useless epiphanies, along with punches to the chin, were fast becoming the bane of his existence.

"Do you remember the story Grelow told us on the boat?"

Pointing out the flaws in Arsenius's questions wasn't exactly proving profitable for Vantix, but he was nothing if not stubborn. "No," he replied sulkily.

"Yes," the other two replied simultaneously.

"Well Vantix, let me sum it up for you. Grelow caught a family stealing his things, changed the mother and father into vampires and let them loose on their twelve year old son." Arsenius's eyes were hard as he continued, "Would you like to know how the story ends? When my parents came after me they were little more than ravenous beasts. I couldn't out-run them, I knew that. So I used the knife my father had given me for my birthday to defend myself. I killed my parents and it was all his fault."

Slyra and Elik placed a consoling hand on each of his shoulders. Vantix felt sincerely bad about questioning the tanned elf's motives and he felt himself go red. Slyra was the first to break the moody silence. "We should go after him."

"No we shouldn't," Vantix and Arsenius replied in unison.

"She's right," Elik said firmly.

"Since when did you become such a big talker?" Vantix replied hotly, "I know we just heard an inspirational revenge tale, congratulations by the way" he grabbed Arsenius's hand and shook it, "but they don't all end that way. We don't have a chance."

327

"He just tried to kill us and he's the king's right hand man; he can do almost anything," Slyra reasoned, "is that the kind of person you want in a position of power? Think of the horrible things he'll do. For love of the gods, Vantix; he killed Farack! Indirectly I suppose, but it still counts. Don't you want to honour your friend?"

Vantix raised a hand. "1, I can honour my friend much better if I'm alive. As you just mentioned Welbh is the king's right hand man, so essentially you're asking me to embark on a suicidal revenge mission with no possible hope of either revenge or survival. If there was even the slightest chance of vengeance I'd do it, but there isn't and there's nothing we can do about it right now. Someday I'll avenge Farack but not when I'm more likely to die in the attempt. 2, since when did you all start caring about the greater good? We don't know that Welbh is going to do horrible things." His eyes brightened as if he'd suddenly come up with the solution to all of life's problem, "This entire journey Rekil was offering our services to every single villager chancing their arm at getting free help, and you were all just as annoyed by it as I was. Don't pretend to be better than you are. You all just want revenge. If there was any justice none of us would have survived this trip. Good people like Rekil, Farack and Terif would have collected our share of the money and given it to the homeless, or the needy, or something."

It looked like Elik was about to say something but there was no stopping Vantix mid rant. The older man walked away.

"Since my life is my own, I'll not waste it in a vain attempt to save other people," Vantix finished dramatically.

Arsenius stared at him. "Normally, I'd agree with you," he offered, "but when you say it like that it just comes across as selfish. Maybe it's time we thought of turning over a new leaf."

From somewhere nearby there came a distressed whiny, and they looked up to see Elik returning.

Speaking directly to Vantix, he said: "Your horse seems to have inadvertently died somehow," he wiped his sword clean in the grass before sheathing it, "Now you can stay here in the middle of Ghostwood, without a horse, or you can come with us."

Vantix contemplated staying here in defiance, then he realised that would be punishably stupid. He smiled wearily. "How could I resist such an offer?"

Chapter 37

Trune's rapid acceleration up the ranks of the Derranferd army was exactly the sort of propaganda the army's marketing department loved. For several hours yesterday he'd had to pose for them to paint different posters of him over and over again, sometimes saluting the crown, other times stamping on a Fardashian soldier who happened to be wearing a shirt with the words *"I Support Regicide"* written in red paint. Subtlety wasn't their strong suit.

A twenty two year old achieving the rank of captain was unheard of, unless it was in one of those all child communities but people generally found it hard to take them seriously.

With his own soldiers ready to brutally enforce his every command, nothing could obstruct his path to glory. His men were the elite, the indoctrinated if you will. They believed their sole purpose was to honour the nation of Derranferd, to bring glory and pillaged goods to its table. They'd be the first into battle today; the first to punish these deceiving, king-murdering Fardashian vermin.

The two main armies would meet and exchange lethal pleasantries on the plains in front of the castle and if Fardash waited for Derranferd to come to them, it would be a simple matter to for them to flank the invaders. To prevent such an occurrence Trune's elite had been sent.

They'd separated from the main army yesterday in order to approach from the east. As their comrades moved into formation on the battlefield, Trune and his men stole into position; looking down on the ambush squad on the hill below them.

Sneaky, conniving, Fardashian rats! Trune thought to himself, seemingly oblivious that he was doing the same thing. Although he only had 90 men to their two hundred, he also had the drop on them. They'd spent long enough watching the battlefield; it was high time they noticed him. Gesturing for his men to ready their bows, he aimed his own at a specific target along the line. If he took out their leader, they'd be like any other disorganised mob; violent, unsupervised and not good at making up impromptu chants. "Fire!" Trune ordered.

Along with jokes and epiphanies, ambushes are really one of those things in live that could use a music sting. It needn't be some sort of operatic masterpiece, just a simple two note melody to show recognition for the art form that is the ambush.

Ninety out of the two hundred Fardashian soldiers lying in wait didn't get up again. Those that did experienced a moment of blind panic, many of their number lay dead, their leader among them. Some just ran.

As for Trune's men, they simply dropped their bows and drew their swords. They'd pick up the ranged weapons later, after the slaughter. Rushing at the enemy they made no attempts at injury. They aimed to kill.

Trune was the first to clash with their foe, ducking under an axe and dragging his sword across the man's chest. Whirling round to face his next, he got the feeling this was going to be an exceedingly good day.

*   *   *   *   *

The first sounds of battle reached Minos's ears. Sounds that seemed to come from where their ambush party was waiting. "Gods," Minos groaned; this was already setting itself up to be a less than pleasant day.

He and the rest of the Cannonbridge guards had escorted the fleeing townspeople here to take refuge in the keep and escape the destructive rampage of the Derranferd army. Although they'd tried to weasel their way into the cellar with the townsfolk, the prince had refused to hear any such suggestions. According to him they had a greater calling, one that went beyond defending the idyllic town of Cannonbridge. All able-bodied men had to fight for their province.

The sounds from the eastern ridge weren't overly promising, mostly because it's hard to tell who's winning when clashing forces are hiding behind a hill. Derranferd had clearly known about the ambush, which didn't bode well in any case. Again Minos found himself wishing for a cosy little place to ensconce in the castle's cellar.

A roar erupted from the other side of the field, capturing his attention and holding it at knife point. The entire Derranferd army rushed toward them. He readied his axe. Unfortunately at this point, some of his Fardashian brethren ran forward, prompting the rest to follow. Minos was dragged along with them, unwilling to let himself be trampled by the waves of running soldiers.

He was fairly certain he was being dragged to his doom.

* * * * *

Two heavily armed forces got in my way, seems reason
enough to abandon anything, never mind a quick quest
for revenge that only three of your members are truly
invested in. Nevertheless it failed to make the list of
"Reasons why things don't go according to plan" but
only because Slyra and Elik proved impossible to deter.
Still it was rather a shock to the two colossal forces.

"What's going on here?" Vantix asked, unconvinced
his eyes were correctly reporting the scene before him.
There seemed to be a lot of random acts of violence
going on of late, but two armies clashing was another
thing.

"It looks like an invasion," Arsenius replied blandly.

Sometimes when Arsenius was younger and living in
the desert, he'd sometimes make fatal errors that would
put his life in danger. A perfect example of this would be
the time he used his water skin for target practice, losing
not just his only supply of hydration but also killing the
camel that he'd hung the water skin on. Whenever he was
plagued by such an occurrence, he'd felt a deep sinking
feeling in the pit of his stomach, which usually indicated
whose fault it was.

As he stared out at the battlefield, Arsenius noticed a
deep sinking feeling in the pit of his stomach, indicating
whose fault this was. That couldn't be right. As he turned
to his friends the feeling got stronger, a sign of their guilt.
"I think this is our fault," he said aloud.

Vantix eyed him as if he was an idiot. "How could this
possibly be our fault?" he demanded curtly.

"I have a strange feeling in my gut that it is."

Vantix laughed without mirth. "Are we supposed to
base all our decisions on your stomach's condition?"

"We'll probably be able to use this to our advantage," Elik mused, "Should actually make it easier for us to gain entry to the castle. Slyra you'll need this." He handed the young witch one of his lighter swords.

She took it and nodded her thanks. Vantix held on tight with his heels as she spurred the horse onward, wishing that he'd displayed more forcefulness when she'd refused to let him take the reins.

The Fardashians wore a simple green tunic over chainmail, whilst the Derranferdians wore blue and yellow over either plate or chainmail, depending on their rank. It was to the latter that the group temporarily pledged their allegiance.

Vantix's short swords were already drawn when he slid off the back of the horse. Swinging both swords at the nearest green tunic, he signalled which side he was on. Of course, this also meant making enemies of all the others, but he was okay with it.

Elik's sword came round in a circle, disarming the soldier and cutting off his hand at the wrist. The soldier fell to the ground, searching amidst the trampled earth and armoured feet for something. Whether it was his sword or his hand Elik couldn't be sure, he was busy contending with his next opponent.

Slyra and Arsenius made a decent team. Although fairly maladroit with a sword, Slyra could block and stab. Her powers evened the odds, but reverting to magic was her last option. The duration of this battle was currently a mystery and it would be important to conserve energy.

As for Arsenius, years of living on his own in a desert full of thieves, murderers and botanists had taught him one thing: swords aren't meant for taking prisoners.

A sword came across from Slyra's side, aimed at her head. Instinctively she opened her palms and energy sent her foe flying high into the air, forcing him to try his luck against a hundred foot drop. She shook her head; it was going to be a long day.

* * * * *

Trune dragged his sword from the man's chest and cleaned his blade in the grass. He'd been the first and last person to draw blood, fighting with a tenacity that most people in their first battle lacked. Ambition is an unmatched fuel.

"Casualties?" he panted, finally getting a chance to catch his breath.

"Seventeen, captain."

With seventy-three men he could easily take a castle, he was certain of it. Though if you asked him at that moment, he would also have told you he could fly and shape solid rock with his fingernails.

"We're taking the castle."

Their path clear, he and his men ran. You had to sprint at times like these. Any other speed was simply unacceptable.

* * * * *

"My lord, it seems a group of Derranferdian soldiers have breached the gate," Welbh informed Balithorn.

"What?" the prince put his head in his hands; he'd expected his men to hold out longer than this.

"Yes, your highness," Welbh reaffirmed, "It appears they anticipated your ambush and dealt with it on the way here."

They were in the lavishly decorated royal study which had belong to King Jandelk. Bookcases lined each wall, creaking under the weight of the rare tomes that filled their shelves. Prince Balithorn sat behind an intricately carved desk, desperately trying put the blame on someone. "You!" he cried eventually, an intense look of loathing adorning his features whilst he glared at Welbh.

"Me, sire?"

"Of course you!", the prince yelled, "It's all your fault! Where is the deliverance you promised me yesterday? Where are these "arrangements" you made?"

Welbh smirked in reply, which made Balithorn decidedly uncomfortable. "It's right here, your majesty," he declared whilst removing his hand from his sleeve.

Balithorn didn't understand what Welbh was getting at. How was a strange, gold hand-bracelet supposed to save them? Realisation dawned and Balithorn felt guilty for several things. He felt guilty that he hadn't recognised how traumatising his father's death had been on Welbh; guilty that he wouldn't get to accompany his troops onto the field; and most guilty of all because he'd entrusted the safety of the nation in the hands of a man who believed unfashionable jewellery was the answer to anything.

"Unfortunately you will not live to see this war won. A Derranferdian soldier made it up here and you didn't survive the encounter," Welbh's voice was flat and emotionless. Immediately springing to action, he didn't give Balithorn time to process his statement.

The Solus's emerald shone and then energy shot from it, burning through anything in its path. It hit one of the bookcases and caused it to topple, crushing Balithorn underneath.

Welbh shook his head; he'd been aiming for the prince. It didn't matter though, this way seemed just as effective.

He took his leave with asking Balithorn's say-so; it didn't seem likely an answer would be forthcoming.

* * * * *

Minos saw him and instantly knew what he had to do. He would kill this dirty treacherous murderer, there wasn't even a single doubt in his mind. Taking his axe in hand, he strode purposefully through the throng of brawling bodies. The little blighter had done enough damage to his town, he could not be allowed do the same to his nation.

Vantix brought both his swords down in diagonal strikes. His foe fell, two deep gashes in his chest.

A big man was striding toward him, axe raised threateningly. Vantix recognised him from somewhere, but he couldn't place it. Unlike the other Fardashian soldiers, who were simply mad at Vantix for killing their comrades, he had a disturbingly purposeful look on his face. It was clear a quick catch-up and drinks weren't on this soldier's mind.

Minos leapt forward and his axe clanged against Vantix's sword. the traitor then tried to get under the sword, but not before Minos's knee came up, catching him in the chin.

Vantix stumbled groggily back, the knee had caused him to bite his tongue and he could taste blood in his mouth as the axe came at him again. This time he side - stepped out of the way, lashing out at the hand holding the axe as he did so.

Minos ignored the initial spasm of pain and the dull throbbing afterward. Grimacing in a grim manner(it's physically impossible to grimace in any other manner), he maintained his firm grip on the axe. He couldn't let go, not until he'd dealt with this traitor.

Vantix tried to feint right, but lost his footing. Upon hitting the ground he instantly rolled out of the way, watching as an axe rammed itself into the dirt he'd been occupying a fraction of a second ago. A boot came down on one of his swords, wrenching it from his grasp.

As the axe came down again, he raised his sword to block and grabbed it with his free hand. Exerting a strenuous amount of effort, he not only held on, but also managed to turn it so the flat side faced him. Then he rolled over, dragging the axe under him.

In theory this is a fine way of disarming your opponent. In practice it just drags your opposition down on top of you. The two of them struggled over the axe, but then Vantix seemed to realise he had his own weapon and wasted no time plunging it into Minos's neck.

Vantix rose to his feet, gathering up his swords. As he regained his breath, Elik came running over. "You see that," he pointed at the distant castle rooftop, "There's somebody up there. Meaning there must be a doorway into the castle."

Vantix seemed to be missing the significance of this revelation.

"I can get in there," Elik persevered, looking for some sort of reaction.

"Congratulations," Vantix smiled wearily.

Elik's wings emerged from under his cloak, flapping twice and launching him high into the air. It was certainly impressive, Vantix had to give him that.

For a moment everything around him seemed to move at double speed, leaving Vantix behind as he stood perfectly still. Nobody intruded on this rare moment of peace, almost as if the battle had gone elsewhere and taken its participants with it.

Then there was a roar, deep, threatening and extraordinarily intrusive, jolting Vantix out of his serene moment of relaxation.

* * * * *

The Drakold's roar seemed to reverberate across the field, drawing all attention to it. Veteran soldiers turned and were instantly terrified; this thing was horrifying.

The monstrous creature on the other hand, could barely contain its excitement. After trailing him for so long, the prey was finally in sight. The blood it craved was within its grasp! He could not be allowed to escape.

He ran, along with most of the Fardashian army. The Drakold was so very close, all the waiting had come up to these next few moments. It gave chase.

* * * * *

Lightning erupted from Slyra's palms, shocking all those around her. Arsenius was crouched on the ground below, hands on his head. When Slyra gave him the all clear he rose to his feet. "You okay?" he inquired, concern evident in his voice.

She nodded. Magic was strenuous, but she was fine for now. Preoccupied as they'd been, they were counted among the few who'd missed the immense roar. As Vantix sprinted by several paces away from them, they finally caught sight of the Drakold.

The monster was a good bit behind Vantix. Some dutiful soldiers of Fardash had mistaken it for some kind of Derranferdian super soldier, though how and why they reached this conclusion in the first place was unclear. As it tossed them high into the air, crushed them underfoot or tore them apart, Arsenius got the impression they regretted that mistake.

He dragged Slyra further out of the way as the Drakold swept by them. It was definitely headed in the direction Vantix had gone.

Fardashian warriors charged at them, preventing the two of them from dwelling on the experience.

* * * * *

From atop the castle, Welbh surveyed the battle. Although some Derranferdians had breached the gate, they were having trouble getting through the barricades in the courtyard.

As he watched the entire left flank of his army fled back toward the castle, but he'd anticipated that. They wouldn't be able to hold out against Derranferd; the numbers were far out of their reach. The only surprising thing about their sudden retreat was that they seemed to be fleeing from some sort of demon.

On his hand the Solus was glowing warmly, as if it sensed it would soon be time to put his plan into action. A plan that would have him hailed a hero and declared king in the same afternoon.

There was something approaching him from the battlefield. At first he'd thought it was a bird, but birds don't wear gleaming armour and cloaks. Welbh knew who it was. How many other people had wings as distinctive as those?

Saying he regretted what he'd done would be a lie; Elik and he may have been friends but that became moot as soon as they murdered his brother. Few friendships can get over something like that. "Elik," he called as the figure landed across from him.

"Ah," his old friend recognised him this time, "You're just the person I was looking for."

Elik's cloak slid from his shoulders, his wings unfolding behind him. They were pitted and scarred in several places, highlighting the trials and tribulations the group had been through. It was understandable that they'd been somewhat unhappy with the method of payment Welbh had offered. Then again, he wasn't exactly best pleased with the services they'd rendered either.

Elik's blade dripped with blood. The blade was thin, curved and obviously sharp. Welbh wasn't in the mood to put it to the test. He raised his hand, the Solus's shine undiminished by the overcast sky. As earlier when he'd tried it on the king, a beam of cutting energy shot forth but all Elik had to do was flap his wings lazily to put himself out of the way.

From his elevated position Elik let out a roar that wasn't particularly human. It had a certain ferocious twang to it that no man could recreate. The stone at Welbh's feet was torn up into the air, followed closely by him. Landing heavily, he felt the wind rush out of him.

As he rose shakily to his feet, Elik dropped to the roof once more. He seemed content to wait for Welbh to regain his breath.

When he was ready he drew his sword. This was going to have to be dealt with the old fashioned way.

* * * * *

Vantix was running full pelt. Having already outdistanced the retreating Fardashian soldiers, he headed for the castle gates. Getting Four-foot thick walls between him and that thing seemed like a good idea.

Being occupied with thoughts of monstrous demons devouring him, Vantix failed to take the time to really appreciate all Castle Fardash has to offer. It's a magnificently engineered castle, shaped like a pentagon with the doorway at one of the five corners. It's vast walls are filled with spectacular stained glass windows and the fluted columns and arches of the inner hallways are not be missed. One stairway at the far end of the castle leads up to all the floors and finally to a massive rooftop, perfect for feasting under the moonlight. All of these factors make it a popular holiday destination among friendly dignitaries, but of course, Vantix didn't know that; he hasn't read the brochure. Plus, there was the whole chased-by-a-demon thing occupying his mind right now.

Behind Vantix, the Drakold's path was once more obstructed by a group of soldiers. Vantix had to hand it them; they were persistent in the face of death. That being said they weren't up to contending with a monster from the Shadowlands. It had a bit of fun, this time impaling a few whilst confident in the knowledge that its prey couldn't escape.

* * * * *

Elik leapt, hovering in the air just above Welbh's blade. However this proved an entirely useless strategy, as Welbh just parried any downward thrusts. As he descended Welbh kicked his feet out from under him, causing a complete mess of a landing.

Without his feet to land upon, Elik crashed heavily against the stone roof. Using one of his wings to throw himself to his feet, he was just in time for his sword to clang against Welbh's descending blade.

Finesse wasn't getting him anywhere, so Elik deemed it best to try brute force. He brought his blade down toward Welbh' face, a move easily blocked. Instead of spinning away and trying somewhere else, Elik put his weight behind the sword. With his free hand he grabbed a hold of Welbh's tunic, trying to pull him toward the sword.

Welbh would have spun away but he couldn't; Elik's firm grip made sure of that. He flinched as both swords were pushed closer to his face, holding them off indefinitely would be a problem. Sensing he only had one option available, he took it.

Elik caught sight of the emerald glowing on the Solus's surface, but only just before it blasted him. As Welbh relaxed, the other man's body landed in a heap at the edge of the rooftop, clothes gently smouldering.

Welbh looked out over the battlefield once more; it was most definitely time to end this. Raising his hand, he watched in amazement as waves of energy shot from the Solus and washed over the castle, battlefield and anywhere else Derranferdian soldiers could be located.

* * * * *

The barricades had given him some trouble, but Trune had persevered. He ordered his men to go over them, any who disobeyed his orders and tried to go through the doorways were slaughtered. It was a very clever tactic in use, this barricade filter, but the problem was the barricades were too flimsy.

As he hopped the last barricade, the majority of his troops hopped it with him. it looked like they'd take the castle. All that remained in their way was a wall of sandbags in the castle doorway, which Fardashian soldiers were using as shelter whilst they fired their crossbows.

Trune dodged another arrow, gripping his sword tight and fighting the urge to smile. Apparently smiling whilst you attempted to kill people was a sign of madness. It was only then that reality gave up its fight against the Solus.

He may have been running, climbing and wielding a sword for most of the day, but his arm seemed to tire from nowhere. It became immensely heavy, dragging him down from the shoulder. Next came his sword arm, his hand cementing in place and preventing him from loosening his grip on the weapon any time soon. Then his feet were immobile, too heavy for him to lift.

He couldn't run anymore, he was frozen in place. Arrows bounced off his stone chest as this unbelievably unusual ailment took hold. He wanted to shout, to scream but he couldn't; his vocal chords were just as solid as the rest of him. The obscure ailment spread upwards, encasing his head in stone as he stared at the sky. Remaining like that seemed to be on the cards; frozen in stone with mobility just beyond his reach.

*　*　*　*　*

Arsenius sliced off an arm and turned straight into the path of a stone soldier. The man had been human before and charging at someone, but as his state of body changed the statue couldn't stop itself colliding with the tanned Nospac elf.

Grunting with exertion, he heaved the statue off himself and turned to Slyra. "I think you got the wrong side," he grinned weakly.

She shook her head. "It wasn't me."

"The how-" Arsenius began.

344

The question went unfinished, interrupted as it was by the Fardashian army's sudden realisation that although not covered with a layer of stone, Arsenius and Slyra were not on their side.

A single arrow was launched at them, which Arsenius adeptly deflected with his sword. When several more arrows whistle through the air toward them, the two of them ran.

*   *   *   *   *

Vantix threw himself over the barricade. The courtyard was littered with statues of those who'd been here when it happened. Some were even hanging precariously from the barricades, their weight almost dragging the structures down with them. Since Vantix had never seen anything like it, he was readily willing to blame it on the ten foot tall demonic monster that was following him. He was wrong of course, but nobody actually leapt up to correct him.

Scaling the next barricade, he just evaded an arrow that was fired at him upon reaching the top. Two soldiers were behind cover in the doorway, firing out at him.

The barricade behind him shattered as the Drakold ran into it. Vantix got the distinct feeling that dallying here would be a mistake, then dived straight off the barricade. Grazing his hands and tumbling to his feet, he ran in the general direction of the castle door.

Sidestepping left and right, he dodged two arrows and was over the minuscule piece of cover without breaking stride, continuing unabated straight down the hallway.

The two soldiers watched him run, hurriedly reloading their crossbows for another shot. They were crushed beneath the feet of the Drakold a second later.

Bounding down the hall, Vantix could see a line of soldiers. Stretching from wall to wall, they seemed intent on stopping him. *Good luck to them*, was all he thought, not slowing for a moment.

Just before contact with them, he let his feet fall behind him, sliding on his knees under their sweeping swords. Springing back to his feet, he opted for the straight path down the hall. Stairs were visible at its end and he let the faint hope that demons couldn't climb stairs blossom within.

Behind him, the noises the Fardashian soldiers made indicated that they weren't faring well. Despite the pains numbing his legs, he pushed himself on.

The stairs went up in a spiral, with one door leading out on each of the castle's four floors. The last door led to the roof and Vantix decided to head up there. It might offer a nice view.

Thundering up, he'd reached the third floor before he looked down. The Drakold was at the bottom and it was evident that it couldn't even fit both its feet on the staircase.

However, Vantix's smirk of satisfaction didn't last long. The creature dragged itself up the side of the staircase, then pressed two feet against the wall and hurled itself up to the next floor. This is actually a recognised military method for climbing staircases.

For a moment Vantix froze, terror preventing all mobility and leaving him every bit as much a statue as those in the courtyard.

As the fiend climbed to the steps beneath him, he regained motion capability. Pushing himself as fast as he could go he just managed to stay ahead of the creature, leaving each level behind only seconds before it landed there.

The door to the roof only steps away he lengthened his stride. It was small, only was human-sized and he wondered whether the Drakold would even get through. There were naught but milliseconds to spare, when he reached it, tugged at the handle and realised it was locked.

The prey almost within its grasp, the Drakold tossed itself across the gap.

When a ten foot tall monster launches itself at you and your back is to a wall, you really only have one option. Reflect on what you've done and what you've achieved, curl yourself into a ball and wait for the end. You'll be devoured in a minute.

* * * * *

The doorway to the staircase, along with its surrounding masonry, came raining down around Welbh and he had to raise a hand to shield his head. The massive creature he'd observed demolishing his soldiers came flying through, along with a teenager who was curled up into a ball.

"What the hell is that?" Welbh shouted at the barely conscious body of Elik. He was sick of all these complications. Muttering something incomprehensible, he raised his arm. The Solus was still shining.

The Drakold's every sense went crazy as it grabbed its prey and pinned him down. It could smell that exotic ecstasy-inducing blood running through his veins. The prospect of it made the creature let out a delighted roar. It raised a clawed hand.

Vantix struggled beneath the fiend's grasp. He knew it was hopeless. The clawed hand was already raised and he couldn't reach his weapons. His early life flashed before his eyes, but it was interrupted by a shot of green energy hitting the Drakold square in the face, knocking it off its feet and subsequently freeing him.

It was only then Vantix noticed Elik. Resisting the urge to check on

his friend was a lost cause; he was always inquisitive when it came to injuries. Especially since there seemed to be smoke coming from his downed companion.

Elik's shirt had been torn away and a few burns had taken up residence on his chest, but it wasn't actually that bad.

Vantix looked up at the hand that was raised threateningly at his head. The Solus was there, glowing with a sinister hue. Or at least, that's what it seemed like to him.

"If you're a friend of his," Welbh spat, "you obviously aren't a friend of m-"

This sentence wasn't cut off by any disturbance from Vantix. Instead, it went unfinished due to Welbh being picked up by the Drakold and shoved into its mouth. Vantix winced at every crunch and muffled scream, as he backed away slowly, hoping that the monster would be full after its meal.

He was eyeing all possible exit points (even if most of them involved plummeting to his death it still seemed better than Welbh's fate) when the behemoth before him spat something out. The Solus clanged against the ground and Vantix noticed the damage Welbh had done with it.

The Drakold's horn was no more than a stump now, the Solus had cut it clean off.

Yet it still seemed intent on impaling him. *Maybe it has an exceedingly sharp forehead,* Vantix thought.

Both his short swords were somewhere amidst the rubble, meaning he only had his crossbows and the broadsword he'd stolen from the glasrobes to choose from. Reaching slowly for the crossbows at his belt, he moved further away from Elik. After all, he didn't want his wounded friend to be trampled to death.

A crossbow now in both hands, he fired from the one on the left. The arrow lodged itself in the Drakold's shoulder, causing it to roar and rush at him.

Vantix gave an involuntary yelp and his other crossbow went off. The arrow hit the demon in the face and bounced off. It has been pointed out previously that although stylish, miniature crossbows are definitely impractical.

The monster tried to grab him but he managed to shuffle away from its outstretched claws. However, a back swing from its arm sent him skidding away along the roof. Vantix groaned as he lay on the ground; he was going to be covered in bruises in the morning. At the same as he rose to his feet, the monster wheeled around for another go. Vantix drew his broadsword, an expression of grim determination planting itself on his face. This might be the end for him, but he wasn't going out without doing his fair share of damage.

The Drakold charged, and Vantix reacted perfectly. Jumping over the diving monstrosity, he lashed out with his sword. The creature shrieked as blood spurted from its now empty eye socket.

Snarling venomously, the fiend swatted aside Vantix's sword thrust and head butted him in the chest. It probably hadn't had time to adjust to the whole no-horn thing yet, which explained why it was surprised to see him thrown back along the roof instead of mounted on its head-spike.

Vantix dragged himself along with his arms, the villainous miscreation before him relentlessly following him step for step as he shuffled along the ground. A few of his ribs were broken and the creature had made both his legs numb, leaving his chances of defending himself at zero.

The Drakold took the last few steps toward its prey. Everything had boiled down to this moment; it could feel it. Bringing its clawed hand down on its defenceless prize it felt a moment of utter joy, something to which demons are unaccustomed.

Vantix grabbed his sword and plunged it deep into the monster's heart, extinguishing all life in there. The people who found them surmised what he'd accomplished and rewarded him, with gold, carpets and other things rich people tend to have. He lived out the rest of his days in the lap of luxury.

By Vantix's standards this vision wasn't far off.

Vantix's hand settled on something and he brought it round to strike his demonic executioner. It was only then that he saw what it was.

The clawed hand made contact with the emerald side of the Solus and seemed to crack it, but only for a moment. As he watched, time slowed, all colour was drained from the surrounding scenery and sounds drowned out by a deafening, humming silence.

In an instant colour, sound and properly flowing time shot back into the world. Exploding from the Solus and propelling itself straight through the Drakold. The monster fell, a gaping cavity in its chest. It wouldn't be getting back up.

Getting slowly to his feet, Vantix slipped the Solus onto his hand. The artefact was emitting strange, pulsating warmth. He scrutinised it curiously.

"Hey!"

Soldiers were pouring up the staircase, armed, dangerous and with a firm misunderstanding of the situation. If he'd known how to work the Solus Vantix might have given it a go, but as it was there were too many of them.

Grabbing Elik's barely conscious body and Nasrode's sword, Vantix hoisted his unconscious friend up onto one shoulder and ran for the edge. The first of the arrows were just being fired as they jumped off the roof.

The soldiers looked down and saw nothing there. Nobody hanging from a ledge a few feet below, nobody flying off into the sunset, just nothing. It baffled them, perplexed them and even went so far as to obfuscate them, until they came to their senses and abandoned any hope of understanding.

Chapter 38

It had been hours before anyone had found Balithorn, and for a while it seemed their victory would be marred by the death of the only remaining member of the royal family with the ability to govern. They'd been extremely lucky; the only damage was to his right leg, left collarbone and nose, all thoroughly broken by the bookcase.

He sat on his throne, right leg raised and left arm in a sling, thinking about the events of the day. Below him the higher ranking members of the army sat. He'd thanked them, congratulated and given them a sumptuous feast. Now his mind turned to other things.

Where is Welbh? This thought kept popping into his mind and pondering it gave him no answers. Despite the attempted regicide, Welbh lived up to his promise of deliverance. At least that's what Balithorn surmised. The promise and then the extraordinary manner of their victory couldn't just be a coincidence; the gods hadn't granted them many favours within memory, so there must be other forces at work.

Also a source of mystery and concern, was the ten foot tall monstrosity on the roof. It was hideous, dead and had a gaping hole in its chest. Apparently it was from

Derranferd and had attacked the castle. What it was, how it had got onto the roof, and whether there were more of it, were matters all up for discussion. They all looked to him for answers, seeming to forget that he spent the battle trapped under a bookcase.

Those statues all over the plain and courtyard had to be disposed of as well. He was tempted to pass them off as decorations and donate them as a complete set. The Nospac were into statues; maybe they'd take them off his hands.

The entire room quietened as he raised a hand. He'd just remembered something someone had said to him a couple of days before the battle.

"It has occurred to me that the entire Derranferd army was eradicated today. Although our loses were substantial, we could easily replace them with conscription."

There were stunned whispers around the hall; no king had ordered conscription in generations. There must be a purpose behind it, some plan to make it acceptable.

"Since conscription will replenish the army," the prince continued, "I see no reason why we wouldn't have adequate forces to take Derranferd as our own. It is ours; what we deserve as recompense for the destruction they brought to our lands. Its resources, coupled with our own, should bring prosperity to our nation. Enough to make us strong again. After what we achieved today, I believe the other nations will be less inclined to push us around much longer. From now on we command respect."

This was greeted by cheers.

"From now on we take what we want."

More cheers.

"We will spread out and take control, and all will bow before the might of the Fardashian empire!"

A roar of approval ripped through the room, people clapping and beating the tables. There would be glory for the taking.

The prince leaned in close and whispered to the nearest advisor, "Begin conscription immediately. We invade before the week is out. Make the necessary arrangements for my coronation as well, an empire should have an emperor."

* * * * *

Far away from the turmoil of Ballisca, a lone god stares out across the kingdom he has created. It's beautiful, perfect even. A true marvel of godly engineering. The place he's looking out upon isn't Ballisca, but it isn't heaven either. He'd left there long ago.

This is his world; a world where everything lives according to his command. There is no life here unless it is by his decree, no death without his consent and above all, there's no free will save that which is granted by him. Mountains crumble, oceans evaporate and steel is dust beneath his fingertips. He is Hastore; one of the almighty three and at this point in time, he's rather troubled by the events unfolding in Ballisca.

Shoes click against the marble flooring as Shank entered. "It seems

they were unable to recover the Solus," Shank tells him.

"Who?" he asks.

"As far as I can tell, it's in the possession of someone named Vantix."

"What happened to Lintous?"

"He's dead, Lord Hastore."

"Good, I was sick of his interfering."

Hastore tutted to himself; it felt wrong to wish death upon people. Still it hadn't been his fault, and he switched back to the matter at hand. "This Vantix," Hastore asked, "Is he the one I spoke to?"

"Yes my lord, but he has since regained human form."

Hastore gave an irritable grunt. This complicated matters even further. Nevertheless, he couldn't simply sit around as his siblings did; the situation with the Solus needed to be rectified. Their faith in their creations had been unfounded and once again Hastore was forced to pick up the pieces. Secrets like the Solus couldn't linger among mortals where anybody could misuse them. They needed to be locked in a chest, moved to a hidden valley, guarded by dragons and then submerged in eternal silence. If necessary, the valley could then be flooded.

"What about our guest," Hastore wondered aloud, "does he know?"

"I don't think so, my lord," Shanks replied.

"Then don't tell him. And get me everything there is to know

about this Vantix. I want to be well informed when I meet him."

Shanks bowed and left, the discussion over.

* * * * *

Seeing as they'd arranged to meet in the tavern, Slyra and Arsenius were perturbed by the lack of Vantix and Elik. Still, they bought drinks and settled in at a table in the corner.

"So what will you do now?" Slyra asked as she was struck by a thought.

"Already trying to get rid of me, eh?" Arsenius said, disappointment evident in his voice.

"No, I'm not, I just," Slyra blushed as she realised he was winding her up, "What I mean to say is, you've fulfilled your oath and avenged your parents, what's next?"

He shrugged in reply. "I haven't really thought about it."

The conversation ended there but not because they didn't have any more to say, or because they wanted to listen to *"Mantis the hero without a soul"* which the bard was playing. Conversation ended because two figures entered, one leaning heavily on the other. Even this far away and with a cloak over Elik's wings, they were still unmistakeable.

Seeing the two blood encrusted men enter caused the tavern's patrons, who'd already been celebrating the victory over Derranferd, to erupt into cheers and raise their glasses to the battle weary newcomers. They weren't made from stone so obviously they'd been fighting for Fardash, right?

They reached the table after countless pats on the back and being offered more drinks then are possibly consumable in one night. "Slyra, if you wouldn't mind," Vantix nodded toward Elik.

Slyra nodded her consent and placed a palm on Elik's chest. Healing energy raced from her fingertips, assuaging all the injuries inflicted upon him. After a moment he stood up on his own and requested the strongest drink available from nearby patrons eager to reward this victorious soldier of Fardash.

"Is that about you?" Arsenius indicated the bard playing *Mantis the hero without a soul.*

"Typical," Vantix smiled wearily and rolled his eyes, "It's only been a few days and they've already got my name wrong. Almost makes you want to give up."

"I know what you mean," Elik sighed into his beer and gestured to their surroundings, "I wanted so much more than this."

Arsenius spoke up. "Didn't Welbh say you'd find what you were searching for in Port Daichwater?" His curiosity forced him to add, "What are you looking for?"

Elik stared into his drink for a moment and answered, "I don't know. A life, a family, a home maybe. Everything from my past; everything I've forgotten."

"And you deserve it. In fact, we all deserved so much more than this," Vantix corrected himself before adding, "Could you just bear with me for a moment? I'm new at this."

He looked over both his shoulders, before removing the Solus from his pocket and setting it on the table. He then proceeded to throw up his hood conspiringly. Leaning in close, he whispered:

"I've got a proposition for you....."

31676775R00214

Printed in Poland
by Amazon Fulfillment
Poland Sp. z o.o., Wrocław